Lauren Jackson lives in a small coastal town in Australia. Her hobby of writing stories developed into a passion when she discovered the website Wattpad at age fourteen. Since 2012, she has garnered thousands of followers and millions of views on her stories, which have helped grow and develop her love of writing. Lauren loves to write sweet (sometimes dark . . . you never know what you're going to get!), steamy romances, and is always writing a new book.

laurenjacksonauthor.com
@laurenjacksonauthorr
@laurenjacksonauthorr
groups/5495306513812797/
https://www.goodreads.com/user/show/18315357-lauren

ALSO BY LAUREN JACKSON

Standalone
Meant to Be

Red Thorne series
Die for You (#1)
Live for Me (#2)

Stratton University series
Break The Rules (#1)

LIVE
FOR
ME

LAUREN JACKSON

PENGUIN BOOKS

UK | USA | Canada | Ireland | Australia
India | New Zealand | South Africa | China

Penguin Books is part of the Penguin Random House group of companies
whose addresses can be found at global.penguinrandomhouse.com.

First published by Penguin Books, 2024

Cover design by Nikki Townsend Design © Penguin Random House Australia Pty Ltd
Cover images: sword by oksana2010/shutterstock.com, rose petals by
Amazingphotographs13/shutterstock.com, moon (back cover) ID 177062435 © BulbSpark |
Dreamstime.com, green leaves and red roses with blood by Trevillion.
Author photograph by Lauren Jackson
Typeset in Sabon LT Pro by Midland Typesetters, Australia

Printed and bound in Australia by Griffin Press, an accredited
ISO AS/NZ 14001 Environmental Management Systems printer.

A catalogue record for this
book is available from the
National Library of Australia

ISBN 978 1 76134 881 5

penguin.com.au

*We at Penguin Random House Australia acknowledge that Aboriginal and Torres Strait
Islander peoples are the first storytellers and Traditional Custodians of the land on which we
live and work. We honour Aboriginal and Torres Strait Islander peoples' continuous connection
to Country, waters, skies and communities. We celebrate Aboriginal and Torres Strait Islander
stories, traditions and living cultures; and we pay our respects to Elders past and present.*

To those who have strong personalities,
a weakness for broken heroes, and have
never stopped loving vampires.

Content Warning

Thank you for choosing to read *Live for Me*.
I really hope you enjoy it!

Some of the content may be triggering to some readers.
Content warnings include profanity, explicit sexual scenes,
descriptive scenes of death, violence, and brutality.

I hope you enjoy the story.

PLAYLIST

'Anti-Hero' – Taylor Swift

'Tears of Gold (Stripped)' – Faouzia

'Prisoner' – Miley Cyrus, feat. Dua Lipa

'Devil Doesn't Bargain' – Alec Benjamin

'So Good' – Halsey

'NDA' – Billie Eilish

'Slow Down' – Chase Atlantic

'You Put a Spell on Me' – Austin Giorgio

'Love Me to Death' – Nikki Idol

'Cravin'' – Stileto, feat. Kendyle Paige

'I Did Something Bad' – Taylor Swift

'Control' – Halsey

'Animals' – Maroon 5

For complete playlist

PRESENT DAY

1

CORA

The Fighter

DEAD BODIES ARE BEING found around town again.

That situation was supposed to be resolved months ago, but I have a feeling Red Thorne is a place full of unresolved mysteries.

With two fingers, I lightly push against the jaw of the dead teenage boy sprawled in front of me. His head lolls to the side, and I narrow my eyes at the jagged puncture marks that are carved into his flesh. He wasn't just bitten, the vampire dragged their fangs down so that there was no way he would survive the bite. Dried blood stains his skin and the grass beneath the back of his head.

'If this was you, I'm going to kick your ass so hard you won't be sitting for a week,' I say, when I hear the sound of feet hitting the ground behind me.

'I'd like to see you try,' Theo replies in a deep voice.

Standing, I turn to face him. His blond hair is especially messy, looking windswept and like he hasn't brushed it in a few days. Or weeks, knowing him. He towers over me, and offers me his trademark crooked smirk.

The temptation to prove my point almost wins the battle inside me, but with a sharp exhale I turn back to the corpse at our feet. Planting my hands on my hips, I stare at him, unsure of what to think.

'This seems a little familiar,' Theo says.

He's referring to the very pissed-off vampire, seeking revenge on Theo, who built a small army of newbie vamps and left a trail of dead bodies. Since that case was resolved, the missing people and dead bodies had completely stopped, and the town had returned to its creepy, but normal, self.

Until a few weeks ago.

'Whose girlfriend did you kill this time?' I ask, raising an eyebrow.

'I've been on very good behaviour lately,' Theo retorts, crossing his muscled, tattooed arms over his chest. 'Much to my own disappointment.'

'You don't think . . .' I trail off, anxiety rising in me, gripping my heart in a painful fist. 'It's not . . .'

'I don't think so, Cor,' Theo says quietly, shaking his head. 'If Kian was here he would make himself much more known than this.'

'He likes to play games. This,' I gesture to the body, 'is a game. Leaving corpses out like this, for anyone to find.'

'Seems a bit beneath him,' Theo argues. It seems preposterous that a person being murdered in cold blood, left to bleed out and die for anyone to find, could possibly be *beneath* someone, but he is right. Kian is much more theatrical. 'He's more the type of person to kill the university chancellor at our graduation with a massive live audience, or something.'

An unnatural chill inches down my spine. 'I hate that you're right.'

'I'm always right.'

'If anything, you're mostly always wrong, but sure. Whatever helps you sleep at night.'

Theo rolls his eyes. Bending down, he scoops the dead boy into his arms, flinging him over his shoulder. I peer around, thankful no one has walked by us, since we are right near town, on one of the most popular walking tracks.

It's quiet as we walk, since our footsteps are as light as a feather. My eyes dart around us, constantly monitoring for the tiniest of movements, but it seems we are the only ones in the woods tonight. It used to be quite busy out at night, but since these dead bodies started popping up every few nights for the last month, most people stay indoors now.

Theo sings in a low voice, something about having a pocketful of sunshine.

'You're a bit twisted, you know that?' I ask him.

'We're all a bit twisted, girlfriend.'

'Don't call me that,' I mutter.

Theo peers back at me. 'You sounded so much like your sister just then.'

My stomach clenches at the mention of Raya. I miss her so fucking much. I'm glad she is away from Red Thorne for this. She deserves to be happy, and off enjoying her life. I'm incredibly thankful for Hunter, and his commitment to making that happen. Raya deserves the world, and he is willing to go to every length to give it to her.

'What's with the new hair?' Theo asks.

Drawing me from my thoughts, the question prompts me to glance at my long, now-black hair that cascades down my shoulders. The ends are a dark ruby red since I thought that with my vampire-black eyes, and the fact that I wear mostly black clothes, I needed a little colour to spice it up. I spontaneously dyed it this morning. I've always had a natural dark brown, the exact same as Raya's, but I felt like it needed to change. Since I have changed so much inside, I needed to alter the outside to match. It feels kind of nice. Like shedding old skin.

I shrug, running my tongue across my teeth, feeling a little antsy, although I don't know why. 'I needed a change.'

'Suits you.'

'Thanks.'

We get to the clearing, and Theo tosses the body to the ground. It lands on the harsh dirt with a sickening *thump*. Theo is gone and returns within a moment. He generously douses the body in petrol, and my thumb rubs up and down the side of the lighter as I wait for him to finish and back away.

I land by Theo's side as the body erupts into flames, the heat splashing across my skin. I feel a little uneasy as I watch the fire consume the flesh, the smell filling my nostrils, making me resist the urge to gag. Considering we have done this a few times now, I should be used to it, but I don't think the sight of a dead body being eaten by flames, and the gut-wrenching smell that comes with that, is something I will ever get used to. I often wake up at night, the heat of fire on my skin, the smell invading my lungs, only to realise I'm alone in my bed. I suggested burying them, but apparently burning bodies is the best way to make sure a vampire stays dead, given the many stories passed around that buried vampires have a habit of reappearing. A shiver rockets down my spine at that thought.

'Reminds me of old times,' Theo says. 'Me and Hunter used to do this. Bonding time, I called it.'

I screw my face up. 'That's terrible, Theo.'

Withdrawing a long-neck from his jacket, he offers me one. I blink down at it. 'Drink?' he asks when I don't take it. I turn my incredulous gaze toward him. 'What? It's a bonfire.'

'You're fucked,' I mutter, but I take the drink regardless.

We watch in silence. I take a long sip, grimacing at the bitter taste.

'Well. This has been fun.' Theo drains the remainder of his. 'Shall we keep the good vibes going?'

I give him a deadpan stare.

Grinning, he turns, and I follow him. After everything, Theo has become numb to the harsh reality of life. He can turn almost every horrible situation into a joke. At first, it made me so furious with him, I could barely make eye contact when he talked to me, but now I see it's a coping mechanism. He has just as much trauma as me, and this is the way he finds relief.

Surveying the area, I chew my lip, my mind spinning. We need to find out who is doing this. I need to know if it's Kian. If it isn't him, who else would it be, and why? After what happened to Theo, it makes me paranoid not knowing who is behind this, since the vampire world seems small when it comes to revenge and death. I already have the sensation of being watched, so this is only ramping that up.

'What are we going to do about this?' I ask, trailing behind Theo as we wade through the trees. There's hardly any light offered from the moon tonight, but thankfully my eyesight enhances when I need it to. 'What's our game plan?'

Theo shrugs. 'We have a case to solve, Detective.'

'No shit,' I grumble. 'I mean, where do we start?'

'We need to get to know people. Ask around. Someone is bound to know something. You're always out and about, you need to start networking.'

I screw my nose up. 'I don't like people.'

'You're going to have to suck it up, girlfriend.'

Spreading my lips into a thin line, I mull over his words. They make sense. If we want to find out who is doing this, and hopefully put an end to it, I'm going to have to start asking questions. Which means talking to people. Getting to know them. *Ugh.* Sounds awful.

'And you?' I ask. 'What will you be doing?'

'The same thing, obvs,' he replies, kicking a stick and sending it soaring ahead of us, disappearing between two trees.

'Uh-huh.'

'What else have I got to do?' he asks, slowing down a fraction so that we fall in step, side by side. 'Minus hanging with you.'

'Harassing is a better word.'

This is another thing Kian has done that doesn't sit right with me. Restricting Theo to this town, refusing to let him leave. I shudder at the thought of being trapped here. I've been there with Kian – held in his claws, so tight it's suffocating. I've felt the walls closing around me. It's something I wish to never experience again. But while I know it infuriates Theo, he still manages to enjoy himself here. I kind of admire that about him.

It's unsettling that Kian has so much power over those he turns. It's been said that some vampires have particular gifts beyond the usual perks of being undead. Kian appears to have an enhanced ability when it comes to compulsion. A maker is always connected to and influential over the ones they turn, but Kian takes that a step further.

If I have a gift, I would say it's my speed and precision in a fight. Or maybe that is just Kian's training. If being crafty and silent is a gift, that is certainly Theo's.

'What do you think they want?' Theo asks, his voice changing to a more serious tone he rarely uses. Sarcasm and inappropriate jokes are his way of dealing with everything, but every so often he drops that wall with me.

I sigh. 'I don't know. To send a message, maybe. What message, and to who, I have no clue.'

'Hopefully nothing to do with us,' he says.

'That's wishful thinking.'

Kian.

A shiver rolls through me at the thought of him, and my mind wanders to the letter he sent me . . .

I haven't forgotten about you.
You still owe me nine years.
I'll be coming to collect.
See you soon, Cora.

Goosebumps scatter over my skin and I glance around me, as if expecting him to step out from the shadows.

Unease swirls in my gut at the thought of it. It would be foolish of me not to assume this is linked to him, but Theo also makes a valid point. This seems . . . beneath Kian. Maybe that's the whole point. Perhaps he wants to throw us off? Purposely confuse us? *That's* something he would do.

My eyes dart to Theo. I never told him about the letter. He should know, especially if Kian turns up again – which I don't doubt he will. Half-turning to Theo, I open my mouth to tell him about it, when a stick snaps. There's a sudden rustling in the trees that has my chin jerking up, and both of us freezing. Theo tenses beside me, and I quickly press my hand to his mouth, ensuring he doesn't do or say anything that will give us away, if we haven't already done that.

Theo's tongue runs against my hand, and I yank it away, giving him a withering glare.

'Focus, you loser!' I mouth to him.

His smirk widens, only annoying me further.

A cat lands in front of us, its yellow eyes blinking up through the gloom. Its midnight black hair makes its body blend into the shadows. I exhale, slumping my shoulders. Sensing something off about us, the cat hisses, darting off into the darkness as fast as it can. I think we scared it just as much as it scared us.

'So scary,' Theo whispers, re-enacting my frozen face and rigid body.

'Fuck you,' I mutter.

'Anytime, girlfriend.'

'Stop. Calling. Me – *ah*!' My feet suddenly fall into a hidden hole, and I tumble downwards. I land elegantly in a low crouch, my eyesight focusing as the world around me brightens slightly, letting me see where I am.

Brushing dirt off my clothes, I peer around, wondering where the hell this pit of darkness has come from. We walk through this forest almost every night, and we have never noticed it. When my foot hits something, I glance down, yelping when I see a skull facing me.

I shriek, leaping backward, hitting my shoulder against a hard rock. I spin, then discover the rock is in fact the shoulder of another skeleton, and I scream again.

A *whoosh* to my left has me whirling around in fright to see Theo. He grips my shoulders, his firm hands lending me a little bit of comfort, and I force the panic out of my mind.

'Are you okay?' he asks.

Nodding, I swallow, trying to calm myself down.

Theo slowly turns, taking in the piles of bones at our feet, and the skeletons leaning up against the dirt wall. They look like they have been here for a while, but it's hard to tell how long.

'This is creepy as fuck,' he says.

'Get me out of here,' I whisper, closing my eyes, attempting to convince myself that the walls aren't *actually* pressing in on me. An awfully familiar tightness encloses my chest, and my hands tremble as I lift them to cover my face.

When I reopen my eyes, we are back in the forest.

'It's fine,' he says. 'You're fine.'

I nod slowly. 'I'm a little claustrophobic.'

'Yeah,' Theo agrees, brushing his hair from his eyes. 'You're shaking, Cor.'

'Let's just go.'

He hesitates a heartbeat of a second before nodding. We continue to exit the forest, thankfully at a faster pace. I breathe a quick sigh of relief when we make it back to the pavement. Theo wanders over to the patch of blood from the body, doing his best to scrub it out with his foot, and then covers it with leaves.

'I know you're not someone to let anyone inside those highly built walls of yours,' Theo says once he has successfully gotten rid of the evidence. 'But you can talk to me. About stuff.' He looks away for a moment. 'I understand better than you think. About Kian. The way he makes you feel. The things he asks you to do. The lack of control and power.' He hesitates. 'The way you also want his approval.'

My lower lip trembles and I clench my jaw. Theo and I have never discussed this. Hell, I don't think we've ever had a heart-to-heart about anything that matters. Not that I would admit it to him, but that's what I like most about our friendship. The fact that we have both been through some serious shit but can still laugh and have a good time.

'I really appreciate that, Theo,' I murmur, swallowing hard, not liking the burning sensation creeping over my eyes as tears threaten. 'Thank you.'

When I look up, his easy smile is back on his face. 'What's on for the rest of the night?'

'Sleep. I'm exhausted.'

'Why are you working so damn much?' Theo asks, his face muscles visibly jumping. This is a conversation we've had several times over the past few weeks. He doesn't understand it.

'I want to,' I say, even though we both know that isn't it. 'Thanks for your help tonight.'

'Mmhmm,' he says, shaking his head, indicating his disagreement with my new way of life, but like always, I choose to ignore his opinion. 'Night, Cor.'

'Night, Theo.'

Despite everything going on in Red Thorne right now, I still take my time walking back to my house. I'm positive the eyes I feel on me are Theo's, making sure I get home safe. I don't ever let on that I know he's there. It's comforting to know I'm not truly alone.

Tugging the sleeves of my jumper over my hands, I shiver slightly, the events of the night repeating in my mind on a continuous, irritating loop. Trotting up the stairs of my porch, I slip inside, triple locking the door. If a vampire wants to get in, there isn't much stopping them, but I still feel better knowing that all the doors are deadbolted.

My phone rings, and I read Mya's name across the screen. I met Mya through work when I first moved back and she's become very special to me. As someone who didn't have many friends as a human, let alone as a vampire, when I found someone I genuinely click with – here of all places – it was such a relief. Without Raya around, I've really missed having a close girlfriend.

Smiling, I answer. 'Hey,' I say.

'Hellooo,' Mya replies in her sing-song voice. 'Are you home?'

'Yup,' I reply, wedging my phone between my cheek and my shoulder as I yank off my boots. With all the corpses turning up, we have made a promise to each other to call and check we made it home. It seems morbid, but that's Red Thorne for you. 'Are you?'

'Home, tucked into bed, reading my monster romance smut.'

I snort. 'Good Lord. At least that's better than the one from last week. What was it again, a woman and a . . . chair?'

'Hey, don't knock it until you try it!' she protests.

'Right . . .' I trail off, unconvinced. 'How was your family dinner?'

'I . . . didn't go.'

'Mya,' I laugh, shaking my head. 'You're going to be in trouble.'

'I knowwww.' She exhales, and I can picture her nose screwing up like it always does when she is flustered, or embarrassed. 'I just can't face my father right now. He is so angry with me.'

'Are you ever going to fill me in on what this big falling out was about?' I ask, placing her on speaker as I move around the kitchen, tidying my bench. Having a spotless house has become a hobby of mine. A way to pass the time, and occupy my hands. I must have rearranged my house furniture, and everything in my cupboards, at least a dozen times. Organising and keeping things clean makes me feel like a normal person again, and that is exactly what I need after the year I've had.

'It's complicated,' she replies, yawning, which makes me yawn. 'I'll tell you one day. It's a long story.'

'I'm holding you to that.'

Movement to my right captures my attention, and I glance out the window. The boy next door is moving around his house. When he steps into view, I turn my back to him, not wanting him to know I was looking. He's a close friend of Mya's and I secretly think she is trying to set us up. She talks about him nonstop to me, and because I'm refusing to acknowledge Kian, I've probably misled her into thinking I'm looking for someone, when I most certainly am not. I can't think anything of the sort right now, when he still consumes me, in more ways than one.

'Cor?' her voice murmurs, bringing me back to the present.

'Huh?' I ask, berating myself for once again letting my mind drift toward Kian, the one person I do *not* want to be thinking about.

'Never mind.' She chuckles. 'What are you up to?'

'I've got a hot date with my bed.'

She laughs, and it's soft and whimsical, which has become a comforting sound to me. 'Sounds good. Okay, I'll see you tomorrow. Sleep well.'

'You too.'

The first thing I do when I get off the phone, like always, is turn my music on and crank it up to a volume that effectively drowns out my thoughts. Peeling off my clothes, I shower, and get ready for bed. Plucking a blood bag from the fridge, I collapse onto my mattress.

I'm deep in thought, despite the music. I take long sips of the blood. It's nothing like getting it directly from the source, and most of the time it has a bitter taste that makes my insides feel like they're about to shrivel, but it does the job.

Hunger satisfied, with my favourite music playing, I finally untense my shoulders, and close my eyes, hoping that nightmares don't plague my dreams tonight.

My legs dangle from the roof of my house as I gaze upward at the sky.

As much as I love the night, and the moon, there is something particularly special about the quiet calm of the early morning, and the stunning vibrancy of the sky as the sun slowly rises. As a vampire with a deadly creator who has more enemies than not, I often wonder which sunrise will be my last.

Given that I likely have a target on my back, I should be on the move, keeping my head down, and fleeing from a town like this, but living life on the run doesn't appeal to me. If someone is coming for me, and they take me down, I will gladly go. I don't deserve justice after the things I've done.

An image of Alex – Raya's best friend – flashes in my mind, and my stomach roils as I remember so acutely his neck snapping in my hands. Guilt plagues me for many of the things I've done, but that particular moment will haunt me until the day I die.

'I'm so sorry,' I whisper, bringing my knees to my chest, hugging them. I lightly rock back and forth, Alex's eyes so vivid in my mind.

Then my mother's face appears, like a slideshow of the poor decisions I've made. The acceptance on Alex's face, despite the pain, knowing his death was coming. My mum's head bent, blood dripping over her skin. She was in that car because of me. Her blood is on my hands, too. Tears roll down my cheeks.

'I'm sorry, I'm sorry, I'm sorry,' I whisper over and over, my voice broken and hoarse as I sob, soaking in the pain of it all.

I weep for several long moments, letting the pain consume me, before drawing in a ragged breath. Placing the lid firmly back on my container of emotions, I force myself to push away the images flooding my mind, and re-open my eyes.

A few moments is all I'm allowed to grieve, and then I have to move on. I can't let my past ruin my future, no matter how much I hate myself for the things I've done, and the events I've set in motion with my foolish decisions.

Trailing my finger down the spine of one of my journals, I pull out the very first one from the tote bag beside me, flipping to the front of the book, where I begin to read.

I am completely and utterly obsessed with him.

I've never experienced anything like this. He is magnetic, and charismatic, and everything I want in a person.

Handsome, mysterious, has the world at his fingertips. And he wants me. He will do anything to have me.

I can't wait to conquer the world at his side.

The feel of my skin burning snaps me back to reality. The sun is directly before me now, and I exhale, slapping the journal shut. Leaping elegantly from the roof, I land in my front yard. Entering the house, I make a beeline for the stereo and crank the music up loud, trying to push all thoughts of Kian, Alex, my mother – and the other faces of victims killed either by my hands or by Kian's as I watched – from my mind. I shouldn't read the journals. I shouldn't remind myself of the mistakes I made that led me down this path, but I can't get him off my mind, no matter how hard I try.

After a shower, I lean against my kitchen counter, peering down the street, sipping on a blood bag. No matter what blood I have, it all tastes like dirt, only easing my hunger to the point where it's just bearable. I don't know how to make it better. A part of me knows I need to drink hot blood, right from the source, but I can't bring myself to even think about it.

A bang on my front door startles me. Stalking over, I swing it open to see the boy from next door standing there, looking weary and pissed off. Dark bags underline his eyes, making his face appear puffy, and a little bruised.

'Do you realise you have neighbours?' the boy barks, his expression hard. 'It is *way* too early in the morning to be listening to whatever death-metal garbage that is playing right now.'

I blink at him in surprise. The boy finally meets my eyes, and the reaction is immediate. He steps back, alarmed. Licking my lips, I narrow my eyes, probably making them look even more eerie.

'Nice to meet you, too,' I say bluntly. He's lucky I know he is a good friend of Mya's, otherwise this would have gone very differently. 'Turn the music down. Got it.'

'Thank you,' he says in exasperation, eyes moving back to mine. A crease forms between his brows, as if he is thinking hard about something. 'And also, you can close a door quietly, you know. You don't have to slam things. Same with your cupboards in the kitchen.'

'For fuck's sake!' I exclaim in frustration, and my gums tingle, threatening to release my fangs. That happens when I'm angry.

Sometimes it's out of my control. 'Anything else you want to complain about?'

'Yes,' he snaps. 'Don't forget that while you might like to stay up all hours of the night, others don't!'

My mouth falls open and fury sweeps through me as he glowers at me.

Turning, he stomps down my steps, and back toward his house. Running my tongue over my teeth, I slam the door shut. Then, just to spite him, I open it and slam it shut again even harder.

My first instinct was to grab him by the collar of his shirt and tell him exactly what I think of his attitude, but I'm trying not to let my anger rule me. I'm also trying not to use compulsion whenever I want to. I promised myself I would live as normal a life as I can get, and attempt to make up for the shit I've done in the past.

I want to be a good person. I *need* to be. For myself, but also for my mother, whose life was stolen from her, and for which I am solely to blame. Becoming a vampire has given me a second chance at life. I don't want to screw it up, despite everything that led me here.

Gritting my teeth, I lower the music, feeling whatever was left of my good mood completely evaporating. Well, if I'm honest, I was never in a good mood.

Collapsing onto the lounge, I stare up at the clock, watching it slowly tick.

I hope all this will get easier.

2

KIAN

The Enforcer

MY HAND PLUNGES INTO the man's chest.

His eyes widen in pure terror as I lean close to him, curling my fingers around his heart, squeezing it. He chokes on a sob as he tries to rear backward, but my grip on him tightens.

Down here in the basement, it's dank and reeks of mildew. I can smell it with each inhale, and it leaves a bitter taste in my mouth. Blood and urine coat the air, potent and gut-churning.

'Tell me what you know, or I will rip your heart from your chest.' I sneer down at the cowering man beneath me. Torturing him happens to be killing two birds with one stone. He is suspected to be a direct link to someone I'm looking for, while also rumoured to be involved in an underground operation happening a few towns over, where my sources say at least three vampires are being held. My sources are never wrong. 'I won't ask again.'

'I don't know!' He chokes on his breath, spit pooling at the corners of his mouth as he sharply inhales, desperate to get air into his lungs.

'I don't believe you,' I growl, shooting a steely gaze at him, my lips twisting into the cruel expression I've mastered over the years.

'The last I heard of one of them being alive was from last year,' he manages to get out, voice quivering, his face turning an unhealthy shade of purple. I loosen my hold ever so slightly, and he wheezes, jerking and spasming against my hand.

I don't feel bad for him. His involvement with a group who thinks rounding up vampires and killing them – or worse – means he does not deserve any mercy from me. I need to extract answers from him, and then take his life as if I'm the grim reaper and his soul is mine to claim.

These groups don't just torture vampires. They starve them, use them, force them to do things. I have been chained, beaten, and starved before. I am in a position to save vampires now, and I intend on using my power to do just that. The rise of witches is increasingly alarming, and they're becoming less forthcoming when being taken and questioned. It's infuriating. It's like they're mimicking what us vampires do, trying to outsmart us with our own moves.

The moans and whimpers of the others pull my attention from the man, and I scowl in their direction. That's one annoying thing about holding prisoners. The constant crying and screaming. Well. I enjoy their screams. It's particularly delightful when they really deserve it.

'Where?' I seethe, leaning closer.

'Red Thorne.'

I hiss in exasperation. Red Thorne. The bane of my existence. Everything leads back to that place. Its history of supernatural creatures continues to invade my life over and over.

'Who?' I demand. 'Who was there?'

'A witch! The only one left from that coven, I think.'

I have been trailing the last remaining witch of a particular coven for what feels like a lifetime. 'I need more than that.' My eyes snare his but whatever magic is in his system refuses to let my compulsion work. Sweat beads across his forehead as he struggles. 'Is there something you're not telling me?'

A dazed expression falls across his face. 'No.' He shakes his head. 'That's all I know, I swear it,' he gasps, eyes shaking as they roll back into his head. 'P-please . . . I gave you what you asked for.'

My lips curve, offering him a cold, empty smile. 'Not enough.'

I yank his heart from his chest. Life drains from his eyes as he collapses to the ground. I toss his heart next to him with a wet sounding *splat*. I love to watch as the light goes out in someone. The feel of their blood on my skin. Their heartbeat becoming fainter with each struggling breath.

Killing and causing harm has become some sort of addiction for me.

Unhurriedly, I walk toward the sink, washing the blood from my hands.

'You,' I snap. The human I picked up last week appears before me, staring at me with a dazed expression. 'Get rid of this.' I lazily gesture to the dead body at our feet.

'Yes, sir.'

Strolling around the room, I push up the sleeves of my shirt to my elbows. Round, fearful eyes swivel in my direction. Flashing them a leering smile, I lean forward, bracing my hands on my thighs.

'Who wants to go next?'

More cries. Sobbing. Wails of pain. Smiling, I walk toward a girl huddled in the corner, purposely trying to make herself as small as possible. Yanking her up by her arm, I drag her along and throw her onto the chair in the middle of the room. She stumbles, catching herself just in time before she falls.

'Do you have information for me, or are you going to be just as useless as your friend?' I snarl, looming over her, my fangs dropping down. She recoils at the sight of them, trembling so much the chair legs rattle against the cement ground.

All of them are a part of the one coven. All as guilty as the next. They are involved in things they have no right to be involved in. All of them must know something, and I am determined to find out exactly what that is.

'Th-there might be some still alive, and u-using cloaking spells to conceal their identities,' she forces out, teeth chattering almost violently.

'No shit,' I spit, the anger surging through me like a tidal wave. 'You don't think I fucking know that? Tell me what I want to know, or you'll join your friend down there.'

'You're going to kill me anyway,' she cries, something fierce flashing in her eyes, and for a moment I almost applaud her bravery.

'It can be fast and relatively painless,' I offer. 'Or, I will kill you so slowly, so excruciatingly, you will be *begging* me to end your life.'

Gulping, her eyes flutter closed. 'It's true. Our friend was in Red Thorne. I'm not sure if she is still there. She moves from town to town, always changing her identity. Last I heard, she was there, and I think she has her coven there, but some of them are under-cover.'

Making a humming sound in my throat, I nod. My finger twitches, the urge to reach out and snap her neck almost winning, but I force myself to retract my hand. She slumps, looking weary as she slowly blinks up at me, trying to figure out what I will do next.

'You're not telling me anything I don't already know. Try harder.'

'Apparently there is a witch who comes from a powerful family, but she isn't practising witchcraft. I don't know why, but maybe she knows something. Maybe there is a reason she doesn't practise. Her family would know something . . . I'm sure of it.'

I stare at her, deadpan. 'A witch who can't even control her own magic? That is of no interest to me.'

Sweat drips down the side of her neck, and my eyes watch it carve a line across her throat, before slipping beneath the collar of her shirt. My fangs tingle in anticipation, but I don't act on the impulse. There is only one source of blood I crave – which I refuse to acknowledge – and my body loves to remind me of it. It shouldn't be possible that I want *hers*, but I've known for quite some time that nothing about our situation is normal.

'Can you contact your friend?' I ask, narrowing my eyes as I stare down at her expectantly.

She shakes her head, chest heaving as she struggles to get enough oxygen into her lungs. 'No. She doesn't trust anyone. She doesn't think it is safe to let any of us know where she is.'

My upper lip curls. Perhaps this little witch isn't as clueless as I first thought. Running my teeth across my tongue, I step back. 'I see.' My jaw flexes. 'Prove it.'

'What?' she squeaks.

Lunging forward, I locate the phone jammed into her pockets. With the signal blocker I have down here, no phones except mine have any reception. I pull my own out and disarm the blocker via the app. The human's phone brightens to life in my palm as a series of notifications chime.

Passing it to her, I wait for her to take it.

'Call her.'

Lower lip trembling, she wordlessly takes it, and pulls up the contact 'red'.

'Red,' I say. 'What is that for?'

The girl trembles, shrugging when she fails to get her words out clearly. She tries again. 'Code red. I'm supposed to call her in emergencies only.'

'This is an emergency,' I snap.

With shaky hands, she jabs her finger onto the name and presses the speaker option. It rings a few times, and a voice answers.

'Bailee? Are you okay?' the woman asks, her voice low, and a little breathy, as if she has her hand curled around her mouth, attempting to conceal this phone call as best as she can. There's significant background noise – a busy street, perhaps. Faint music fades in and out, and I listen carefully.

As fast as a whip, I pull a blade out from where I had it concealed, and press it against the girl's throat. She screws her eyes shut as she rocks back and forth, desperately trying not to let out the sob I know is on her lips.

'H-hey,' she says, and I release a low grumble at the sound of it. She jerks upright, almost dropping the phone. 'Are you okay? Where are you?'

Silence. I close my eyes for a brief moment. She blew her cover immediately. I would have compelled her if her magic would allow me to. I'm gifted beyond most when it comes to compulsion, but a witch's magic overrides even my extra ability.

The line goes dead.

I tsk, shaking my head. 'You blew your cover.'

She whimpers, cringing away from me.

'What do you know about the farm near North Pines?' I demand.

'Nothing!' she sobs, leaning as far as she can away from me. 'There're no vampires there!'

'Bullshit!' I bark at her, voice as menacing as I can make it. 'My sources tell me there are at least three. What is your little motley group planning for them?'

'T-they're harnessing their blood.'

Anger spikes through me. 'For what purposes?'

'There are witches who are paying top dollar for vampire blood by the litre. They're using it for some sort of experiment.'

'What experiment?'

'I don't know, I swear I don't know.' She is almost hysterical at this point, her words bleeding together incoherently. 'All I know is that it's something that witches have done in the past for humans, and they want to try and manipulate vampire blood. That's it. That's everything they've told me!'

'Vampire blood?' I repeat slowly, staring at her pensively. 'Why vampire blood?'

'I don't know.' Her eyes dart to her phone, and her finger is close to pressing a button on it, one that I imagine would alert people of her location.

Yanking her off her feet, I slam my fangs into her neck and rip out her throat. The scream that tears from her lips lasts only a second before she drops to the floor in a pool of blood. I peg her phone to the ground and it splinters into pieces.

My eyes rake over the last three remaining prisoners.

Without a word, I turn, leaving them all shivering, and whispering, their eyes on my back. Once outside, I take in a deep breath, trying to clear my head. I've been doing my best to focus on my mission, but I keep getting distracted. My annoying little infatuation with a certain someone keeps occupying my mind.

Recalling what the witches said, my thoughts creep back to Red Thorne.

Perhaps it's time I pay the town a visit.

After all, I'm due to collect what is owed to me.

Twisting in my sheets, I squeeze my eyes shut, trying to block out the memories resurfacing. During the day, it's easy to keep busy, with so much on my mind, but during the night everything creeps back up on me.

Darkness consumes me once more, and I turn, burying my face in my pillow as the memories bombard me.

Terror laces the air.

I quicken my pace, precise and silent, as I hunt her. She pauses, looking around, her eyes darting across the road.

She knows I'm here.

Pushing ahead, a low, inaudible sound falls from her lips and I launch myself into the air, landing on top of the building that looms over us as she shoots a hex or spell behind her, hoping to catch me in it. She must know I'm far too clever to walk into a trap as mediocre as that.

Her short honey-coloured hair whips around her face as she glances over her shoulder. Her pulse thundering, the witch hurries down the street, attempting to put as much distance between herself and me as she can. She fumbles for her pocket, and curses when she realises her phone isn't there.

This seems too easy. How did a witch as unprepared and flighty as this take down one of the strongest, most ruthless creatures I know? My own witch friend is reliable, and has never let me down with her intel, so I trust the information she provided is correct. Ignoring my gut feeling of something being off, I continue watching my target for a few moments.

Staring down, I twist her phone around between my fingers, until it is nothing but shattered glass, and pieces of metal and plastic.

Her breath releases in short, sharp spurts as she rushes down the street, hoping to lose me. Peering over the edge of the building, I enjoy listening to the slam of her heartbeat, and the smell of her sweat as she turns her hurried walk into an outright run. I study her small delicate hands. These hands don't seem capable of performing the necessary magic to end the vampire who created me, but I know better than anyone to never underestimate my opponent.

Bounding off the roof, I land in front of her.

She barely has time to scream before my blade is slicing open her throat. Her blood sprays over me, hot and thick. She clutches her neck, stumbling backward as blood bubbles out of the cut. Recognition flashes when she meets my eyes, and I enjoy the terror in them.

'For Aithan,' I say coldly, closing the small distance between us, upper lip curling menacingly. 'All of you will pay the price of his death.'

I drive my fangs into her neck. A choked sound escapes her as I drink long and hard, consuming a deadly amount, although the throat wound secured her death regardless. She struggles for one final breath before I snap her neck, like it's a mere stick, and toss her to the ground. With her head bent, and her eyes lifeless, I smile down at the corpse, the stench of magic poisoning the air enough to make me feel sick to the stomach.

'One down,' I crow.

For good measure, I disfigure her body, pulling apart her limbs with a squelching tug, ensuring there is no way for another witch to resurrect her. Stringing the body up on the alley wall, I place the body parts back together, as if she is still in one piece, so any locator spell they use for her will still work.

'Beautiful,' I marvel, licking her blood off my lips.

Turning, I briskly walk back down the alley, and out onto the street. A few people pass me, their eyes turning my way. I know blood must be splattered across my face, and down my white shirt. I wear the witch's blood with pride. I hope they report back to the coven.

In fact, I'm counting on it.

Strolling into my house, I kick the door shut and enter the kitchen, feeling agitated, and a little restless. The witch's death feels entirely unsatisfying. Usually avenging a death brings me an addictive thrill, but this felt . . . too easy, and uneventful. Doubt creeps into my mind as I mull over the last hour. The way it was so easy for me to steal her phone, to guide her toward that abandoned alley, and to kill her so effortlessly.

The taste of the witch's blood is still on my tongue when the front door flies open. Spinning, a woman appears through the doorway, eyes narrowed in my direction. Bouncy curls fly around her face as wind that was not there a moment ago whips around us.

'You killed her,' the woman spits at me, voice dripping in venom as she directs those pained eyes in my direction.

Having people avenge their lover's death is not uncommon for me. A regular Thursday. I quirk a brow, dragging my tongue across my lip.

'She killed my maker,' I shrug. 'An eye for an eye.' Her lower lip trembles with rage as she struggles to control her emotions. The anger rolls off her in waves, and I offer her a thin smile, glaring at her distastefully. 'I can smell her magic on you.'

'Her name is Susannah!' The witch shrieks, barely able to contain her fury.

'Was.' I smile, the unhinged one that people often tell me reminds them of a wolf. My lip curls. I'm not a wolf. I'm a fucking vampire. 'Her name was Susannah.'

Her body trembles as she steps closer to me. Tilting my head, I assess her. I am exceptional at covering my tracks when I want to, although more often than not, I purposely leave a trail, simply because I enjoy the chaos that ensues. In this case, I didn't. Witches are a pesky nuisance that I don't have the energy for, but she must have used some sort of locator spell to find me. One beyond the basic spell, since my witch friend has made finding my location very difficult. It's worked so far, so this witch must be a powerful one. I can sense it.

'Demon bloodsucker,' she snarls, breathing ragged. 'You just signed your death warrant.'

If stares could kill, I would be deceased on the floor. The untamed magic coats the air, making my skin prickle.

'Come closer,' I sneer. 'Let me see if your blood is sweeter than hers.'

A tortured scream leaves her as her hands shoot forward. I dart out of the way, appearing behind her. I'm so close to snapping her neck when she spins, launching a spell that hits me square in the chest. I stumble backward, feeling whatever she threw at me deep in my bones. Everything inside me rattles.

'You think Susannah killed Aithan?' she says, voice shaking. 'My sweet Susannah would never hurt anyone. I killed him, and I'd do it again.'

Something sharp is stabbing me in the chest, but there is nothing there. Her words sound close but distant at the same time. My vision swims momentarily and I grapple to hold on to my depleting strength.

'I wanted to kill you,' the woman whispers, leaning down, meeting my eyes. I force myself to stare back at her, ignoring the increasing urge to close my eyes and give in to the darkness. 'But a quick death would have been too kind. Enjoy rotting from the inside out. You chose the wrong coven to fuck with. We ended Aithan, a vampire that was not able to be killed for over a century. You didn't think I could find you?' She spits at me. 'Your pride and ego killed you, you foolish, naive demon.'

I'm unsure if she disappears into thin air, or I somehow lose time, but she is gone after my next blink.

With considerable effort that makes me feel human again, I push off the ground, annoyed that I feel a little shaken from the *encounter. Stumbling into the bathroom, I yank off my shirt and stare at the faint mark on my chest. My stomach sinks as I eye it, hearing her voice like an echo inside my skull.*

Enjoy rotting from the inside out.

A rage, so potent and violent, surges inside me and I let out a ragged scream as I launch my fist into the mirror, shattering it. Her words ring through me, as if she is whispering them into my ear.

You just signed your death warrant.

Choking on air, I wake with a harsh jolt, my hand on my chest. An eerie coldness inches down my spine, and I swing my legs over the edge of the mattress. Burying my head in my hands, I press hard against my temples.

I will track that witch down, and I will find her.

I will get my revenge.

3

CORA

The Fighter

IT'S FRIDAY NIGHT, and we are busy, as usual.

I float around between tables, scanning my eyes across the groups, pretending I'm looking for plates to clear when I'm in fact trying to figure out which groups to question. It's noisy here. The jukebox has been playing nonstop, and with the laughter and chatter filling my head, I'm finding it hard to concentrate.

Since I'm overdue for a feed, I'm feeling more tired than usual. I'm looking forward to a nice, quiet night with a warm bath and a blood bag. My insides clench, the need for blood direct from the source throbbing in my veins, but I ignore the desire. There is a pit of nausea in my stomach that keeps flaring up. I ache for Kian, and it makes me sick to my fucking stomach. I don't know what kind of spell he has me under, but I want to snap the thread.

Closing my eyes, I lean my hip against the counter and take a moment to centre myself. Swallowing, I focus on clearing my mind. Eventually, the loud noises fade into the background, and my shoulders relax. Sensitive hearing comes in handy in a lot of situations, but it certainly can be distracting and overwhelming.

Opening my eyes, I flinch when a face is staring back at me. Unkempt long brown hair. Pale blue eyes that look like two pools of shimmering water. He adjusts the beanie on his head, and pushes the sleeves of his black hoodie up his forearms.

'Howdy, neighbour,' he greets me.

I feel my smile flattening. His own smile widens at my reaction, as if seeing me annoyed is amusing. With the natural charisma of a vampire, I often have people falling over their feet to get my attention, but it seems like he is the opposite.

Mya, my only friend here – Theo doesn't count since he literally can't leave town – has a lot of friends, and I really don't care for any of them. My neighbour is one of the few she hangs out with and insists I will 'love' when I get the chance to 'know him better'. The last thing I want to do is to get to know anyone better, but with a killer on the loose, I'm trying to step out of my antisocial comfort zone so I can find some answers.

'Hello,' I say a little coolly.

'This is my friend Eli,' Mya pipes up, rushing around behind me, as if she hasn't been talking about him nonstop for the past two weeks. She has beautiful long red hair. Strawberry blonde may be more accurate. Soft green eyes that are round and kind of adorable. Light freckles dusted across her nose and upper cheeks. I always hated freckles when I was younger, and a few times I attempted to 'scrub' the tiny little birthmark I have on my cheek, hoping if I cleaned it hard enough, it would eventually disappear. No such luck.

'We've met,' I say, pressing my lips together, trying not to scowl.

Blood rushes to my ears, hunger gripping me so tightly, I can hardly focus on anything else. Things seem to be getting worse with my self-control. It's like I'm losing my grip on it more and more each day, becoming more easily impacted by the moon, and blood, or lack thereof. My head pounds, and my vision blurs as my eyes move to his neck. A buzzing sensation fills my mind as I picture Kian moving behind Eli, black eyes hooked onto mine, his fangs extending in two long points, blood lightly trickling from them.

'Table for one, please,' he says, his voice sounding like nails scratching down a chalkboard, with the way my head is screaming.

'You can just find one yourself,' I say a little distractedly, clenching my teeth, trying to swallow my random surge of anger. Since when do I get this damn hungry? It's like I have been living on an unsustainable diet and my body has had enough, but I don't understand why it feels like this. Vampires drink blood. I drink blood every day. It might not be from the vein, but plenty of vampires survive on blood bags. What is the problem?

He raises a dark eyebrow, pointing to the sign above his head that says, '*Welcome. Please wait for one of our friendly staff members to assist you to your table.*'

'Funny how I don't feel welcome, nor do the staff seem friendly.'

Sighing, I yank a menu from the counter and briskly walk past him, balling my shaking hands into fists as I force the cravings and anxiety down.

I shouldn't have allowed him to speak to me like that this morning. I'm a vampire. I should have just compelled him, but I'm *trying* to be a better person. The temptation to go against my own rules, though, sometimes almost overpowers all rational thoughts.

Kian would be so ashamed of me.

I don't care what he thinks.

I don't.

I really, really don't.

'Here you go,' I say, stopping at one of the free tables.

'Thank you.' He grins, dropping down into the seat.

'What can I get you?' I ask.

He raises a brow. 'I haven't exactly had a chance to look.'

Gritting my teeth, I turn, walking away. I've decided I dislike him. Anyone who can't handle my music is an immediate red flag.

Secondly, he didn't introduce himself, didn't ask politely for me to lower the volume of my music, and now, he's bothering me at work.

He's just here for dinner . . . A rational thought sneaks through, and I massage my temples, hoping these cravings calm down, because it's making me feel out of sorts.

When the restaurant is busy, and short-staffed like we are now, it makes me wonder why I do this to myself. I could very easily not work, but I recall my conversation with Hunter about vampires who don't keep busy. How boring and endless the days can be. Besides, tiring myself out helps me sleep, and keeps the dark thoughts at bay. At least somewhat.

I tune in and out of conversations as I wander around, trying to pick up any information that might be useful.

A throat clears, which I ignore, since I'm listening to a group of guys talk about a house party they're planning to attend after they finish their burgers.

Snap.

Ignoring the blatant attempt to get my attention, I continue listening carefully, mentally taking note of the address, and some other key bits of information I need on who is going, what the theme is, and what time they are meeting the others.

'Hello?' his irritating voice calls out.

'What?' I whip around, glaring down at Eli.

'I'm ready to order.' He smiles sweetly.

Exhaling, I re-focus, reminding myself that I'm working, and technically, he has done nothing wrong. This is what I am here to do.

'What do you want?' I ask, trying not to sound as exasperated as I feel. It's not his fault that I am completely out of my mind right now. He is just the poor guy who happens to be in the wrong place at the wrong time. And it doesn't help that we started off meeting each other on the wrong foot.

'A smile.' He grins.

'You're very annoying.'

His eyes shine with amusement. 'I don't think that's what you're supposed to say to paying customers.'

Exhaling, I lift my chin, forcing a smile onto my face. 'What can I get you?'

'I would like the special burger, and a large Coke.'

'Is that it?'

'Yes.'

He opens his mouth to say something else, but I turn abruptly and stride back to the kitchen. I realise I forgot to write it down. Although I don't need to jot down people's orders to remember them, the chefs need it. I yank my pad off the counter and quickly scribble his order onto it, shoving it onto the already full rack.

'No rush on this order,' I say to the head chef, pointing to the ticket.

His eyes flick toward Eli, and he grins, revealing a few missing teeth. He has wicked tattoos that paint up his arms and neck. He is a nice guy, burly and strong, and I'm positive he is an alcoholic since I smell alcohol on him more often than not, but he is one hell of a cook – or so I hear from the chatter of the customers. People line up down the street for his specials. We have a kinship, he and I, and we enjoy mocking the annoying people who come here. In another life, we probably would have made great friends.

'Got it,' he replies in his usual cheeky-but-gruff voice.

'Hey girl,' Mya says when I appear back out the front. She gives me a tired smile as she re-makes her bun. Her hair falls to her waist when she doesn't have it piled messily on the top of her head. 'What are you up to tonight?'

Leaning on the counter, I shrug. 'I'm not sure. There's a party over on the West Side that I'm thinking of going to.'

'It's my friend's party,' Mya replies, using one of the napkin holders as a mirror to check her reflection. She has too many friends. Satisfied with her hair, she spins to face me. 'I was going to ask if you wanted to come with me.'

'Oh,' I say, a slight thrill zapping through me at the thought of someone inviting me somewhere. Due to my RBF (resting bitch face) – or so Raya refers to it as – and my overall 'don't come near me' attitude, I don't tend to make friends as easily as others. Mya is cool. She works hard, doesn't annoy me, and has great style, which is something I always respect. 'Sure. That sounds great.'

'I'll meet you at your house after work?' she suggests.

'Sounds good.'

Grabbing the order, I make my way over to my neighbour's table, and set the plate and drink down a little too roughly. He has a notebook out, which has pages and pages of notes scribbled in a semi-messy scrawl. I'm dying to know what he is writing about. It must be something significant to be able to write so much on it.

'Thank you,' he says, eyeing some of the soft drink that has spilled onto the table from the way I put it down. It's easy to forget my own strength sometimes.

'What are you working on?' I ask.

He turns to look at me. 'People usually introduce themselves before they start asking personal questions.'

'Eli,' I huff.

'Are you always this rude?' he counters.

I bristle. I've heard that all my life. I release a breath, realising how unnecessarily hostile I've been. I need to change my attitude if I am to make friends, and figure out what the hell is going on around here.

'Sorry,' I say after a long moment. 'I've had a really rough . . . year.'

Eli looks surprised at my statement. I guess most people only have a bad day, or perhaps a bad week. I'm not normal though, and it's hard pretending to be.

'Sorry to hear that,' he says, holding out his hand. 'I was also being rude. I handled it all wrong this morning.' He offers a lopsided smile. 'I'm Eli.'

'Cora.'

He jolts a little when our skin connects. I narrow my eyes when he lets go, leaning back, suddenly appearing nervous. It's not uncommon for a reaction like this, since our skin is abnormally cold. Some humans are very heavily affected by our alluring nature, and others not so much.

'So?' I press. 'What are all the notes about?'

'I'm writing a novel.'

'You are?' I ask in surprise. 'That's cool. I love reading.'

'Me too.'

I take a moment to sweep my eyes over him. He is attractive. Tall, muscled, with a slightly arrogant air around him. Unfortunately my type, not that I am in the right headspace for anything of the sort. I don't think I will ever be able to get over the all-consuming feeling that I have for Kian. I refuse to acknowledge it, and I'm trying to move on. Deep down, I know I never will.

'What's your novel about?' I ask.

'It's a mystery thriller. Still in the planning stages.'

'Cool,' I say.

'Yeah.'

I turn to leave again, when I catch a scent that makes the burn in my throat roar with severity. I snap my head back to him, my eyes dropping to his leg. My mouth waters as the hunger I've been ignoring all day climbs up my throat.

Eli frowns at me, his gaze moving to his leg, which he subconsciously rubs. My hands curl into fists at my side. Going from

drinking a lot of blood directly to blood bags has made me feel
irritable and restless. More than usual. There's also a persistent pit
in my stomach that seems to be growing, and I refuse to acknowledge it has anything to do with Kian.

'Are you bleeding?' The words are out of my mouth before
I can stop them.

His lips part in surprise for a moment. 'Uh, yeah, I fell over.
No big deal.'

My blood rushes to my ears, and I feel the urgent rise and
fall of my chest. I jerk my chin, hastily rushing away from him,
and out the back, probably looking totally strange. I stumble out
into the fresh air, gulping it down. My hands tremble as I drag my
fingers through my hair, trying to force down the hunger. After a
few long seconds, the ache eases. Shaking my head, I return inside,
and head over to the counter.

'Is that your boyfriend?' asks Haley, another co-worker who
I tolerate.

'No,' I reply quickly, not even looking up. 'He's my neighbour.'

'Who is your neighbour?'

I straighten, turning quickly, to see Theo walking toward me.

'Oh,' I say. 'It's you.'

'Greetings,' he replies. 'I'm bored.'

'Are you now?'

'Mmhmm.'

'We're going to a party,' Mya pipes up, and I shoot her a glare.
She ignores me, smiling widely at Theo, and I make a face at her
when she flutters her eyelashes. 'You should come.'

'A party?' Theo perks up. 'Count me in.'

I point a finger at him. 'Only if you behave.'

'Where's the fun in that?' he asks.

'Yeah, Cora!'

'Shut up, Mya,' I mutter.

Theo and Mya spend the rest of the shift flirting with each other, but I have been adamant he is not allowed to bite or sleep with her, since I actually like her and don't want her to run off after having a bad situation with him.

As I go about my jobs, I feel eyes on me. I glance up, noticing Eli studying me with a puzzled expression on his face. He always does an awkward tight-lipped smile when I catch him staring, then he returns to his note-taking. A laptop sits on his table now, and I'm itching to know what he is typing.

I don't like how much he is staring at me, but to be fair, I have acted nothing but odd since we have met, so I can hardly blame him.

'When do you finish?' Theo whines, drumming his fingers against the surface of the counter. 'I wanna party.'

'Ten minutes.'

'Can't you finish now?'

'Can't you wait ten minutes?'

Rolling his eyes, he collapses onto the stool beside him. Sometimes I feel like having Theo around is like babysitting a toddler. I never know what he is going to say or do, and I constantly have to keep an eye on him, and make sure he is somewhat entertained. It's exhausting.

Noticing that Eli has finished, I make my way over and take his plate.

'Going out tonight?' he asks, leaning back into the booth, propping his elbow up.

'Yeah.'

'Sounds like it's going to be fun,' he says.

I pause, my eyes meeting his. 'Are you trying to get me to invite you?'

'Sure, I'd love to come to the party with you,' he replies. His easy-going smile has me faltering for a moment. 'Thanks for asking.'

I blink at him. 'Fine. Meet out the front of our houses in thirty minutes.'

'Roger that.'

Shaking my head, I head out the back to dump his plate and glass, wondering why the hell I just agreed.

So much for having a quiet night.

My throat is on fire.

Swallowing, I swipe at it, as if touching my fingers to my skin will somehow help ease the pain building.

In my rush to get to the party, and with Eli hovering nearby, I didn't get a chance to feed before we left, and the hunger clawing through my chest is enough to make me feel a little light-headed.

Yanking the red cup out of Theo's hand, I down the drink, hoping it will make a difference, but the burn only worsens.

'Okay,' Theo says as I hand him back the empty cup. 'Sure. Have some of my drink.'

Dragging the back of my hand across my mouth, my eyes roam over the room, trying to take in my surroundings. All I can hear is heartbeats in my ears, and pulses thrumming underneath the tender skin of the throats around me.

Theo eyes me with a suspicious frown. 'I think you need another drink,' he says pointedly, and we both know he doesn't mean alcohol.

'I'll be right back,' I mutter, pushing past him.

On my way to the kitchen, I pause as I pass a group. Tuning my enhanced hearing to focus solely on them, I catch snippets of what they are saying. I can't lose focus. This is why I am here.

'Does your dad know anything?' one of them asks, and my eyes flit toward one of the girls, who is looking up at a tall guy beside her.

He shakes his head. 'You know the police stay out of vamps' business. They run this town.'

'So it is vampires, then?' she asks, looking a little paler than she did a moment ago. She tucks her short brown hair behind her ears.

'Of course it is,' he answers with an exaggerated eye-roll. 'They're all the same. Bloodthirsty killers.'

His head turns and, suddenly, he is looking directly at me. His eyebrow piercing glints in the lighting, and I assess his face quickly, forcing a flirty smile onto my face. His eyes rake over me approvingly, and he walks away from the girl beside him, even though she is mid-sentence.

'Hey,' he says once he reaches me, offering me a lazy smile.

'Hey yourself.'

'Are you new here?' he asks, his eyes unashamedly moving over my body.

'No, not really.'

'How have I not run into you yet?' he asks, finally meeting my eyes once more.

'You tell me.'

Running his tongue over his bottom lip, he nods. My vision blurs. I need to focus, to dig for answers, but I can't.

'Want to come join my friends?' he asks.

Damn.

This is the perfect opportunity to do snooping, but I can't get myself under control. I have no idea who anyone in the group is, though they're all human as far as I can tell. Locals, probably.

My eyes scan his face, storing it in my memory so I can find him later, when I kick these cravings to the curb.

'I'll be right back.'

I beeline to the kitchen and grab the first can of alcohol I see. Apparently alcohol is meant to ease the craving for blood. I need to do something about it. I've been avoiding drinking straight from the source, scared I may lose control, but it looks like I've left it too late now.

Deep bass vibrates the walls; it feels as if the speaker is inside my skull. I release a breath of laughter. I wonder if that's how Eli feels when I crank my music up at all hours of the night. My eyes close, and I sway a little. Being hungry makes me not only physically weak, but mentally, too, apparently, since I'm now siding with Eli.

'I'll take one as well.'

Letting out a yelp, I spin around, noticing only then that Eli has followed me. I must be really out of it to not have heard or sensed him behind me.

He gives me a strange look. Clenching my jaw, I reach over, fetching another one of the drinks, and pass it to him. Our fingers graze, and his eyes track the movement as I quickly pull my hand back.

'Are you cold?' he asks.

'No.'

'You sure?' His eyes move down my body, taking in my tight black dress that stops mid-thigh. Considering it is also sleeveless, it leaves a lot of my skin exposed. A human would be cold, but since I don't feel things the way others do, I'm totally fine. I didn't think anything of it when I put it on. 'Your skin is like ice.'

'I'm fine.'

Ignoring my comment, Eli shrugs out of his leather jacket, and hands it to me.

Offering him a small smile, I take it, sliding it over my shoulders. Instantly, I'm enveloped in the warm, woody scent of

Eli's cologne. Involuntarily tightening the jacket around me, the roar inside my body becomes almost deafening. I need blood. *Now*.

The hunger flares inside me, and I groan a little.

'You okay?' he asks in concern.

'I . . . need to go,' I choke out, pushing past him and rushing up the stairs.

I stumble into the bathroom and a girl shrieks in alarm. She's positioned between a guy's knees, her hands on his belt.

'Get out,' I wheeze.

The guy looks like he is about to argue, but a deep rumble reverberates from my chest, and I know my eyes must be black. They scramble to their feet and shoot past me. I shove the door, only for it to bang back open. I glare at Eli, who steps inside the bathroom, closing the door behind him.

'Can I help you?' I growl, narrowing my eyes into slits.

He squints, stepping closer to me. 'Your eyes . . .'

'What are you doing here?' I demand. 'You don't just follow girls into a bathroom.'

'You don't seem okay.'

'That is none of your concern.'

'I came to this party with you and you're Mya's friend. It *is* my concern.'

I breathe hard as we stare at each other. Then, I push him back against the wall, diving toward his neck. Eli lets out a sound of surprise, tensing for a second, before a breathy exhale leaves him.

This is the first time I have had blood directly from the vein since I was with Kian, and it feels fucking incredible. I drink long and hard, taking too much, too quickly.

I reel back, determined to release him, when he quickly presses his mouth to mine. His wild heart beats feverishly in my ears as I drag my lips across his jaw, down to his neck, the impulse to take more almost overwhelming me. My fingers curl around his hair, pulling his head back, exposing his tender flesh. My fangs snap out, and I sink into him in one fluid movement.

'Ah,' Eli murmurs.

I haven't been intimate with someone like this for a long time. Suddenly, I crave feeling his hands and mouth on me, even though I know it will be nothing. I'm just desperate to rid Kian from my mind. In fact, I wish Kian was here right now, his mouth leaving hot trails of kisses down my skin, the way his hands would possessively grip my ass, pulling me closer to him . . . I mentally shake myself. What the hell am I thinking? He is a monster. An evil force who bulldozed into my life and ruined everything in it.

Eli's blood is much sweeter than the blood bags, sending shockwaves of longing through me with each mouthful. Something niggles in the back of my mind, though. Everyone says blood from the vein is so incredible, there is nothing like the high it gives you, and yet every drop I taste never quite hits the mark. Eli's blood is certainly better than cold blood bags, but it still isn't as good as I need it to be, and it's infuriating.

Despite the pure bliss that would be coursing through him, his hands continue to trail down my sides, toying with the end of my dress. Grinding myself against him, the fabric inches further up my thigh. Suddenly, Kian's face enters my mind, and it feels like I've been doused in icy cold water.

Pulling back, I lick my lips, tasting the sticky sweetness coating my skin.

The necklace around my neck burns white-hot, and I let out a sound of shock as I stumble back. I clench my jaw, yanking it off my skin. Kian gave me this, and told me to never remove it. I cringe at it every time I see it. With its thick black band, and black stone, it reminds me of a dog collar. Another way to exert dominance over me.

'I knew you wanted me.' Eli smirks, and I realise I have totally forgotten about him.

Whatever blood lust haze I was under fades quickly. I yank him forward, leaning in close.

'Forget this ever happened,' I command, locking eyes with him and throwing a strong wave of compulsion straight toward him.

Eli nods. I practically shove him out the door.

Staggering over to the sink, I lean heavily on it, staring into my reflection. My eyes shimmer back at me. My gaze drops to the necklace and, for a moment, I swear it tightens around my throat.

4

KIAN

The Enforcer

AS I PASS THE '*Welcome to Red Thorne*' sign, I barely spare it a glance.

The usual chill is in the air as clouds appear in front of the mouths of anyone I see. Everyone is bundled up in layers. I dig my hands into my pockets, prowling along the perimeter, the smell of fresh blood thick in the air. There isn't any brightness in the sky tonight, and it seems to be getting darker the deeper into town I go.

Murmurs of conversation, laughter, and the sounds of gravel crunching underneath shoes fill my ears as people crowd the street, going from one place to the next in a hurry, everyone too scared to be out on the streets for too long. I love watching them squirm. The darting gazes, their nervous tics, their elevated breathing. Tasting the anxiety on humans draws out something purely dark inside me, fuelling my predatory instincts.

My first stop is the house that Hunter used to reside in, which Theo still inhabits. I peer into the dark window. Hunter is long gone – parading around London with his girlfriend. I have more important things occupying my mind, but I haven't forgotten him, or his bonded blood mate.

The scent of Theo is strong. Although attached to him – as I am to anyone I turn, much as I despise it – I don't think of him much. Not like a certain black-eyed girl with a sharp tongue, and a body I'm dying to touch again.

My eyes blink back at me from the reflection of the window. A powerful surge courses through me, and I groan, doubling over for a moment. Cora. I'm highly attuned to her thoughts and feelings – it is maddening. A maker can also vaguely sense things about the vampires they turn, but with Cora, it is extremely heightened.

With the way my blood heats up, I can tell she is feeding. Interesting. She hasn't tasted human blood straight from the source since she left me. Is she having the same trouble consuming blood that I am? Does all the blood taste awful to her? I have a few theories ticking away in the back of my mind as to why this is happening, but I don't want to accept any of them.

My fingers trace the necklace around my neck. A black stone, attached to a leather band that hugs my throat. I press my thumb to it, the corner of my lip twitching as I feel her reaction as strongly as though she is in front of me, and I am watching it in person.

In a blur, I'm strolling down Cora's driveway. My mouth waters as my senses get invaded by her. Slipping far too easily inside, I drop onto the couch, sitting in the dark. Leaning back, placing my hands behind my head, I wait.

I sense her presence before I hear her. She bids goodnight to the human who lives next door. My eyes lock on him as he slopes across the yard, disappearing into his house. My eyes narrow.

He touched what is mine tonight.

Cora strides inside, and a shriek leaves her lips when she sees me.

'*Mio tesoro*,' I purr, keenly feeling her presence like a physical touch.

My treasure. My precious, darling treasure.

She stiffens, and I feel the fear in her shoot through my body like someone has just prodded me with a taser. A mouse who has stepped into the lion's cage. Those round, glittering eyes. Hair – now an opaque black with ruby red tips, making her eyes even more striking – falls down her shoulders in loose waves. Those cherry-red lips that I can't ever get off my mind.

'Kian,' she whispers, frozen as she gapes at me, eyes locking onto mine, shining in the darkness.

'Did you miss me?' I drawl.

She stands still. Too still. Barely blinking. She is waiting to see what kind of mood I am in. My lips tilt. She is a fucking beauty to look at. How I found this diamond amongst dirt, I do not know, but I don't intend to ever let her go.

A dark chuckle leaves me when she fails to reply. 'No?'

'What are you doing here?' she asks, lifting her chin, a guarded expression on that pretty, heart-shaped face. Her defiance makes me want her even more. My fingers twitch and the urge to reach for her is almost uncontrollable. I have spent many hours working on detaching my emotions from my impulse control, attempting to have complete control over my reaction to being around her. Now everything I have worked on unravels before me.

'I came for you, of course.'

'Me?' she mutters bitterly.

My eyes appraise her slowly and deliberately, drinking in every feature that has been haunting my mind since I saw her last. My longing for her is unrelenting, and I am determined to squash it – make it cease to exist – but being back here, in front of her, makes that seem like an impossible task. The gnawing in my gut that has been growing worse finally feels at ease – like my muscles were bound up tightly and at long last relax.

It makes me want to hate her.

I wish I could.

It would make everything a lot easier.

'You are mine.' I shrug, voice intentionally cold. 'I own you.'

Her jaw flexes. 'I am no one's.'

'No,' I growl, leaning forward, digging my elbows into my thighs. 'You. Are. Mine.'

The muscle in her jaw twitches as she stares at me. Grinning, I lean back, enjoying the sight of her for a few more seconds. I really could stare at her all day and never get bored of it.

'New hair,' I comment.

'Yes,' she replies, tone clipped, appearing on edge, as if she isn't sure I'm happy with the change. My mouth twitches. She cares about what I think, and it must infuriate her that she does.

I move faster than she can blink. Her breath stutters as I twirl a piece of hair around my finger. Silky. Smooth. Like always. Breathing her in, it's as if something inside me had been almost empty, and having her near swells the reserves of my soul. Heat flares through my veins. Vampires do not feel temperatures, but when I am around her, everything is different. Being back here with her is intoxicating, making it hard for me to focus. *Nothing* makes me lose focus.

'Suits you, *mio tesoro*.'

Her eyes flutter closed, and I track the slight tremor in her hands.

'Do you tremble out of fear, or are you fighting your desire to be close to me?' I ask, tilting my head, eyes tracking along the slender curve of her throat.

She is stunning in every way. I have met a lot of beautiful people in my life, it's granted being a vampire, but something about Cora captivates me in a way that's almost unnerving. I pride myself on being detached from people, even my own blood, but she has gotten under my skin. When she left me, I thought letting her go would ease the ache that builds inside me whenever I'm near her, but it's only made it worse.

Much worse.

In the beginning, I thought my infatuation with Cora was simply due to the fact that I had her in my clutches. She was mine to do whatever I wanted with, my own little bird trapped in a cage. But I quickly realised it was more than that. No one has impacted me the way she does. I have a visceral need for her to be *mine*. More than what we are now, not that I like admitting that to myself, let alone anyone else.

She scoffs. 'I *loathe* you. Don't kid yourself into thinking it is anything else.'

I breathe a laugh. 'Loathe . . . love . . . such a fine line, no?'

'Not in this case,' she mutters, turning that steely gaze to me. 'Is it you that's been killing people around town?'

'Believe it or not, I have been too busy to care about what is going on in Red Thorne,' I say, stepping back from her and dropping onto the lounge again, draping my arm on the back of it. Her eyes are narrowed as she watches me carefully, as if she's not sure whether she should try to run, or listen to what I have to say.

I wouldn't mind if she did run. I love a good chase.

'Why do I find that hard to believe?'

I lift a shoulder. 'Because you think my world revolves around you.'

'Doesn't it?' she counters.

I inch my lips up. 'Perhaps it does.'

She does an impeccable job of neutralising her expression, attempting to mask any feelings she might be having, although I can sense them keenly. I admire that about her, since it is something I do so often myself. We are twin flames, Cora and I, not that she would agree.

'What are you doing here?' she asks on an exhale, folding her arms across her chest. 'Come to kidnap me? Drag me back, kicking and screaming?'

Leaning forward, I tap my fingers together. 'I want you to tell me everything that is going on around here.'

She purses her lips for a moment, fixing me with that heated stare I enjoy.

'Not much,' she says after a moment of hesitation.

Raising a brow, I stare at her. 'Not much?'

'That's what I said.'

I tsk my tongue, shaking my head. 'Don't you trust me?'

She releases a laugh. 'No.'

'You hurt my feelings,' I say, fighting off the smile creeping its way onto my face. 'Come on, now. Tell me what is going on.' Leaning forward, latching my eyes onto her. 'I insist.'

She straightens a little, unable to resist answering my direct command. It is particularly useful that I can have so much influence over my turned ones. My compulsion still works on them – albeit not as strongly as it works on humans, but well enough. It works especially well with Cora.

Aithan showed me the craft of how to do this. I don't know another vampire that has managed to do it. It takes a very strong will and mindset to pull it off, but if anyone could do it, it was Aithan. I have tried to teach Cas, but he hasn't managed to perfect it yet. Cas insists certain vampires have particular gifts, but I'm not sure how true that really is.

'Dead bodies keep turning up. Theo and I are attempting to network with people to try to find out what they know.'

'Any leads?' I question.

She shakes her head. 'No. We haven't had much time to investigate.'

'I want you to be my eyes and ears here. Find out everything you can.' I watch her intently, and she meets my gaze. 'I need you to find out if there is a witch here. Most likely blended in with other humans. Sometimes it can be hard to tell if someone is actually a witch.'

She raises a brow, her eyes flickering as they move to my chest, then back to my eyes. Cora has known about my unfortunate situation for a while now, but she doesn't quite know the extent of it.

'No luck, then?'

'Are you worried about me, *mio tesoro*?' The corner of my mouth lifts in amusement.

Flashes of memories bombard my mind, and I know she can feel the tension between us just as strongly as I can.

'Is that all?' she asks abruptly, lowering her gaze.

'One last thing,' I say, standing once more, looking down at her. 'If another man touches what's mine again, I will carve the flesh from his skin and use it as a wall decoration.' Placing my finger under her chin, I tilt her head back, forcing her eyes to meet mine. 'Is that clear?'

She swallows. 'Yes.'

Running my thumb across her jaw, I trace back and forth as she shivers.

'It's good to see you again, *mio tesoro*.'

5

The Prisoner

TIME MOVES DIFFERENTLY HERE. At least I think it does.

Wherever *here* is. For a prison cell, it doesn't really look the part. Soft sunrays spill through the blinds of a tall window. The walls are painstakingly bare.

I get fed three times a day. The mattress is comfortable. I enjoy the music that can be heard through the door and is softly playing more often than not. It's honestly quite nice for being held captive.

I just wish I knew how long I'd been here, or what the hell was going on in the outside world.

My head is fuzzy, like my thoughts are quicksand, and the harder I try to grab a hold of one, the faster it slips through my fingers.

I'm quite sure something in my food is keeping me in a docile state, but I'm too hungry and fatigued to not eat, and, besides, being a little groggy makes the time feel even further warped, and as if it goes by relatively fast.

A few times I tried to escape, but there is no use. With every attempt, someone new stopped me, making me realise I truly don't know what lies beyond these doors.

Besides, I don't have the energy for it anymore. My strength is depleting with each day, it seems.

My eyes move to the clock on the wall, and I release a heavy exhale.

I wish I knew what they wanted with me.

BEFORE

6

CORA

The Fighter

THE SUNRISE WAS INCREDIBLY beautiful today, and yet, even the stunning sight can't pull me out of the vortex of dark thoughts spinning through my mind. The warm rays on my cheeks can't dull the ache behind my eyes.

Pulling my gaze back to the letter in my hand, I stare at yet another denial of financial aid for university. I've put it off for years, working just to keep afloat, while applying for any support I can that would allow me to work less, and go back to study.

Wiping away the tears from my cheeks, I inhale a shaky breath. I told myself that this was the last one I would apply for. So I guess I'm giving up.

Scrunching the paper in my hands, I toss it into the closest bin, and turn my back against the warm sun. A complete opposite to how I feel. I've been soldiering on, working three jobs, attempting to help Mum keep a roof over our heads in this getting-worse-by-the-day economy we are living in.

Last week, I found Mum passed out in bed, an empty bottle of wine on the floor. Drinking herself to sleep is becoming a weekly occurrence. Under her bed – amongst more empty wine bottles – I found a letter from the real estate agent. Our rent has increased by thirty percent. We were already struggling as it is, and now this.

Sometimes, I feel like the weight of this world is too much for me. I can feel my knees buckling as the days go on. I just . . . can't do this anymore.

My head throbs, and my body aches for coffee, but I force myself to walk past the cart. If I want one, I will make it at home. Although I know the cupboards are bare, I did buy milk last week. I hope there's enough left for at least one coffee.

Detouring to my PO box on my usual run was supposed to be a good start to the day, but instead it closed off my last escape route from this life of drudgery. Deciding to stretch out my run a little more, I take the scenic route home. I run until I can no longer breathe easily, and my lungs burn. I'm desperate for the numb feeling it often brings me, but today there is too much heartache and pain for it to cover.

As I push open the door to our apartment building, I do one final swipe down my face to rid it of any tears or streaks on my cheeks. The elevator clunks and clangs as it slowly takes me to my floor, and I focus on steadying my breathing.

When I walk inside, Raya is sitting cross-legged on the dining-room chair, spooning cereal into her mouth. My eyes drift to the empty milk container on the bench, and I let out a slow, shaky exhale.

My sister and I look so similar it's almost like looking into a mirror. But she has a shine in her eyes and a bright smile that comes naturally, whereas mine is growing more forced with each day.

Our apartment is cosy and cluttered, but it's home. I'm here, with the two people I love most in the world, and I want it to be enough.

It *should* be enough.

'Morning!' I say chirpily, leaning down to press a quick kiss to her temple. 'How did you sleep?'

'Fine.' She smiles, leaning back so she can peer up at me. 'How was your run?'

'Great! It's a beautiful day. What have you got planned?' I yank my ponytail out, shaking it over my shoulders, combing my fingers through the long waves.

'My friends are all going to the movies,' Raya says, shrugging nonchalantly, shifting her gaze back in front of her.

'That sounds fun! You're going, right?' I ask.

She shrugs again, looking down at her hands, where she picks at her nail polish. 'I didn't get a chance to ask Mum for money.'

My stomach clenches. Pulling out my wallet, I look at the last remaining fifty-dollar note I have been trying to hang on to. I have a bit of money in my account, but after groceries and helping Mum with bills, I'll be down to nothing by tomorrow. Beaming down at my sister, I hand her the note.

'Go. Have fun.'

Raya's wide grin makes the anxiety in my chest ease a little. 'Are you sure? Do you need it?'

'Nah. Go enjoy yourself.'

'You're the best!' She bounds to her feet, wrapping her arms around me. Holding onto her tightly, I hug her back, suddenly feeling a whole lot better about giving the money to her. This is my little sister. She deserves the world. She is such a kind, strong, caring person. I want her life to be great. Not all of us should have to suffer.

Dashing over to the kitchen bench, she swipes her phone from it, her thumbs moving quickly across the screen as she texts her friends. A sensation – that feels much like jealousy – burns my eyes, and I turn away from her, heading to my room. I've distanced myself from my friends. It got to a point that I was humiliated being around them. They're all succeeding and achieving things that are out of my reach. When I had to cancel on them multiple times due to not having enough money – although they never realised that was the reason for me bailing – they eventually stopped asking me out.

After a shower, I step into my denim shorts and off-the-shoulder shirt that is two sizes too big for me, but is the only clean shirt I can find, reminding me how behind I am on basic chores. Once I tick a few of my jobs off the list, I allow myself to sit on my bed and journal for a while. It's the one place I can pour out all my inner thoughts. My struggles, the dark thoughts, the pain I harbour inside me, that no one probably can tell is even there. The one place I can truly *feel* and be honest without judgement.

'I'm craving a coffee. You want one?' Raya asks, poking her head around my door.

Smiling dryly, I shake my head, ignoring how much I truly would love one. 'I'm fine, but I'll come with you.'

There is a coffee shop just down the street, and I know I could use the money I gave Raya to buy myself one, but I don't want to eat into the money she will need for the movies tonight, because if she asks for more, I don't want to admit that there isn't any. She's old enough now that I could be truthful with her, and she is one of the most understanding and empathic people I've ever met, but I just want to shield her from all the shitty parts of life for as long as possible. As the older sister, I feel it's my job to do so.

The security guard, Gavin, is hovering by the door and beams at Raya when he spots her. His shifts are seemingly growing more sporadic through the weeks. He used to always be here, but it is less and less lately. In fact, this is the first time I've seen him this week. Considering how low-budget this building is, it's a miracle they even hired one, but I think the safety complaints and concerns were a nuisance to the landlord. Having security will probably only be temporary, to calm down the complaints, and then he will cut Gavin loose.

'Morning!' Raya chirps, her pretty smile lighting up her face.

Smiling, Gavin nods at her. 'Good morning.'

'Lovely day outside,' she says conversationally, and his smile widens, his eyes taking on a tenderness that Raya easily brings out in people. She has that infectious, sunshiny personality that makes you want to smile and forget about everything else. That's another reason why I don't want to burden her with things she doesn't need to know about. I would hate for that sunshine to dim.

She's just so damn *cute*. Like, you just want to squish her cheeks and give her a tight squeeze kind of cute.

Raya moves ahead of me, and the security guard's eyes swivel to mine, his smile fading. He gives me a firm look, lips thinning.

Gavin and I don't speak since I shouted at him once. A man got inside the building and broke into the apartment right next to ours, robbing the place of everything worth any value. There were marks on our door where he had tried to get into our apartment, but thankfully I was home, and when I spotted him through the peephole, I ran out with a knife, and I think I truly terrified him. He ended up tripping over and spraining – or breaking – his ankle in an attempt to get away from me. I managed to keep him on the floor, since he couldn't get up anyway, until the police came.

Everyone congratulated me for it. We had free food for weeks from the neighbours. But the way I saw it, I did Gavin's job better than he did, and he should know that his mistake could have cost someone their life. Since then, he gets this awful expression on his face when he sees me, like he wishes he was anywhere else but here.

After Raya gets her coffee, and my stomach grumbles at the incredible smell of pastries wafting toward me from the display case, we return to the apartment. We both sit at the table – Raya painting, and me journaling. We often do this, sitting together in a comfortable silence.

Within an hour, Raya leaves, and it's like she takes all the light in the room with her. The small amount of contagious energy she lent me evaporates all too quickly. Everything that has been circling around in my mind rushes back to me. I collapse onto the lounge, bursting into tears.

I cry, and I cry, until there are no more tears left.

'Come on!' Ange calls, her fingers wrapping around my wrist as she drags me toward the club.

I shiver, the air nipping at all the skin this dress doesn't cover. Almost tripping over my own feet in these gigantic heels, I stumble after her.

I can't seem to shake myself out of the depressive episode I've been in for what feels like months now. When Ange reached out unexpectedly to invite me to her birthday celebrations, a night out on the town sounded exactly like what I needed. I had been feeling so down about the lack of friends in my life, I honestly couldn't believe it when the notification popped up on my screen. I just couldn't say no.

Glancing down at my dress, I surreptitiously run my palm over a stain that I haven't been able to get out. I've worn this dress so many times, it's starting to fall apart.

My mind has been racing with everything going on, and I'm convinced I'm having some sort of quarter-life crisis. Everyone else is at university, engaged, having babies, or travelling around the world. Here I am, less than two hundred dollars in my bank account, mental health in ruins, and trying to avoid eviction for Mum and my sister. It seems like no matter how hard I try, and no matter what I do, I can never keep my head above water.

When tears spring to my eyes, I shake my head. Tonight is about letting loose and having fun. All my problems will still be there tomorrow, so there's no point in wallowing now.

The line is long, and I cross my legs uncomfortably as we stand outside, the urge to pee almost overwhelming me. My head is buzzing from all the pregame tequila shots. A guy we met at a bar we were just at has taken an interest in Ange, and has been shouting everyone drinks all night. I can't complain, I really felt like a drink but couldn't have even bought one for myself.

Wincing, I glance down, adjusting my weight from my right foot to my left. The straps of my heels are biting into my skin, and I can see the blood underneath them. My feet are killing me now. I cringe at the thought of how they will be after dancing for a few more hours. I'm desperate for another drink – I need it to numb the pain – and I pull out my phone, glancing down at the digits on my online banking app, a glaring sign that I cannot afford to be out tonight.

The line finally moves and we make our way inside. The music blares as we walk down the hallway. My heart physically hurts when I pay the entrance fee, following my friends into the club. I haven't been out in so long, I let myself succumb to the peer pressure. Just this once.

The air feels damp and warm, such a stark contrast from outside, and suddenly I feel flustered. The music is so loud, I wince, rubbing my ears as if that will somehow attune them to the volume.

'I need to pee!' I shout at them.

'I'll meet you at the bar,' Ange tosses over her shoulder, hurrying toward the line. Her long, wavy blonde hair disappears as she is swallowed by the sea of people. I can hardly think straight; the techno music feeling like a sledgehammer inside my head. Shaking it off, I roll my shoulders and try to seem less tense.

Turning, and attempting to ignore the piercing pain of each step, I head toward the bathroom and almost cry in frustration when the line is even longer than the one outside the club. If only I could just enjoy being out with my friends, no problems with money, no sore feet, no urge to pee every five minutes.

Huffing, I mentally slap myself. *Enough*, I berate my mind, as if I have two voices inside me – one desperate to let loose and have fun, while the other torments me with all the stress I'm trying to pretend isn't there.

By the time I am finished, and step back out near the dance floor, I can't see any of my friends. Not near the bar, not dancing, not in any of the booths that I pass. My eyes roam through the space. The dance floor is so tightly packed, there's a good chance they are somewhere in there.

Trying not to panic, I push through the crowd. An elbow swings into my head and I wince, rubbing my forehead as I continue toward the bar. I'm tempted to ask the staff if they saw my friend, but I doubt anyone would remember a blonde girl, since there are at least a hundred of those here.

Now my head is throbbing, as well as my feet.

When a couple next to me in line bumps into me, making out so passionately that the person behind them takes their spot, I swallow down the lump lodged in my throat. I miss the attention from guys. Being held. Having someone there to be by my side. With my schedule, boys have been low on my priority list. Everything other than surviving has been low on the list, honestly.

Being out tonight is supposed to be serving as a distraction from how much my reality sucks right now, and here I am, letting my thoughts and feelings ruin this, too. I want to shake myself.

My eyes burn, and I rub them, before remembering I have mascara on, and I've quite possibly just smeared it all around my eyes.

'Hello,' a deep voice purrs right beside my ear, causing me to whirl around in surprise.

My gaze connects with eyes so dark they look black, and my heart drops into my stomach at the intensity of them. He's tall. Really tall. Towering over me with impressive height and broadness from what looks like many years of workouts and training. His lips are tilted in a seriously hot smirk, with a jawline as fierce as the end of a blade. He looks intimidating as hell, and it has my pulse *racing*.

'Hi,' I breathe, a little starstruck by his looks. It's like seeing a celebrity out in the wild and just *knowing* they're famous, even if you don't actually recognise them.

'Drink?' he asks, gesturing to the spot that has opened up in front of me, where the bartender is blinking at me, a look of impatience on his face.

'Yes,' I manage to choke out, trying not to look as flustered as I feel.

His smirk widens. 'And? What are you drinking?'

'Oh,' I say, a blush spreading down my neck. 'Vodka raspberry.'

The man leans forward, repeating my order, and the bartender swiftly moves around behind the counter, preparing the drinks. The man easily invades the entire space, causing a few heads around us to swivel in his direction. The bartender slides the drinks across, and the man leans forward once more to grab the glasses. He turns, not pulling out his phone or wallet to pay. I peer over his shoulder, but the bartender has moved on to the next person. Perhaps he comes here so often he has a tab.

He is dressed in all black, his clothes fitting him perfectly, showcasing the hard muscles underneath. I frown for a moment, my eyes sweeping over him. He looks too good to be in a club like this.

When his eyes connect with mine, the corner of his lips twitches.

'Want to come sit with me?' he asks, causing me to lean forward, completely captured by those eyes. It must be a trick of the light, but I swear I can see the black rippling, like a sea of dark glitter.

Nodding, I follow him toward a booth in the back corner. I do another quick scan of my surroundings, confirming I can't see any of my friends.

When I sit, my eyes travel upward, and the way he looms over me makes my heart speed up a little in excitement. His eyes drift downward, slowly travelling over my body, down my legs, landing on my feet.

'You're bleeding,' he says, voice silken, causing a shiver of desire to roll through me.

'Stupid heels,' I reply, unable to tear my gaze from his when they snap back up to mine. 'I'm Cora.'

'Nice to meet you, Cora.' His voice is deep, rumbling like the sound of distant thunder in a storm. Leaning his forearm onto the table, his fingers tap against the glass of his drink, eyes fixed on mine with a piercing intensity. 'I'm Kian.'

7

KIAN

The Enforcer

DESPITE THE BEATING THIS man just took, he has a sharp gaze that is unwavering as I lean toward him, resting my hands on my knees.

Blood drips from his chin. His nose is broken and one eye is swollen. He spits blood at my feet, and I ignore the flare of hunger inside me. Squashing down the urge to bite into his throat, I level him with a fierce stare.

The blood I'm craving isn't his, but sometimes my body forgets that.

'Tell me. Now,' I growl, my voice deep and menacing, my tone dripping in the most vicious tone I can muster.

'I ain't telling you shit,' he hisses, scowling at me with venom swimming behind his eyes.

Huffing in frustration, I step back and wipe the blood from my hands.

It has been a hell of a week. Running a hand through my hair, I stalk out of the room, leaving the man chained to the floor. The ache for blood washes through me, almost knocking me over. I've been lazy with feeding this week – my mind preoccupied – and now the consequences are knocking at the door.

'Kian,' a voice says.

Glancing up, I see him. One of the only people in the world I would consider a friend. His white-blond hair is stark against the darkness of the room. Tall and wiry with skin whiter than paper, making his shadowy black eyes look demonic and unnatural in his angular face.

'Cas,' I grunt.

His eyes drop to my blood-soaked hands, his lips tilting. 'Having fun?'

'Loads.'

'What the hell happened?' Cas asks, peering around the lounge-room of the house I have rented for the week, as if it might hold answers for him. A trail of blood zigzags across the floor from when I dragged the man across it. Cas eyes it, and then swivels his gaze to mine, smirking in amusement.

A cigarette is slipped behind his ear, and he swiftly plucks it out of its spot, lighting it. A lot of vampires smoke. Both smoking and drinking can help ease blood cravings. Some vampires feel that more strongly than others and use either or both as a coping mechanism. I think it's weak, and they should train themselves to just deal with it – like I do – but I allow Cas to get away with certain things that I would judge others for. As much as I don't like having people close to me, Cas is an exception.

'I've got someone in the basement.'

Cas smiles, his trademark thin smile that somehow looks sarcastic but severe at the same time. 'Of course you do.'

'Another day, another supernatural to torture.' I sigh theatrically, shaking my head. 'Never ends.'

'Apparently not,' Cas remarks, eyes moving to the blood once more. 'How did they kill him?'

Dropping onto the lounge, I hang my head, hating that it hurts me somewhere deep inside whenever someone mentions the vampire who created me. He was killed earlier this week. I felt it the moment it happened, like a stake through my chest.

'It was a coven of witches,' I answer. My jaw flexes, and I pull at the shirt that's spread across my chest, like it suddenly feels too tight.

Cas slowly nods, not bothering to question how I found this out. It's what I'm best at. Tracking, and killing.

'I did suspect,' he says.

After becoming a vampire, there was no one I could trust, except Aithan, the vampire that turned me, and Cas, who he turned at the same time. Aithan was a strong, vicious man. Brutal, efficient. A man – a vampire – that I respect. *Respected*.

I knew there was a history between him and witches, but I didn't know how deep that war ran until I felt his death like a gunshot, and the pain of it is lingering like a human hangover that seems to last for days. I tracked the coven, and I got my fangs into one of them, and then all hell broke loose.

'I never thought of him dying, you know,' Cas murmurs, staring ahead, a sullen expression on his face. 'He was someone I just thought would always be there.'

'I know.'

'It hurt.' Cas winces, touching his chest, as if protecting a gaping hole.

That's how it feels for me, anyway. I don't know much about the connection a vampire has with the vampire who created them, but it is something significant.

I glance down at my own chest. A dark mark lies there now. It's been there since the witch cursed me. Another eerie sensation rolls through me and I try to shake the feeling off, refusing to believe any of the worst-case scenarios my mind is concocting.

'Yeah.'

'Who've you got down there?' Cas asks, jerking his chin toward the door that leads to the basement.

'The only person I've traced from where Aithan got killed.

I think he is friends with one of the witches. They've covered their tracks well, but I'm trying to get him to fess up. He has some anti-compulsion magic in him though, which is making the process . . . slow.' Scrubbing a hand across my jaw, I lean back onto the lounge. 'But I'll get it out of him.'

Cas chuckles, shaking his head at me. 'If anyone can force someone to talk, it's you.'

'Mm,' I mutter noncommittally.

'You good?' Cas asks, concern clouding his features as he glances at me.

'I just feel . . . weird.'

'Me too. The after-effect of the death of a vampire's maker can linger for a while. It can be really extreme sometimes. I've been doing a bit of research about it.' Cas leans back against the wall, crossing his ankles.

I resist the urge to roll my eyes. Sometimes Cas speaks like he is reading directly from a textbook. To be fair, he does spend a lot of his time researching – especially about vampires. He has an insistent need to know absolutely everything he can. I suppose we do have one particular thing in common; we like to be the smartest person in the room. We developed that way of thinking from Aithan. He practically drilled it into us.

'Yeah, I get that, I think that's a part of it but . . .' I hesitate, unsure how to say what I want to say. I'm not one to really discuss anything like this with anyone, but with Cas, it's different. He's my ally, and due to his obsession with learning all he can about vampirism, he is probably the best person to ask. 'Have you ever had a hyper-fixation on someone before?'

He raises a brow. 'Can you be more specific? A human?'

I nod. 'Yeah. Like . . . something draws you to a place where they are, but you don't know what. The smell of their blood is different from others. Their presence is . . . intoxicating.'

When I drag my eyes to meet Cas's, he has a startled look on his face.

'You're feeling that for a human?'

I grimace. 'Unfortunately.'

'Never thought I'd see the day . . .' Cas mutters, genuinely looking shocked. 'Well. Of course it is a natural instinct for a vampire to hunt prey, and humans are our prey. We can easily get hyper-focused on one target until that prey becomes ours. Whether that be a mate of some sort, or simply a meal.' He shrugs. 'I think it's normal. I know I'm certainly drawn to some humans more than others.'

'You're right,' I say with a nod. 'That must be it. I just haven't experienced it before but I'm sure that's all it is.'

Cas shrugs. 'No harm in exploring it. I know you don't let anyone get close to you, but I don't see the issue with it. You have all the time in the world, after all.'

'Mm.'

Shoving himself off the wall, Cas pushes the sleeves of his shirt up, rolling his neck. In the pale lighting that has slipped through the blinds, his skin has a silvery colouring to it, his bleached hair looking more white than usual. He inclines his head toward the basement door.

'May I?' He grins, his eyes darkening into an opaque black. 'I feel like getting my hands dirty.'

Lazily gesturing my hand in the direction of the top of the stairs, I nod. 'Go for it.'

A scream splinters the air a few moments later and I smile, sinking back into the lounge. My eyes drift closed, and my mind wanders to the other night.

I don't know why I've chosen that night, and that town, but I feel I am drawn to the girl. She walks right past me, eyes scanning her surroundings, and if my heart was still beating, it would stop in my chest. Long dark waves cascade down her back. A tight-fitting dress hugs her figure. Her blood smells so sweet, I can practically taste it in the air. Everything inside my brain stops functioning for a solid thirty seconds. Her scent is delicious, washing over me to the point I step back, as if an electric shock is coursing through my body.

Something I can't describe rises inside my chest. A feeling I've never experienced before. I can't help but drop everything and follow her, like I am being pulled by a magnetic force.

As she smiles up at me, my eyes trace the delicate curve of her throat, watching her pulse.

My God, I need to have her.

When I place my hand on her as I guide her toward the back, I decide right then and there, she is mine.

8

CORA

The Fighter

I STARE AT THE blood on the floor.

Exhaling, I lean down and press the tissue against the cut. I need new shoes but I have nothing left in my bank account until my next pay. If only I was the same size as Mum, or Raya, but for some reason I was blessed with being two sizes larger than the both of them. It makes no sense, since Raya and I are so similar in shape and height, and Mum is much the same.

Cleaning up the mess, I attempt to get my shoe back on and wedge a clean tissue between it and my skin. The pressure of the shoe still hurts, but at least the rubbing is less intense with a barrier there. Wiping the tears from my eyes, I fix my hair, and walk back out into the restaurant.

My mind has been consumed with the handsome stranger I met the other night. He was nothing but a gentleman. We exchanged conversation, shared a few drinks, and he got me into an Uber safely to get home. It was the first moment where I've felt *something* for so long. Well, something other than anxiety and stress. My own thoughts are like a rock, pulling me further and further down as I try to crawl my way out of the darkness, and yet the entire time I was with Kian he made me forget about all my problems. I didn't realise how much I needed that.

I can't quite put my finger on what felt different about him. Perhaps the in-your-face attractiveness, but I don't think that's it. Perhaps the sensual confidence that oozed from him, with the air of mystery. Something almost . . . not human, which sounds completely ridiculous to think.

The more I think about it, the more I wish he had kissed me, or even asked for my number. I'm desperate to see him again, but I have no clue how to contact him. Only having his first name to go off, I've had no luck locating any of his social media.

Dipping my fingers into my pocket, I pull out the dried rose petal he gave me. A dark blood red with a shimmering black border that bleeds down the petals. I run my finger over it. If it wasn't for this, I would think I'd imagined that entire encounter between us. He was just too good-looking, too seductive, too charming to seem real. But he is, because he left me this, and as much as I don't want it to get ruined, I couldn't bear leaving it behind today.

'Heyyy,' Melissa, my co-worker from hell, chirps, making a beeline for me.

I quickly pocket the petal carefully, hoping she doesn't notice it, while I inwardly groan. I've been avoiding her all night. She always asks me to cover her shifts, or stay back so she can leave early. I appreciate the money but she always seems to ask when I'm having the worst day. It also seems like I have been having a lot of 'worst days' lately.

Her shiny blonde hair tumbles down her shoulders, which she flicks out of her face. She is a bubbly, perky girl who always makes me feel like a storm cloud on a sunny day. I attempt to match her energy, but it's like putting a black cat beside a golden retriever.

'Melissa,' I say, brushing past her.

'I was wondering,' she begins and I push my tongue against the inside of my cheek in annoyance, spinning to face her. 'Do you think I can head off now, and you cover the last hour of my shift? I know you're due to finish in a minute, but I just have this suuuuper important appointment I can't reschedule.'

I blink at her. 'You're just asking this now?'

Her smile widens, ignoring my comment. 'Come on, Cor. Pretty please. I'll owe you one.'

'I think you've reached your capacity of "owing me one",' I say flatly, a headache pulsing behind my eyes. I've already been here for nine hours. My head is aching, my feet are killing me, and I promised Raya I would be home tonight to cook dinner and watch a movie with her, since we haven't seen each other much over the last two weeks with all the extra shifts I've picked up. 'I can't tonight. I need to get home.'

'Come on, Cora. Please!'

'She said no,' a deep voice says from behind me, and I feel his presence without turning to see him. His chest hits my back and I see Melissa's eyes widen. 'Do it yourself.' She opens her mouth to retort, when he steps even closer to me, causing a shiver of anticipation and a slight thrill to roll down my spine. 'Leave her alone.' Her mouth snaps shut and she turns, disappearing out the back.

My mouth feels dry. Slowly, I pivot, and crane my neck to stare up at him. My stomach flip-flops as those black eyes land heavily on mine. The pure liquid heat that scorches though my body at seeing him is unlike anything I've ever felt. Dressed in a leather jacket, and a black tee, with his hair stylishly messy, I almost go weak at the knees. He looks like pure sin.

'Hi,' I breathe.

'Cora,' he drawls, his lips curving upward. 'It's nice to see you again.'

I'm breathless as I gaze up at him, wishing I didn't look as dishevelled as I feel. No one feels nice after a nine-hour shift of running around, barely able to pause to have a drink of water.

This was my first bathroom break I've had all day, and it is only because a customer complained about the blood leaking out of my shoe.

'You too,' I murmur, swallowing, hoping to regain some moisture inside my mouth. I vaguely recall mentioning to him where I work, but I'm still surprised he is here. I was wondering whether I would ever see him again.

His eyes trail down my neck, making me flush. They keep travelling down my body, and it's like my skin is alight with fire. His eyes pause at my feet. 'You're bleeding again,' he comments.

I glance down, and wince to see half of the now-bloody tissue is dangling out of my shoe. That's an attractive look. Covering my face, I inhale, trying to get a grip on my breathing. I desperately don't want to fuck this up with him. Whatever is even happening. But with how much my life is spiralling right now, I feel like it's all too possible.

My heart sinks at my desperation. The man spent a few hours with me, and here I am, already imagining that something is happening between us and thinking of ways I'm going to sabotage myself.

'Wow. I wish you hadn't seen that,' I mutter, glaring at the tissue.

A ghost of a smile flickers across his face as I peer between the gaps of my fingers. 'Blood doesn't faze me.'

'That's a relief,' I say with a smile, slowly lowering my hands.

'When do you finish?' he asks, and I find myself leaning forward, staring into his eyes.

Shifting back in alarm, not realising how close I had gotten, I look at the clock above the till, my heart increasing speed when I realise my shift technically finished two minutes ago, meaning I have no reason *not* to go with him if he asks.

'Now, actually.'

'Excellent,' he purrs, dragging his tongue across his lower lip in a seductive way that has me clenching my legs together. *God, I really am desperate.* 'Would you like to have a drink with me?'

I nod. 'Sure. I don't look my best, though . . .' I trail off, staring down in dismay at my faded uniform, which hangs off me since I've stopped eating enough.

'You look perfect,' he whispers, and it's so quiet and deep I almost don't hear him.

My head snaps up, and we lock eyes. Delight fills me at his words, and suddenly, I feel tears welling. No one has said anything like that to me for a long time. Smiling, I nod again. 'Oh . . . thank you.'

Holding out his arm, he smiles. 'Shall we?'

Circling my arm around his, I let him lead me out the door. It doesn't even occur to me that all my things are still in my locker out the back.

'Were you hoping to see me again, Cora?' he murmurs, turning to face me when we get out onto the street. I relish the evening air that washes over me, cooling my heated cheeks. His eyes drop to my lips, before inching their way back up to hook on my gaze again.

'Yes,' I whisper.

He looks pleased at that. 'Good. As was I.'

'Why?' I ask, blurting out the word before my self-control has a chance to stop it.

His lips twitch. 'I can't seem to get you off my mind. That is very unusual for me.'

My lungs contract. The way he stares at me is like a wolf sizing up his prey. That should scare me, or at least intimidate me, but it makes me feel . . . excited. Gazing up at him, I smile, enjoying the way his eyes assess every movement I make.

'Well,' I say, sweeping my eyes over the busy street, trying to regain my composure. 'Now that you have me, what do you plan to do with me?'

Leaning forward, he traces a finger down the side of my face. I gasp at the coolness of his skin. Tucking a piece of hair behind my ear, his lips inch into a smirk.

'You have no idea the things I have planned for you.'

Tilting my head back, I laugh. A true, genuine laugh that I haven't heard from myself for a long time.

When I sober up, I face him, to see him staring. He's always staring. Watching me closely, as if memorising every movement of mine, like he is storing all the information he can about me in a file inside his mind. It should freak me out, but the way his eyes track me, almost like he's fearful I might slip from his grasp, does something to me that I can't quite explain.

We walked around the park near my work for over an hour, talking, getting to know each other. He has a rich, deep voice that I could listen to all day. I'm utterly fascinated by him. The way he speaks, the way he moves. The snippets of information he shares with me about himself. I drink it all in and I'm thirsting for more.

Italian heritage. No kids. No partner. He travels a lot for work. What work he actually does, I'm still unsure, but the way he dresses and holds himself, I imagine he is comfortable with money. He's guarded, like me, but seems to be open to sharing things about himself – within reason.

Then the last hour or so we spent in a bar, and I had one too many glasses of wine, and my head feels light and floaty. I had forgotten what it feels like to let loose and have *fun*. To not wince every time I need to pay for something, to not mentally calculate everything in my head, to not worry about tomorrow. He makes me forget about all my worries, and it feels fucking incredible.

'It's very pretty,' I say, glancing at him, leaning onto the table. We are secluded in a booth at the back of the bar. The air is warm, carrying a soft murmur of conversation and music, but all I notice is him.

'Hmm?' he replies in that deep voice of his. It's such a pleasant sound. I never knew I could be attracted to a voice until now.

'The dried rose petal. It's unique. I've never seen a rose with those colour petals.'

'Ah.' He nods, staring at me, something I can't quite decipher sparkling in those hauntingly pretty eyes of his. 'Yes. I do it myself.'

'It's beautiful.'

The way his eyes sweep over me, assessing every detail, makes me smile coyly up at him. He brings his hand up to my face, his thumb caressing my cheek. Desire courses through me. I've never felt anything like this, and I don't know how to handle it. This man makes me feel like I'm a teenager again with hormones coursing through me.

'I have never given one of my rose petals to someone before.'

I straighten, eyes snapping to his, since they had drifted to his lips. What pretty lips they are. I've never thought that of a man before, but everything about him is just *pretty*. I don't know how else to say it. Handsome? Gorgeous? An eerie beauty is perhaps the most accurate way to describe him. A sort of pretty that is almost brutal, with his dark brows, black eyes, and sharp jaw. His skin is . . . too smooth. Too perfect, and unblemished. I can't pull my gaze away from him, no matter how hard I try.

My tongue darts out, moistening my lips, and his gaze tracks the movement.

'Really?' I whisper.

'Mmhmm.' He nods, his hand dropping, much to my dismay.

I like the feel of his skin on mine. Cool and smooth, like marble. Since he makes my cheeks burn with heat, it is a soothing feeling having him touch me.

'Why me?' I blurt, my mouth having a mind of its own.

He shrugs, digging his hands into his pockets. 'I'm trying to figure that out.'

I raise a brow. 'Trying to figure me out, you mean?'

'Something like that.'

'Well. I'm an open book.'

'Are you?' he questions, a dry smile twisting his lips. 'You don't seem all that open to me.'

I smile. 'I am, if you look hard enough. Unlike you.'

'Unlike me?' he echoes, looking curious.

'You are very mysterious, Kian.'

'Is that so?'

'Yes.' I nod. 'I like it, but I'm dying to know everything about you.'

He chuckles, and the rich sound of it sends goosebumps rippling across my skin.

'So, you move around a lot,' I say, twisting my fingers together as I look ahead, suddenly feeling a little nervous about asking this question. I don't know if I'll like the answer. 'Are you here for long?'

Kian is quiet for a moment. 'That's a good question.'

I glance over at him. 'You're not sure?'

'Not really,' he admits. 'I guess you could say I'm working remotely right now. So I can move on whenever.' Those unsettlingly dark eyes rest back onto mine and I swallow, feeling flustered. 'Or I could stay.'

My breath is short as I nod. I don't know what it is about him that makes everything he does, every interaction, seem so much more intense than usual. Like every movement, every word he says, every meeting of our eyes is deliberate.

'Do you enjoy travelling?'

'Yeah. I like the anonymity of it. Meeting new people, experiencing new things, and then being able to just move on.'

'Does it get lonely?' I ask, hoping he doesn't take offence at the question.

He shrugs. 'You meet people wherever you go.'

'I suppose so. I guess I can't imagine life without my family.'

'Do you have a big family?' he asks.

I shake my head. 'Not at all. It's just me, my sister, and our mum.'

'House of women,' he comments.

'Yeah.'

'Your father?' he probes. 'If I may ask.'

'Not in the picture.'

'I see.'

'You're the opposite, I guess. A massive family, but in a different country.'

He nods. 'Yeah.'

'Do you see them often?'

'No, not often. I have an app, where I can check in on them.'

'What do you mean?'

'Well. My brother set it up. I hack his cameras to check in on them. He basically monitors them, to make sure they're safe.'

I jolt back slightly, alarmed. 'You spy on them?'

'Let's just say there's a family history that may put them in danger, so it's a necessity.'

'Er . . .' I say, unsure how to digest that information. Clearing my throat, I decide to keep the conversation rolling, although my mind is stuck on the words he just said. 'What's your brother like?' I ask.

'He's . . .' He hesitates. 'A very kind, considerate person. Nothing like me.'

I breathe a laugh. 'I don't know what you mean. You seem to be both of those things.'

Kian flashes a smile at me. 'You're the only person to have ever said that.'

'I'm sure that's not true. Do you and your brother get along?'

He exhales. 'I keep him at a distance. He doesn't think I'm there for him, but I do check on him a lot. I've helped him more times than he will ever know.'

'Helped him? With what?'

'When he has let his control slip.'

My brows furrow. 'His control?'

'He's been in quite a few dangerous situations that I've helped him out of. He just wasn't aware it was me watching over him.'

I blink at him. 'I'm not really following.'

He waves a hand at me, dismissing my confusion. 'Don't worry. It's complicated.'

'What do you mean your brother has an app to watch the family?' I blurt, unable to move past that. I'm a little uneasy at how casually he admitted to that, as if it's the most normal thing in the world to be monitoring the people you love through cameras.

Kian is beginning to look a little frustrated with my questions, but I'm desperate to know more about him. He is so damn intriguing.

'It's just a safety thing. Since they're so far away.'

'Right . . . you don't go see them in person?'

'Not often.'

'You're a bit of a lone wolf, then?'

He snorts. 'That's ironic.'

'Is it?' I smile, brows arched in confusion, crossing my leg over the other. 'Why's that?'

Kian shifts closer, and I stare into his eyes, a little entranced. He lightly touches his finger on my cheek, across the little birthmark there. He runs his thumb back and forth over it, and my skin erupts with tingles.

'Forget I said anything about the cameras. About monitoring my family. What I said about my brother. You will only remember when I ask you to.'

There's a quiet pause and I suddenly can't remember what we were just talking about.

'Can I say something that is potentially absurd?' I whisper.

'Sure,' he says casually, studying my eyes for a moment before glancing away.

'It feels like we met at the exact moment I needed to meet you.' I swallow, shaking my head, unsure why I'm saying anything like this. For some reason, I seem to want to blurt out every thought to him, as if he is pulling them from me with an invisible string. 'That probably sounds bizarre because we literally just met.'

I'm reluctant to meet those dark eyes, fearing I've totally blown everything.

'I'm starting to think that, too, Cora.'

My head snaps up at the sound of my name on his lips. It does something to me. Something I can't quite put into words, but all I know is that I want to hear him say it again. I'm leaning forward, it's as if he is drawing me closer, although he hasn't moved a muscle.

'Come on,' he says, capturing my hand in his, threading our fingers, like it is the most natural thing in the world. 'I want to show you something.'

'What is it?'

'A place I like to go.'

'A place?' I echo.

'Yeah. I like to go there to think. It's quiet. Peaceful. I discovered it only recently, but I really quite like it.'

Fighting back a smile, I trail after him, attempting to keep up with his long strides. Heads turn our way, almost every pair of eyes watching us, but Kian doesn't seem to notice. We spill out onto the street, walking for a few minutes until we get to a gigantic building that is looming over us with impressive height. I peer up at it, not having ever been this close to it before. I don't often come to this part of the city.

'Hold on,' he whispers, and I jolt in alarm when he is suddenly right behind me, his mouth pressed against my ear. Circling his arms around my waist, suddenly wind rushes against my face. By the time I blink, we have somehow been transported from the street to the roof of the building.

I let out a shriek, stumbling out of his arms, gaping around us.

'How . . . what . . . ?' I can't seem to form a sentence as my heart gallops in my chest. I feel dizzy. A ripple of fear moves through my body, and I shiver, stepping back from him, creating some distance between us.

He grins, amusement shining in his eyes, and I baulk at the sight of it. The grin is utterly beautiful on his handsome face. Heat flames my cheeks as I gape at him for longer than I should, taking in every inch of that perfect smile, my mind racing at all the thoughts bouncing around my head.

A thought enters my mind, and my heart stops.

He is not human. He can't be.

'Don't worry about it,' he murmurs, eyes connecting with mine. 'Don't be afraid.'

And just like that, I'm not worried about it, and I'm not afraid.

'How did you do that?' I ask, feeling calm, and somehow relaxed, the tenseness in my shoulders easing.

'I guess you could say I'm gifted.' He shrugs, walking toward me, his long strides easily eating up the distance between us. I catch my breath, stumbling back, hitting the edge of the building.

'Gifted?' I raise a brow, painfully aware of my blushed cheeks and racing heart, although it is slowing down since he told me to not worry.

'Cora . . . I have learnt a lot about you in a short amount of time,' he says, taking a step closer to me, leaving barely any space between us. I inhale sharply, his scent that seems so familiar from seeing him recently, but so unfamiliar at the same time. A scent I can't quite describe. 'I want to ask you one thing.'

'Okay,' I say cautiously, swallowing, my throat suddenly feeling dry.

'Are you happy?'

He barely whispers the words, and yet, he may as well have shouted them at me with the way I flinch.

Rolling my lips, I want to look away, but can't seem to get my eyes to obey. I'm taken back by the question, and force an easy smile onto my face. My go-to 'everything is just fine' smile that has become a part of my personality at this point.

'Y-yes,' I eventually stammer. 'Of course I'm happy.'

He shakes his head, drawing closer once more. 'I don't believe you.' His eyes bore into mine with unsettling scrutiny. 'Tell me the truth.'

'No,' I murmur on an exhale. 'I'm not happy. I haven't been happy for a long time.'

He considers this, eyes watching me carefully. 'If you had the chance to leave your life behind, would you do it?'

My spine straightens and I look at him sharply. 'I don't understand what you mean.'

'If you could live a better life, and were given the opportunity to do so, would you do it?'

Another shiver rolls through my body. He is so close to me now, I can feel his presence like a physical touch. Tilting my head back, I stare at him. His hand snakes around my neck, his thumb traces my throat, and I clench my thighs together to stop my knees from weakening. His touch sends me spiralling into a hot mess of emotions, emotions I can't seem to get control over.

'Yes.' I whisper, watching those dangerous eyes of his, enjoying how they seem to impossibly darken, even though they are already as black as the night sky. The pressure of his thumb on my skin increases, pulling a slight gasp from my lips at the feel of it. His tongue slides across his lower lips as his eyes scan my face one final time, making my skin tingle under his gaze. 'I would.'

9

KIAN

The Enforcer

AS SHE WALKS DOWN the dark street, I can't help thinking how easy it would be to snap her neck.

Cora would be gone, and so would these strange feelings festering inside me, growing stronger and more insurmountable, like a plague. She would be dead. Problem solved.

I don't understand how I went from having no attachments to anyone, to being utterly consumed by this human. The paranoid part of me wonders if it is the witches somehow concocting something. A way to draw me out, so they can finish me off. I don't entirely believe that theory though, as much as I would like it to be that simple. There's an innocence about the girl, but I can see the darkness in her, a darkness so similar to mine. It's simmering beneath the surface, begging to be released. I can feel it.

I've been doing some research about this, but finding answers about vampire legends can be difficult, since the majority of humans don't know we exist. Finding a reliable source is difficult, too, given the topic at hand. I'm not giving up, however. I will find out what it is about her that has me going mad. If the witches are involved, it will be the last thing they ever do.

The moonlight bounces from her silky hair as she moves quickly and quietly through the streets. I keep a few metres behind her, as silent and hidden as a shadow. Watching her has become a particular enjoyment for me. Studying her, observing her surroundings, learning more about her day-to-day life.

What a sad, pathetic life it is.

I could give her the world.

Gritting my molars, I swallow down a dark laugh that threatens to rise. I don't give anyone anything. I look out for myself, and that's what I've always done. Who is she to deter me from the way I have always been?

Moving as quick as lightning, I come up behind her, my hands closing around her throat. It would have taken only a second to snap her neck, but my body recoils like I've run head-first into a brick wall. With a sharp inhale, I jerk back, melting into the darkness once more as she spins around, eyes wide, breathing frantic as she gropes at her throat.

Her gaze lands on the spot I'm hiding in, and she steps forward, eyes narrowing.

Loud laughter yanks both of our attention from each other, and she glances toward the group that stumbles out of the bar closest to us.

When she looks back at the spot I was just at, I'm already gone.

I try to walk away. I really do.

The way her pulse thunders as she hurries down the street makes me feel more alive than I have in weeks. I stalk her, carefully and quietly, moving like the wind. When she feels my touch on the back of her neck, she sprints ahead.

I land in front of her, and she screams, running straight into me. My fangs snap out and I throw myself at her, only for my fangs to lock back into my gums, and my limbs to freeze, as if someone is holding me back. But there is no one there.

Growling, I drop her to the ground and sink into the shadows, furious and confused with myself, not bothering to compel her, since she didn't see my face, although I probably should, since she's terrified.

I'm at war with myself. A part of me wants to kill her, and end whatever this fucking madness is that is consuming me. The other part wants to hold her close, and protect her. Claim her as mine. I have never had a partner since I turned, and for some reason, my brain has decided that she would be a good one to have.

Gritting my teeth, I disappear into the night, feeling utterly lost, and confused.

Cora looks like her mother.

Tilting my head, I study the woman. She fights off a yawn as she strolls down the street, glancing at the shop windows she passes. She looks older than I'm guessing she is, with lines round her mouth and eyes, and an overall fatigue about her. A woman who works too much, and isn't kind to her body.

I've decided to do some digging into the family. Cora's father has a new family, and they live on the opposite side of the country. Nothing exciting to report there, his background is clear, and there is nothing tied to any sort of witches or covens. Her mother doesn't have any close family since she is adopted. I'm frustrated that it has led to a dead end, because something isn't right with the way I feel for Cora. No one gets under my skin, and I really don't like that she has.

My hand moves to my chest, and I place my palm over the mark on my skin from the witch. Whatever she has done to me, it's getting worse. Is it poisoning me? Am I starting to hallucinate? Are all these feelings for Cora a result of my mind crumbling away bit by bit? Are the two linked, both designed to drive me into oblivion?

The wind picks up, blowing a bunch of leaves in front of my feet, and I'm so focused on how similarly the woman walks to

Cora that I step right on top of one, and it crunches. Her head whips back, but I'm not there by the time she turns. Her eyes bounce around the empty street before she shrugs it off and continues walking.

After a few moments, I let her hear me.

She whirls around. When she turns back, she screams.

'Hello,' I say, staring down at her.

'Where the hell did you come from?' she exclaims, stepping back, clutching her chest.

My God, she looks even more like Cora closer up, only with sun-damaged skin and faint streaks of greying hair. She's pulled her hair back into a tight bun off her face, so it's hard to tell if her hair falls in the same way, but I imagine it does.

Narrowing my eyes into slits, I step closer to her. There is something about her, and I can't quite put my finger on what it is.

'Who are you?' she demands, frowning up at me.

Exhaling, shaking my head in disbelief, I meet her gaze. 'What are you?'

Screwing her face up, she looks an equal mixture of affronted and shocked at my intrusion. 'What?' Stepping back once more, her brows pinch together sharply. 'You're invading my space.'

I give her a cold, leering smile, and my voice sounds hollow even to my ears. 'Am I?'

Her brows bend further toward each other as she eyes me. I barely take one step back from her.

'Answer the question,' I say, pushing my coercion onto her with more force than I normally would. Her body jerks at it. I'm unsure whether it works or not. Or perhaps it is affecting her, but not to the full extent I need it to.

'I'm a mum,' she says.

I raise a brow. 'And what else?'

'I don't know what you mean.'

My lips flatten into a line. 'Are you human, or not?'

She looks at me like I've grown an extra head. 'Yes. I am human.'

'There's something not right about you.' I sneer, stepping closer once more, making her cower away from me. 'What is it?' Grabbing her arm, I yank her toward me and inhale against her skin. She recoils from me, and I let her go so abruptly, she falls to the concrete pavement. Throwing her hands out to catch herself, her skin tears on impact, and my head snaps toward the smell of her blood.

A slight gasp leaves me as I blink down at her. Tilting my head, I crouch, ignoring the way she cradles her hand to her chest, glowering at me with a hatred I'm used to seeing. It's difficult to decipher exactly what is different about her blood, due to the amount of alcohol poisoning it, but there is something not right . . .

'Well,' I say, conversationally, a wry smile forming on my lips. 'What do we have here?'

10

CORA

The Fighter

THE APARTMENT IS EMPTY when I arrive home.

Peering around, I feel momentarily lost. There is always someone home. The television is always murmuring, and there is always a sound coming from the kitchen. At this moment, I feel a such pang of overwhelming sadness that I sink to the floor, my eyes roaming the space.

'You're sitting on the floor because . . . ?' A voice trails off, and I jump in alarm, not having heard Raya open the front door. She is staring down at me with a curious expression on her heart-shaped face.

'Not sure why.' I shrug, pushing to my feet, forcing a casual smile onto my face.

'Sore feet, again?' she asks, kicking off her shoes and walking over to the dining room table where she drapes her handbag over the back of one of the chairs.

'Yeah. They're more sore than not these days.'

'I got some more bandaids.' She pulls a packet out of her bag and tosses it toward me.

'Oh, thanks.'

'What's for dinner? Is Mum going to be home tonight?' Pulling her hair around to the side of her face, she begins to plait the long waves.

'Mum is bringing something home. She shouldn't be too far away.'

'Oh, yay.' She beams. 'Family dinner. It's been a while.'

My stomach clenches. Nodding, I force a smile. 'Yeah. It has.'

Raya heads toward the bathroom when the front door opens again, and Mum walks inside, groceries hanging off her arms. I rush to help and we manage to unhook them from her and place them onto the kitchen counter miraculously without any of the handles breaking. I look down and notice four bottles of wine, explaining why that bag is so heavy. I scowl at it, knowing she spent money she can't afford to waste on that. I'll find her passed out later tonight, dead to the world.

'What happened to your hand?' I ask in alarm, looking at the peeled back skin and red-raw scratch across it, instantly distracted from my vicious thoughts.

'This jerk got all up in my face!' she exclaims, shaking her head. 'I don't know what the hell was his problem.'

'Oh my God.' I frown, concerned. 'Are you okay?'

She waves me off. 'Yeah. It's fine. Just very odd.' She exhales, pressing her fingers to her temple. 'Everything is seeming odd this week.'

'Oh?' I ask, unloading the cold items into the fridge. 'What else?'

'I've just felt really weird . . . like someone is watching and following me. I swear I keep hearing footsteps and then I turn around and no one is there.' She looks perplexed as she shakes her head. 'I think I'm losing it.'

The colour drains from my face. My eyes move to her hand. 'That is weird . . .' I say, my voice sounding far away. 'What did the man look like?'

'Hmm?' she asks, distractedly.

'The man from earlier?' I ask, throat dry as I attempt to appear nonchalant, but knowing I certainly don't. 'What did he look like?'

'Well —' she begins, but Raya strolls into the kitchen, her damp hair falling down her shoulders, her skin red from the obscenely hot water she insists she needs to feel 'cleansed'. She plucks a grape from the packet and pops it into her mouth.

'What are we talking about?' Raya asks.

The strained look on Mum's face vanishes into thin air and the forced, bubbly smile – the one I recognise that is often on my own face – replaces it instead.

'Nothing, Pumpkin. Just complaining about my day. How are you?' She leans forward, kissing Raya on the forehead, and tears spring to my eyes. I can't remember the last time she did that to me. For years now, I've gotten to see the truth behind her struggles, and the harsh reality of life, whereas Raya lives in this perfect bubble. Anger boils to the surface. What I would give to trade places with her.

'Also,' Raya says, and I realise I've completely missed the whole conversation, as I was too busy sending death glares to Mum as she smiles bigger and wider toward Raya with every word she speaks.

It isn't fair that I've been burdened with everything from such a young age, and Raya hasn't, especially since I'm not much older. I don't mind that Mum shares things with me, but the contrast with how she treats Raya, to me, is startling, and I don't know why it has worked out this way. But that's just the way it is for me, and I'm used to it now.

'I totally forgot about this museum trip I agreed to go on. Do you have any spare cash I can use for the weekend?'

'Sure, honey.' Mum smiles, and gives me a pointed look.

With my jaw clenched tight, I stomp over to my bag and pull out my wallet. I'm down to one hundred dollars. Sighing,

I pull it out and toss it on the counter. Mum picks it up and hands it to Raya, who completely misses the entire exchange as she sticks her head in the fridge, looking at the new groceries inside.

'Thank you!' she chirps, pocketing it.

My earlier feelings fade as I moodily glare out the window.

'If you could live a better life, and were given the opportunity to do so. Would you do it?' a voice whispers, filling my head. I shiver at the sound of it. My eyes drift closed, and I picture Kian's handsome face. I imagine him taking my hand and pulling me after him, whisking me away into the night. A slow, small smile creeps across my lips.

On second thought, I can't wait to get away from this hell.

11

KIAN

The Enforcer

THE SOUND OF THE blade gliding against the sharpener echoes around the room.

Pulling it toward me, I inspect the edge, satisfied with the sharpness of it. Standing, I slip the dagger into its position at my side. Whirling around, I stalk toward the window, and lean heavily on the frame, staring out at the full moon.

I always feel particularly restless during a full moon.

My phone rings, and I stare down at the screen, seeing Sofia's name across it. One of the few people I tolerate.

'Sofia,' I say, leaning against the wall. 'What did you find out?'

'I'm good, thanks for asking,' she replies snippily, and I roll my eyes. 'Not much, honestly. She's not a witch.'

'Then what is she?' I demand, frowning. 'Her blood is different. I could smell it.'

Sofia is a witch. A very powerful one who often does favours for me, and in return I help her when she needs it. A witch and a vampire forming an alliance is unheard of, since we have been at war for centuries, but since we are both considered the black sheep of our family, we have some things in common. An understanding, if you will.

It makes sense that Cora's mother isn't a witch, since I

seemed to be able to compel her somewhat, but it was as if my coercion was weaker than usual. I've noticed a similar thing with Cora. I can compel her, but not entirely, like I can with most humans.

'I'm not quite sure, but I have a theory,' says Sofia, snapping me back to the present as my mind wanders – like it has been a lot lately.

'Go on.'

'I need to do more research on it. I'll get back to you.'

I scoff. 'What was the point of this call, then?'

'To stop you from harassing me or showing up at some ungodly hour of the night in some weird way, like you often do.'

'I don't do that,' I sneer.

'You do. It's rather annoying.' She sighs. 'I'm working on it, Ki. In the meantime, lay low, and avoid the entire family. I don't know what's going on, but something is weird about them, and their blood. Just stay away, until I can figure it out.'

'Uh-huh.'

'I mean it, Kian.'

Hanging up, I slip the phone into my back pocket. Glancing down at the time, a slow smile pulls across my lips. I have never had a problem filling my day. I always have plenty to do, and yet today has crawled by at a snail's pace, and I have found myself glancing at the time on more than several occasions, waiting for the moment to see her again.

Shrugging into my jacket, I drain the last bit of whiskey in my glass, and slip out the door. With my blood reserves full, and the moonlight shining down on me, I can't help but have a little pep in my step. I haven't felt anything like this since I was human. Dare I say it, I feel . . . excited. A part of me tries to shake this off. I'm not human anymore, so I'm not supposed to feel these kind of things. I shouldn't feel anything at all.

I'm aware I'm blatantly ignoring Sofia's advice, but honestly, it feels like I have no control to stop myself right now. Must be the full moon.

Purposefully, I have not given Cora my number, or any way to contact me. I know it's confusing her, but the increasing sense of how much she wants me is thrilling. I can see the lust in her eyes and the heat of her skin. Fuck. How I haven't lost control and tasted her blood yet is beyond me. I deserve some sort of award for my divine patience.

I have never wasted time with a human like this, and I don't understand why I am doing any of it, but I just can't shake her from my mind. Tonight of all nights, I should try to ignore this, given that my self-control is particularly weakened because of the full moon, and yet, I can't ignore the call to go to her, whether it be what Cas said about the hunting instinct, or the darkness I sense about Cora that seems so like my own. Whatever it is, I can't deny the pull of her.

The bag I have in my hands sways against my long strides, and the roar of the heartbeats of the humans around me thump loudly in my ears. There's a lot of loitering around the front of the bar that Cora works at, and I stride past a group, my shoulder jamming into one of the guys that drunkenly stumbles into my way as he gestures to his friend while telling what sounds an extremely exaggerated tale.

'Hey!' the guy shouts, gripping my arm.

Whirling around, my eyes flash. The guy blanches, almost falling over backward, and the inebriated group dominating the path all fall silent, letting me past. The security guard steps out of my way, barely able to make eye contact with me.

'Hold this for me,' I demand, thrusting the bag I have in my hand to him.

Wordlessly, he takes it.

I stride through the door, locating her immediately. My mouth waters as my eyes trace her curves. The alcohol and sweat dousing the air fades into the background as the scent of her blood overwhelms me, almost drawing me to her straight away, abandoning my plans entirely.

I've timed this perfectly. She has her schedule printed on the wall of her bedroom, and since I have been in and out of there a few times without her knowing, I memorised it, so I know she is due to finish now. She makes her way out the back and I tune my ears in, carefully listening to her idle chit-chat with whoever is out there as she grabs her things. After a moment, she reappears, pulling out her hair from its ponytail, shaking it down her shoulders.

Her eyes snap to mine, and my lips curve.

'Cora,' I say.

'Kian,' she replies, breathless.

'I didn't know you worked here,' I say smoothly, gesturing around the bar. 'It's my lucky night.'

A blush kisses her cheeks. 'I have a few jobs. Customers joke they see me everywhere.'

My cheek spasms at the thought of men purposely stalking her at work. I ignore the fact that that's exactly what I am doing.

'I was hoping you might want to go on a date with me.'

A shy smile stretches across her lips as she nods. 'I would love that.'

'Are you free now?'

She looks surprised and delighted at my words. 'Now?' Her flush deepens. 'Sure.'

'Excellent.' Holding out my arm, she takes it, and my mouth waters at having her so close to me.

As we exit, I swipe the bag from the security guard's hands, and don't miss her eyes darting to it as she frowns momentarily, but doesn't question what it is.

'Have you been here before?' I ask, pointing across the street to what looks like the nicest restaurant of the lot.

She shakes her head. 'No.'

Ah. I forgot the financial constraints. Of course she hasn't eaten here.

'Shall we?' I ask.

She presses her lips together as she eyes the restaurant, and I can practically see the thoughts written across her face. She is concerned about the bill.

'I'd like to buy your meal, and a nice bottle of wine. If you will let me.'

Her eyes grow watery as she smiles. 'Are you sure?'

'Of course I'm sure, otherwise I wouldn't have offered.'

'Okay,' she relents, looking a little hesitant, her eyes glancing down at her uniform. 'Thank you.'

With my hand on her back, I guide her across the road. It seems like every pair of eyes turn toward us as I guide her to the table, and pull out the chair for her. I take the seat across from her, and the waiter leaves the table beside us mid-order, turning a big smile in my direction.

'Good evening, sir,' he practically falls over his feet to get to me as quickly as he can. 'What can I get you?'

'Whatever is the nicest wine that you think my date would appreciate,' I answer.

He nods. 'Certainly. I'll be right back.'

The people at the table next to us complain about the rude waiter, as Cora watches the entire encounter with a baffled expression on her face. My God, she is gorgeous. A stunning woman, despite the faded clothes, and thinness from lack of eating. It doesn't dim her brightness.

'Did you see that waiter left the other table to come serve you?' she questions, stunned.

'I've been here before. He must have remembered me.'

She raises her eyebrows. 'You must have left an impression.'

'I tend to.' I smirk.

Dinner goes smoothly, and I feel a weird sense of joy providing Cora with a fine meal such as this, since she would probably walk by this restaurant every day, unable to ever come here. I force myself to chew and swallow the food, to keep up appearances.

Cora eats the entire meal quickly, and looks sheepish when her plate is completely emptied.

I grin at her. 'You liked it?'

'I didn't mean to scoff it down like that. I skipped lunch today, and it was really delicious.'

Something twists inside my stomach at the thought of her not being able to afford to feed herself. This will not do.

'No need to apologise. I'm glad you enjoyed it.'

'The wine is great,' she praises, smiling. 'Do you like it?'

'I do,' I reply. 'I'm more of a whiskey man, but I do enjoy the occasional wine. Do you drink often?'

Something flashes across her eyes, and she can't hide the scowl that forms before she quickly masks it. I realise that must be a sensitive question. When I went to her house, I noticed a lot of empty wine bottles around, and since Cora doesn't seem to drink much, and her sister is younger than her, I guess that it is her mother. Maybe that's what made her blood smell so potent.

'I do, but only occasionally.'

'I see.' Leaning back in my chair, I appraise her, enjoying how much happier she looks now, compared to when she was finishing work. It must be exhausting working three jobs, on little to no substance to provide her energy. I'm unsure how she manages it. 'What do you like to do for fun?'

Sadness creeps into her eyes and she offers me a small smile. 'I don't have much time to myself for fun at the moment.'

'If you did have the time, what would you do?'

'I like to write. Journaling, and creative writing. I like to create worlds and scenarios that could never possibly be my reality.' She laughs softly. 'It's a nice escape.'

'I was never much of a reader, but I do appreciate a good story.'

'I also used to dance. I really loved it.'

'Why did you stop?' I ask.

'I wasn't able to manage classes around my schedule, or afford them.' She groans. 'Sorry, I'm not meaning to sound so tragic. I want to be honest with you, but it just makes my life sound so depressing.'

'Don't do that.'

Her brows pinch. 'Do what?'

'Apologise for having to sacrifice your own happiness for others.' Her lips part as she gazes at me. Leaning forward, I trace my thumb along her knuckles, causing her to shiver. 'Don't ever feel like you can't talk to me about the reality of your life, or the problems you face.'

'Thank you,' she whispers, hastily taking a sip of her wine, and I think it may be an excuse to not look me in the eye, since hers have a shine to them from tears threatening to spill over. She clears her throat, blinking a few times. 'What about you? What do you like to do for fun?'

I resist a smirk. I hardly think telling her that killing and torturing vampire hunters is a favourite pastime of mine would be a good idea.

'I used to be really into boxing, but I haven't done it in a while.'

She blinks. 'I didn't expect you to say that.'

A flash her a grin. 'Why, you don't think I could fight?'

Her eyes dip over me, and it makes my stomach do a strange flip-flop motion. 'Oh . . . no, I don't doubt you can fight. You're just dressed so nicely. You're very elegant, and boxing can be such a violent hobby.'

My smile widens. 'I can get my hands dirty when I want to.'

She grins. 'Oh yeah?'

'Mmhmm.'

'Maybe you'll have to show me your moves one day.'

Oh, I intend to.

Pushing my tongue against the inside of my cheek, I nod. 'Sure.'

Once we finish the bottle of wine, we head out onto the street, and it is busier than it was an hour ago. Cora picks at her nails as she looks down, eyeing her clothes again. It appears to really be bothering her that she is in her uniform, although it does not matter in the slightest to me.

'Do you need to be home any time soon, Cora?' I ask conversationally as we fall in step with each other. The breeze moves her hair back from her face, and the scent of her has something electric rocketing through my body.

She shakes her head. 'No, not really.'

'I'd like to take you out dancing, if you're up for it.'

She brightens at this, despite the dark circles under her eyes indicating how tired she must be.

'I would love that, but I think I need to change.'

'Let's get you a new outfit, then.'

Her mouth forms an 'O' before she quickly snaps it shut. 'What?'

I point to the store near us. It's closed, but I can see a woman walking around, adjusting clothes on the rack. 'Let's go here.'

'It's closed.' She frowns.

'That won't be a problem.' I march up to the door and rasp my knuckles on it. The woman startles, whirling around. I wave. Lips tugging down, she points to the closed sign. My smile fades, and I pin her with a stare that has her straightening, and digging around her pockets. She hurries to the door, unlocking it.

'Sorry to be a bother, but we are desperate for a new outfit. It's not a problem. Is it?' I ask her, a forced, cool smile etched onto my face as my compulsion bores into her with an intensity that has her taking a step back.

'N-no,' she stammers nervously, lines crinkling around her eyes. 'Come in.'

Cora is speechless as we step inside the store. The woman glances at her, but quickly ducks her chin, casting a nervous look to me, as if worried I might turn around and snap her neck at any moment. To be fair, that's a possible reality.

'Whatever you want, I will buy it for you.'

Cora's jaw practically unhinges as she gapes at me. She moves her eyes around the clothes. I'm guessing she hasn't set foot in a store like this for a long time, or perhaps ever.

'Kian . . .' she says uneasily, a flush creeping down her neck. 'I can't accept any of this. You just bought me a wonderful dinner.'

Facing her, I touch my hand to her arm, watching as goosebumps spread across her skin. She tilts her head back, heart thundering in her chest.

My eyes stare intently into hers. 'Let me spoil you, Cora. You deserve someone to look after you.' Holding up the bag, I give it a little shake. 'I have something for you.'

She opens her mouth, closes it, and then opens it once more, as if unable to process her thoughts into words.

'A gift. For you.' I say.

Her face lights up, and it does something weird to me. God forbid . . . do I feel delight?

'A gift?'

Turning to face her, I hold it out. With a smile so dazzling, it's almost blinding, she takes the bag from me. Withdrawing the box, she places the bag neatly at her feet. She opens it, and her mouth drops open.

'Oh my, Kian,' she murmurs.

Red-bottomed diamond stilettos glitter underneath the street-lamp. Money is nothing to me, but to her, I've gifted her something she never could have afforded in her wildest dreams. They will look exquisite on her, especially when she wears that cherry-red lipstick I adore.

'Your feet will never hurt again,' I say, my voice firm. 'You will look back at those times, and laugh at how far you've come.' I lightly touch the shoe, which her eyes are still glued to. 'These are nothing compared to what I can gift you, but this will do as a starter.'

'Oh,' she whispers, eyes wide. 'Kian . . . I cannot accept this. These would have cost thousands . . .' She shakes her head in bewilderment.

'You're worth it, Cora,' I murmur, feeling almost uncom-fortable at the feelings inside my chest at seeing her so filled with elation. Other people's happiness means nothing to me, so I don't know why I'm experiencing this weird, warm, gooey sensation in my chest.

Whatever the witch has done to me must be making me ill. Tears spring to her eyes, and I place the lid back on the box and return it to the bag.

'Now,' I say, stepping back and looking down at her. 'Pick an outfit to go with them.'

Following the darkness of the room, I skate along the edge and push a couple off a chair I want. They huff but don't argue when I send them a withering glare. I settle onto the seat, leaning against the wall, watching what is mine.

Absolute perfection. Every inch of her.

I've never, *ever* thought that of someone. If anything, I look at everyone as almost a failure. Most people never rise to their full potential. There is always a fatal flaw about them, but when I look at Cora, I see nothing but beauty, and wit, and my God, she is going to belong to me.

As if sensing me, her eyes sharply meet mine. The smile hasn't left Cora's face all night as she dances, dressed in the tight, strapless black dress she picked out from the store. It fits her like a second skin, hugging every curve, allowing my eyes to devour her, and imagine what is underneath the dress.

We have been to several places, but this time, I enjoy stepping back and admiring her. After a few minutes, I beckon her to me.

The scent of her invades me as she strolls over, stopping between my legs. My hands find her hips, dragging her closer.

'Kian,' she says, and the way it falls from her lips, like pure smoke, has me tightening my grip on her in a possessive way.

'Cora,' I say in the same tone, enjoying the way the blood rushes to her cheeks, matching the cherry-red lipstick she has on.

'I love spending time with you.'

'Me too,' I say in a low voice. 'You wanted me to be here. So I am.'

She breathes a laugh, chewing her lower lip, the red looking stunning in comparison to the white teeth. Teeth I wouldn't mind biting into me, while I touch and caress every part of her body.

'Oh yeah? You think so?'

'I know so.'

'How do you know that?' she asks, tilting her head.

'Because you want me as much as I want you.' Her lips part as she stares at me. I offer her a lazy smile, plucking a rose petal from my pocket. She smiles as I place it in her palm. She rubs it softly between her fingertips. It suits her. The smoky red, with darkness bordering the perfect petals. They remind me of her. 'Want to get out of here?'

Her hands land on my chest, and the sensation that spears through me is enough to make me quiver. Her thumbs run over my muscles, and I groan, gripping her so tightly, I know I'm going to leave bruises.

'Lead the way,' she murmurs, slipping the petal into her purse.

The music, the voices, the laughter, the clinking of glasses – it all fades away. I guide her toward the back alley. The moonlight bleeds across my skin, and I feel a wave of something alter my brain chemistry, like a sledgehammer is being taken to my wall of self-control. Fucking full moons.

We stumble over each other as I slam her against the building. She lets out a squeak of surprise as I dive toward her mouth.

Ah, fuck.

She's much better than I imagined.

My hand slips into her hair, tugging on it, and she moans into my mouth. Heat drips through me like a white-hot poker and I grind my hips against her, loving that sound from her. I haven't kissed someone so hard and so passionately . . . ever. Literally *ever*.

My mouth moves across her cheek, down her jaw, and I inhale her perfectly sweet scent. My fangs snap out almost painfully and, without warning, I plunge them into her neck. A shocked gasp elicits from her.

'Kian . . .' she whispers, and I reel back, staring at her.

Her eyes are wide as she breathes hard, looking fearfully at my mouth.

'Don't be afraid,' I insist, and she slowly nods. 'It felt good. Right?'

'Yes,' she admits, licking her lips, eyes focused on my fangs.

Groaning, I pin her harder against the wall as her blood pours into my mouth, overwhelming me in a way that has my head spinning. I drink long, and hard, feeling blissfully high as I take and take and take. She tremors beneath me, and I feel her grinding her hips sensually against my raging erection.

'You want me to touch you?' I breathe against her.

'Yes,' she gasps, the sound of her racing pulse taunting me to make it beat harder and faster.

Shoving her dress up, I push her thighs apart, slipping my hand between them. She cries out at my touch, and I almost collapse in pleasure as I feel her wetness coating my fingers. The taste of her, the scent, the feel of her body wrapped around mine – it's too much.

This one taste will never be enough. I'm going to crave this girl for as long as I walk this earth. She is never escaping me.

Moving my arm, I slam my wrist against her mouth.

'Taste me,' I command, a hint of compulsion coating the air, and I see the way her eyes widen and accept my words simultaneously. 'Rip my flesh.'

Her eyes flicker to mine moments before her teeth sink into my skin, and my God, seeing my blood coat those pretty lips of her makes me *feral*.

The suction of her lips on my skin almost undoes me.

Using my vampire speed, I move my hand quickly and expertly across her clit, and within moments, an orgasm crashes through her, and I take one last hearty gulp of her blood, as I feel my own release explode. She sags against me, and I fall limp against her, my forehead pressed into her temple as the bloodlust and orgasm combine in a fiery clash in my body, flooding through my system like a tidal wave.

'*Pregate alle stelle*,' I groan, lowering her to her feet, and stepping back.

She is a shaking mess, my blood smeared across her face, her hair everywhere, and her heartbeat erratic. She trembles as she stares up at me, blood streaking down her neck, soaking through her dress in scarlet ribbons. She has never looked more beautiful than she does at this moment.

'Holy fuck,' she whispers, licking her lips.

Bracing my hand against the wall, I sweep my hair back, feeling so light-headed I might collapse. My eyes move to her neck, and I stare at the delicious warm blood coating her skin. My fangs tingle, and I feel her staring at me, wide-eyed.

'What are . . .' She trails off, brows pinching together. 'You have . . . *fangs*.'

I nod.

'I don't understand.'

Running a hand through my hair, I lick my lips. 'I'm a vampire.' My lips twitch as her eyes widen impossibly more. 'Yes, they're real.'

Her heart slams inside her chest, and I can practically see her mind spinning with this information. She opens her mouth – probably to say vampires don't exist – but she snaps her lips together, eyes glued on my fangs for a long moment.

'Are you going to hurt me?' she eventually whispers, her pulse thrumming musically in my ears.

'Cora,' I say, as gently as I can given how wild I'm feeling right now. 'It's okay. I'm not going to kill you.' My eyes bore into hers. 'You're fine. You're not hurt. You won't remember all the details of this when you wake up in the morning.'

And then a group of people appear, walking through the other end of the alley, and I stagger back. A sharp pain splinters through my chest, and her face crumples with confusion. She opens her mouth to say something, but without a word I turn. I run all the way back to the house I'm staying in. I shove through the door and fall to my knees, struggling to draw breath as the tightness in my chest constricts to the point it feels like someone has their hand around my throat.

Something is happening to me. Something intense, and beyond anything I have ever felt or known. Is this somehow linked with Aithan's death?

Collapsing onto my back, I claw at my chest. An ache spreads through me, and I retch, Cora's dazed round eyes appearing in my mind. My body is begging me to go back to her, to care for her, and I feel fucking sick at the thought of that.

I don't owe anyone anything. I don't have attachments. I don't *feel* things.

Running a shaky hand down my face, I blink up at the moon that is leaking through the blinds.

What the hell is happening to me?

12

CORA

The Fighter

I JERK AWAKE WHEN I feel someone shaking me.

Raya blinks down at me, a line furrowed between her brows. I feel groggy, and rub my eyes as I attempt to sit up, but my head spins violently. I collapse back onto my pillows, feeling exhaustion deep in my bones.

'Cora?' she exclaims in concern, eyes searching my face. 'What's wrong?'

'Tired,' I mumble weakly. 'What time is it?'

'Seven. Your alarm woke me up because it just kept ringing and ringing,' she explains, gesturing to my phone. 'What the hell happened to you last night? What's on your neck?'

My eyes feel so heavy as I concentrate on her words. Reaching for my neck, my fingertips graze across my throat, and it feels alarmingly tender.

'There are bruises all over you.'

Looking down, I see I'm dressed in my usual oversized t-shirt. I showered, apparently, but have no memory of it. In fact, I don't even recall getting home. What was I doing last night?

'Bruises?' I croak, pushing onto my elbows.

I feel hungover. Slowly, memories flash through my mind of finishing work and spending the evening with Kian. I remember talking, flirting, drinking . . . I sit bolt upright. Raya barely moves her legs out of the way as I stumble to my feet, and into the bathroom. I lean heavily on the sink, staring at the array of dark marks and bruises across my skin.

'Jesus,' I wince, my eyes widening.

I definitely *didn't* imagine his fiery kiss, and feral moans. His fingers combing through my hair, his lips on my skin, his fangs . . .

I want to laugh at the thought of fangs because this is the real world, and that kind of shit is straight up out of a teen drama show. My eyes travel to the floor, where the dress I wore last night lies crumpled, blood soaked through it. My stomach jolts. Swiftly picking it up, I shove it underneath the pile of clothes waiting to be carried to the laundry.

When I stand, I feel light-headed. Reaching to lean back on the counter, I try to catch the fuzzy snippets of last night that keep fanning through my mind.

'Are you okay?' Raya asks cautiously, stepping into the room, and I'm thankful I managed to get rid of the clothes in time. I have no idea how I would explain the blood. I don't even really understand it myself. 'Are they hickeys?' she says with a slow smirk.

Chewing my lip, I consider her words, before nodding. 'Yeah. I . . . made out with someone and it got really intense.' Her face morphs into horror, and I quickly put my hands up. 'No, no, nothing like that. Just a really passionate make-out session.' I gesture to my neck. 'As you can tell. I must have drunk too much wine. The night is a little blurry. I remember we made out on the street and then I think I just . . . came home.' I rub my temples. 'Maybe I felt too drunk to do anything else.'

'Oh,' she says softly. 'I hope you're okay. Did you have fun at least?'

'Yeah. I was having a blast.'

'Who's the guy?' she asks.

I shrug, appearing as nonchalant as possible, trying not to show the panic on my face as images of blood, and fangs, bombard my head so violently, I almost stagger back into the mirror.

'I don't really know much about him. I didn't get his number or anything.'

Raya chuckles. 'Damn, girl. At least you had fun. You look really tired though, why don't you go back to bed?'

I shake my head, trying to rub the sleep from my eyes. 'I'm fine, I have too much to do.'

'Rest,' she insists. 'I'll make you coffee and some food.'

'You don't need to do that.'

'You go above and beyond for me, always. Let me return the favour.'

Usually, I would protest more, but I'm too damn tired. Dragging my feet, I fall back onto the mattress and sink underneath the covers as Raya leaves the room. Something touches my skin, and I jerk, yanking back the covers. A series of dried blood-red rose petals are scattered through my bed. Swallowing, I pull the blanket back up, rolling my lips into my mouth. Did I put those there?

My eyes droop shut, sleep clawing at me in a fight for dominance, and I have no energy inside me to resist. Darkness borders my vision before swallowing it entirely.

Cool fingers trail up my arm. My gaze lifts, meeting his unwavering black eyes that seem to glitter underneath the starry night. I fall back onto the ground, and he braces himself on his palms, hovering over me.

Strong, muscled arms caging me in. Every time I inhale, it's all him. Every breath, every movement, every touch – it all gravitates to him.

'Did it hurt?' Kian whispers, a dark strand of his hair falling across his forehead. Such a harsh contrast against his lightly

tanned skin. In some light, it seems eerily pale, and in others like he once spent too much time in the sun.

My lips part, as I gaze up at him. 'Not during it, no.'

'Would you do it again?' he asks, fangs lengthening into two long points. Desire trickles through me and I straighten my spine, shifting my seat. My hands – having a mind of their own – move to touch his chest. I breathe a sigh, enjoying how he feels under my fingertips. Pure, hard muscle.

'Yes,' I breathe.

'Do you want to be mine?' His voice is silk, caressing me in the most gentle, intimate way.

'Yes.'

'Good,' he murmurs, tongue dragging across the edge of his fang, lowering himself down to my body. I arch my back, eagerness spreading through me like a tidal wave, seeking his touch like a moth to a flame. 'Because your soul is mine to claim.'

I wake from the dream with a gasp, to see Raya closing the door.

Goddamn . . . that felt so real.

A mug of coffee is beside me, and a breakfast tray is placed on my bedside table. I shrink under the covers, eyes turning to the ceiling. My body trembles lightly as the fangs stay vividly in my mind, like they've been broadcast on a projector behind my eyes and there is no off switch.

Last night felt like a twisted dream. A nightmare, even. But the coiled knot in my stomach tells me this is happening, and it is very, *very* real.

I feel agitated.

Fidgety. Anxious. My energy level is still abnormally low, even after two strong coffees.

Exhaling, I smear extra concealer under my eyes. Slipping my jacket over my shoulders, my eyes hooking onto the shoebox peeking out from underneath my bed. I grab the shoes and stuff them into my bag, shaking my head, still unable to comprehend the extravagant gift he gave me. Those shoes cost more than my mind can comprehend, and he gave them to me so casually, like it truly cost him nothing to get them. With my thoughts spinning, I head to the door.

The TV murmurs softly. Raya has a bowl of popcorn in her lap as she watches a movie. Mum is snoring softly on the recliner, an empty wine glass beside her.

Thankfully, I was able to swap shifts with someone. I was supposed to be on the lunch shift, but I couldn't drag myself out of bed. Now, I'm working the night shift. I'm still chronically fatigued, but I'm out of bed, which is progress.

'See you tomorrow,' I say to Raya, leaning down and pressing my lips to her temple.

'Have a good night,' she smiles.

'You too.'

My eyes move to Mum, and then the empty wine glass, feeling an anger rise that threatens to consume me. Grinding my molars, I stalk past her, unable to stand the sight of her sprawled out on the lounge like that, her mouth agape, soft snores emitting from her.

The sun has barely sunk into the horizon, and yet the hallway has a dark and ominous feel to it as I make my way to the elevator. Leaning wearily on the wall, I allow my eyes to close for a few seconds. When the doors clang open, I attempt to shake off the exhaustion and stride through the front doors, Gavin and I avoiding each other's gaze.

Once outside, the cool night wind washes over me. The hair on my arms raises when a dark shadow reflected behind me in a window startles me. I whip around, but there is no one there. My eyes flick back to the reflection, and it's just me standing there, eyes wide, skin flushed.

A shiver rolls down my spine and I tighten my jacket around me, feeling as if there are eyes on the back of my neck. My skin prickles. This is the exact feeling Mum was describing. What is going on?

As I get to the bus stop, I nervously twist my fingers, my eyes scanning the empty streets around me. When a throat clears somewhere to my left, I jolt, spinning around to see a man walking his dog. He side-eyes me as he moves past. When I hear the familiar sound of the squeaky brakes of the bus from further down the street, I breathe a sigh of relief, practically sprinting up the stairs when it arrives.

Collapsing onto the seat, I perform slow circles with my fingers on my temples, trying to breathe through the tightness in my chest. I've felt unsafe travelling to and from work before, but this newly heightened sense of paranoia is intense, and very unwelcome.

The lightest of touches brushes against my ear.

'Cora . . .' a faint voice whispers, and the sound is close, and invasive, like the voice is actually inside my head.

Jumping in alarm, I turn in my seat, my eyes landing on the empty rows behind me. Swallowing, I face the front again, my stomach clenching with nausea.

My shift flies by in a blur, but the eerie sensation of being watched never fully fades, and I swear I felt the touch of fingers against my back when I was alone in the bathroom. I shudder thinking about it, and cast my gaze nervously around the street when I step out onto it in the early hours of the morning.

The crunch of gravel underneath boots makes my head snap up. A man walks toward me, hands dug deep in his pockets. I tense, taking a few steps back, panic climbing up my throat. His shifty gaze bounces from me to our surroundings.

'What's a pretty girl like you doing out here all alone?' he asks, a crooked smile stretching across his thin lips.

Spinning, I take off at a run, and my heart plummets into my stomach when I hear him chase after me. My heartbeat is loud in my ears as I push myself to move faster, mentally thanking myself for running as often as I do.

Darting down a side street, I dive behind a pile of boxes. Somersaulting and hitting my head on the ground, causing me to bite my tongue, I still, trying to quieten my laboured breathing as I listen for his footsteps. They slow, and I slam my hand over my mouth, begging him not to hear me. Peering through a thin gap between two boxes, I see him looking around. Eventually, he scowls, turns and skulks back down the street. After a few minutes of silent tears tracking down my cheeks and waiting for the trembling to stop, I try to stand. The adrenaline leaves my body in a rapid whoosh, and I stagger, the fatigue I've been suffering through all day coming back with a vengeance.

Forcing my eyes to focus, I step back out onto the street, swinging my gaze around, ensuring I truly am alone once more. I barely take a step toward home, when someone roughly yanks me back. I slam back against the pavement, hitting my head so hard, black dots dance across my vision.

'Thought you got away, did ya?' The man leers down at me, dirt and grime coating his skin. A wave of his pungent scent crashes over me, and I gag at the smell of it.

The man is stronger than I expected, holding me down with a grunt of effort as he straddles my waist. I kick and flail, landing a few solid hits into his face. The weight of his body on top of mine causes bile to rise in my throat.

'You're a little too lively for my taste,' he spits down at me, his fingers closing around my throat. 'Smile for me, I want to see it while your life drains out of you.'

Choking on my own breath, I glower up at him, swiping aggressively at his hands.

'Go. To. Hell,' I hiss through my teeth.

My hand hitting his arm grows weaker as the pressure in my head builds. Hardly any air is being inhaled through my lips as his hands constrict my throat. My eyes flutter as I let out a few choked sobs, giving one last desperate attempt to pry him off me.

Hands appear either side of the man's head. With movement so fast I barely catch it, the man's neck twists with a sickening crack. One of the hands lazily flicks him off me, as if the man is as light as a feather. Glorious air bursts through my body, and I splutter, rolling to my side as I heave.

My entire body is shaking as the figure beside me slowly lowers into a crouch. My eyes squeeze shut for a moment, but I already know who it is.

'See how easy it was for me to protect you, Cora?' he whispers.

The huskiness of his voice makes me shudder. Swallowing, I lift my gaze to his. When our eyes meet, it feels like I have been struck by lightning. Tension crackles through my body. A rush of warmth and safety fills me at the sight of him. Strong hands. Long, veiny arms. His broad, muscled chest. That deliciously dark hair that always looks windblown, in a stylish way. That half-smile, half-smirk that looks sexy as hell.

'Yes.'

'Did you feel helpless?' he asks. 'Powerless?'

Tears fill my eyes, and I nod stiffly.

Reaching out, he runs his fingers lightly through my hair. The gesture is so tender, and so comforting, that more tears spill down my face. I can't remember the last time someone comforted me. It is always the other way around.

'I can make sure that never happens to you, or anyone you care about, again,' he murmurs. 'Would you like that?'

Breathing hard, I nod. 'Yes.'

'Here,' Kian says, his fangs snapping out, making me jolt in surprise. He presses the pad of his thumb against the edge. A round drop of blood oozes from the slit, and he extends his arm toward me. 'Take it.'

Hesitantly, I inch forward, sliding my tongue across his thumb. The taste of him is instant and recognisable from last night. As if someone has tipped a warm bucket of water over my head, I feel every pain point inside of my body ease. Every tense muscle unknots. Every bruise clears. Every cut disappears. The headache and intense fatigue that clouded my brain all day completely lift, making me feel strong. Stronger than I've ever felt.

I should be scared. I should be running from him. But if anything, I feel safe with him, and I haven't felt truly safe for a long time.

Nodding, he stands, thrusting his hand out. I take it, letting him pull me effortlessly to my feet. His thumb tenderly runs a line down my hand. I stare down at the man on the ground. He's completely motionless, his head bent at an awkward angle. His eyes, open and unblinking, stare ahead at nothing.

A darkness rises inside me, curling through my veins, caressing them with an intimacy that feels familiar. A flare of anger has me stepping toward the man, upper lip curling. I want to punish him for what he did to me. What more he wanted to do.

'There's time for that,' Kian says, tone soft and reassuring, instantly putting a lid on the anger that seems to be spilling over inside me. 'All the time in the world, if you want it.'

Facing him, I tilt my head. His skin seems to shimmer, his eyes sparkling as we stare at each other. He is otherworldly, this man. Incredibly handsome, insanely powerful, and *he wants me*.

'Come with me,' he says, tugging on my hand. 'I can make your life a hell of a lot better than it is now.'

And just like that, the weight in my chest, all the stress, all the anxiety, it melts away, and I let him in. I follow him.

If only I knew.

13

KIAN

The Enforcer

I LOVE WATCHING HER.

Cora's eyes roam around my house. Well, the house I'm currently living in. It seems strange to have someone here as a guest. Someone who isn't a vampire, a meal, or someone to torture answers out of. This might be the first time in years that I've ever had just a . . . guest, other than Cas. He comes and goes as he pleases, but he is practically family at this point. Closer to me than my own blood, although the distance between me and my family is all my own doing.

'I like this,' she observes, running her fingers along a photo frame that holds a few of my dried rose petals. The petals are tainted with darkness and black droplets drip from them, looking like a twisted version of blood. It's one of my favourite pieces I've created. It travels with me everywhere I go. 'Such a pretty rose, but it's warped in this eerie darkness.' Smiling, she glances over at me. 'Suits you.'

I flash her a smile of all teeth. 'I made it. I always bring it with me, since I move around a lot. I don't exactly have a "home", but that piece is special to me.'

'I like the idea of you always giving me petals when you haven't done that with anyone else. Almost like our special thing.'

I smile, and the movement feels out of place on my face. 'Never thought to do it before.'

Turning, she pins me with her curious gaze, and I feel like she has the ability to snatch the breath from my lungs. A pretty heart-shaped face, long dark hair, and those stunning emerald eyes that have seen too much hardship for a girl her age.

Thanks to my blood, the dark circles under her eyes have disappeared. Her skin has the pretty, flushed colour it often has when she is around me. She seems to have life about her again, and for some goddamn reason, it brings an emotion to the surface inside of me that I do not like. *Happiness*.

I've wanted many things in my life. Power, wealth, blood, control. A partner has never been on the list. I've had my fair share of blood-filled rolling around in a bed, or street, or wherever the hell I've ended up, but they have never led to anything, and the thrill has always ended with the act itself. I've never craved someone's touch before like I do now. *Why?* What has this girl done to me? What kind of spell has she put me under? I'm furious at this attachment.

I just wish I could kill her and stop this temptation before it blossoms into something beyond the infatuation I'm already feeling, but the thought of any harm coming to this girl makes my heart feel like it's being cleaved in half. A muscle in my chest jerks at the mere thought, and my stomach roils.

I've never been overcome with this kind of lust before. The way I want to touch her, hold her, and kiss her . . .

'What are you thinking about?' she asks, tilting her head, a shy smile on her pretty lips.

'Just thinking about how much I want to kiss you,' I admit. 'And other things . . .' I trail off, running a hand through my hair. I fall back onto the lounge, enjoying the way her heart trips in her chest, and the heat flares across her cheeks and neck.

'Oh yeah?' she asks, her voice husky and sexy as fuck. Blood rushes to my groin – or at least it feels like it does – and I squirm, the temptation of her almost unbearable.

'Yeah,' I reply. 'Come here.'

I spend a generous amount of time tracing her body with my eyes as she walks toward me, those long, lightly tanned thighs endless and gorgeous. I wonder how they would feel wrapped around me as I moved in and out of her . . . I groan, biting my teeth into my closed fist as she sensually inches closer and closer to me, growing more confident with each step, which is somehow turning me on even more.

The soft click of her shoes fill the space. The shoes I bought her. The glitter under the dim light overhead, looking perfect on her, like I knew they would.

The rational part of my brain – that seems to become dormant whenever I'm in her vicinity – shimmers beneath the surface, telling me that I could end all this right now. It could stop here, I could make her leave, and never see her again. I can make myself disappear as easily as snapping my fingers.

My heart squeezes. I don't know why, but I feel this deep in my soul – I can't leave her. There is something beyond anything I could imagine rooting me to the spot.

This girl, she is mine, and I am hers, and I am simply incapable of walking away.

When she is close, I inhale deeply, and the scent of her does something unspeakable to me. Like it alters my brain chemistry.

Curling my hands around her, I tug her onto my lap. She parts her thighs, and I shove the little dress so far up her body I'm blessed with see-through, lacy fabric that can be barely classified as underwear.

'Did you wear this, hoping I might see it?' I ask her, licking my lips, her eyes hooked on my mouth as she nods, pupils dilating.

'Yes,' she murmurs, and I gently run my finger against the line of her underwear, grazing her skin. Her hips jerk at the sensation, and she throws her head back. I enjoy watching the dark waves tumble down her body.

Her skin feels impossibly hot, penetrating through my pants. Running my fingers up and down her smooth thighs, I lazily watch the tremors roll through her body, her panting filling the room, making me almost lose my mind.

'I want them off,' I drawl, slipping my finger in and ripping the underwear off her with the slightest of flicks. She gasps, her eyes following them as they launch across the room. 'Ah,' I breathe, my eyes trailing over her bare flesh. 'Better.'

It's all supposed to be about owning her, controlling her, having her at my mercy, and yet, here I am, wishing for something *more* than that. Since when do I want someone by my side?

Moving my hand, I feel her wetness, and I groan in longing. She moans as I slip my finger into her entrance, rubbing in soft circles that has her arching her back, almost making her flip backward off the couch. I secure my hold on her with one hand, while I play with her with the other.

Her hands move to my upper arms, squeezing them, eliciting an untamed growl from me as I push my hips into her ass. She grinds herself onto my hand, her soft moans filling the air around us, and I feel what little grasp I have on my control completely slipping.

In one fluid movement, I use one hand to lift her, and the other to yank my pants down. She gasps at the sight of me. Moving to her knees, she braces herself with one hand, her fingers curling around my neck, while the other moves to my . . . sweet Jesus, I am about to explode.

Nothing, and I mean nothing, like this has ever happened to me. Sex has always been fine. Enjoyable, thrilling, I suppose – when there is blood involved. Lots of it. But nothing has felt like this. Intense, and so . . . intimate.

A slur of Italian falls from my lips and my head falls back, her small hand moving up and down my length. Precum leaks from my tip and my hips thrust upward to meet her movements. I grip her so hard, she chokes on her breath.

'You like that?' I grunt, harshening my hold. 'You like a little bit of pain?'

Her breathing is heavy, eyes desperate, chest heaving. After a moment of hesitation, she nods. My lips twitch. That's all I needed to hear.

Slowly, I pull out one of my daggers. Her eyes widen, and her hand keeps moving, and the sight of the two combined is enough to send me over the edge, but I refuse to release so soon. Not when I have so much more I want to do with her. I expertly flick my fingers, my shirt ripping straight down the centre.

I press the blade into my neck. My blood spills across my skin, and her breath hitches.

'Take it, *mio tesoro*,' I murmur. 'As much as you want.'

She licks her lips, eyes darting from my eyes, to my chest, back up to my eyes.

'But,' I drawl, tilting my head, shifting so the dagger tip is lightly pressed against the soft skin on her arm. 'I must take from you, too.'

She gulps, eyes widening, but offers a miniscule nod.

Moving my blade to her throat, I press it hard against the skin, feeling a wave of delight wash through me at the crimson streak that rolls down her collarbone. She moves, sinking onto me, and I hiss, constricting my hand so hard I fear I might pop a bone out of its socket.

The feel of being inside her is indescribable. I let out a shuddering breath as she settles, getting used to my size. Pulling her to me, she starts rocking her hips as I drag my tongue across her neck. When her lips move against my chest, tasting my blood, I almost black out from the insane pleasure that overcomes me.

'That's it,' I groan, bouncing her up and down my length as I take my fill of her blood, loving the sensation of her doing the same to me. I've never let a human taste my blood. Ever. That is something that is sacred, and to be earned, and no one has ever been worthy. Until now. 'You take me so well, *mio tesoro*, so fucking well.'

She rears back from my chest, moving harder and faster. I slam myself upwards, spearing into her in the exact right spot. She screams my name, the sound shatters through me like I've just fallen head-first through a glass window, and I feel her clench tight around me. My own release spurts out hot and fast, filling her up, as pleasure takes over me.

When I blink back from the high, she is slumped over me, breathless.

Blood. Is. Everywhere.

Running down her dress, smeared across her thighs. Up my arms, streaked down my chest. The sight is almost enough to make me lose control again. She leans back, still seated on top of me, and I can practically feel the energy and post-orgasm high buzzing through her.

She pushes herself off me, and I groan when I see my release dripping down her thighs.

'Oh,' she says softly, looking dazed. She pushes her hair from her sweaty forehead, stepping back, completely naked for me except the sparkling shoes, which make her look so fucking incredible, although she does not need help in that department. My eyes ravish her, memorising every line and curve she has to offer.

I go to stand, and the sight of her sends me to my knees. My gaze drinks in every inch, and I pull her to me, pressing my forehead into her stomach, trying to process everything surging inside me. I've never felt so much, and all at once. Her fingers comb lightly through my hair, and I exhale shakily, feeling unsteady, and intensely alive, all at the same time.

Tilting my head back, our gazes lock, and I startle, positive I can see something swirling in her eyes, but then it's gone just as quick as it appeared.

Her touch is tender, stroking my hair. My eyes shutter closed, and I lean forward, holding her to me, as if her soothing touch is unlocking an emotion that has been buried deep inside of me, desperate to have been released.

'Cora,' I whisper heavily, tightening my grip. 'You're going to ruin me.'

And all my plans, a voice whispers in my mind.

14

CORA

The Fighter

'YOU'RE NOT LEAVING.'

My head snaps up as Kian towers over me, eyes narrowed. I glance down at the shoes in one hand, my bag in the other. Every nerve feels like it is crackling from the aftermath of what we did together. The moment was quickly broken when he stood abruptly and left the room. I guess he didn't want to hang around to cuddle. I suppose I don't blame him. The one or two times I've had a one-night stand, my flight-mode was activated and I was out of there before the poor guy had a chance to catch his breath.

'I'm not?' I ask, brows raised.

He looks annoyed. 'No. You're not. Why would you think you are?'

Straightening, I roll my shoulders. 'Because the last time we did something like this, you disappeared without a word. No explanation, nothing. I just expected the same, I guess. And you . . .' I trail off, gesturing to the door he exited through so swiftly. 'Left.'

His cool mask slips for a moment before he manages to school his features. 'I'm struggling with this,' he admits, pointing at me, and then to himself. 'I've not done this before.'

'Sex?' I echo, incredulous.

He laughs. 'No. I mean have sex with . . . feelings, I guess.'

I can't stop the smile that takes over my face. 'Oh.'

'Feelings. They're rather annoying,' he says with a huff.

'Are they?' My smile widens.

He grunts, folding his arms across his chest. 'And. Well. I have something to tell you.'

'What's that?'

'I'm not exactly a normal guy.'

'I gathered that much already, Captain Obvious.'

He raises a brow. 'Captain what?'

'Never mind. You were saying?'

He exhales. 'You understand that I am a vampire, yes?'

Slowly, I nod, though the word 'vampire' being used so casually still throws me. All my life I've thought of these super-natural creatures as works of fiction. It's hard to wrap my mind around the possibility of it being reality, but the evidence is right in front of my face, so there is no point denying it.

'I have some questions.'

'Go ahead.'

'Vampires are predators. Right?' I ask.

'Correct,' he answers. 'Yes, I kill people. No, I don't intend to kill you. In fact,' he steps toward me, eyes flashing, and I back up quickly. His gaze darts to mine. 'Don't be afraid.' Swallowing, I nod, feeling the panic that was engulfing me slowly ebb away, as if he has the ability to control how I feel. 'I want to turn you. So that you're like me.'

'Turn me?' I echo. It feels strange not to have some sort of reaction to this. But I like how calm I am. I've never felt so clear-headed.

'Yes,' he says with a stern stare, eyes flitting over my face, studying every inch of it for my reaction.

'Will it hurt?' I ask.

He nods. 'For a bit.'

'I will need to leave my family?' I ask, brows pulling together.

'Yes.'

The world tilts. Stepping away from him, I walk to the arm of the lounge and sit on it. My eyes move to look at the blood marking my body. I can still feel where he was inside me. It was like nothing I have experienced before.

I want more.

I *need* more.

'We can plan it,' he suggests. 'Make it seem like you passed away. We can compel them to grieve and move on.'

I jerk back, feeling like he has slapped me. 'What? Compel them?'

Kian offers me a cool smile. 'I can be rather persuasive, and I can make people forget things. It's a gift of mine. Something you will be able to do, as well.'

My mouth falls open as the seriousness of this dawns on me, his words going over my head as I get stuck on what he said about my family thinking I've passed away. 'They will think I died?'

He nods. 'Or, we can make them forget you ever existed.'

I gasp, my hands flying to my mouth. 'No!'

He shrugs. 'Well. Back to option one, then.'

It irks me a little that he is so nonchalant about this. I understand that this isn't his life, or his family, but I would expect a little more compassion.

Will I think like him, once I turn? Will it change me? Will I lose touch with humanity? It blows my mind that I am even able to think rationally right now, but it's his words, and his mind influence. Is that the right term?

'I need to think about this,' I whisper, shaking my head. 'This is a lot to process right now.'

'I thought you wanted this,' he says sharply, walking toward me. 'You said you would take the chance to leave your life. You're miserable here. I can make that all go away.'

'By leaving them?' I whisper, tears burning my eyes.

'Yes, but that won't matter so much when the world is at your fingertips. I will take you places you have only dreamt about. We will be able to conquer great things, you and me.'

'I can't leave them.' I shake my head. 'I just . . . can't do that. They're all I have.'

His eyes darken. 'You have me.'

I release a breath of laughter. The connection we have is undeniable, but we've only just met. Am I really considering uprooting my entire life, and world as I know it, for this stranger?

'Forget about everyone else for once,' he snaps, and whether he means to or not, his compulsion smacks into me like a force field, and I flinch at the feel of it. I can still think for myself, but he is somehow guiding my thoughts in the direction he wants. My head spins at the feel of it. A part of me wants to resist it, while the other – more dominant part – is more than happy to give in. It's easier to give in.

All the worry and concern regarding my family vanishes. My lips part as I realise how simple the answer is when I actually think about what *I* want, instead of feeling so concerned about everyone else.

'Hmm?' he asks, tilting his head, a wry smile on his lips. 'What do you think now?'

'Let's do it,' I whisper.

The warm water runs down my skin, and the blood pools at my feet momentarily before slipping out of sight through the drain.

Kian's hands move across my skin. Once more, it is soft, tender touches, lingering stares, and the tension building to the point where I can hardly focus. Both hands run across my shoulders, his thumb and fingers massaging into the spot where I often get tense. Breathing a sigh, I lean back into him, feeling a wall of muscle behind me, and then something else that has my breath quickening.

'Again?' he murmurs with a deep chuckle.

Pushing back into him, I rub against his erection, and he makes a low grumble. His hands slip down my sides, one disappearing between my legs. He releases a sound I can only describe as a content sigh.

'Wet and needy,' he whispers. 'You want more, *mio tesoro*?'

'Yes,' I whimper.

Bending me over, he moves his fingers inside me for a few moments, before I feel the tip of him against my entrance. When he pushes inside, I gasp, clinging on to the wall, almost slipping. His punishing grip secures me in place as he thrusts hard and fast into me. I yelp at the sensation, not expecting him to be so rough, and surprised at how much I enjoy it.

Leaning forward, his chest against my back, he loops his arm around, hand bracketing my throat. He squeezes and the pain of it feels delicious. His other hand skates down my body, moving to the front of me, his finger sliding between my thighs, pressing straight onto my clit. The reaction from my body is instantaneous, and I moan. I hear the distinct sound of his fangs dropping as he bites my shoulder, pumping in and out of me with harsh brutality. I push back, matching his rhythm, enjoying how in sync we are. The pressure around my throat tightens and tightens, as does the movement of his fingers. Within seconds, I've completely come apart, the orgasm roaring through me with a savage crash, and my scream sounding distant as it rips out of my throat. I feel his release inside of me at the same time, and his whispered sweet nothings in Italian have me feeling like I might melt.

'Fucking perfect,' he groans, doing a few more slow thrusts before sliding out of me. I immediately miss the feel of him inside me, and almost fall when my legs turn to jelly. He captures me easily, spinning me so I face him. 'I can't get enough of you.'

'More,' I whisper, and his eyes flash hungrily. 'Give me more.'

His fangs release as he props me against the wall. Wrapping my arms around his neck, my legs around his waist, I sink onto him, and we both moan again.

On and on it goes, endless moving in and out of each other. Long, passionate kisses, hair pulling, biting, whispers and promises to each other that would probably sound fantastical to anyone else, since we really only just met, and he is not even *human*.

And yet, I can't stop, and I don't want to.

I want more.

I always want *more*.

It's been days.

I haven't left his house, or his side. Other than a few texts to Mum and Raya, telling them I'm house-sitting for Ange while she is away, the outside world doesn't exist. It's an endless whirlwind of sleeping, fucking, sharing blood, occasionally pausing for me to eat, only to start all over again.

My appetite for him is insatiable.

'When?' I murmur, my eyes rolling back into my head as his tongue slides over me.

Lifting his dark gaze to meet mine, head between my thighs, he tilts his head. 'When what?'

My eyes shift to the scars scattered across the tops of his shoulders, which run all the way down his back. Vicious, raised lines that can only come from torture. He was very vague about what happened, but I know it was before he was turned, and that's why he gets nightmares. He doesn't like to talk about it, but I know something horrific happened to him, and those scars are a horrible reminder of that. Every night he has been in a fit of distress as he sleeps, but when I lay a hand against him, it seems to calm him. The way his arm curls around me, pulling me flush to his body, like I am his most prized possession, makes me feel warm, giddy, and valuable.

'Cor?'

My eyes snap back to his, and I mentally shake myself. 'If you do turn me . . .' I say slowly. 'When would it be?' I ask, my fingers bunching up the side of the sheets.

'Hmm,' he murmurs, his lips vibrating against my most sensitive area. I convulse at the feel of it. 'I'm enjoying having you all to myself.' His head dives toward me again, and I cry out at the sensation.

I get lost in the feeling of him again. Hours go by before I eventually pass out, wrapped in his arms. Full and sated.

In his arms, no one can touch me. I'm safe. He is the most dangerous thing I know, and he wants me. I am his.

I am going to be his forever.

Hours later, we are laying in Kian's bed, our limbs tangled together, which is my new favourite place to be.

Sometimes I wonder if I'm in a weird fever dream, because this is just too good to be real. Whisked away by a perfect, handsome stranger, who fulfils all my darkest desires, all the while promising me unlimited power, wealth, and freedom?

Turning, I stare at him.

'Hello,' he mumbles, eyes closed, a faint smile on his lips. 'You're staring.'

'You're too pretty not to stare at.'

He snorts, rubbing a hand down his face, the muscles in his arm flexing deliciously as he does. His bare chest is hard and smooth, the sheet draped messily across his lap. His hair is dishevelled, and it looks so handsome on him, as if he has let a part of

himself unravel in front of me. A tiny gap in the perfectly meticu-
lous wall he has surrounded himself with.

Shifting, he moves to face me, reaching out to dance his fingertips along my arm. He pauses at my wrist, running his thumb
across the smooth skin there.

'What is it?' I whisper, watching him.

'I have a business,' he says, voice soft, and a little raspy. 'People
who are under my protection wear a mark, and my enemies know
to look for this mark. They know if a hand is laid on my people,
their life will be taken as a consequence.' He swallows, eyes
trained on my skin. 'A little half crescent moon. Right here.' His
finger taps it lightly. 'May I lay the mark on you?'

My heart trips in my chest as his eyes lift to mine. His expression is often precisely composed, guarded, like he uses every ounce
of control he possesses to make his mask blank, and emotionless,
not allowing anyone to see the real him. But his eyes tell a different story. They possess heat, fire, vulnerability, tenderness . . . it's
enough to steal the breath from me. Such intensity and intimacy,
all for me. Only for me.

Rolling my lips, I arch a brow. 'Are you asking me whether
you can brand me?'

His tongue drags across his lip as he fights off a smirk.
'Precisely.'

'You want to brand me as yours so the whole world knows
who I belong to.'

Something flashes in his eyes, and a deep rumbling sound
emerges from his chest. A feral, predatory smirk tilts his lips.

'Yes,' he grunts, nodding. 'Because you are mine. Aren't you?'

Heat inches up my neck, my breath hitching, but I'm nodding
furiously, because there is no point denying it. With a sweep of his
hand, he yanks me to him, covering my mouth with his, devouring
me with enough heat to spark a fire.

'Let me mark you,' he growls, pulling me beneath him, the sheet falling away, our bare skin pressing together. The tip of him nudges my entrance, and I feel dizzy with lust as I open myself for him. '*Mio tesoro.*'

I repeat the words, rolling them around my tongue. 'What does it mean?'

'My treasure,' he answers.

'Okay,' I whisper, swallowing, tingles erupting through my body. 'Do it.'

His fangs descend, and they bite into my skin, eliciting a hiss from me at the sharp sting of it. He pushes inside me, stretching me around his thick length, and I arch my back, a moan slipping past my lips at the feel of him, combined with the pain on my wrist. He carves his fang around my skin in a half-moon shape. When he finishes, he thrusts brutally into me, and I gasp at the harshness of it, digging my fingers into his hips.

I'm aware that this is dangerous. He is fucking me like he owns my body and my soul. He has just branded me as his, claiming me like I am a possession, not a person. A treasure. His *tesoro*.

It's probably wrong. He's a walking red flag. He's more dark than light. More monster than man, because he's admitted he's killed people, and has countless enemies, and that he will have to dedicate utmost time to keep me safe from them. These are all signs I should run from him.

But I'm hopeless to stop any of this, because I don't want to stop.

He slams inside me, dominant and hard. I cry out at the sensation. Kian buries his face in my neck, sliding his fangs deep into it as he moves inside me.

Suddenly, he lifts me, flipping so that he is on his back as he plants me down onto his face. My breath catches as I grind against him, leaning forward to grip his thighs as I move over him, my mouth taking his length.

My orgasm rises and releases at such a rapid pace, I have no time to come to terms with it as I climax, drenching his face and tongue, grinding on him as he lets me ride the wave he created.

Flipping me once more, the world a blur around me, I'm on my back and he is over me, his hand pumping up and down his length before he spurts across my face, spraying me with his hot release.

My tongue snakes out, licking it off my lips, and his eyes darken as he watches me do so, very clearly enjoying the sight of his cum smeared all over me.

I'm panting, chest rising and falling, as we gaze at each other.

After we shower, and collapse back onto the bed, I'm tightly tucked against his chest, my thoughts turning over in my head. My cluttered, small apartment with my family is supposed to be my sacred place. The place I long to be. The place I call home. I'm beginning to realise that Kian is my new home, and I am not mad about it, because here I am treasured, protected, and safe. I'm being looked after, not the other way around, and it's such a goddamn relief to take a break from everything.

When we fall asleep, tightly in each other's embrace, neither of us have nightmares.

When I wake the next day, I can tell things are different.

The little bubble we have been in has to break, because I can't go without seeing my family much longer without creating suspicion. We also need to get started on the plan. The thought of leaving them behind doesn't worry me anymore, and I know it's because Kian compelled me to feel that. I would never just walk away from them, but when I try to explore that feeling, my train of thought vanishes, like my brain is a whiteboard and someone has wiped it clean.

It's like he has swept away my consideration of other people's thoughts and feelings, only able to focus on my own, and, honestly, it's a blessing to no longer be burdened and weighed down with the concerns of others. Always feeling like I have to think of them first, before myself. He's allowing me to be selfish, and I fucking love it.

I take a long look in the mirror. I'm practically glowing. I haven't looked this healthy in years.

'How much time do I have with them?' I ask once I'm back out in the living room, where Kian is sitting, throwing a knife up in the air. It spins and he catches it, repeating the motion, but his eyes are on mine.

'A day. Maybe two.'

Swallowing, I nod. 'Okay.'

'I will tell you the time and the place. You all need to be in the car. I will organise the rest.'

I almost hyperventilated when he told me that someone will die for me to turn. It makes sense that nature demands a balance, but I don't want someone to die because of *me*. But like before, Kian swept my worries under a rug that I have no ability to lift up to pull them back out.

Other than saying goodbye, there is nothing else left to do.

As I make my way home, my jacket on, my hair down, I practically skip along the street. I can't help daydreaming about what lies before me. Endless days of talking, laughing, making love, exploring, getting to know the deepest, darkest parts of each other. I finally have someone who sees me for *me*. Someone *I* can depend on. Who wants to love me, to hold me, and protect me. It feels incredible, and I can't *wait*.

Don't forget, Kian's voice whispers, and I shiver. It feels like his mouth is against my ear, but when I look over my shoulder, there is no one there. *You want it to be easier on them. So make it easier.*

My entire attitude has changed toward them, and when I walk in the door, I almost backpedal. Raya is laughing at something my mum is saying as she stirs the pot on the stove. It's so rare for all three of us to be home at one time, I simply gawk at the scene in the kitchen. Smiles on both of their faces, rosy cheeks, and soft music humming in the background.

'Sweetheart!' Mum beams when she notices me. 'I've missed you. Come over here and give your mother some love.'

I blink at her. She hasn't treated me like this for so long. Maybe I should go away more often. Why does she start treating me like I'm her daughter now, just when I've decided to leave?

I'm supposed to make them distance themselves from me. To make it easier. I can't do it. Not yet.

Slipping out of my jacket, I beeline toward her, and she wraps her arms tightly around me. She kisses my hair, holding me close. My lower lip trembles. I try to recall the last time she hugged me, and I truly can't remember. Does she sense some sort of difference within me? Can she sense something is about to happen?

'How are you, sweetheart?' she asks, stepping back and cupping my face, and I'm so thrown by it, all I can do is stare at her, speechless. After a moment, I shake myself out of it, smile briefly and dip out of her hold, feeling a little overwhelmed.

'I'm good. How are you both?'

The easy conversation that follows makes my heart thud painfully. I almost can't go through with it, but Kian's words repeat in my head, getting louder and louder.

My phone buzzes, and I look down at the screen.

Kian. Not long now . . .

15

KIAN

The Enforcer

I NEED TO KILL SOMEONE.

The familiar restless itch has been absent since I've been with Cora, and it's freaking me out. I'm not myself. I've gone soft. Something must be wrong with me. I'm sure if I go about my usual ways, I'll snap out of whatever delusion has taken over me. The timing of my maker's death, and my encounter with that dreadful witch are no coincidence – it must have fractured some part of my soul or tainted my mind. That has to be it.

This is all a part of the game, I remind myself. *Lure her in, gain her trust, turn her. She will be loyal and I will have complete control over her.*

Having someone completely loyal to me will be helpful. Other than Cas, there are not a lot of people I can trust, and I need someone that can help me, especially given this . . . predicament I am in, thanks to that damn witch.

As I stand in the shadows, I quietly watch people walk right by me, not having a clue there is an evil lurking so close to them. When a man who keeps taking photos of women who aren't paying him any attention passes me, I snake my hand out, pulling him off his feet and into the darkness with me. He barely has time to cry out before I stab him. Over and over and over. The distinct slicing of blade against skin, the blood squirting over my hands, the struggled drawing of breath. It's like coming back to a happy place, or memory. Smiling, I watch him choke and gasp. He reaches for me, and I use his shirt to wipe my blade.

Lifting my hand, I lick the blood from my fingers. Instantly, my stomach coils, and the blood comes back up. I heave, leaning over the guy, throwing up across the grass.

Fuck. It's confirmed. For some unknown reason, I can only drink from her. I've been dragging out turning her in fear that I'm somehow going to end my only blood supply, but Cas with his famous research has explained to me that it doesn't work like that. He seems to trust the words of older vampires, but I don't like making assumptions about anything. I purposefully kept her in my house for days as I stored a significant amount of her blood. I have a fridge full of it. It was so easy to drain her, and then compel her to forget. The more time I spend with her, the easier it is to compel her, as her trust for me grows and grows. With the amount she was replenishing herself with my own blood, I was able to take more than I expected. If I end my supply of blood by turning her, I can sustain myself having one drop of the fridge blood for what I've worked out to be quite a long time, as long as I can store it correctly.

There's an eerie silence once the man's heart stops beating. Blowing out a breath, I drop my fangs and plunge into his arm. I swallow one mouthful and reel back. The reaction is instant but this time I'm ready for it.

Gritting my teeth, I struggle to swallow it but force myself to keep my lips tightly shut, not allowing any of it to slip out. It bursts out of me and I let out a growl of anger. Closing my eyes for a moment, I calm down, and try again.

Again and again I attempt to force the blood down and eventually, I manage a few drops. If I keep working at this, I should be able to stomach blood that is not hers long enough to keep me alive, if something goes wrong when I turn Cora, or if the blood of hers that I have stored gets damaged, or goes bad somehow. I need to cover all bases.

Returning to the house, it feels cold and empty without her here. Scowling, I pick up one of her jumpers, prepared to throw it across the room. Instead, her scent infiltrates something deep inside me, and I pull it to my face, inhaling deeply, feeling at ease finally, since I have been tense all day. Ever since she left earlier, there's been a pit growing in my stomach. That, combined with whatever the fuck the witch has cursed me with, is a lot for me to handle, and getting far too hard to ignore. I don't want to deal with any of this, but it is out of my control.

I must admit, having Cora here was an exceptional distraction from the outside world for a while, but time is ticking, and I need answers about this curse, or whatever it is the witch did to me. At first, I was feeling a little depleted, but being around Cora has made me feel strong once more. I like the idea of having someone loyal to me, like Cora, to have my back. After all this time of refusing to let anyone in, this is it. The time has come. I need someone to watch my back, and . . . help me . . . if this curse continues to attack and weaken me, which I have no doubt that it will.

There is Cas, but he lives his own life, and whatever we have is not as deep as a maker and their turned. I have turned people before, and it hasn't felt like anything, but something tells me that Cora will be different. I know it.

Moving through the darkness, I make my way to their apartment. I linger outside, my eyes zeroing in on her window. All the lights are out, and everything is calm. She is sleeping. Dreaming of me, perhaps, as I am thinking of her.

It requires a lot of strength not to go to her.

In the end, I fail.

Silently, I scale the wall, and swing myself up to the window. Pressing my hand to the glass, I inch it up. It makes a squeaking sound, so I pause. After a beat, I keep going, and slide through the gap.

The ache ceases, and I kick my shoes off, crawling into the bed beside her.

'Am I dreaming?' she whispers, reaching out for me.

'Yes,' I murmur. 'Go back to sleep.'

'It feels so real,' she mumbles, touching her fingers to my chest.

Pulling her to me, I wrap my arms around her, and for a moment, I switch my brain off; everything that is telling me to run away, to cut her off, to get my head back in the game. I cradle her to me, and bury my face into her neck, breathing her in.

I am so *fucked*.

I was supposed to leave.

Sneak out unnoticed. But of course, I don't listen to myself, and instead, we move against each other in a tangle of limbs, and kisses, and touching, and my hand is over her mouth, muffling her moans as I bury myself in her.

Her body beneath me, her dark hair cascaded across her pillow, nails clawing up my sides as I claim what is mine over and over, makes me wild. I have never felt this kind of joy. I didn't know it existed for someone like me.

When the bed hits the wall, I flip her off the side, and continue on the floor. She giggles, locking her fingers around the back of my neck.

'What?' I smile, moving my mouth toward one of her nipples and sucking on it. I release it sharply with a loud *pop*.

She moans softly. 'This is making me feel like I'm a teenager. Hiding things from Mum, sneaking a boy in.'

'I'm not a boy.' I smirk. 'I'm a ruthless vampire. Don't compare the two.'

'I wouldn't dare,' she replies, a lazy smile on her face.

Gripping her, I twist her body so that she is on her knees, yanking her hips back to meet my thrusts. She mewls, arching her back, pushing into me with a pressure that has me close to climaxing. Twisting her hair around my knuckles, I tug her head back, leaving hot, wet kisses down the side of her face, while my other hand slips to the front of her, circling around her clit in the way I know she craves. She jerks in my hands, and my thrusts plunge deeper, both of us releasing at the same time in a euphoric wave that blacks us both out.

I jerk awake a moment later, both of us on our backs, and I have no idea what just happened. Peering down, I see her head resting on my chest. Her fingertips trace invisible patterns on my skin. A shiver rolls through me as she traces over my bicep, and I turn my face to her, watching as she moves her finger back and forth, an indescribable sensation of possessiveness and desire swirling inside me. Reaching out, I pull her closer to me, even though she was already tucked against my side.

'What is this?' she murmurs, tracing her finger over the dark mark on my chest, making me shiver.

Swallowing, my gaze lowers to it. 'A problem.'

'What do you mean?' she asks, frowning.

'It's a situation I'm dealing with.'

'Are you okay?'

I nod. 'Yeah. I'm fine.' Pressing my lips to her forehead, I exhale softly. 'Nothing to worry your pretty little head over.'

'It seems like something.'

'I had a rather unfavourable run-in with a witch. She has done something to me. A curse, or something. But I'm fine. I'm sorting it out. I'm going to find her.'

Her eyes widen. 'A curse?'

Stroking my fingers through her hair, I smile softly. 'I'm fine. Okay?'

Swallowing, her eyes intently stare into mine for a moment before she slowly nods. 'Okay.'

It's silent for a few long moments.

'I've never felt this way before about anyone,' she whispers, biting her lip softly. 'It's kind of scaring me.'

Swallowing, I resist the urge to pull away from her. This kind of talk, expression of feelings, is not my thing, but I can't stop my hand from moving to her cheek, caressing her soft skin. It's warm under my hand, and her face fits so perfectly against my palm.

Such a pretty little thing, in the hands of a predator, and she has no idea. Has no idea how bad, rather.

I'm torn between wanting to end her life, to stomp out the feelings in such a vicious, violent way, ensuring there is no possibility they can linger, and then the other part of me, which wants to own her, keep her so close, that she becomes truly mine and no one could touch her, or take her from me.

I'm going insane. I have never had thoughts like this in my life. How have I fallen so fast, and so hard? Insanity . . . it must be.

'Me too,' I admit. 'I've never wanted to have someone before, but you . . .' I pause, twisting her hair around my fingers, enjoying the sight of her hair tangled amongst them a little too much. 'I can't resist you.'

'I can't quite comprehend that.'

'What do you mean?' I frown, my eyes darting back to hers, and I assess them carefully, seeing the uncertainty in them.

'Well . . . you're absolutely perfect. Every inch of you. You're powerful, wealthy, strong, handsome, and I'm nothing special. The opposite of everything you are. I just don't understand what you could possibly see in me.' Her eyes move to the ceiling, and she exhales, cheeks darkening in embarrassment. 'I don't mean to sound insecure, it's just hard not to notice that you're . . .' She flails a hand lethargically at me. 'Obviously very attractive and powerful. I am just so very plain and human.'

'There is nothing plain about you,' I say, meaning every word. 'Although you are very beautiful, it's what is in here.' I tap my finger against her chest. 'You're brave, selfless, and tainted with a beautiful darkness that I recognise all too well. You are smart, witty, and best of all, you will challenge me.' My lips tilt, and I release a breathy laugh. 'And that excites me. I do love a challenge.'

Her eyes widen, and she seems taken back by my response. 'You think all of that, even in this short amount of time that we have known each other?'

'I don't measure the length of time for how best you know someone.' I answer, my voice coming out a little too-matter-of-factly. 'Sometimes, you can simply *feel* it.'

'Huh,' she murmurs. 'I've never thought about it like that, but that's a good point. Depending on the situation, I think you can find out everything you need to know about a person when you first meet them.'

'Yes,' I agree. 'If you study them close enough, you can see past the facade.'

'And you?' She smiles. 'Is everything so far a facade, or are you truly a gentleman?'

I bark a laugh, unable to help myself. 'A gentleman? I don't think anyone has ever called me that before.'

She gives me a puzzled look. 'I don't believe that.'

Covering my amused smile, I run my fingers through her hair, enjoying the silkiness of it as it slips through my fingers.

'I wish it could be different,' she murmurs.

'Hmm?'

'I don't want to leave them behind, and start a new life without them.'

I exhale, allowing my eyes to drift shut, the bubble that had formed around us popping abruptly, and my signature scowl twists onto my lips. I must have reached my quota of discussing feelings. Remarkable that I lasted this long, really.

'I know.'

'Do you miss your family?' she asks.

'No.'

'Not even your brother?' she questions.

My frown deepens. I didn't mean to let it slip that I have a brother, but I must have. I got too carried away in acting like the nice guy, apparently I disclosed some real truth about me.

'No.'

'You don't get along?'

Tapping my fingers restlessly, I huff. 'I've always been competitive by nature, and my brother always seemed to have everything so much easier than me. He was handed things that I had to spend so much time and energy to earn. I suppose I grew a resentment for him, and he never understood that. But they don't, when they are the ones who have it easy. They will never get it. What it's like to be on the outside, looking in.'

'You basically just summed up my entire life.' Cora gives me a wry smile. 'I love my sister, but I sort of resent her . . . and it's my own fault that she has been wrapped up in this perfect bubble. I played a part in it.' I swallow. 'My mother . . .' She shakes her head, a pained expression forming. 'I just don't get why I'm treated like a slave. Like a partner in motherhood when I was only a child myself.'

My lips part as I stare at her in surprise. 'I didn't realise we had so much in common.'

'If you resented your brother, why did you turn him?' she asks.

'I didn't turn him.'

'But you turned his best friend, and you knew he would turn Hunter,' she points out.

I blow out a deep breath. I don't even remember telling her all of that. It seems I've gotten carried away with telling her the truth, and that was never a part of the plan. She seems to just extract it from me, with that soft, warm look she gives me. Makes me want to split open my chest and bleed out every bit of pain I've ever endured, just to have her understand what I've been through, and why I am here now. Shock courses through me at that thought, and I mentally scold myself for being so weak.

'Well,' I begin, clearing my throat. 'I'm going to be honest with you, and I haven't been honest about a lot of things for a long time.'

'Okay,' she whispers.

'I needed my brother to be a vampire. When you're a vampire, especially one like me, you tend to have enemies. He needed to be able to protect himself. I also needed to keep him at a distance and publicly claim I do not speak to him, or care for him, so that there would not be a target on his back.'

'A vampire like you?' she implores. 'What do you mean by that?'

'I run a business that gets me in some hot water,' I reply. 'I worked by the side of the vampire who turned me, but since his passing, I now run it.'

'What kind of business is it?'

'Vampire business.' I wink.

She rolls her eyes. 'Come on, you can tell me. You know you can trust me.'

I almost laugh. Trust. Something I don't take lightly, but I find myself almost compelled to tell her.

'Basically, we go after vampire hunters. There's a lot of solo hunters out there, with their own agenda, but lately it's becoming more popular for them to form a group. Vampires are being held on farms, and basically tortured and used for certain things, and I oversee the missions to extract the vampires, and eliminate everyone involved. The problem is, the people involved are powerful. They have connections. Shifters, werewolves, witches, you never know who they have in their pocket.' I chuckle, shaking my head. 'It makes no sense that they trust some of the other supernaturals that are just as bad as us, but vampires have a pretty bad rep of being . . . ruthless.. Most view us at the top of the food chain, and think getting rid of us is the best thing to do, even if it means trusting other creatures to do so.'

'Wow, okay,' she murmurs, nodding, absorbing all of that information. 'So, your brother thinks you hate him?'

'Yeah. Well. I do,' I chuckle. 'But, also I don't.'

'That whole situation sounds complicated. Have you ever considered explaining any of that to him? He might understand? It could be better than him thinking you loathe his very existence . . .'

'I prefer to do things alone. The less he knows, the better.'

'Sacrificing your relationship with him is worth saving his life?' she asks.

My fingers stop moving and I furrow my brow at her words. I never really looked at it like that, but yes, that's exactly the choice I've made.

'Yeah,' I mumble. 'I guess it is.'

'You really think if people were to come after you, they'd go for the people you love?' Cora asks, her voice timid.

'I know so.'

'How's that?'

'After a raid at one of the farms out west, I oversaw the operation. It was my face, my name, they were all whispering to each other. One of the men who orchestrated the whole thing escaped, and word got out. They couldn't find me, so they found my best friend. He was still a human.' Swallowing, I force myself to keep talking, even though I have never told anyone about this, except Cas, who had to pick up the pieces of me after it all. 'We had plans that night. I arrived just a minute too late. He died in my arms.'

'Oh my God . . .' she whispers, tears filling her eyes. 'I'm so sorry, Kian. That is terrible. You know for sure it was them who did it?'

I nod. 'Yeah. They left me a message.'

And then I slaughtered their entire family, but I decide to leave out that little detail.

'It makes sense now.'

'What does?'

'Why you're so scared to let anyone in. You can't bear to lose them, and you don't like how vulnerable it makes you. Better to have no one to lose so nothing can hurt you like that again.'

My heart squeezes. Pressing my lips together, I exhale.

'I'll have to do the same to you,' I whisper, shifting my eyes to our entwined hands. I pull mine from her grips, twisting our fingers together, enjoying the feel of her heated skin contrasting against the coolness of mine.

'What?' she asks, pushing onto her elbow, staring down at me.

'I can't walk away from you, but I can't let you in.'

She frowns, her forehead creasing adorably.

'I want you to forget everything I've just said, and you will only remember if I say to you "I need you to remember". This applies to once you've turned as well. Any moments of complete vulnerability, you need to temporarily erase, until I tell you to remember. Do you understand?'

Her eyes glaze over momentarily, and she nods. 'Yes.'

I study her. 'What was the last thing you remember me saying just now?'

She blinks. 'You think it's funny I called you a gentleman.' I relax, the muscles in my shoulders unwinding. 'So, will I get to meet your other family one day?'

'Can we not do a family history lesson right now?' I mutter, gently pushing her off me, and getting to my feet, my tolerance for conversation fast fading. I'm feeling agitated now.

I don't like this. I don't want to get close, to trade secrets, and share things with her that I haven't ever dared to say out loud before, but she clouds my judgement, the words pouring out of me without my control. I need to cut this off immediately once she is turned, because the thought of growing to love this human makes me feel ill. I do not want to depend on anyone. *Ever.*

She pouts. 'I just want to get to know you.'

I turn, my usual snarky retort on my lips, before I remember I'm playing a role. Instead, I smile.

'I know. I'm sorry. There's going to be a lot of time for that. Promise me you'll stay with me after I turn you.'

'Where would I go?' She frowns.

'Just promise me.'

'I promise.'

'That's not enough,' I counter, sitting on the edge of the mattress. It groans underneath my weight, and she scrambles to her feet. She pads over to me, dropping down between my knees, hands resting on my thighs. 'Swear on it. Make a blood oath.'

'A blood oath?' she breathes, raising a brow. 'Is that like a promise?'

'Mmhmm,' I murmur, using my nail to create a slit on my finger, before raising it. 'But you can't break the promise.'

Unless it comes from me. But I don't tell her that. It's rumoured that breaking a blood oath causes instant death, but I have never actually tested the theory. I probably should have before entering one with her, but time is of the essence. I want to turn her. Now. This curse is eating at me more and more each day, so I want her trained and ready to help me when I need it.

Swallowing, she turns her hand, allowing me to do the same. She hisses as I perform the cut. Raising her arm, our fingers press together, and I smile.

'Ten years,' I say, eyes connecting with hers. 'You're with me, by my side, no matter what. For ten years. Then, if you wish to leave, I will let you go.'

'You will protect Raya.'

A flicker of irritation flashes through me, but I nod. 'I promise.'

'I won't want to leave,' she says firmly, pressing our fingers harder together.

A smirk inches across my mouth.

'Sure.' I shrug, retracting my hand. 'If you say so.'

16

CORA

The Fighter

WHEN I SLIDE INTO the passenger seat the next morning, my heart is hammering to the point I might pass out.

I've purposefully been bratty to Raya, and I've been harsh to Mum, more than I ever have been before. I can see their hurt in their eyes, but it needs to be like this. It's all a part of the plan.

Mum needs to get her shit together and look after Raya while I'm gone. If I'm able to, I will send her money and make sure she is safe and cared for, but I still need Mum to do what she is expected to do as a mother. She can't let herself sink further into this numbing oblivion. I won't be there anymore to pick up the pieces.

The guilty thoughts surrounding what is about to happen fade from my mind, and I exhale heavily. It's odd not caring about what others want. Kian compelled me to not consider other people's feelings when making this decision for myself. After spending my entire life putting other people's wants and needs over mine, no longer having guilt and worry about others is like breathing a breath of fresh air.

Yawning, I rub my eyes. I couldn't sleep at all. I spent most of the night writing in my journal, leaving tidbits of information behind. I carefully write out the words, leaving breadcrumbs for Raya, for the time when she might be able to come find me.

I don't intend on leaving my sister forever. Closing my eyes, I rest my head back, trying to get myself under control.

Hugging my arms around myself, my knees bounce up and down as I gaze out the window.

'Road trip classics, please!' Raya requests, leaning forward between the two front seats, draping her arms over them. She is still as chipper as ever, ignoring the way I've been acting. I admire her for it. If the roles were reversed, there is no way I wouldn't have reacted just as harshly back.

'We're going to the markets. Not exactly a road trip,' Mum points out, but passes the phone to me regardless, though I don't miss the annoyed side-eye she gives me, since we technically haven't been speaking. This isn't the way I want to leave things, but the things I said to her had to be done.

My mind drifts to the conversation Mum and I had last night, when Raya was out for dinner with a friend.

'I need you to stop this!' I snap, yanking the bottle from her hand. I throw it into the sink and the bottle smashes, the liquid pouring down the drain.

'No!' Mum shrieks, and she leaps for it, cutting her hands as she desperately tries to pick up the broken bits of glass, as if she can possibly mend it and stop the wine from gushing out. 'Why did you do that?' she sobs, blood filling the sink as she cries, ignoring my hand on her arm as I pull her back. My stomach sinks at the sight of her, so desperate, and so unstable, but I don't feel guilty anymore about leaving. I know it's Kian's influence over me, but it still feels odd not having that soul-crushing feeling of leaving my family.

She whirls around to face me, hand poised to strike my face, and I smack it back from me so hard, she stumbles, falling with a crash to the ground. She breathes rapidly, looking up at me, her hair having fallen out from its bun.

'Look at you,' I spit at her, shaking my head, disappointed beyond words. 'Drunk, screaming at me, and you would have just hit me if I'd allowed it.' I lean down, jabbing a finger in her direction. 'I know life sucks, and it's hard, but you are my mother, you are an adult, and you need to get your shit together. You need to step up and look out for Raya, because if something happens to me, she will need you!'

My mother bursts into tears, and so do I, but I turn my back on her so quickly, she doesn't see, and I stalk out of the room, knowing I've just taken it way too far.

The phone screen brightens and a photo of the three of us smiles up at me, making my stomach roil painfully. I feel sick at the words I said to her, the way I acted, and what I am about to do. Quickly swiping into the app, I select the playlist and put it on shuffle. As we cruise down the road, my fingers tap restlessly against my thigh.

The music starts blaring from the speakers, and my eyes are glued to the road. I tense as each car passes. It's not until we get out onto the highway when I realise this is where it's going to happen.

I can barely breathe as the car gradually increases in speed. Raya sings, dancing in the back seat, and my mum joins in, doing her best to not show the rift between us to Raya. It's all about keeping Raya in her perfect bubble.

I nervously peer over at them, a strained smile on my face. Guilt grips my stomach at the thought of a stranger having to die because of this, but as usual, the calming thoughts of Kian flood my mind, and the guilt evaporates, as if it was never there.

When I look back, the next few moments all seem to happen in slow motion.

I sense him before I see him. Kian steps out from a spot on the side of the road, throwing a rock up into the air and then catching it. When the car coming toward us gets closer, with a quick flick of his wrist, the rock careens toward the other car, shattering the glass. The driver loses control, heading straight for us.

'Mum!' I scream out of genuine reaction to seeing the car rushing toward us, but it's too late.

Our cars collide with a brutal force. Glass erupts around me, there's screaming, and I feel everything all at once. The force of being thrown forward, the glass slitting into my skin, the heat of the road metal clashing with metal . . .

I jolt awake with a gasp, feeling pain *everywhere*.

My eyes are heavy as I force them open.

The car is on its side, and my head is aching. It's unbearably hot, and there's an unsettling silence. The visor hangs loosely off its hinges in front of me and I meet my own gaze in the mirror. Blood streaks down my face, and it feels like I've broken my nose from the impact. My neck is so stiff and sore, I can barely move it as I look around the car.

I choke on a gasp as Kian sits in the back seat, blood smeared across his lips as Raya lays there, eyes closed, dark hair billowing around her face.

'Kian!' I whisper, my throat burning. 'What are you doing?'

'I needed to see what her blood tasted like compared to yours.' He grins, and I feel cold at the empty, cruel smile that tilts his lips. A smile like that doesn't belong on such a handsome face. My eyes turn to her wrist as I notice the same mark that brands me is now on her, too. 'Delicious, but not quite as divine as yours.'

My head is fuzzy. I can barely focus on what he is saying.

A siren wails in the distance and I drag my eyes from him to the front seat, where Mum is. A scream tears from my lips when I see her head bent backward, blood streaming down her neck. A gaping wound lies there. A bite.

Suddenly, I'm yanked from the car, and I scream again, agony I've never felt ripping through my body with an intense severity.

'What have you done?' I gasp, barely able to stand as Kian pulls me to him. Collecting me in his arms, he sweeps me off my feet and the world tilts. His fangs drop down and he drives them into my neck. I scream, desperately trying to get him off, but he's far too strong, and I'm dizzy with the pain.

My eyes fly open when he stops, and he pulls out a blade. Flipping it effortlessly, it glints in the sun that is beginning to peek through the clouds. He pushes the blade into my chest and I choke on my breath at the pain.

A wicked smirk lights up his face.

'See you on the other side, *mio tesoro*.'

17

KIAN

The Enforcer

HER FOOTSTEPS ARE AS light as a feather.

Cora walks unhurriedly down the hallway, eyes roaming around, searching for me. When I breeze past her, she startles, whipping around, but I'm already down the stairs. Swallowing, she cautiously moves down them.

She has adjusted well to being a vampire.

I've been hard on her.

Intentionally cruel – to keep her at a distance – but forceful with her training. She needs to be tough if she is by my side. She needs to hold her own. Sink or swim.

Crashing into her, I slam her against the wall, my hands closing around her throat. She fumbles for her dagger, and I snap her neck, ignoring the ache inside my body from doing that to her, as if I hurt myself in the process. She crumples to the floor, dark hair spilling across the tiles, her eyes staring up at the ceiling.

Tsking my tongue, I step back, looking down at her. I was hoping she would stop me in time. I am purposely going slower than I want to, taking into consideration she is new, but I need her to adapt *quickly*.

I leave, and it's a few hours later when I return to the house. Stepping inside, my eyes move to where I left her on the ground, seeing nothing but empty space. I barely have time to take another step when she launches at me, a dagger plunging into the side of my neck.

'Fuck,' I growl in surprise, whirling to face her. The little brat had been hiding somewhere up on the ceiling. Pulling the knife out, my lips curve. 'Element of surprise. That's a very neat little advantage to have.'

Another dagger flies at my face, and I fix her with a bored stare as I sidestep it. Another one launches at me.

Smiling wider, I move out of their path.

There is something about this woman throwing daggers at me that really does it for me.

As I advance on her, she backs up as fast as she can, hitting the wall so hard, the photo frames knock off it. Slamming my hands either side of her, I cage her in. Studying those pretty eyes for a moment.

'Good,' I say. 'You're getting more creative, and quicker.'

Sneering up at me, she lifts her chin. 'One day I'll get you.'

I release a bark of laughter. 'I don't think so.'

'You act like you're the most powerful vampire there is.'

Pushing off from the wall, I shrug. 'How do you know I'm not?'

She glares at me. 'You're so full of yourself.'

My lips twitch. This is the most emotion I've seen from her in a while. A little bit of the fire that I know is in there. It's always simmering at the surface, and I'm desperate to have it unleashed.

'You might think I'm unreasonable, but you will develop skills that will save you countless times in your life, and you will be grateful for this.'

'Grateful?' she echoes, releasing a dry laugh. 'I don't think it's possible for me to feel anything of the sort toward you.'

'Oh no,' I croon, staring mockingly down at her. 'I gave you eternal life, the gift of getting what you want from others, incredible speed and strength. Skills others would die to learn.' Tilting my head, I continue. 'I'm ensuring no one poisons you, or makes you suffer.' Sneering, I bare my fangs at her. 'I'm such a monster for giving you all of those things.'

'You're a liar, and a murderer.'

'You say that like it's an insult.'

Her mouth falls open as she glares at me in outrage. 'Don't you care *at all* for human life?'

I arch a brow. 'No. I don't.'

'Do you forget you used to be one?' she exclaims, shaking her head in disbelief.

'How could I forget?' I snarl, stepping toward her once more. 'Being powerless, weak, and vulnerable. All. The. Time.'

'You have a warped outlook on life.'

I stare at her. 'Perhaps, but it isn't necessarily the wrong outlook.'

'Who says?'

'I do.'

She scoffs. 'You're unhinged.'

'And?' I probe. 'There's nothing wrong with that.'

'There's everything wrong with that.'

'How so?'

'You're unpredictable and dangerous.'

'Ah.' I offer a thin smirk. 'My two favourite things to be.'

'And psychotic.'

'Thank you.'

'Argh!' she exclaims, shoving me back from her, eyes narrowing into slits. 'You're infuriating.'

She stalks down the hall, and I throw one of her daggers back at her. Whirling around, she ducks, and throws one back to me just as fast. I catch it, blood spilling down my hand as I do.

'Good,' I say firmly, nodding.

Shooting me a withering stare, she disappears around the corner, and my smile grows.

She is going to be absolutely *lethal*.

18

CORA

The Fighter

THE SOUND OF MY own screams wake me.

Snapping my eyes open, I peer around, baulking when I see Kian lurking in the shadows, that predatorial smirk on his face as he strolls into the room. Shrinking under the covers, I pull them up to my chin, feeling the coldness in the air straight into the marrow of my bones.

A violent rage washes through me at the sight of him. How can such a pretty face be so cold and cunning? My fingernails sink into my palms as I ball my fists, absolutely seething by doing everything I can to not lose control right now. It won't end well for me.

I was hoping the anger I felt toward him would become more manageable as time passed, but it's like it's festering inside of me, clawing at the walls to get out, and I'm moments away from letting it consume me.

This isn't the man I thought I was falling for. There is nothing remaining in him. He is an empty shell. A cruel man. A spider, who caught me in his web.

'Get up,' Kian says coldly, his eyes sweeping over my dishevelled hair. 'We have business to attend to.'

It's been three months since everything happened. The car accident, turning, and then adapting to everything. Kian has been training me, and for fleeting moments I swear I see the other side to him – the Kian I first met – but then it's gone just as quickly. I think I'm just desperate to see good in someone where there is none, and I'm in denial about it. It's a difficult pill to swallow knowing I uprooted my entire life for a man who doesn't care about me.

He's a killer.

He's a liar.

He's a manipulator.

One day, I'm going to kill him.

Silently, I peel the covers back and stand. I make a point of keeping my distance, basically scraping against the wall to avoid touching him. His eyes follow me as I pass him and slip out through the door. I'm dressed and by the front door a few minutes later, and he appraises me for a moment. He looks like he wants to say something, but decides against it, gesturing for me to exit out the front door.

Initially, I didn't believe Cas and Kian when they said breaking the blood oath would kill me instantly, but I have been digging wherever I can, and I fear they are right. It's not worth the risk. I need to do my time, learn everything I can about it, and use this information against him.

I've met a few vampires since being dragged around with Kian and they all say the same thing about a blood oath. In the beginning, I assumed Kian had gotten to them first, but I've asked too many now, it's not possible for him to have gotten to all of them before me, especially when a lot of the vampires have been strangers we meet on a night out.

Both of us dressed in skin-tight black clothing, we probably look like we are about to rob a bank. It sort of feels like it, with so many daggers stashed all over me.

'You are about to see a raid first-hand,' he says, eyes darting to mine. 'You're ready.'

Not a question. Nodding, I continue staring forward, keeping alert. We move through the woods at a speed that would look like a blur to the human eye. Following his lead, we run for a fairly long time, covering an unearthly amount of distance before he eventually comes to a stop on the edge of a forest.

I have no clue where we are. There's a lot of land, and there don't appear to be any close neighbours. Anyone walking by would never suspect anything unusual about the place. The house looks completely normal, and I imagine the inside probably does, too. It's what is below the ground that holds the prisoners.

'Where's your team?' I question, scanning the area, not seeing anyone else arriving.

'We can handle it.'

My head snaps to him. 'You're taking me on a raid with no back-up?'

His lips curve. 'You're with me. You don't need back-up.'

Swallowing, I drag my eyes from that stupidly handsome jawline, and rake my gaze over the farmhouse before us. Off to the side, there is a door in the ground, one that wouldn't be noticed unless you had enhanced eyesight, like vampires do.

'In and out,' he instructs. 'Quick, and silent.'

'But you always say these places are full of poison. I still react to them,' I say nervously, gnawing my lip.

'Then don't get poisoned.'

With a *whoosh,* he jets forward. Gritting my teeth, I follow him. The door is open by the time I get there and I descend the stairs silently. The air is tainted with something that makes my stomach churn.

Three guards stand by the doors. One is already dead by the time I reach the bottom step. His blood is sprayed across the ground in a gut-wrenching display. Kian moves so quickly, like a snake striking. The next guard is down before I can blink. Kian is intensely brutal and precise when he fights, leaving no room for mercy. He often brings people back from these farms to torture answers out of them, but the guards generally don't know anything important, and are just strung along by the people who are the managing the operation.

The third guard gasps, swinging his crossbow up and aiming. Kian dances out of his way, a gleeful smirk on his face. The man breaks out in a sweat as his eyes dart around the room. When he finally notices me, with surprising speed, he launches the arrow toward me.

Kian steps in front of me when I remain frozen, and he knocks the arrow out of the way. Turning to face me, he glowers down at me, his upper lip curling in anger, making me recoil from him. Something twists in my stomach as I sense his disappointment.

'Hesitate like that again and you're dead,' he hisses. 'Have you learnt nothing?'

Another arrow whizzes toward us, and Kian doesn't even look back as he flicks it away, like it's merely an insect. His skin blisters immediately from the poison it must be dipped in, but he doesn't flinch, or even act like he felt it. It makes sense. He is attempting to build my resistance up to everything too, and it's incredible how nothing affects him like it should.

'He's yours,' Kian snarls, fingers digging into my jaw as he forces me to meet his brutally black eyes. 'Kill him for what he has done.'

Releasing me sharply, he steps back. The guard's eyes are ping-ponging between us, as if he doesn't know who to aim for. Kian suddenly disappears, and the man whimpers softly, eyes searching the area.

Then he looks back at me. And the arrow is pointed at my chest.

'Kill him!' a voice whispers, sounding like it is inside my head.

My eyes drift to the cages. A vampire lays sprawled on the ground, skin sunken in, and such a pale colour, it's almost translucent. My throat tightens at the sight. Moving to the next cage, this time, my heart squeezes. A young girl, who mustn't be much older than twelve, looks on the brink of death. Even worse than her neighbour.

The arrow flies toward me.

I move.

The guy panics, turning around in circles, his back to me. My focus sharpens, and I imagine all the times Kian has shown me the exact way to go for the kill. Forcing myself to move, I whip out my dagger.

Kill or be killed.

My dagger drives straight through his back. I'll never forget the squelching sound of the blade sinking into his flesh, and the pressure of it on my hand. A garbled sound escapes him and I wrench my hand out, seeing his blood coating my skin. He falls to his knees, clutching his chest, before he collapses.

A numbness inches through me as I stare down at my trembling hands, and the man's blood on them.

Kian appears so suddenly, I flinch.

He smiles.

'Perfect, *mio tesoro*,' he purrs. 'Well done.'

I'm trembling so hard, my teeth knock together. Panic seizes me at the realisation of what I've just done. There's a pressure increasing in my chest, climbing up my throat, threatening to choke me.

'Oh my God . . .' I murmur, hand pressing against my chest as I stare down at the dead bodies around us.

Kian plays with the end of my hair for a moment before he

slides his hand around my throat. Gliding his hand to my jaw, forcing me to meet his eyes.

'I just killed a man,' I whisper, my head feeling light.

Kian nods slowly, lifting my chin. He has a cold smirk twisted onto his mouth, but his eyes flicker as they assess me, looking as if he may want to comfort me. Thinking better of it, the corner of his mouth inches down, and whatever I thought I saw vanishes.

'And there will be many more.'

Cool fingers run down my arm, his equally cool breath fanning my earlobe as he presses his chest into my back.

It's only been a few weeks since my first kill, but it feels like a lifetime ago. I stare down at the man, the numb feeling I often get when I'm about to kill, or watch someone be killed, spreading through me like poison.

'Is this him?' Kian asks, and a shiver inches down my spine at his voice. Like ice clinking in a glass of water. Or a cup of life-threatening poison.

His fingers dance across the edge of my shoulder, and I refrain from shuddering in disgust at his hands on me. A part of me relishes having him close, his hand somewhat of a comfort, and the other part of me loathes him so much, I see red. It's hard to hate someone, only to have the core of me crave his praise. It makes sense that I am loyal to him, since he created me, but I never would have sold my soul to the Devil if I'd known what the true cost would be.

'Yes,' I reply.

The man cowers before us, the scent of his fear and sweat drenching the air around him, so potent I can taste it on my tongue.

'I'm sorry, I'm sorry,' the man whimpers, rocking back and forth on the ground, his head wrapped up in his arms. His long hair is matted, falling limply down his shoulders. I wrinkle my nose when I detect urine soiling his pants.

'Not so fierce now without your weapons.' Kian smiles down at him, revealing two very sharp fangs. His voice indicates an undertone of friendliness, as if he has a reasonable bone in his body. But those calculating eyes size up the man before us like he is a mouse, and we are the lions caging him in. 'Tell me, how long have you been hunting vampires?'

'N-not long,' the man stammers.

Joseph, a vampire hunter. Amateur vampire hunter, I should say. He wounded one of the humans Kian was keeping around. He was aiming for me, but I heard him coming. I stepped out of the way, and the human Kian has been toying with for the past week got an arrow to the heart. Kian has no care whatsoever for the human girl the man struck in the chest, but the fact that he had the audacity to aim for me has sentenced him to death. People have died by Kian's hands for a lot less.

Kian makes a tsk sound with his tongue in disagreement. 'I don't think you're telling me the truth.'

'Two years,' Joseph chokes out, teeth chattering together as he violently trembles. Sweat drips down the back of his neck, landing in a soft splatter on the cement floor.

Drip. Drip. Drip.

'And in these two years of hunting,' Kian continues, gliding across the floor as he paces calmly, hands resting behind his back. The basement we are in is dark, damp, and filled with mildew. I can smell it with each inhale, and it leaves a dirty taste in my mouth. Wherever we make home – however temporary it may be – Kian always makes sure there is a basement in the house. It gets used every time. 'How many vampires have you killed?'

'I don't know,' Joseph whispers.

Kian glances at me, silently asking if I've heard the increase in Joseph's heartbeat. I give a subtle nod.

'Do not lie to me, Joseph,' Kian snarls, his voice deepening to one that plagues my nightmares. A crisp coldness that can be felt in the marrow of my bones.

'Ten,' Joseph gasps, tears streaming down his cheeks as he peers up at us, pleadingly.

Kian nods. Turning, he moves his empty gaze to me. 'Stab him ten times. Each one for the vampire life he stole. Then let him bleed out.'

'No!' Joseph screams, his terror palpable.

The man reaches for a loose rock beside him – the floor is filled with debris – and aims for the back of Kian's head. Kian crouches beside him as the rock soars. The sound of Joseph's leg snapping upon the impact of Kian's hand splinters the air with a sickening crunch, and then a few seconds later, the rock connects with the wall.

Joseph's tortured screams echo in the old basement, bouncing from the walls, making my ears feel like they're on the verge of bleeding.

Nodding, I swiftly pull out my rubber-handled dagger, and it glints in the dim lighting. A gift from Kian to me. 'Mio tesoro' is engraved in it, and it gives me a tiny thrill every time I look down at it. Something deadly in my hand that is truly mine.

Kian steps back, looking delighted at getting his hands dirty. Screams of pain feed his dark soul. Joseph clambers backward, trying to get away from me, but my strong strides eat up the distance between us with a speed his human eyes struggle to comprehend.

I sink the dagger into his thigh, the leg that Kian has just fractured. Joseph howls in pain, curling over onto his side as he gropes blindly at the gaping hole. The scent of his blood hits me with a severe pulse, almost knocking me over. I haven't fed for a whole day. This is a part of Kian's test. If I feed right now, I get punished. I do not feed while I work. We must not mix business with pleasure when it comes to these kinds of situations.

My teeth clamp down onto my tongue, my own blood filling my mouth as I plunge the dagger underneath Joseph's rib, sliding it across, feeling the metal graze the bone. He struggles to draw breath in his panic, his lightly tanned skin growing paler by the second. In and out, I pull the dagger, and stop precisely when I have reached ten wounds.

'Come,' Kian says once I have finished, his voice leaving no room for hesitation. 'Leave him to die.'

I rise to my feet, my eyes glued on the man as he jerks and spasms, the blood oozing out of him and onto the dirty floor. Pocketing the dagger – still drenched in his blood – I follow Kian up the stairs. The scent is overwhelming, burning my eyes, and making my throat ache something severe.

It won't always be like this, I remind myself. *Things will get better.*

At this point, the guilt stirring in my stomach is a constant churning that makes me feel ill, but overall, I'm growing more numb as the days pass, as if each kill fractures a piece of my soul, and I'm slowly allowing the darkness to creep inside me.

I'm learning to live with it. It's something I have to endure. I signed my own fate, and now I must reap the consequences. There is no one to blame, but myself.

Lifting my chin, I walk into the kitchen, feeling Kian's watchful gaze on me. Removing the dagger, I rinse it under the tap, and then wash my hands.

'You have good self-control, for a young vampire,' Kian says quietly.

Twisting on my heel, I face him. 'I learnt from the best.'

Kian offers me a lip-twitch, which is the closest thing to a genuine smile he has shown me since he turned me, and suddenly became a stranger. He nods. 'You must be hungry.'

I don't reply. I don't need to, he can tell how hungry I am, and how much strength it cost me to not give in and feed just now.

'I want to go out tonight,' Kian says, leaning casually onto the door frame. His hands slide into his pockets. 'Will you join me?'

I want to laugh, but I resist the urge. He enjoys asking me things like this, as if I have some sort of freedom or choice in the matter.

'Of course,' I say, because I have fought and fought with him in the past, and I can't win, or get myself out of this. I made a blood oath. Ten years with him, by his side, doing as I'm told. I don't like to admit I've given up, but it's just easier doing what he says. I've started really trying in our practice fighting, and I'm learning an incredible amount from him. I'm studying him, just as much as he studies me, and when the time comes, hopefully I will be skilful and strong enough to kill him. I just need to bide my time. A part of me wonders if I truly could kill him, because of the strong attachment I do feel for him, but I like to delude myself into thinking I would be able to, if it comes down to it.

Looking pleased, he pushes off the frame. 'Human One,' he calls out down the hallway. Soft footfalls can be heard as a teenage girl hurries into the room. She is young, and it kills me to see her innocent, doe-eyed expression as she stops in the centre of the room. She's dressed in a silky red dress that is completely backless. Kian intercepted their limo on the way to their school formal last night. Apparently, the limo friends all are a part of an interconnected group who orchestrated a massive operation that killed thirty-one vampires. So Kian decided to get back at them the worst way imaginable. I can't think about that right now.

If I try to run, I die. These people are dead, whether I am here or not. I just need to survive, and get through this.

'Take her dress,' Kian says. 'You will wear that tonight.'

Every part of my insides curls in on itself as I walk over to the girl. She shakes as I slide the straps off her shoulders. The dress pools at her feet, and she steps over it. I pluck the dress from the floor and hang it over the door. The girl is completely bare now. Bruises litter her skin from Kian's earlier attack, and my eyes move to the floor, my stomach clenching to the point of nausea.

'Now feed,' Kian demands, lazily gesturing to the girl. 'I want you in full strength tonight.'

My fangs snap out, and I yank the girl to me. Shutting everything out, I let the numbness filter through my veins like poison. She cries out, and her cry morphs into a scream when I bite her. The sweet warmth of her blood floods my system, not as bitter as most of the blood has been, and I groan in longing at the taste of it. This is the longest I've gone without feeding for a while, which must make the blood taste better. When I first turned, I couldn't keep any blood down, but I've gotten better at controlling it. Kian saunters up behind her, taking her other side. The girl's tight grip on my arm softens, and fades into nothing as she slumps forward into me.

Kian tosses her backward, as if she is as light as the silk dress she wore moments ago.

With blood-stained fingers, he reaches for my face, trailing his hands down my cheek.

Lifting my chin, I stare back at him.

His lips tilt. 'I truly am going to have so much fun with you.'

PRESENT DAY

19

The Prisoner

I STARE AT THE WALL.

My fingertips run over the raised scars. Scars cover my arms, with a few on my chest, a smaller one on my chin. The ones on my arm are significantly worse than the others. I wish I had a clue as to where they came from.

Low voices can be heard on the other side of the door. Turning, my eyes sweep over it, and I wish I could see through it. If only I could figure out where the hell I am, and why I'm here.

Exhaling, I push off the mattress and move to the window. Pressing my fingers to the blinds, I try to push them away – like I have so many times before – and they don't budge. Squinting, I press my face against the small gaps, but I can't see anything through them except a foggy haze, which doesn't even look real. Like it's an illusion of some kind.

If I had the energy, I would laugh, because that sounds ridiculous to think.

The sound of the doorknob twisting makes me turn, and the door pushes open. A man steps inside, and I tilt my head back to stare up at him, eyes widening at his tall frame. Blinking slowly, something flashes across my mind. I don't think this is the first time I've seen this man, or the first time he has visited me, but I can't recall anything about the other times.

'Who are you?' I whisper.

'That's not really very important,' he drawls, leaning back against the wall, levelling me with a steely, dark look. His eyes are charcoal black, and goosebumps prickle uncomfortably across my skin when they land on me. 'I need to know what you know.'

'What do I know?' I frown, hugging my cardigan closer around myself.

Pushing the door softly shut behind him, he advances toward me. Shrinking back, I hit the wall, as his long strides devour the distance between us. My heart thrums as I try to reel further back. His eyes darken, swirling with an eerie intensity that makes me feel pure terror.

Standing over me, his eyes bore into mine.

'That's what I'm trying to find out.'

20

CORA

The Fighter

WILL THE NIGHTMARES EVER STOP?

I honestly want to know. Will I reach a point where everything I have lived through won't haunt or torment me anymore, or is it always going to be like this?

My eyes stare down at the claw marks over my skin as they heal. I've torn myself to shreds again. Blood soaks the sheets around me, and I shudder at the sight of it. Kicking off the blankets, I practically fall out of the bed. I'm a quaking mess as I stumble into the shower and rinse off the imaginary feel of Kian's touch.

Stepping back into my room once I've finished, I dress quickly, and head out to the kitchen, my skin still feeling prickly. The sun is slowly making its way into the sky. Movement next door captures my attention.

My neighbour Eli sits on the chair on his porch, draped in a blanket. A steaming cup of something that smells like a caramel latte sits beside him. He nurses a notebook and a pen as he scribbles things down. Leaning forward, I try to make out his words, but can't quite decipher them. His words fill the page, and he flips over to the next one, continuing.

Curious, I watch him for some time. His dark hair continually falls across his eyes, and he sweeps it back. My eyes remain glued on him until the sun is well up, showering my kitchen with its golden beams as it filters through the blinds. I don't dare to move, hoping he doesn't notice me here. There is something about him that intrigues me, but I don't know why.

When he turns his head, looking in the opposite direction, I make my escape back to the safety of my room.

A loud bang has me jumping in fright, and whirling around. Theo is at my window, waving at me, as if appearing outside my bedroom window at barely six in the morning is something that is considered normal.

Grimacing, I unhook the latch, and yank it open. The morning air rushes in, filling the space, and I shiver, despite not *actually* feeling cold. The dream of Kian felt so real, it has made me feel uneasy, and my nerves are shot to hell.

'Hello?' I say, although it sounds more of a question as Theo climbs in. 'Why are you here and why are you climbing through the window?'

Theo shrugs, his messy hair windswept. He looks like he is in the same clothes I saw him in yesterday. He rakes his hand through his hair, attempting to flatten it. 'Your neighbour is out the front and I didn't want to talk to him.'

I raise an eyebrow. 'You didn't have to talk to him either way.'

Theo shrugs. 'You were in your room. Made sense to come this way.'

'It really doesn't, but okay,' I relent, shrugging into my jacket, and flicking out my hair. 'What are you doing here?'

'Don't know,' he replies. 'Bored, I guess.'

'It's six in the morning,' I point out.

'Perhaps that would mean something if I went to bed last night.'

Narrowing my eyes, I notice the blood smear around his mouth. 'Looks like you've had fun.'

'I was stalking the train, as usual.'

'Theo.' I sigh, shaking my head. 'I really don't like that you do that.'

'They get so scared.' Theo grins, looking like a kid waking up and experiencing their first Christmas. 'It's so fun. You should try it.'

The train into town arrives at the same time every night. Theo has a terrible habit of stalking the people that arrive, and basically scaring them senseless. He also likes to have a snack – or so he calls it – while he's there.

'I am trying to be a good person.'

Theo steps in front of me, planting his large hands on my shoulders. My head bobbles back and forth as he shakes me a little too aggressively.

'You are a vampire, girlfriend. Time you start acting like one.'

Shrugging him off, I side-step around him. 'I've asked you to stop calling me that, and, trust me, I have done enough "acting like a vampire" to last a lifetime.' I exhale. 'Speaking of . . . I had a visit from a certain someone last night.'

Theo's head snaps up. 'Are you serious?'

'Yeah. He was here when I got back from the party.'

'Are you okay?' he asks, forehead crumpling in concern.

'Fine.'

'Kian's letting you stay here?' Theo arches a brow.

Nodding, I rub a hand down my face. 'Yeah. For now, at least. He wants us to continue figuring out who is killing people. Also, he's still hunting the last remaining witch in that coven he is wanting to find.'

'Ah,' Theo says, looking curious. 'You still don't know what he wants with them?'

I hesitate. I don't like keeping things from Theo, but I know this is not my secret to share. My lips part as I go to speak, but I shake my head and shrug instead.

'Well. At least he's leaving you alone.'

'Yeah,' I reply, not understanding why the thought of Kian not demanding me to go with him disappoints me. The idea is truly nonsensical. I *want* this life. The freedom. The choice of doing my own thing. I don't need him. My heart squeezes at my thoughts and I feel a frown tug at my lips. As usual, I'm at war with myself.

'You're so sad all the time,' Theo pouts, poking his finger into my cheek. I slap his hand away irritably. 'You need to lighten up.'

'No, I need to get ready for class,' I say in exasperation. 'So kindly, get out.'

'Skip.' Theo wiggles his eyes. 'Let's get drunk and make out instead.'

'Theo!' I snap in frustration. Whirling around to face him, I jab a finger into his chest. 'My past haunts me. It keeps me up at night. It makes me sick to my fucking stomach the things I've done to other people. If working hard, and trying to do something in this world, is what I tell you I need to do right now, *don't fucking question it.*'

Theo blinks down at me, shock registering on his face for a moment. Swallowing, he nods stiffly.

'Okay,' he says gently. 'Well, I'll tag along then.'

'What?' I groan, swiping for my bag, and throwing it over my shoulder.

'I'll come to class,' Theo says. 'I'll help you study.'

'You're more of a nuisance than anything.'

'Come on, Cor.'

Exhaling, I throw up my hands. 'Fine. But if you annoy me, in any way, you're done.'

'I will behave,' he promises, with a sultry wink.

Rubbing my eyes, I stalk out of the room, hearing him trot behind me, so close that he bumps into me when I stop.

This is going to be a long day.

*

The sound of my footsteps slapping against the pavement is therapeutic.

Running makes my head feel clear. The fresh air in my lungs and caressing my skin helps minimise the dark thoughts circling in my head. At least for a little while, and that is better than nothing.

Mya and I have been meeting up to go for a run most mornings, and today we decided to meet between classes, since we both had a few hours' break in the middle of the day. I could run a lot longer but I like the company, and I don't exactly need to do it for fitness. I enjoy the numbness it brings me, and that I get to do it with a friend.

'Okay, time out,' Maya gasps, breathing rapidly as she doubles over. 'How the hell have you not even broken a sweat, and I look like I've just finished a marathon?'

Placing my hands on my hips, I turn to face her. 'I run a lot.'

'Yeah, no shit,' she mutters, rubbing her side. Her cheeks are flushed a bright red, and sweat drips down her face. 'I thought I'd get better at this over time, but nope, still hate it.'

Breathing a laugh, I roll my shoulders, staring out at the woods we run by. There haven't been any dead bodies for the past couple of nights. I still have no clue who has been doing it or why. There are a lot of newbie vampires in town, so it honestly could be any one of them, but my gut feeling tells me it isn't.

After spending so much time with Kian, and learning so much from him, it's safe to say I don't believe anything is a coincidence anymore. There is always an ulterior motive, and I need to always be on the lookout.

'Let's walk the rest and go get a coffee?' I suggest as Mya still struggles to breathe normally, her pulse racing to the point it's making me feel fidgety and restless. I can hear her blood roaring through her, making it difficult for me not to look at the pulse in her neck.

'Sure,' she pants, trying to catch her breath.

We take the scenic route through the trees, and my eyes track everything, but it's a quiet day. The vibrant greenery always calms me. I love being in the woods. There's just something so soothing about it.

Birds chirp as we walk by the trees they're perched on, and a few fly through the gaps in the branches. Streaks of sunlight pierce the leaves for a few moments before the clouds move once more, covering the sun back up.

The main street of Red Thorne is busy as we make our way down it. Lots of faces I don't recognise, but quite a few from my classes out and about, probably having a similar schedule to me.

My eyes constantly assess my surroundings, ears tuning in and out of conversation. Surely someone has to know something about what has been going on around here, but I keep turning up empty-handed.

We order our coffees and then make a slow walk toward the apartment building Raya once lived in. Temporarily, at least. Collapsing onto the bench I often meet Mya at, I lean into it, and exhale, my finger running up and down the side of the takeaway coffee cup.

'You know – I genuinely have no clue where this bench came from,' Mya observes, brows dipping as she glances at the plaque.

My eyes follow hers.

In loving memory of Alex Valenti. Forever in our hearts.

A hollow pit forms in my stomach as I stare at the words. I had it made for him just after I got back into town. I'm not sure if Theo has even noticed it, or if he has, he hasn't said anything to me about it. Which could certainly be the case since we don't often discuss anything of importance. Possibly also because Theo never got the chance to know him. I never did, either.

I worry about Theo sometimes. I don't know everything that has gone down with him since he's been turned, but I know there has been some trauma, and he doesn't know how to cope with it.

Vibrations pull my attention back to reality. Mya digs around in her skin-tight leggings pocket for her phone. She stares at the screen, her lips tugging downward.

'Your dad?' I guess, yanking my hair out of its ponytail, letting it fall loose around my shoulders.

She sighs heavily through her nose, declining the call.

'Yup,' she replies. 'He's relentless.'

'Why exactly are you avoiding him again?' I question, taking a long sip.

'He is trying to force me to do something I don't want to do, but I'm the only one in my family who doesn't want to, so I'm basically exiled from them. None of them are speaking to me, except Dad, who only calls me to try to shove it down my throat.'

'Yikes. What is it he wants you to do?'

Mya looks down. 'Help with the family business, you could say.'

'You don't want to be a part of it?'

'No,' she answers, shaking her head. 'I really don't, and he hates me for it.'

'I'm sure he doesn't hate you.'

'He does.'

'What is the business?' I ask.

'It's hard to explain, but basically it would control my whole life and I just want my own identity, you know?'

Nodding, my cheek twitches, acknowledging her comment. 'I know exactly what you mean. I'm sorry you're in that situation. That really sucks.'

'Yeah,' she mutters.

Her phone rings again, and we both stare at her pocket.

'My first thought about him calling you so much is that he cares.'

She scoffs. 'Trust me. He doesn't.'

Shrugging, I look ahead, unsure what to say next, given I really don't know anything about her family, or whatever business they're involved in.

Glancing at the time, I push to my feet.

'We better get going. I want to have a quick shower before this afternoon's lecture. I'm going straight to work after.'

'Me too,' she says, finishing the last of her coffee. Reaching for my cup, her finger presses against mine and a rush of cold fills me. I step away, goosebumps erupting over my skin. Quickly looking around, I wonder if it's the sensation of being watched. Mya deposits our cups into the closest bin. 'See you at work!'

'See you,' I mumble distractedly, peering around me one last time, before jogging back toward my house, feeling the hairs on my arms stand up as I do.

Theo is late.

Exhaling in frustration, I glance down at my phone, the time flashing five minutes past my clock-off time.

'What are you still doing here?' Mya asks, coming around the corner, depositing a bag into one of the rubbish bins.

'Waiting for Theo,' I reply. 'I think I'll head to his house. He might have forgotten we were meeting. You wanna come?'

She shakes her head, yawning. 'I'm wrecked. I'm just going to head home. Have fun tonight!'

'Thanks.' I smile. 'Are you all good?'

'Yeah, just tired. Are we still having coffee tomorrow?' she asks.

We often meet for coffee and a walk on a weekend, whereas we run through the week. I've grown accustomed to drinking coffee, since it is no worse than blood lately. It doesn't do anything much to me, but I like appearing normal, and the routine makes me feel balanced.

'Yep! I'll see you then.'

'See you,' she says, as she disappears through the back door.

Making my way over to Theo's, I'm just strolling through the front door, when there is a fierce *whoosh* that has the collar of my uniform flicking up, as Theo appears, his lopsided smile in place.

'Sorry, got caught up,' he says. 'I'm not surprised you didn't wait, you're not exactly known for your patience.'

I scoff. 'Hello to you, too.'

'Apologies, girlfriend.'

'Call me that one more time,' I warn, gritting my teeth in frustration.

He has done well to not annoy me too much today, but he is probably due to start back up again.

'I have an idea that might make you feel a little better,' Theo says, and I immediately don't like the look in his eye.

'I don't want to go to the train, Theo,' I deadpan.

'Aw, come on,' he nudges me. 'Don't knock it till you try it.'

'I said *no*.'

Blowing out a puff of hair, he side-eyes me, annoyance written on his face. 'Fine. A drink, then.'

'Sure,' I agree. I shrug my jacket on, attempting to disguise the fact I'm still in my uniform. 'That sounds more *legal*.'

'There is nothing legal about being a vampire,' Theo argues, and quickly raises his hands in a peace offering. 'But, yes, being a better person and all that. I'm picking up what you're putting down.'

There's a shiver down my spine just as the door to Theo's bedroom swings open. I straighten immediately as Dante enters the room, shirtless, with blood in the corner of his mouth, and a few flecks over his chest. His long hair hangs around his face, almost to his shoulders.

'What the fuck . . .' I mutter, and when both of them look at me, I realise I've said it out loud.

'Howdy.' Dante waves at me, like it isn't the most bizarre thing seeing him here. Tattoos line the dark skin across his chest. He looks so different from when I saw him last time. Like he is a completely different person.

Narrowing my eyes, I notice the hickeys on his neck, but the moment I spot them, they begin healing, and I wonder if I really did see them at all.

'You remember Dante?' Theo says, running a hand through his hair, his eyes drifting to the now bare back of Dante as he moves around the kitchen, looking far too comfortable right now.

'Er – yes. Hard to forget.'

Dante was a vampire who was wronged by Kian – surprise, surprise – and made it his life's mission to hunt him down and seek revenge for killing his family. Kian told me about when he first turned. How he, Cas, and Aithan went on a blood-lust bender, and he hardly even recalled the night Dante's family were killed, which makes it even *worse*. It deeply disturbs me that human life means so little to vampires, and the more of them I meet, I realise it's just the way they think, even though it baffles me, since we were all humans ourselves. Some of us not that long ago. I still feel so separate from other vampires sometimes.

I feel so sorry for Dante. He turned, becoming a monster, in hopes of defeating Kian, but he has so far failed in his mission.

Apprehension curls in my veins as I watch Dante rip open a blood bag. Turning, he leans against the kitchen bench, eyes finding mine. The tension in the air increases to the point I feel it all around me.

'What are you doing here?' I ask him, folding my arms across my chest, feeling unnerved by this entire encounter.

'Heyyy,' a voice calls, and I snap my head to the doorway, where a pretty, long-legged brunette stands, completely naked. 'Come back to bed,' she whines. Another girl appears over her shoulder. Both of them are covered in blood and hickeys.

'Are we going to play with her next?' the new girl purrs at me, a slow smile stretching over her lips.

'Er – no thank you,' I say curtly, narrowing my eyes at them, my compulsion ringing toward them with ferocity. 'Go back into the room and stay there until you're told otherwise.'

The two girls quickly disappear, and I turn, eyeing the two boys, completely unsure of what dynamic is going on here, but honestly, that's the least of my concerns. This is a normal night for Theo. I never know who he has here.

'I heard Kian has visited you,' Dante drawls, and something in my chest tightens. He's lost himself to being a vampire, I can sense the shift in him. His eyes lack any sort of warmth as he analyses me, with an almost cruel appraisal, actually reminding me a little of Kian. 'I thought we made an agreement that your little group of friends would inform me if he came back.'

Theo's gaze bounces between the two of us, as if the topic of why Dante was even in Red Thorne had never come up. Knowing Theo, he probably didn't even question it. How they ended up here together, though, confuses me.

'So that's why you're here?' I ask. 'You're still after him?'

'Of course I am. He took everything that ever mattered from me, and I won't stop until I rip out his heart, and end him, for good.'

We stare at each other, and I lift my chin, narrowing my eyes. 'I don't have answers for you.'

'I think you do.'

'I don't,' I say, my voice firmer.

His head tilts. 'Yes. You do.'

There's a long pause as we both wait for the other's next move.

'Well,' Theo interrupts, rocking on the balls of his feet. 'This is getting intense, and I'm thirsty. Let's continue this over a drink, shall we?'

I side-eye Theo. He is impeccably terrible at reading the room.

'What is going on here?' I demand, gesturing between the two of them. 'You hang out?'

Theo shrugs. 'Yeah. Just a few times.'

'Since when?' I exclaim.

'Erm, like, just the last week or so.'

'It wasn't exactly planned,' Dante offers. 'We ran into each other, had some drinks, and decided to share a human. It's been fun.'

'What have you said to him?' I ask Theo.

Theo's eyes are on the window, and he doesn't even look like he is paying attention to the conversation, which he proves as much when he glances at me, noticing me staring.

'What?' he asks.

'What have you told him about me and Kian?'

'Oh, nothing, just that he stopped by to pay you a visit. You know, since you're tied to him for so many years.'

'That's so interesting,' Dante muses, slurping long and loudly on the blood bag, even though he clearly has just had his fill of human blood, given the marks on the two humans waiting for them in Theo's room. Kian once told me that vampires can get addicted to the high of blood, consuming such quantities that it can make them delirious. Studying Dante closely, I wonder if he is on his way to reaching that point. 'Means you're a direct connection to him.'

The growing pit in my stomach deepens. 'Whatever is going on in your head right now, Dante, I want no part of it. I've moved on, I'm trying to live a normal life. I don't want to be involved in anything.'

'But you are,' he says, and the glint in his eye is making me even more uneasy. 'You're right in the centre of it.'

'You lay a hand on me and he will kill you,' I warn him, tracking his movements carefully, in case he decides to make a move to come for me. If he's been talking to Theo, he should know Kian has trained me, and he must know when it comes down to it, I'll protect myself, at any cost. 'He will rip you apart in the worst way imaginable.'

'Mmhmm.' Dante's lips curve. Not quite a smile, more of an acknowledgement of my words, as if he expected me to say that. 'That's what I thought.'

'I'm bored,' Theo interjects, and I swear I could throttle him right now. 'We're going out. You coming, Dante?'

The two of us continue glaring at each other and after a long moment, Dante drags his eyes from me, focusing on Theo.

'Nah, I have some friends I'm travelling with. I best get back to them.' Pushing off the bench, he swipes his discarded shirt from the floor, yanking it over his head. I bristle as he brushes past me, an amused look lifting the corner of his mouth as he does. 'Nice to see you, Cora.'

'Wish I could say the same,' I retort sweetly.

He disappears into the night, and my eyes stay watching the darkness for a significant amount of time, unconvinced he's going to leave me alone. If he attacks me, Kian will come for me, and that is exactly what Dante would want.

Another target on my back. Excellent.

'Let's go,' Theo says, completely unfazed, as if he has totally forgotten about the two naked girls in his room.

Turning to him, I slam my hands into his chest, shoving him so hard he falls backward.

Damn, that feels good. I've been wanting to do that for a hell of a long time.

'Ow!' he complains, frowning up at me. 'What was that for?'

'Don't go running your mouth to anyone that shows you the slightest bit of attention. You've now exposed me as a way to Kian, and Dante is unhinged after everything he has been through. Don't you understand he is going to try to use me to lure out Kian?'

'You're being a bit dramatic,' Theo scoffs. 'Not everything is about you.'

'When it comes to revenge, everyone is expendable,' I hiss. 'Including me *and* you.'

Theo pushes to his feet, shooting me an annoyed glare.

'I could fucking kill you right now,' I seethe, my hands balling into fists.

He eyes them dubiously, backing up. After a heated moment of us glaring, he exhales, shoulders sagging.

'Shit.'

'Yeah.'

'I fucked up,' he says.

'Yes.' Pinching the skin between my eyes, I fight back the urge to burst into tears. 'I shouldn't have come here. To this town. I should have tried to run.'

'He will never let you go.'

The tears escape, rolling down my cheeks as I stare out the window.

'I'm sorry,' Theo whispers, walking over to me and placing his hands on my shoulders. 'I'm really, really sorry, Cor.'

'Yep,' I say stiffly.

'Cor . . .' He trails off, squeezing me gently. 'Look at me.'

Reluctantly, I force myself to face him. His dirty blond hair is messy, those pretty, dark eyes soft and pleading. In the moonlight,

I can almost see flecks of jade green in them, which is the colour they were before he turned. Or at least as far as I can tell in the photos he's shown me. He has a shrine of photos of him and Hunter plastered on his wall.

'I wasn't thinking. I get so caught up in the party life that I forget about all the serious problems we face every day. I try to forget about it all, and I know I shouldn't do that, because it can lead to a mess like this. I truly am sorry.'

'It's fine. Just another enemy to watch out for. I'm used to it.'

Theo's hand moves to the side of my face, and he collects the tear on his thumb.

'I've never seen you cry before,' he murmurs. 'I hate that I caused it.'

'I'm a bit of a mess lately,' I admit. 'Kian coming back has really shaken me. I'm feeling lost and confused about a lot of things. I don't know what my purpose is, and that's really quite a scary thought.'

'It's normal to feel like this. Everything is going to work out. For the both of us. We just need to try and enjoy life while we can.'

I let out a breathy laugh. 'Yeah. I guess. Do you know who Dante is travelling with?'

Theo shrugs. 'Two female vampires. He apparently has known one of them for a while, and the other is her girlfriend. That's all I know.'

'Hmm,' I say.

I wonder if when the time comes, they will fight Kian, too? Has Dante accepted that he will not take Kian down on his own?

'What do you know about him?' I ask. 'How did he get turned?'

'Apparently when he was coming back to the beach and Kian had his fangs in Dante's wife's neck, he saw his face. Full moon, of course. Obviously he was quite traumatised from that and never forgot it. When police couldn't give him answers, he did his own research and ended up here. I'm not really sure how he actually got turned, but he said that it isn't that hard to find someone to turn you, if you know where to ask.'

Shaking my head, I rub my temples. 'Right. Now he's just stalking Kian, trying everything he can to find him, and kill him.'

Theo shrugs.

Anger uncoils in my gut, and I stare stonily out the window, trying to get a hold of my feelings. I don't want to be pissed at Theo, but he has really upset me.

'Come on,' he says, nudging me. 'Let's still go out and try to forget about all of this. At least for tonight. Can we do that?'

A night out is something Theo and I often do together, and I wouldn't mind losing myself to the void. If Dante is going to come for me, at least I should have a few hours of fun before he does. A part of me is wondering whether I should let Kian know, but he would probably just laugh. He doesn't view Dante as a threat, merely an annoyance. He's barely a blip on his radar.

'Yeah?' Theo grins, noticing the small smile fighting its way onto my face.

Damn it. I'm smiling because of Kian, and that smug grin of his, and the way he would shrug off the thought of someone hunting him down to murder him. He's simply that powerful, he doesn't need to worry, and I hate how attractive I think that is. I'm not right in the head.

'Fine,' I say, desperately wanting the distraction from my thoughts.

Looping his arm through mine, Theo drags me forward, and I briefly close my eyes and mentally prepare for the night ahead.

'Also, this is a good chance for us to start mingling,' he says.

I nod. 'Good point.'

The main street of Red Thorne is somewhat quiet compared to earlier today, but the bars are overflowing with people inside. I suppose no one wants to be out on the streets alone, but are tricked into a false sense of security being indoors, surrounded by others. Little do they know they're in just as much danger inside.

The best drinking place in town is called 'Code Red', which has a line outside full of people waiting to enter. Theo drags me to the front of the line, flashing his trademark smirk. The bouncer lets us inside without a moment of hesitation. Theo gestures to me to go in first.

The air is full of stale cigarettes, and sweat. The music does well to drown out my thoughts, and I welcome the numbness it brings with it. Theo touches his hand to my back as he guides me toward the bar. He merely has to hold up four fingers, and the bartender drops whoever he is serving to make our drinks instead, without Theo even saying what we want. We have been here together a few times, but it's obvious Theo comes here regularly.

This place has a strange energy to it. Like the air around me is pulsating with something that isn't quite human. To be fair, most of Red Thorne has an eerie feel to it, but there's something about this place that seems to take it a step further. I don't believe this bar has been around that long, but it's a major hit in town, and by far the best place to drink and have a good time.

Ignoring the humans complaining beside us, Theo turns his back on them. We simultaneously grab the shot glasses. We clink them together before I swallow it down, enjoying the sting of the alcohol as it burns its way down my throat.

Theo and I do this too often. Drink too much, ignoring our problems, wanting to numb the pain away. I know it isn't healthy, but I'm not strong enough to handle it any other way yet. I'm trying. Working myself to exhaustion. Filling my day so full,

I barely have time to think. It's helping, but not enough. Nothing is ever enough to chase away my demons.

Theo's hand clamps around my wrist, and he yanks me toward the dance floor. It's so crowded, I bump into a person every few seconds as we make our way through the groups, and into the centre. The only lights are the bright neon strobes that flicker every few moments. The warmth of the alcohol buzzes through me, making me feel light and floaty. In the back of my mind, I remember that we are supposed to be talking with others, trying to gather information, but suddenly that just doesn't seem important.

A couple dances in front of us. The girl's long ruby-red hair captures my attention. My eyes track down her hair, toward her pale, slender neck. My mouth salivates at the sight of it, and the hunger blossoms so violently, I'm walking toward her before I realise what I'm doing.

I can't rid Kian from my mind, no matter how hard I try. I'm convinced it isn't *him*, it's simply the fact that he turned me, and I have some annoying attachment to him because of it. That's all it is. Snapping out of my thoughts, I focus on the girl in front of me. Drinking from the vein with Eli made me feel more alive than I have for weeks. I'm going to try and feed directly, just a bit whenever I need it, and it will also serve as the perfect distraction from my spiralling thoughts.

My hands snake around her hips as I pull her back toward me.

Theo moves between the girl and her boyfriend, his hand dragging down the guy's defined chest, running over the muscles of his stomach. An ache – longing – flutters through me, as Kian's face appears in my mind. Those black eyes, the razor-sharp jawline, the tilted smirk always on his lips.

The girl's skin is hot as I move my lips down her ear, dragging them across her throat.

Unable to ignore the impulse I have been feeling so strongly, I push my fangs into her neck, and groan. I let myself enjoy the heat of her blood, and the rush it gives me.

I've missed drinking directly from the vein. Is it that bad, letting myself indulge every now and then? Plenty of other vampires do it. Hell, all of them, minus a few here and there. If I don't go too far, is it really causing any harm?

Her blood has a tangy taste, contaminated with alcohol, and the pleasurable thrill of something a little extra. Some sort of amphetamine. It doesn't taste as terrible as the other blood I've been having. Still not as good as it should, but certainly better.

I tilt my head back, running my tongue over the edge of my fangs, capturing every last drop.

Spinning the girl, I pull her close to me, quickly healing her.

'You don't remember seeing me, or feeling any sort of bite,' I murmur into her ear. 'You drank too much. Felt a little too high, but you had a great time.'

Nodding sleepily, she leans back, falling into the arms of her boyfriend, who is wearing a matching dazed expression.

Theo and I spend another hour drinking and dancing, before spilling out into the street, feeling high on blood – and a little extra *something*. I'm laughing at an inappropriate joke Theo has just made, my vision a little hazy as the streetlights brighten the outside world into focus.

'Admit it,' Theo beams at me, throwing his arm around my shoulders. 'You're having fun. Second time this week.'

Smiling, I lean into him. 'I'm having fun.'

We stagger and sway together, holding each other up as we make our way down the street, neither of us knowing where we are going.

Movement makes my chin jerk up. If my heart was still beating, it would have stopped in my chest. Kian steps forward, wearing that sinister smirk of his, the one that is etched so deeply in my mind even a lobotomy couldn't remove the image from my brain.

He holds his fingers up. Nine fingers, for nine years. Dragging his finger across his neck, his soulless black eyes bore into mine, the threat as clear as day.

Shaking my head, I blink, trying to sober up, but when I look back to the shadowy spot, he is no longer there, making me wonder whether he was ever really there to begin with.

My blood runs cold at my paranoia.

I am never going to be free of him.

21

KIAN

The Enforcer

THE WHISKEY BURNS MY throat as I swallow it down.

My fingers drum against the surface of the table as I pore over the articles before me. I'm missing something. But what? Flicking through them, my eyes scan the page, absorbing all the dates, details and information I deem important.

This little witch I have been hunting is being particularly difficult. No one hides from me. I trace, I find, I kill. It's the thing I'm best at. Why is this one so difficult? She must be using exceptionally clever magic to cover her tracks. It's the only possible explanation.

I know now not to underestimate her. She killed Aithan, one of the most powerful vampires I've ever met, and then she cursed me – his second in charge. There is no witch in history, or at least that I know of, that has done two such powerful acts, and so close together. The fact that I can't find her, or even find a hint of where she might be, is making me even more concerned.

If I don't find her soon, the curse she hexed me with will kill me, meaning she will have ended the both of us, and that is something that I did not think was possible. Aithan seemed untouchable. So many people had tried before, why was it this time someone succeeded? How did she manage it?

Exhaling, I lean back in the chair, thinking.

My phone vibrates, pulling me from my thoughts. Answering it, I place it against my ear.

'What is it?' I ask.

'Your sources were correct. There's a farm down south that has at least three vampires in cells. Do you give permission to go in?' Lance's gruff voice asks. Lance is a vampire I recruited to help manage the business while I'm preoccupied with hunting down this witch, and trying to understand what is going on with my connection to Cora. He's brutal, direct, and views everything in black and white. The perfect person for the job, and also, a friend of Aithan, which I don't take on lightly.

'Have you scoped the area in the way I taught you?' I ask.

'Yes, sir.'

'You're confident you and your team can handle it? Have you covered all the bases, done all the groundwork that is necessary?'

'Yes, Kian, I'm completely confident with the mission. Everyone is geared up and ready. Just need your word to go ahead.'

I nod. 'All good to go ahead. Let me know if there's any problems.'

'Will do.'

The line goes dead, and my phone slips from my hand as my vision flickers. Leaning forward, I place my head in my hands.

Time is running out for me.

'Human,' I growl.

Soft footfalls can be heard before a girl appears. She sits on the edge of the table. Leaning forward, I sink my fangs into her thigh. She releases a breathy moan. I take as little as possible, reeling back, resisting the urge to spit it out. Blood is tasting worse and worse, no matter who the human is. It appears the longer I am apart from Cora, the worse it gets. Drinking blood used to give me an unbeatable high. One that I was addicted to. Now, I can barely keep it down, and sometimes, I spew it all back up. But I find forcing myself to drink a little bit every day has helped, and I'm able to control the urge to vomit. It's a constant battle, but one I'm positive I can conquer.

I always win. I get what I want. This is no different.

Dismissing her, I stand, feeling shaky, and stumble to my secret fridge, pulling out a small vial of Cora's blood. Staggering into the bathroom, I lean on the counter, staring into my reflection. My skin is sickly pale. My eyes are an inky black with dark circles underneath them. Lifting my shirt, I stare at my chest, and the dark mark that lies there. I feel an unsettling coldness inch through me. It's growing, looking like some warped dark tattoo.

Tension lines my shoulders and I roll my neck, as if that will relieve some of the pressure. I shouldn't be feeling any of these things, but this curse is stripping me, inch by inch, of my power. If word gets out about this, I'm finished.

Unscrewing the lid, I down the small amount of blood. Exhaling with relief, I lean forward, forehead pressed against the glass. It's the only damn thing to make me feel better, and even with me only using tiny amounts, I'm going through it at such a fast rate, I will run out sooner rather than later.

Throwing my shirt back on, I head down to the basement. One of the houses I've been staying in more recently isn't too far from Red Thorne. A safe enough distance away that no one should bother me, but close enough for me to get to Cora quickly if need be.

Muffled cries and whispers can be heard as I reach the door. Stepping inside, I notice a tense silence settle across the room. Striding purposefully forward, I reach for the first prisoner I see, yanking him up by his shirt and tossing him toward the chair.

'What do you know?' I snarl, leaning in so close that his rancid breath fans over my face. Gritting my jaw, I refuse the urge to recoil from him.

'Nothing!' he spits at me. 'I know nothing, and even if I did know something, I wouldn't tell you.'

Anger unfurls inside of me like poison. I savagely bite into his neck, ripping out his throat. I throw him to the ground, and his head connects with a *thump* as it bounces off the cement ground. His blood pools beside his head.

With blood smeared across my mouth, dripping down onto my shirt, I pivot, facing the last two prisoners, attempting not to let any go between my lips. I can't show any sort of weakness to anyone, especially not my prisoners. The last thing I need them to see is me fighting to keep it down.

'I will kill every last one of you,' I growl, my eyes raking over their huddled, quivering forms.

All of these people were names that turned up in my research. I need to find the coven the witch who cursed me belongs to, so I can find her.

'We will gladly die for our families and friends,' the woman says, eyes reluctantly meeting mine. 'We have accepted death.'

'Die, you will,' I retort dryly. 'But for that, I will make you suffer.'

She whimpers as I lunge toward her, circling my fingers around her ankle, dragging her across the ground.

'Tell. Me,' I seethe, a low growl vibrating through my chest.

'I'd rather die!' she shouts back at me.

Whipping out a blade dipped in poison, I carefully edge it out of its holder, before I stab it through her leg, pushing it so far down that it lodges itself into the cement floor beneath her, pinning her there. She howls in pain, clawing at it, trying to remove it. She hisses when she comes in contact with it. It's handy having a witch under my thumb. She has served me several of these blades for my use, as well as the necklace that I wear around my neck, matching the one I have for Cora, allowing me to summon her if and when I need her, and me to her.

The witch draws in a ragged breath as she collapses back onto the floor, writhing in pain as the poison begins to eat her flesh.

Turning, I stare down at the last prisoner. The youngest of them all. Sweat and dirt cling to him, covering most of his dark skin. His chest rises and falls rapidly, his wide eyes blinking fearfully up at me.

'And you?' I inquire, a smirk pulling the corner of my mouth up. 'What have you got to share with the class?'

'She doesn't tell us anything,' he whimpers. 'She said the less we know, the better.'

'Are you lying to me?' I ask, voice dripping with ice as I glare coolly down at him.

'N-no,' he stammers. 'I would tell you, if I knew anything. P-please, don't kill me. Please, please, please . . .'

Crouching down low, I place a hand on his knee, sighing.

'You disappoint me.'

With that, I slam the heel of my hand into his forehead, feeling his skull crunch beneath my fingers.

22

CORA

The Fighter

THE SHEETS TANGLE AROUND my legs as I toss and turn.

A soft groan leaves me as I flop onto my stomach, burying my face into my pillow. Squeezing my eyes shut, I try to push the memories out of my mind, but they forcefully shove their way in.

The door bangs open and Kian falls through it.

Startling, I leap to my feet. Drenched in blood, he rolls onto his back, propping himself onto his elbows, lips curved in amusement.

'Just had a lovely encounter with a werewolf,' he says, combing his fingers through his blood-soaked hair. Parts of his clothes have been ripped off, and the harsh scars that litter his body are slowly healing. 'Haven't had one get that close to me in a while.'

My initial reaction to seeing him like this is to go to him, and care for him. I mentally slap myself. I hate that I feel some sort of attachment to him. I hate this man with a fiery passion, and yet, a part of me longs for him. A part of me enjoys being in his presence. It's sickening.

Kian winces as he shoves to his feet.

'That's taking a while to heal,' I say quietly, taking a small step in his direction, my fingers spasming at my side, wanting to reach for him.

'Yes,' Kian breathes after a long moment of silence. 'It appears it is.'

'Because their claws are venomous?' I say.

'Yep,' he replies casually, calm as usual. 'Be a dear and fetch me a human.'

When I get to the living room, I cringe. Three humans sit, ramrod straight, staring vacantly ahead. They look like robots. Kian compelled them to sit still and not move until he came for them. They've been like that for hours. It's creepy as hell.

'You,' I say, reaching down and yanking on the arm of a girl who looks much the same age as me. 'Come.'

She stumbles over her feet as I drag her after me. Kian curls an arm around her and yanks her to his chest. He bites harshly into her upper arm and the girl moans, her head lolling to the side as he practically inhales her blood and then tosses her away. My jaw flexes and I look away, forcing myself not to react.

'Fuck,' Kian snarls, spitting some of the blood out. I flinch at the sound of it, wondering why on earth he would do that. He hisses when he touches one of the long jagged lines running down his forearm. 'I need you to get this venom out.' His eyes flick up to mine. 'Do you remember how I told you to do it?'

'Yes.'

As fast as I can, I gather the things I need from the kitchen before I'm back by his side, on my knees. I press the scalpel around the edges of the scar, and a low growl vibrates through his chest as I cut deep, moving the edge of the knife through his skin. Kian jerks for a moment, his hand gripping my arm. His touch sends a ripple through me, but I don't budge; I keep slicing until I cut all the poisoned flesh from his body.

He slumps forward, fatigued, resting his forehead into my upper arm. I swallow, revelling in the closeness, and also disturbed at the thought of that. We went from such an achingly passionate start to our relationship to nothing. The moment he turned me, the distance between us became astronomical. He shut down, becoming cold and cruel. I can tell it's his way of keeping himself guarded and protected from whatever chemistry we have with one another, but the string of rejection after everything absolutely crushed me. He barely touches me, except when we train, and having him this close, breathing in that familiar scent, feeling his skin on mine, is like someone gently rubbing a hand down my back. A comforting notion that makes me crave more.

I refuse to acknowledge how messed up it is that I want this from him. I'm so angry with him, I see red. Then there's this other part of me that is desperate for him.

'You have steady hands,' he murmurs, and my head snaps up at the softness in his voice. It's so uncommon coming from him, that I almost can't believe those words came from his mouth. Did the venom cause him to hallucinate? His forehead is still pressed into me, and I breathe him in, letting myself bask in the closeness while it's being offered, even though I despise myself for it. 'That's a good skill to have.'

I'm unsure what to say. I never know whether he wants me to respond or not. Sometimes he wants a conversation, while other times he scolds me for talking to him. It's hard to tell which personality of his is going to be making an appearance. There are two Kians. The one I first met, who is intense and passionate, who wants to offer me the world. Then there is the other, the cruel, cunning man who seems removed from reality. A man who is hungry for power and control. A man who won't let his guard down, not for anyone, and wants only to use others for some sort of ulterior motive.

After a few moments, it appears his strength is back, and all the damaged skin has healed.

Leaning back, he studies me for a moment, and I reluctantly drag my eyes to meet his. His eyes are a demonic black. Almost like darkness is consuming him from the inside out. His hair is dishevelled, leaving stripes of blood smeared across his skin.

'Let's continue with training,' he says, as if he wasn't poisoned and fatigued mere moments ago. Nodding, I leap to my feet. His gaze trails over me. 'Do you remember what I first said to you, when we started these sessions?'

'Strike hard, in the biggest weak spot I can find. Take advantage of how much they underestimate me.'

Kian's lips twitch. 'What else?'

'Never turn your back on a vampire.'

'Stabbing in the back is a technique I'm rather excellent at,' Kian drawls, lazily taking a step closer to me. 'It is the most common mistake people make in a fight.' His head tilts. 'There's one more thing I told you.'

'Don't underestimate your opponent.'

The jerk of a muscle in his shoulder forces me to leap out of the way. His fist misses hitting my face by less than a second as I expertly dance around him.

'Good,' he grunts, whirling to face me. 'But now you know my tells. You're relying on that.'

I grit my teeth. As soon as I conquer one thing, he piles on another.

He grins, amusement glimmering in his eyes. 'Don't look at me like that. I'm training you to be the best.'

'Why are you training me?' I ask, genuinely curious.

'Because you are my weapon.'

I blink, shocked at his words. 'Your weapon?'

'You are loyal to me, and since I made you, I cannot let you die,' he states, lips curved into a half-sneer, half-crooked grin. 'When we are in a fight, I won't always be able to protect you.

You need to protect yourself. With my training, you will be able to.'

Something compresses inside my chest, and I don't know what it means.

He lurches forward, and instead of running away like I usually do, my leg kicks out, connecting with his knee. His leg collapses underneath him and I straddle his waist, knife heading toward him before his hands knock me off. Rolling on top of me, he pins me down, my own knife pressed to my throat.

'If I was someone else, you would have had me,' he croons, lips inching upward into an impressed smirk.

I breathe a laugh. 'But I didn't get you because you're the best. Right?'

He grins, a leering, cold smile. 'That's right. I am.' He leans down close, his breath fanning my lips. 'I always win.'

And then the knife cuts open my throat.

I wake with a gasp, my hands around my throat as I struggle to blink away the feel of his body on mine, and his voice from my head.

Getting to my feet, I peer out the window, but the street is dark and empty. A sudden movement has me baulking in shock. When I look back, nothing is there.

Shaking myself out of it, I go to the bathroom and wash my face.

Glaring into the mirror, I force myself to push all thoughts and memories of Kian to the back of my mind, as I get ready for the day.

He does not get to control me anymore.

On my walk home from work, I think about those startling black eyes of Kian, like usual. He plagues my mind twenty-four seven.

Unruly, black hair. That jawline. His goddamn smirk.

A stick snapping has me whirling around, narrowing my eyes. I glare at the woods bordering the footpath. For a moment, I almost want to laugh. I'm obsessing over the psychopath who may very well be watching me, who lured me into a life of darkness, and who is a cold-blooded killer, when there are dead bodies turning up every night, and the person responsible very well might be a vampire. I'm not naive enough to rule out a connection to one of us vampires in town.

There's a good chance that Dante is stalking me, like he did to Hunter and Raya, when he was first trying to find Kian. Now he knows of our direct link, it is likely he is after me. At this moment, I curse myself for not informing Kian, but I know that once I confess Dante's motive to him, he will kill Dante, and that's more blood on my hands than I can handle. I'm not safe with Dante lurking around, but I don't want him to die.

'Come out now if you value your life,' I taunt, eyes darting around me, trying to catch a glimpse of movement, a part of me wanting Dante to step out of the shadows and get it over with, as the paranoia of when or if he is even coming after me is draining. If he wants to hurt me, let's get it over and done with.

A black cat leaps out of a tree, landing elegantly on its feet. Two yellow eyes blink back at me, and my fists uncurl from their positions at my side.

'Oh,' I say, remembering the cat from the night Theo and I disposed of the corpse in the woods. It wasn't very long ago, but with my days feeling so crammed, time seems to be flying by. 'It's you. Again.'

The cat stays where it is, watching me.

'What?' I demand, planting my hands on my hips, as if waiting for it to *actually* reply. When it continues to watch me, blinking slowly, I expel a harsh huff of air, and turn my back on it, continuing my walk.

'You've really lost it,' a voice says behind me.

'Ah!' I shriek, spinning around, seeing Theo grinning at me. 'Talking to cats now, are we?'

'Where the fuck did you come from?' I snap, angry at myself for not sensing or hearing his arrival.

Theo smirks, looking rumpled as usual, with patches of dirt clinging to him and what appears to be blood splatters on his shirt. 'I was just out and about.'

'Prowling the woods is creepy,' I point out.

'I'm trying to find the killer,' he explains, flashing his fangs as he runs a hand through his hair. 'Have you noticed there have been no dead bodies the last two nights? They must be scared of me.' He exhales, looking down at his nails. 'Probably because I'm so tough.'

I roll my eyes. 'Get over yourself.'

He grins. 'How was work?'

'Fine,' I say. 'Busy. I thought Dante was stalking me just now. You'd know, since you're . . . friendly.'

'No Dante leering at us through the trees, as far as I'm aware.' Theo rolls his eyes. 'What are you doing now?'

'Sleep,' I reply, rubbing my eyes. Peering over my shoulder, I look back at the edge of the woods, but the cat is no longer there. It's unusual for animals to venture close to us, especially a cat.

'Boring,' Theo pouts. 'Here I thought Hunter was the most boring vampire I'd ever met.'

'Go away,' I mutter, continuing my walk.

'Kidding.' He grins, nudging me as he falls into step. 'Kind of.'

'Have you spoken to him much lately?' I ask.

The night wind washes over me, and I'm almost convinced I can feel its gentle caress on my skin, and the coolness of it.

My mind wanders to Raya. A part of me is jealous that she is living her dream with the love of her life. The rest of me knows I don't deserve a happy ever after in my story. I've sinned too much to deserve such a life.

Alex's face pops into my mind, followed by the faces of the other victims Kian has ordered me to kill. I feel sick to my stomach, but I push the images from my mind, and do what I'm best at: giving into the numbness, and acting like I'm fine. They will resurface later, when I'm all alone, and the darkness is taunting me. I can't run away from it then.

'I FaceTime him every day,' Theo says chirpily.

'You're so extra.'

'He's obsessed with me.' Theo sighs theatrically, shaking his head. 'Honestly, he would be lost over there without me.'

'I'm sure he is.'

'Probably cries himself to sleep every night.'

'Uh-huh,' I reply, noncommittal, tuning him out as my eyes sweep around us, still feeling uneasy at the thought that someone could be watching us right now. My skin feels prickly and a shiver rolls through me. When we get to the end of my driveway, I cast my eyes toward the empty, dark house.

'You sure you don't want to come hang out?' Theo asks.

I shake my head. 'Not tonight. Have fun, though.' I turn to leave, but quickly stop. 'Also, if you could try to locate Dante and make sure he isn't going to attack me out of nowhere, that would be good.'

'Stress less. He is not going to attack you. I'll talk to him.'

'I really don't think you can persuade him to give up the very reason he became a vampire. It's literally his life's purpose.'

'I am *very* persuasive —'

'I don't want you to finish that sentence.'

'Mmkay,' he mumbles in amusement, lightly punching my shoulder, a ghost of a smirk on his lips. 'See you tomorrow.'

'Catch ya,' I toss over my shoulder.

Theo is gone within a millisecond, and I stroll up to my porch. Movement to my left has my fangs exploding from my gums, and I hiss, turning. The black cat peers up at me as it walks across my railing, undeterred from my warning. My fangs snap back, and I blink at it.

'You followed me.'

Sitting, the cat blinks at me.

'Aren't you supposed to hate me? Run away?' I question.

I wait a few seconds before exhaling.

The front door opening next door makes me glance over. Eli walks out onto his porch, pulling his hair back into a low bun. He nods at me. 'Hi there, neighbour.'

My jaw flexes. 'Hello, Eli.'

'Whatcha doing?' he asks.

I gesture to the cat. 'I have a new friend, apparently.'

'Oh,' Eli replies, leaning against the door frame. 'Cool.' There's a beat of silence as I avoid his gaze. 'Haven't seen much of you the past few days.'

'Been busy.'

'Right,' he says.

Since our kiss at the party, I feel awkward, and I'm too scared to make eye contact with him in fear that Kian will turn up and behead him for it.

Kian's possessiveness is *not* hot. Absolutely not. It's vile, and disgusting, and . . . images of him with black eyes, blood dripping from his fangs, invade my mind. Him prowling toward me, like a wolf approaching a rabbit.

'You should probably feed it,' Eli suggests, drawing me from my thoughts, pushing the sleeves of his shirt to his elbows. 'And give it some water.'

'Won't that encourage it to stay?' I ask, frowning.

He shrugs. 'Would that be so bad?'

I consider his words. He has a point. Turning to face the cat, it's still seated where it was, watching the exchange between us.

'I don't have any cat food,' I say.

'I can get some.'

'You'll probably get murdered. I'll be quicker.'

'Hey!' he exclaims. 'You don't think I could take on someone with these?' He flexes, and although his shirt conceals his muscles, the shape is still evident. I can't help but smile. I don't know what to think of Eli, but I like and respect Mya, and Eli is her friend, so I shall extend the notion to him. His gaze often lingers on me a heartbeat too long, and I know Kian would *not* like that.

Leaning forward, I squint. 'Sorry, I can't see anything there.'

He smirks. 'You wish.'

'I'll be right back,' I say.

'Woah,' he says, holding up a hand, looking alarmed. His eyes dart to the dark woods just across the road from our houses. 'At least take my car.'

'No need,' I say over my shoulder.

Once I'm down the street, I take off at a fast pace. I'm there and back within a few seconds. Eli's jaw is almost on the floor when I breeze up to him, depositing the packet of cat food into his hands.

Meeting his eyes, I stand close. 'Forget how fast that was. You are not suspicious of me, or anything that I do.'

Those brutally blue eyes hit mine with full force, and a blank expression falls across his face.

'Okay.' He nods.

I stroll back to my house, the cat still where it was before I left. I pause, glancing back at Eli, who is staring at me, his brows dipped inward. The thudding of his heart is faster than it should be. Is he wearing something that is shielding him from my compulsion?

'Apparently cats can jump more than five times their own height,' Eli says, running a hand through his mop of dark hair.

I raise a brow. 'Thank you for that fun fact.'

'Welcome.'

Was the question an attempt to distract me? He seems relaxed enough. If my compulsion really wasn't working, wouldn't he be running from me?

Deciding to drop it for now, I face the cat, as it silently sits on the railing. My paranoia is really hitting hard tonight.

'Are you hungry?' I ask the cat, unsure why I keep speaking out loud to it, as if it will reply to me. Pushing open my door, I fill an empty container of water and place it on the ground. I hear Eli making his way over from his house to mine. He heaves the bag of food onto the counter. I feel his eyes on me as I take a handful, placing it into another container, putting it beside the water.

'Girl, or boy?' Eli asks.

'It's a girl, I think.'

'What should her name be?'

The cat enters through the front door, her big eyes flitting nervously around the room. She stops, watching us for a moment, before slowly walking toward the two containers. Keeping an eye on us, she leans forward and drinks.

'Midnight,' I say, casting my eye to the clock. 'Because it's midnight, and also she's as dark as the night sky.'

Eli makes a sound of agreement. 'Suits her.'

Leaning back onto his hands, his finger brushes mine, making me jerk my hand away. The sound of his heartbeat slams in my ears. He's nervous?

'Have you eaten?' he asks, voice a little raspy.

'I'm starving,' I murmur, eyes trailing across his neck.

'I'll cook you dinner?' he suggests.

My eyes drop back to the cat who is starting to eat. I feel nothing for Eli. Or anyone, for that matter. Kian consumes me, and I hate it. It's a moment like this that makes me wish I was just a normal girl, able to do normal things. I sealed my fate the moment I met Kian, and let him lead me into the life of darkness I so desperately wanted at the time. I didn't know quite how dark it was going to be, but I followed his lead, nonetheless. I will never be normal again.

'That's nice of you, but I'm fine. I'm just going to go to bed.'

'You sure?' he presses, and I narrow my eyes at the slight pushiness in his tone.

'Positive.'

'Okay,' he relents, pushing off the counter. His hair falls across his eyes and he sweeps it back. 'Night, Cora.'

He crosses the room in a few long strides, and I study him closely.

'It was nice,' I say, forcing my voice to sound a little flirty. He pauses, looking back. 'The other night,' I add. 'What happened, in the bathroom.'

I don't miss the way his foot shifts as he inches toward the door. A lopsided smile crosses his face, making him seem a little goofy. 'Yeah. It was.'

Ice forms in my veins. He flashes me a wink and disappears out the door. I stare at the door, mind racing. I compelled him to forget everything that happened when we were in the bathroom, which means it didn't work.

He knows what I am.

23

KIAN

The Enforcer

MY BACK IS AGAINST the wall. Blending in with the shadow, I keep my eyes glued on the apartment.

I've trusted no one since turning except Cas and Cora, but Sofia is earning a place in my inner circle. She has become a highly valuable person to me. A witch who doesn't want me dead. Possibly the only one to exist.

Sofia has provided location spells on some of the last relations of the coven I'm searching for. Although she can't seem to find the exact witch I need – a witch as powerful as her will not be easy to secure – she has been very helpful with other plans I have needed her for.

Her car cruises down the street and swings into her driveway. The garage door is closing when I move across the road, slinking in through the gap. She shrieks when she turns the light on to find me leaning against one of the storage shelves, smirking at her.

'By the stars!' she exclaims, slapping a hand to her chest. 'Don't you know how to use a damn front door?'

I shrug. 'This seems much more fun.'

Scowling, she grabs her groceries. She inclines her head to the last few bags sitting on her backseat.

'Make yourself useful, then.'

A smile threatens to form. She is one of the only people in the world who could speak to me like this and get away with it. Collecting the groceries, I follow her inside. Incense fills the air, and soft jazz music begins to play from the speakers. Her house is cosy, and littered with so many plants, they take over most of the furniture and living space. She has crammed a lot into a small space, but this must be how she likes it. I can't think of anything worse.

With a flick of her wrist, all the candles in the room spark to life, and I eye one of them for a moment. It's dangerously close to the sleeve of my shirt.

'So,' she says on an exhale, resting her hip on the counter, levelling me with a weary look. Her honey-brown curls are pulled back into a bun on the top of her head. She pulls her glasses off, tossing them onto the kitchen bench. 'What do you want?'

'I need advice.'

She raises a brow, looking at me in amusement. 'Advice?'

'Can you cast a silencing spell, charm, or some shit,' I grumble.

She snorts. 'Sure, let me whip out my wand.'

'I'm serious.'

'Yes, you're always very serious.' She nods, talking to me like I am a grumpy toddler throwing a fit.

She makes a sweeping gesture with her hand, her mouth moving, but no words coming out. A cool wind rushes through the room, blowing out some of the candles she had lit. Pursing her lips, she jolts her fingers, lighting the candles once more. A shiver inches down my spine. Being around witches always leaves me with a vile feeling swirling in my gut.

'I am about to tell you some sensitive information.'

She rolls her eyes. 'And if I betray you, you will kill me, and the people I know and love. Yeah, yeah. What is it?'

I breathe a laugh, leaning forward onto the counter. 'I haven't told you the reason I am hunting this witch.' Sofia's eyes narrow curiously as she nods. 'She came after me. I killed her . . . girl-friend. Lover. Whatever she was.'

'Of course you did.' Sofia's mouth twitches, before blowing out a breath. Every time we have a conversation it seems to age her five years. 'And? What about it?'

'She came after me, naturally. They all do, but she was powerful, and it took me by surprise. It appears she has cursed me.'

Sofia's eyes widen. 'Cursed you?'

'Yeah.' Peeling off my shirt, I stand under the light, and Sofia gasps, her hands flying to her mouth.

She steps closer, eyeing the dark marks on my chest. 'Oh, you're so reckless,' she whispers, shaking her head. 'How have you stayed alive this long?'

I give her a deadpan stare. 'Is that necessary?'

'Why must you always do careless shit?' she mutters angrily, and slaps me on the shoulder.

'Ow,' I say, even though I felt nothing.

'That is a death curse,' she hisses, jabbing a finger at me. 'You've signed your damn death wish.'

'I already guessed that. How do I fix it?'

'You can't.'

I glare at her. 'What do you mean I can't?'

'I mean . . . it's a death curse, Kian. You can't just undo it.'

'What do you mean?' I repeat with a snap, slamming my hands down onto the counter. She gives me a pointed glare as the bench rattles, and I lift my hands, shooting her an apologetic look. I forget how easily I can break things.

'I mean, *she* could fix it. Which is why, I'm guessing, you're hunting her down,' Sofia says, biting her lip. 'But you will probably die before you find her.'

'Thank you for that helpful statement,' I mutter. 'Can't you slow it down, or do something to prevent it from eating away all my power? If word gets out that I'm weak, people will come for me.'

Sofia studies my chest, looking thoughtful. 'This is some dark, *dark* magic, Ki. There isn't much I can do.'

'There has to be something,' I growl. 'Think harder.'

'Don't be an asshole.'

'I came to you for help. So help me.'

'You think I'm not trying to think of something?' Sofia snaps in a huff. 'My God, you're annoying.'

We glower at each other for a long moment before I push off the counter and begin pacing, my mind whirling.

'There is one thing,' she murmurs, and I stop, swivelling my gaze to meet hers. 'You're not going to like it, and I don't think it'll even work for you. Given your charming personality and whatnot.'

I make an annoyed face at her. 'What is it?'

'You said your brother is bonded, right?' she says, stalking across the room, toward the bookshelves lining the wall.

'Yes.'

Running her fingers along the spines, she inspects them, taking a few out and looking at the cover, searching for something.

'I remember reading something about bonded vampires. I did a lot of research on it, actually. Trying to understand it.'

'And?' I press.

'There was something . . . something about blood . . .' she murmurs to herself. She stops, yanking a massive book out, and drops it onto the coffee table. Sinking to the floor, she begins to flick through it. It's not any standard textbook I've ever seen. It's so old, the pages are yellow and stiff. She flicks through them carefully. 'I'm sure there was something about bonded blood magic being able to do amazing things. Miracle things.'

Collapsing onto the lounge, I watch her eyes scan over the pages.

'But given the way you are, I imagine you'll have a hard time finding someone to bond with you.'

'Rude.'

'Just sayin',' she mutters.

My mind is reeling as I mull over her words. I have been researching bonds extensively myself since I heard about Hunter and Raya. Cora's face appears in my mind, and I jerk in surprise at the clarity of it. It's been something I've wondered about for a while now, but I have tried my hardest to refuse it. Of course I want someone loyal to me, but I never signed up for it to be the other way around.

'What?' Sofia asks, eyes lifting as she frowns at me, noticing the reaction.

'If I was bonded to someone, I would know it. Right?' I ask slowly.

She shrugs. 'I'm assuming so. Why?'

'I have turned a few vampires, and there's one I seem to have a very strong connection to. I can sense her emotions, and sometimes, it even feels like I can feel her heartbeat. Which makes no sense since she doesn't even have one.'

Sofia's eyebrows shoot up. 'Is this the vampire you had me make the necklace for?'

I nod.

'Have you always felt this?'

'Yes, but I tried my best to ignore it.'

'I think the curse can affect the bond. You were cursed before you turned her?'

'Yes.'

'Did you blood share with her before you turned her?' she quizzes me, like she is conducting some sort of interview.

I think back to all the times I toyed with Cora, driving her crazy, hoping she would chase me. The memory of us feeding on each other multiple times flickers across my mind, and I hang my head between my hands. Once again, my own pride and strength have overshadowed rational and logical thinking.

'Yes. We did.'

'Hmm . . .' She trails off. 'Interesting. Very interesting.'

'Is it?' I ask dryly.

'I think you *are* bonded to her, and this curse has hindered it. Like, if you weren't cursed, you would be bonded. But you're . . . tainted. So it hasn't fully formed.'

My jaw twitches. 'Is that possible?'

'Mmhmm,' she says, returning to reading. 'Does feeding from others taste terrible?'

'Yes,' I mutter, the truth hitting me like a sledgehammer. I've known for a while now that there is something different with Cora, something I refused to acknowledge. It looks like my denial has come to an end.

'And are you sleeping around?' she asks.

Running my tongue across my lips. I went from living in a sex and blood haze, to nothing. No desire, with anyone. Only her. It's driving me up the wall. *She* drives me up the wall.

'No. Not anymore.'

'Because she's the only one you want, right?' Sofia smirks. 'The only one that can scratch the itch?'

'Do you have to say it like that?' I grimace.

She grins, enjoying my despair far too much. 'You need to feed from her. Even though she's a vampire, her blood is what your body is craving. It should slow down the curse. At least for a while. It'll buy you some time, until you find the witch.'

'Well,' I say, chuckling darkly, furious that she is confirming everything I have already suspected. 'That's just great.'

'Isn't it terrible when there are consequences to your actions?' She smiles sweetly.

'Remind me why I keep you around?' I sneer, revealing my fangs. She ignores them.

'To keep you humble. Someone's gotta do it.'

Exhaling, I stare ahead, processing everything that she has said. I guess in a way, it makes sense. There has to be an explanation for everything that has been happening to me. My life changed when I turned Cora. I was drawn to her like a magnetic force.

'You know . . .' I trail off, frowning. 'Isn't this a little strange?'

'Which part are you referring to?'

'My brother bonding with a girl, and then me bonding with her sister. Technically the other way around, but . . . doesn't that seem odd? Of all the people in the world. Both of us finding sisters and having something happen that is only talked about in history. Something that apparently is so rare that most people never knew it existed in the first place.'

Sofia stares at me. 'It seems like a pretty big coincidence, huh?'

'Can't be. There has to be more to it.'

'I think there is,' Sofia agrees.

Sighing, I rub my eyes. 'I need a drink.'

Standing, Sofia wanders to the fridge, withdrawing two beers. She tosses one toward me, and I sink into the lounge, leaning my head back, fatigue plaguing me.

My life just got a whole lot more complicated.

24

The Prisoner

EACH DAY I'M LOSING a part of myself.

I stare down at my hands. What have I done with these? What did I do for work?

My eyes run over the scars on my skin. How did I get these?

Everything is so cloudy in my head. I need to stop eating the food, but every time I try not to, I find myself halfway through the meal before I realise what is going on. Like I'm under some sort of obedience spell. Or maybe I really am just losing it . . .

Laying back, my eyes trail over the ceiling, tracing the intricate patterns on it. It's an old house that has been renovated, but the renovations were done a while ago, and whoever did it kept true to the old architecture.

Footsteps pass my door and I swivel my head, watching the shadow move across the small gap between the bottom of the door and the floor. The steps pause, and I wonder if they are listening to see if I'm moving around. After a few beats of silence, they move on.

When I try to recall the face of the person, my eyes blur intensely, and a headache pulses behind my eyes.

Sighing, I roll to my side, gazing at the wall.

I wish they had just killed me.

A gasp leaves me as I'm bombarded with the feeling of a crushing weight, loud sounds, and screams. The weight of something on my body. My teeth sinking into my tongue when my head hit something hard. My skin being ripped from something small and vicious, piercing it.

My pulse races as I hold my hands to my chest, trying to breathe, the memory crashing through my mind with vengeance, but everything is just blurry enough that I can't quite make them out.

Vicious fingers bite into my jaw, and words growl into my face.

What words?

Who said these things?

Hot tears spill down my cheeks as I release a sharp cry, the pain from whatever happened feeling so fresh and raw, like it just happened to me, but I know it's the memories trying to break through. If this really did happen, it must have been some time ago.

Screams. So much screaming.

My fingers touch my throat, recalling how hoarse and raw it was at the time.

At the time of what?

Pushing into a seated position, I throw my legs off the side of the mattress, leaning forward and pressing my forehead to my knees, attempting to bring my heart rate back down, as my head is feeling light. Dots dance across my vision and I squeeze my eyes shut, forcing the spins to slow.

What the hell happened to me?

25

CORA

The Fighter

RESTING MY HIP AGAINST the bar, I stare across the room, deep in thought.

'Want me to wait your table?' Mya asks, drawing me from my thoughts.

'Huh?' I ask.

She smiles. 'Don't worry.' She glides toward the table that falls under my section, and I sigh. I can't focus tonight.

'You summoned me?' a voice says.

I glance over to Theo, who is leaning on the counter, flashing his trademark smirk at one of the girls sitting at the closest table to us. She blushes, ducking her chin, and his smirk turns to outright leering as his eyes darken.

'Focus,' I snap at him. 'You're here on a mission.'

'A mission?' he echoes, arching a brow. 'Do tell.'

'I need a party to happen, and I need a certain person to be there.'

'Throwing a party is my speciality, so you've come to the right person.' A wicked gleam lights up his eyes. 'Tonight. The house. I'll make it happen.'

I nod, feeling relieved that it was that simple. 'Great. Thanks.'

'Who needs to be there, and what for?' he asks.

Leaning forward, I glance around. 'I compelled Eli to forget something, and he didn't forget it. I'm hoping I can get him alone and find out what's going on. I don't trust him. He's always making notes and watching me. I have a bad feeling about him and with everything going on, I think it's worth investigating.'

Theo raises his brows. 'I don't need an excuse for a party, but what's the reason for it? Why don't we just ambush him?'

'I don't want him to be suspicious. He might not be working alone.' Lowering my gaze to my feet, I flick my hair out of my face. 'And I'd feel better if you were there.'

'Aw.' Theo grins.

'It will be a good excuse to have you close by if I need you, but far enough away that he might give me some answers if he thinks it's just me and him.'

'Okay. Mission accepted.'

'Thanks. Appreciate it.'

'Girlfriend, you better be prepared to party.'

I scowl. 'Don't call me that. Any updates on Dante?'

Theo shakes his head. 'Nah. You're safe.'

'I don't feel so convinced,' I mutter, eyes darting to look out the dark window. 'Have you seen him?'

'Not since when you did.'

'Great.'

'It's all good,' Theo says dismissively, as usual, unfazed. 'See you at the party.'

He winks, before elegantly standing and strolling toward the table of girls who have been ogling him the entire time he's been here. Exhaling, I switch my brain off and continue my shift. My throat screams at me. As usual, I'm thirsty, and blood bags are seriously not cutting it. I swear they're getting worse and worse. My hands tremble as I swipe my things from my locker, and punch the alarm code in.

The streets are deserted as I walk out. Theo disappeared with two of the girls from the group. I can only imagine what they would be up to. I hope he still has time to pull the party together. I'm sure he will. If there's one thing he does well, it's throw a party. I'm going home to refresh and will meet him at his house.

When I get to my driveway, the hair on my arms sticks up, and I turn, glancing over my shoulder. My eyes sweep the street, searching to see if Theo has randomly followed me home. It's late, and eerily quiet. After another scan, I confirm no one is there.

Stepping inside, I shrug out of my coat, and hang it up. When I turn, I choke on a gasp, as a man stands there, black eyes boring into mine.

'Finally.' He smirks. 'You're here.'

My fangs snap out. I don't recognise this vampire, and by the way he is looking at me, he is no friend of mine.

'Who are you?' I demand. 'Did Dante send you?'

'Who?' he asks as his own fangs flash between two dark lips.

Frowning, I brace myself, ready for an attack. 'Tell me who you are.'

'Your worst nightmare.'

I bark a laugh. 'I was trained by your worst nightmare. I hope you're prepared to fight.'

His tongue drags across his lower lip. 'I was counting on it.'

He is a blur as he moves toward me, and I dart out of his way, sliding across the room on my knees. I'm spinning as he lunges at me, roughly yanking me back at the same time I launch, making our bodies collide in a thundering crack. My hand scrapes against his chest as his hands tighten around my throat. A strangled gargle escapes me. I raise my hands and dig my thumbs into his eyes. He screams into my face as I sink my fingers deep into his eye sockets, curling my fingers and feeling them pop.

An enraged roar tears from him and he flings me across the room. I manage to land on my feet, my back smashing into the wall as I steady myself.

'I'm going to make you scream.' He sneers, moving so fast I can barely form a thought. Blood streaks down his cheeks, and his eyes are bloodshot as they attempt to heal.

Darting out of his way, I almost make it to the door, but his hands wrap around my hair. His fingers clamp onto my shoulder, reefing me backward, and I feel my bones snap upon impact. I grit my teeth as I fall to the floor, him rolling on top of me.

'Now!' he shouts.

The front door is flung open and a human enters. A boy I recognise from one of my classes. My eyes widen as he rushes toward us, a blade in his hand. I bring my knee up, jamming it into the vampire's groin, but he barely flinches, holding me down with a vice-like grip.

Bucking my hips, I manage to dislodge him as the human throws himself toward me. Instead of getting my chest, the blade slams into my thigh, and a sound I don't recognise rips from my lips as I drop to the ground. White-hot agony like I've never felt spears through me, and I howl in pain. I blindly reach for the blade and the burn eats at my flesh, shredding off my skin instantly, to the point where I see my bones. My scream is piercing as it fills the room, panic swelling inside.

The vampire smirks in triumph, lazily getting to his feet, dusting his hands. Turning his back to me dismissively, he faces the human.

'Well done. Chest is preferred, but you did well considering.'

Fuelled on adrenaline alone, I'm at his back before the words finish leaving his mouth. He turns as I plunge my hand straight into his chest and yank his heart out. A sharp gasp leaves him as he stares at me, stunned.

'You don't think I've dealt with pain?' I hiss, breathing ragged. 'I am Kian's progeny, and you know what he always says?' I lean in so close, our noses touch. 'Never turn your back on a vampire.'

He clutches at his chest, clawing at it, trying to get it to heal. I toss his heart onto the floor, and it lands with a *splat*. The vampire collapses, his lifeless eyes staring up at the ceiling.

The human's frightened eyes meet mine, and he trembles so violently, his teeth chatter. Every inch of colour has evaporated from his face as he blinks at me. I open my mouth to demand what he knows, when suddenly his teeth sink into his own tongue and he bites down. His scream is muffled as he jerks and spasms, his tongue falling out of his mouth, hitting the floor. Blood spurts down his face in angry scarlet ribbons.

I stare at him, narrowing my eyes. Kian has used that trick many times, compelling humans to bite off their own tongue so they can't spill secrets. It's clever, and all too familiar. Ice fills my veins. Was this orchestrated by Kian?

Moving forward, I snap his neck, and his body crumples.

Another death at my hands. More blood than I can bear.

My body is shivering from the fierce ache in my side, and I hit my knees as I fall. Clenching my jaw, I push to my feet and stagger toward the door, my fingers curling around the necklace, summoning Kian.

I wish I could fight this on my own. I don't want to need him, but I do. He is an expert at this, and at this moment, I know he can help me. He will come. Something flutters in my chest at the thought of it. I know deep down that when I truly need him, he will be here. I wish that didn't thrill me as much as it does.

I don't know if I black out, or if time is moving differently right now, but it seems like seconds later that the door whirls open, and Kian stands there, black eyes landing on mine. He looks impossibly large, filling every inch of the frame as he looms over me.

Messy dark hair, black eyes, his shirt plastered against his torso deliciously.

'Kian,' I sob, his name falling from my lips as I reach for him.

Collecting me in his arms, he eases me down, inspecting my leg.

'Fuck,' Kian growls, fury swirling in his stormy eyes. 'Who did this to you?'

I nod my head toward the dead vampire and human. His fangs flash as anger pours out of him. I tap my hands against his arm.

'The blade,' I gasp.

Kian lowers his face toward my leg, staring at it with his mask of no expression. 'Poison.' Yanking out a black rubber glove from his pocket, he slips it on. He shifts my head so I'm resting in his lap, and then he pulls it out in one harsh yank. I scream, burying my face into his thigh as the pain coils deep inside me, feeling like it's grating against my bones.

I roll off him, feeling weary and weak, like the poison has drained out all of my strength.

'Get it away from me,' I whisper, putting pressure on my leg, trying to squash the pain radiating from it. My head feels light as I struggle to remain conscious.

Kian calmly stands, throwing the blade onto the kitchen counter. He removes his glove, and as he washes his hands, his eyes are trained on the blade. He's back within a few seconds.

My vision flickers and I'm not sure if I pass out again, but suddenly my head snaps up as the sharp feel of the knife slaps me back to reality, and I clamp my mouth shut to stop the scream. I press my forehead into his chest, breathing hard. He does it fast and expertly, cutting away all the poisoned areas. My skin automatically starts to heal. Glancing down, I see that my hand is almost back to normal as well.

'I need blood,' I whisper. 'There's a blood bag. In my fridge.' I swallow, my eyes drifting closed.

'Drink from me.'

Forcing my eyes open, I gaze up at him, his dark eyes soft and muted. He tenderly touches my face, his thumb caressing my lower lip, and my insides melt at it. Very rarely does Kian allow this between us, but when he does, I crumble at it, as much as I hate myself for it.

'Do it, *mio tesoro*,' Kian murmurs. 'Trust me.'

I'm not sure if I'm understanding this, or if I'm delirious from the poison, but I don't question him.

My fingers curl around his arm, and my fangs sink into his flesh. The deliciously sweet blood explodes in my mouth and I groan in longing and pleasure as it rolls through my system, healing everything that has broken, and filling me with a sense of warmth. This tastes better than human blood, which is impossible.

A part of me that has craved his touch cries in relief. Since he turned me, we have not crossed this line. I was too filled with anger and hate, and he didn't allow me to get too close to him, but all of that doesn't matter right now. I just need him.

Kian releases a breathy exhale and tilts his head back, his dark hair falling out of his eyes, and my God, it is a beautiful sight seeing him like this. His eyes roll as his fingers trail up my arm. He shifts, and I feel the hard length of him press against me. Lust roars through my body at the feel of it, and I moan. Every bit of power that was drained from me returns with a powerful force, swelling inside my limbs.

Flattening him onto his back, I rip open the bottom of his shirt, and drag my tongue across his stomach. I pause, seeing dark marks across his skin, worry gnawing at me.

'Don't worry about it, *mio tesoro*,' he purrs.

As if he has compelled me, all worrying thoughts and concern for him evaporate as I continue kissing across his chest, and down his stomach. He pants, writhing underneath my touch. I was almost dead a few seconds ago, and now, all I can think about is Kian, the warmth of his blood, and the grip of his firm hands on me.

Murderous, lethal hands that are skilled in the art of death, caressing my body with such tender softness, like I'm fragile, and he is doing everything he can to keep me together.

The high of the blood surges through me, and I sink lower. His hips push toward my mouth as he arches his back, his fingers tangling in my hair.

'You want me to?' I whisper, hooking my gaze onto his.

'Fuck yes,' he raspily replies.

Smirking, with a quick flick of my fingers, I unbuckle his pants and drag them halfway down his thighs. Curling my fingers around his length, I wrap my mouth around his tip, dragging my tongue over the head of him. He hisses, his grip on my hair tightening.

My tongue moves up and down the length of him as I push him down my throat. His breath is ragged as he groans, twisting beneath me, his hips jerking as he struggles not to release. I move my head up and down faster, and he can't even get the words out to warn me before he spills onto my tongue. Savouring his taste, I spend a little more time licking up and down, before I move to rest on my elbow.

Leaning forward, his hand curls around my throat as he drags me up his body. His mouth dives toward mine and I groan at the taste of his lips. My head feels light, and I'm dizzy from the blood lust.

Kian throws me onto the ground, peppering my cheeks and jaw with kisses. I twist my head, exposing my neck to him.

'Bite me,' I whisper.

No moment of hesitation. His teeth pierce my skin, and I cry out, my fingers gripping his shoulders, scraping down his sides.

I can feel the slick of blood underneath my fingertips as I claw too hard. I don't know why him taking blood from me is so damn erotic but it's turning me on like crazy. I didn't expect it to feel this damn good.

Releasing my skin, he reels back, breathless. My blood drips from his mouth, and my fangs snap out. He gazes down at me, eyes glittering with darkness. Reaching out, he traces the line of my jaw, before gently running his thumb over my fang. His eyes dart to mine as he presses the pad of his finger against the point. His blood slowly drips into my mouth and I moan loudly.

Moving down my body, he pushes open my thighs. Gripping my underwear, he tears it off me. He leaves hot kisses up the inside of my thigh.

'I need another taste of what's mine,' he drawls, before his tongue drags up my centre. 'It's been too long.'

I whimper, nails dragging against the wooden floor. My legs hook around his shoulders as he continues to devour me. Just as he sucks hard, he slams a finger inside me, and I feel myself tighten around him. My lips part, and I swipe my tongue across my lip, collecting the rest of his blood. The pressure and speed increases. Within a moment, I completely come undone. Shuddering, my head flings back, hitting the floor. Kian drags the back of his hand across his mouth as he collapses beside me.

Pushing onto my elbow, I stare down at his chest, watching the dark lines recede.

'Oh,' Kian says softly, watching it as well. 'She was right.'

'Who?' I ask.

'A witch I know. She said your blood might help me. With the curse.'

Something inside me is swelling with urgency and desperation. A deep sense of longing and lust for the man in front of me. His gaze rakes over my face, and I've never seen utmost adoration like the way he is looking at me right now. I want to save him. Protect him from every bit of darkness that is threatening to steal him from me. In my groggy mind, it doesn't occur to me that *he* is the darkness.

I've seen this kind of look from Hunter, when he was looking at Raya, but now it is being directed at *me*.

My lips part, and our gazes connect.

And then my front door bangs open.

26

KIAN

The Enforcer

THEO GAPES DOWN AT US.

My eyes follow his eyes, and I see that I'm practically naked, Cora's clothes lay in ripped shreds around us, and we are both coated in dark blood. Well. I didn't expect my night to take a turn like this. I was already on my way to Red Thorne when I felt Cora's distress. I got here as fast as I could, and she had managed to take down her attacker. Brutally and efficiently, like I taught her. I've never been more proud.

'Er . . .' Theo begins, scratching his head. 'I think I missed a few chapters. Since when are you two hooking up?'

Cora has transferred what remains of my shirt from my body onto hers. Desire courses through me at seeing her in my clothes. The taste of her on my tongue is enough to make me hungry for more. So sweet, so perfect. More than I could have ever hoped for.

Lazily, I pull my pants up my thighs, and stare down at the blood streaking my chest, hoping it is covering the dark mark enough that Theo can't see it, not that he would have any clue what it is. It does look like a tattoo, so hopefully that's what he assumes, if he does notice it.

Since turning Cora, there have been moments here and there between us, but I was firm about keeping boundaries. I could feel something growing inside me for her, and I tried everything I could to squash it down. Now, it's more rampant than ever, and I know I've seriously fucked up allowing myself to get this close to her. To feel her. To *taste* her again.

It all makes sense now. We're bonded. The connection can't be ignored, even though I have tried my absolute hardest to. It gives me a slight sense of satisfaction knowing that it's practically impossible to dampen my desire for her, so technically, I have not been as weak as I originally thought.

I feel different. Like every nerve in my body is alive and hyper-sensitive. Everything seems sharper, and the smell of the blood taints my nose. I feel fucking incredible. It's at this moment, I realise how awful I *had* been feeling. I feel more like my vampire self than ever. I roll my neck, feeling a smirk inch up the corner of my lips. I feel like I'm strong enough to take on the entire world.

There's something else. I stare down at my hands, rubbing the ends of my fingers together, having the most strange sensation of not feeling real. Waves of *something* pulse through me. As if her blood has twisted with mine. My chest feels light, and I know some of the curse has lifted, or at least, has loosened its grip from around my throat.

When Cora's gaze meets mine, there is a buzz of electricity underneath my skin. An intense feeling washes through me, and I struggle to control the urge to run to her, and hold her. I shake my head, feeling dazed and a little confused at my feelings. Is this an after-effect of her blood? It must be. I'm not soft. About anyone, or anything.

'I was attacked,' Cora explains, folding her arms across her chest in an attempt to conceal her breasts. My eyes trace the delicate curves of her body, and the blood in mine heats up.

'By Kian's dick?' Theo asks.

Blinking out of my thoughts, I snort, unable to help myself. Theo grins in amusement, enjoying my acknowledgement. Cora's jaw flexes, and I can't tell if she is angry at me, herself, or both. She might also be embarrassed Theo found us like this, given it is me she has just been caught with, of all people. I'm the big bad wolf, or so they say. I rather hate that analogy. I'm much more superior than a wolf.

'No, jackass. A fucking rogue vampire with a human companion that was in my class. He was waiting for me when I got home.'

Theo's jaw drops. '*What*?'

She nods. 'The human stabbed me with something that was laced. I couldn't remove it. It literally melted my skin off.'

Theo's jaw is practically on the floor. 'Far out.' His eyes bounce to mine. I say nothing, meeting his gaze, challengingly. I haven't been alone in a room with my turned ones for a while. It feels weird being here with them. 'You pulled it out?'

'Obviously.'

His lower lip twists, resting between his teeth as he stares at me for a beat too long not to be considered awkward. 'Nice.'

Theo has a lot of things he wants to say to me. I can feel it simmering beneath the surface, ready to burst. He wants to be by my side. He wants my attention. He craves it. Tilting my head, I assess him. He is a good fighter. Strong, but he lacks the control I need in someone I can rely on. He isn't like Cora. My darling treasure. Lethal in wit and battle.

'How's life?' I ask him tauntingly. 'Enjoying Red Thorne?'

Theo's hands curl into fists. Forcing him to stay here was mainly to keep an eye on Hunter, and keep tabs on him for me. Now, that purpose has shifted to him watching over Cora. I don't like the idea of her not being with me. I like it even less now that she has been attacked, and I was late getting here, since I was across the fucking country.

His eyes drop to my chest, and I inwardly groan, hoping he can't see the mark.

Cora sighs, closing her eyes for a brief moment, like she is carrying the weight of the world on her shoulders, and I desperately want to go to her. I snarl at my own thoughts. Goddman fucking bond interfering with my life. I already have a mountain of shit I'm dealing with, a bond couldn't have picked a worse time to make an appearance.

'What happened here?' Theo questions, gesturing to the tongue that's lying on the floor beside the human.

'He bit his own tongue off.' Her eyes lift to mine. 'Your speciality.'

I stare at her for several seconds, trying to decipher the onslaught of feelings I sense from her, compared to the guarded expression she's wearing. I can practically hear her train of thought inside my head.

'Why would I organise an attack on you?' I ask, genuinely intrigued by how she is feeling. She is always keeping me on my toes, this one. It's what I like about her.

'Some twisted game of yours?' she suggests, tone bitter.

'I'd send someone a bit more brutal, *mio tesoro*. One vampire and one human? You can fight them off in your sleep.'

She lifts her chin, watching me in suspicion.

'Well,' Theo says awkwardly, eyes darting between us. 'I should go . . . are you all right, Cora?'

'Fine.' She sighs, waving him off. 'Looks like I don't need that party after all.'

'Need me to stay?' he asks.

'No,' I answer for her, not taking my eyes off hers.

'Okay . . .' Theo says, and I can sense the hurt rolling off him. He slips out the door, disappearing into the night.

I walk over to the dead vampire and begin to pat him down.

Digging my fingers in his pocket, I pull out a piece of paper. Glaring down at it, I read the messy scrawl.

I'M NOT THE ONLY ONE WHO KNOWS ABOUT YOUR WEAKNESS, KIAN. YOUR DAYS ARE NUMBERED.

Gritting my teeth, I scrunch the piece of paper up.

'What is it?' she demands.

'Possibly a clue,' I lie, appearing as casual as I can. Lying is second nature to me, but I despise doing it to her. She is too observant and, deep down, I know she would do anything for me, like I would for her. We both hate it as much as we love it. 'I will find out who did this.'

She scoffs, and I turn to face her.

'You think I did this?' I question.

'Yes. I do.'

'I did not orchestrate this attack on you,' I say in a low voice. 'I wouldn't do that.'

'Wouldn't you?' she asks.

'Ensuring your safety has become . . . important . . . to me,' I manage to choke the words out, feeling like I had to pull them out of my mouth. Discussing my feelings doesn't quite come naturally to me, but the bond has other ideas. How fun.

Her eyes flash with surprise, and confusion.

'What's going on with you?' she whispers.

'You know what's going on with me.'

'You're dying.'

Exhaling, I run a hand through my hair.

'The marks on your chest. It's all getting worse. Isn't it?' Her voice is so low, it's barely a whisper.

Slowly, I nod.

She's before me in a blur. I recoil from her soft hands,

stumbling back. She bites her lip, her eyes watering as she takes in the look on my face. Hurt crumples her features before she stonily slides the walls back up.

'Oh,' she says, a bitter laugh escaping her. 'Back to business. Right?'

'I have to go,' I say tersely.

'Don't let the door hit you on the way out.'

Closing my eyes, I exhale a long hard breath. 'I don't like this, *mio tesoro*. I don't deal with emotions well.'

'No shit.'

I give her a wry smile, opening my eyes. 'Stay safe. Don't get into any more trouble.'

'I'll try not to.'

Cora's hair is messy as it frames her face. She offers me a half-smile, and I feel my muscles unwind a little. I have no idea what to think, or how to act around her, after what we just did. After what I let just happen.

'I'll send someone to fix this,' I say, gesturing to the mess.

'It's fine.'

'I will send someone,' I say more forcefully. 'I want you to stay at Theo's tonight. You shouldn't be alone.'

'Why don't you stay?' The words fall from her lips and she looks as shocked as I feel at the sound of them. Her eyes close for a second as if she is berating herself for saying that. I think we are both a little more than surprised to see her softening toward me, after everything that has happened. After what I've done. What I've led her to believe. As much as it hurts me to continue pushing her away, it's what I must do.

I look at her sharply. 'No.'

She presses her lips together. 'Okay.' She feels as confused as I do about everything. 'I don't know why I asked. I don't want you to stay. I hate you.'

'Sure you do.'

'I do.'

'I hate you, too.'

She breathes hard, her gaze narrowed.

Stepping close, I press a soft kiss to her temple, and then I flee into the night.

27

CORA

The Fighter

I THINK THERE IS something really wrong with me.

We blood shared. That is the reason why I suddenly became delusional last night and did those things with Kian and then had the audacity to ask him to *stay*. The rejection stung me more than I care to admit, and I've been repeating every moment of when he entered my house last night in a constant loop inside my brain, growing more anxious and frustrated by the minute.

Theo strolling into the room snaps me out of my thoughts. He peers down at me, rubbing the back of his neck.

'Get any sleep?' he questions.

Shaking my head, I look away. 'No.'

The mattress groans as he sits on the edge of the bed. Leaning forward, the tips of his fingers press together.

'Do you want to talk about it?' he asks quietly, his rare serious side coming out, and instantly I feel a little uneasy. We joke and laugh and avoid our problems together, not face them head on and discuss them.

Covering my face, I melt into the pillows. 'I'm humiliated.'

'Why?' he asks in surprise.

I peer through the cracks of my fingers. 'I did things with him, Theo. He's a monster.'

Theo nods. 'He is, but it's normal to feel things toward him.

He turned us, we have some sort of attachment to him.' He pauses. 'I'm no saint, and you're friends with me.'

'That's different. He has done unspeakable things, and I do not forgive him for any of it. He has some sort of . . . spell on me, or something. I don't know what even happened or how the hell we ended up like that.'

'With all the time you spent together, maybe you developed true feelings for him.'

I side-eye him. 'He is evil, Theo.'

'Doesn't change what I just said. He can be who he is, and you can still have feelings.'

Groaning, I bury my face. 'I can't have feelings for him. I *can't*.'

'Maybe you can convince yourself of that, but I don't believe it.'

Snapping my eyes open, I glare at him. 'You're not being very helpful.'

'No, you just want me to lie to you to make you feel better, which I'm not going to do.'

'I hate you.'

'I know. It turns me on.'

Ignoring him, I rub slow circles into my temple, sitting back, my mind mulling over last night's events. Being back around Kian has rattled me. He affects me like no one else ever has, and it really scares me how much I am drawn to him.

I can't accept my feelings for him.

He is a monster. More morally grey than not.

It really sucks that he is sexy as hell. I'm sure it would be easier to ignore these growing feelings if he wasn't. Getting to my feet, I head to the bathroom to freshen up before detouring to the lounge and collapsing onto it.

I hear the patter of paws cantering across the ground before Midnight neatly leaps onto the lounge, crawling across my lap.

When I packed my bag and left to come to Theo's last night, she was following me, and since she let me pick her up, I brought her along. She slept on the end of my bed the entire night, and it was quite comforting having her there. It made me feel less alone.

Rubbing her head against my hand, I scratch behind her ears, smiling down at her. Since I turned, animals have steered clear of me, so a cat showing me affection makes me tear up. It makes me feel a little more human, and after everything I've been through, it's nice to feel something other than this numb state of acceptance I've become accustomed to.

The sound of a FaceTime call reluctantly pulls my attention from the cat. Theo is holding out his phone, the camera facing him as he walks toward me, plopping down beside us. A moment later, Hunter's face appears on the screen. It's nice to see his warm, genuine smile. It throws me just how much he looks like Kian. There are definite differences between the two, but many features are the same, as well.

'Greetings.' Hunter nods, and his brows rise when his gaze lands on me, and the cat. 'Er – is that a cat?'

'Yah,' Theo replies, not providing any further explanation.

'She tolerates me for some reason.' I shrug, seeing his expression growing more confused by the second. 'Don't ask me why.'

'Okay then.' He shrugs back, looking at us both weirdly.

The phone fumbles and then Raya appears. My heart squeezes at the sight of her and tears spring to my eyes. Damn, I'm feeling emotional today.

'Hey!' She beams, and the shine in her eyes makes a little of the pressure on my chest lift. 'What the . . . is that a cat?'

'Yes.' I laugh, realising now I haven't filled her in with half of what's been going on around here. Although we don't FaceTime nearly as much as Hunter and Theo, we usually aim to speak at least once a week. 'Long story. How are you?'

'I'm really great!' She smiles, and Hunter stands beside her.

Raya rests her head on his shoulder. They're so sickly sweet, it makes me feel like I need to go brush my teeth. 'School is fantastic. We spend the weekends exploring different countries. It's honestly incredible, Cor. I wish you were here with me.'

Rolling my lips into my mouth, I smile sadly. 'I'll join you, one day.'

'I hope so. You deserve to be experiencing this.'

'Well, some of us can't *leave*,' Theo mutters sourly, pouting.

'How are things?' Raya asks, both of us ignoring Theo. 'Any word from *him*?'

Theo pins me with a bitchy look, which I don't acknowledge. I force my familiar fake smile onto my face.

'Nope! All quiet over here.'

Raya frowns. 'Really? Kian hasn't reached out *at all*?'

'No.' I smile. 'Thankfully.' Tucking a piece of hair behind my ear, my gaze drifts to the cat, who is blinking up at me, as if she is also judging me for lying. I stare back at her for a moment before returning to the screen. 'Tell me more about your school.'

The next half-hour is spent with Raya filling us both in on everything they've been up to, and it's a welcome distraction. Hearing her voice is soothing, grounding me in a way that is desperately needed. It's nice seeing her so happy and healthy. It's all I've ever wanted for her.

'You sure you're okay, Cor?' Raya asks in concern, and I don't like how her eyes keep darting to Theo, as if she can read the truth in his expression. To be fair, he isn't exactly being subtle with the way he is side-eyeing me.

'Fine,' I say automatically.

A frown tugs at her lips, and I brighten my smile impossibly more, to the point where it feels completely unnatural.

'Don't worry about me, little sis. All good here. I'll talk to you later.'

When the call is finished, a deafening silence echoes around the room as I avoid Theo's eyes.

'Well,' Theo says. 'I feel like an asshole for lying to my best friend. What about you?'

'I don't want them to worry,' I say, not wanting to feel even more guilty than I already do with all the secrets I seem to be piling up.

He pins with me an intense stare that makes me feel uncomfortable. 'Right. Because I'm sure that will be great for you when something happens and they have no clue about anything.'

'Always the optimist.'

'You don't keep me around to sugar-coat things.'

'I don't keep you around, period. You just keep showing up,' I mutter.

He scoffs, his hand going to his heart. '*You* turned up on *my* doorstep last night.'

'Because Kian told me to.'

He quirks a brow. 'He did?'

'Yeah. He didn't want me alone.'

'And yet, didn't take you,' he murmurs, running his thumb and forefinger down his chin thoughtfully. 'Weird. Very weird.'

'He's distracted. It's probably easier having me here, where he knows the town like the back of his hand.'

'Do you think something seems . . . off . . . with him?' Theo asks, brow furrowed. 'He seems like he isn't as unhinged as he has been in the past.'

Swallowing, I shrug, looking away. 'Still seems crazy to me.'

'Uh-huh,' Theo mutters, disbelievingly, and I don't like the way he is staring at me. It reminds me of the way Kian watches me, as if they can see everything I'm hiding, even though I'm trying desperately not to show anything.

'I have to go,' I say, pushing to my feet.

I dress quickly and gather my things. Theo's eyes are on my back as I head toward the door. I wave over my shoulder and slip out, rushing down the steps. I need time alone to process everything that has happened in the last twenty-four hours. I can't think about Kian dying, it makes me panic, and not be able to breathe – even though I don't really breathe like normal – and my heart is erratic, but it no longer beats . . . he makes it feels like it does, and . . . and . . . I fall to my knees, my chest constricting.

I don't even know what part of town I've ended up in. The sun shines bright down onto me, and my skin burns. It's an unusually sunny day, considering Red Thorne is known for its cloudy skies and cool temperatures.

Without thinking it through, I curl my fingers around my necklace and squeeze. It's barely a minute before he's in front of me. He bends to his knee, those dark eyes settling onto mine.

'Breathe, Cora.' Hearing his voice relaxes my muscles and he pulls me to my feet. 'Look at me.' My eyes move to his, and his eyes soften when they meet mine. 'I'm here. I'm okay. I need you to breathe.' The tightness in my chest loosens, and suddenly, there's air, and sunshine, and I feel okay. Moments ago, the world was crumbling, and I couldn't keep up with trying to pick up the pieces. Slowly, I sink to the ground, and burst into tears.

Dropping beside me, he pulls me toward him, crushing me to his chest, and I bury my face into him, gripping his shirt like it's a lifeline.

'You're dying,' I whisper.

He runs a hand down my back, and it makes me cry harder. He hasn't held me like this since we first met, and my heart feels like it's tearing open and flooding through my body in a painful river of emotions I've tried to desperately keep on lockdown.

'Don't worry about me, *mio tesoro*. I'll figure it out,' he murmurs, his voice feeling like silk caressing my skin.

I pull back, staring up at him. 'What if you don't?'

'And here I thought you hated me,' he whispers, his expression unreadable, but his eyes are soft, offering the tiniest bit of vulnerability.

'I do.'

He smiles, his crooked smirk that I love so much. 'Yeah. It seems like it.'

'You came,' I say, sniffling.

'You summoned me.'

'You got here so quick.'

'Yes.' He nods. 'I was only a town over. I felt your panic.'

'You left.' I swallow. 'I asked you to stay, and you left. You push and push and push me away, lashing out at me, hurting me all the time, trying to keep me at a distance.' Another traitorous tear rolls down my cheek. 'But I call, and you come. Every time.'

There's a significant pause as he exhales, sitting back. He tilts his head, looking up at the sky. I didn't even realise he had moved us into the shade.

'I don't let anyone in, Cora.'

'And yet, here you are.'

'Here I am,' he says.

'I can't tell if you care, or simply feel obliged.'

'I don't feel obliged to anyone. You know that.'

My heart sinks, causing physical pain to radiate through my body. He winces, as if feeling it, and sighs once more, heavier than before. Drawing his knees up, he rests his elbows onto them, bracing his head in his hands. He rakes his fingers through his unruly hair, and my own fingers twitch in desperation to do the same.

'I care,' he mutters in his low, deep voice, and when his eyes move to mine, it's just as it felt when we first met. Magnetic, like we are drawn to each other and it is completely out of our control. 'I care a lot, and it fucking scares me.'

'Because you don't want to care.'

'Precisely.'

'I don't want to care, either,' I say.

'I know.' He swallows, jaw ticking. 'I've made you forget.'

'What?' I ask, blinking away the blurriness in my vision.

'I care for you so much it hurts.' Curling his hand around mine, he pulls it to his chest. 'I will figure this out because the thought of my death hurting you is enough to make me fight with everything in my power to survive this and be by your side. I will find a way to live for you.'

'Live for me?' I question, pressing my lips together.

'By your side. Forever. I've had to make you forget things about me – about us – but when the time is right, it will all come back to you, and it will all make sense. The things I did, why I did them, and how important you are to me.' He presses his lips to my hands. 'But I can't show you. Not yet.'

'Why?' I shake my head, tears continuing to fall. 'I don't want to forget anything.'

'I know. But you have to. For now.'

'No,' I plead, my fingers latching around his, and he slowly pulls them apart, my heart squeezing as he does. 'Don't do this.'

With two fingers, he brings them to his mouth, pressing them softly against his lips and then tips them toward me.

'Forget everything we just discussed. You're still angry with me for last night. You're still confused about how you feel.'

Blinking, I look around, momentarily lost. My eyes snap back to Kian, who is watching me silently, a hard look in his eyes. He steels himself as I narrow my eyes, anger forming a hard knot in my stomach.

'You've done unspeakable and unforgivable things. I can't ever forgive you for what you've done,' I say haughtily.

'Then don't,' Kian says, pushing to his feet, his gaze dropping from mine. 'It'll make it easier on both of us if you don't.' Looking down the path, his jaw is tense. 'Don't get hurt. Don't make me come back for you.'

I scoff, glaring up at him. 'Trust me, I won't.'

Rolling his tongue on the inside of his cheek, he finally looks down at me. 'Stay safe. I mean it.'

'Yes, sir.'

The corner of his lips twitch, and then he is gone.

I hate myself even more for everything I just did.

Work sucks.

Why did I sign myself up to this, again?

I'm on my last hour of my shift, and I feel like I'm well and truly back to reality. Dealing with grumpy assholes all day makes me feel like I've gone back in time to my life before Kian, and as crappy a day as I've had, I've enjoyed the humanness of it. Long days, cranky customers, annoying co-workers. It's nice to feel normal again.

It also helps that Mya spends some nights with me. We often drink too much wine, watch comedies, and complain about our life choices. Having a friend like her really makes me feel like a normal person again, and I am extremely grateful for that. As incredible as being a vampire can be at times, I truly miss just living a normal life, although I wish the normal life I'd had before was different. I used to think I'd do anything to go back to it, but now I'm not too sure. I was so unhappy, and not myself.

The last two days have really shaken me. Having Kian appear back here has brought up all the feelings I've desperately tried to suppress, and my mind is in shambles. When we first met, it was a fiery passion-filled whirlwind, and then it went from one extreme to the other. Once I was turned, he killed my mother, hurt my sister, and completely changed. Despite a few moments here and there, he has kept me completely at arm's length, so to see this soft side reemerging, I feel like I've been hit with whiplash. It's as if there are gaps in my mind, and I can't work out how that happened, or if it's even possible.

My heart, and my brain, are very traumatised and confused.

'What are you thinking about?' Theo asks, throwing the end of a rolled-up straw at me. It connects with my forehead and flops onto the counter. My eyes follow it, and I release a heavy exhale.

Theo is here so much, he's practically an employee. I originally thought he was just bored, but I've now put two and two together. Kian has asked him to stick by me, just like he had Theo watching over Hunter when he was here.

'Reminding myself that Kian tortures people, and killed my mother.'

'Your ex-boyfriend killed your mum?' Mya exclaims, whirling around with wide eyes.

Whoops. I forgot people can hear me when I speak.

Since Theo and I often forget the people around us actually pay attention to the things we do and say, Mya has learnt a few things. I haven't bothered compelling her to forget because I really like her, and consider her a friend. Well, if I was to have any friends, I'd pick her, is basically what I mean. Therefore, she knows I have an 'ex-boyfriend', and that he is 'definitely no good', and I'm 'kind of scared of him even though I still think he's hot' – thank you, Theo.

'Not literally.' I wave her off dismissively. 'Figure of speech.'

She gives me a weird look, understandably flabbergasted at what I just said.

'Okay then . . .' She shakes her head, moving around the counter to serve the group that just sat down at one of the tables down the back, casting a frown over her shoulder at me.

Theo watches Mya. Her long strawberry blonde hair falls down her back in loose curls, and her hips sway as she walks. She is gorgeous in an effortless way.

'Eyes off,' I snap.

'I can look and not touch,' Theo purrs, leaning forward, interlocking his fingers.

'I don't trust you.'

He smirks. 'Turns out, I don't trust you either.'

Rolling my eyes, I push away from the counter and move out the back to restock the fridge. When I step inside the cool room, I press my forehead against the chilled wall, letting my eyes drift closed.

'We're going out.'

Rolling my head to the side, I peer up at Kian, who strolls toward me. He pushes the sleeves of his black shirt up to his elbows. My heart splinters every time I look at him. My feelings for him developed so strongly, and so rapidly, only for him to not be at all the man I thought he was.

'I'm not going anywhere with you,' I whisper, my voice broken and completely devoid of emotion. It's been days since I turned, and I've been a mess for the entirety of it. With my heightened emotions, I've been screaming, crying, throwing up, back to screaming again. Now, there is nothing left, and I feel numb. A part of me doesn't believe any of this has really happened. Surely it's some horrific nightmare that I'm due to wake up from any minute now.

'Haven't you pouted long enough?' he drawls in that cold way of his that makes my insides shrivel. Those black eyes are haunting and endless. What I once thought were mesmerising and pretty, now I think are terrifyingly empty.

'You killed them,' I choke out, my eyes burning. 'You killed my mother. You killed everybody in that other car. You would have killed Raya if given the chance.'

His shoulders are stiff as he eyes me. 'You will lose a lot of people now that you are a vampire. You get used to it.'

'I hate you.'

'Okay.' He shrugs, looming over me. 'How long until you're ready? I'm thirsty.'

'Didn't you hear me?' I snarl, my fangs snapping out. His eyes drop to them, and that infuriating smirk of his twists onto his lips.

'Oh yes, I heard you,' he replies in a flat tone. 'I think the entire fucking town has heard you moping around. Snap out of it, and move on.'

'How can you live with yourself?' I say, shaking my head in true disbelief that I'm really here right now, in front of this soulless man. A vampire who tenderly touched me, whispered promises into my ears, held me close to him. Tricked me into becoming his slave for ten fucking years.

The man I fell for is nowhere to be seen. Maybe he never truly existed.

When the hell did it all go wrong?

Kian is quiet for a long moment. His eyes swirl, and I study them closely, trying to decipher what he is thinking. I can't tell if this cool exterior is an act, or if he truly is completely devoid of emotion.

'Feelings. Emotions. They don't exist to me. I care about living, surviving, and feeding. That's what you should care about, too.'

'Why did you do this to me? To them? What did I do to deserve any of it?' I ask. I wish I could talk in that cold, harsh voice like he does, but instead I sound broken and vulnerable. Like every inch of pain is painted across my face.

Kian's head tilts, as if he is considering my words. He leans forward, hands coming down either side of the lounge. He is so close, the tips of our noses almost graze.

'I let you get too close,' he murmurs, and I feel the weight of his words like a stone in my gut.

With that, he pushes away from me, striding toward the door that leads to the basement.

'We're leaving in five minutes. Be ready.'

'You making out with the wall or . . . ?' a voice asks.

Jolting, I turn around. Theo grins at me, looking far too pleased with himself at that silly comment. I glower at him. Once again, he has snuck up on me. Either he is way more stealthy than I've given him credit for, or I'm losing my edge. Perhaps both.

'Stop following me.'

'Why would I do that? It's fun catching you doing all kinds of weird things.' He grins, leaning on the door frame. 'Daydreaming about a certain someone?'

'Yes,' I admit. 'But not in the way you're thinking.'

'Oh?' he hums, looking curious.

'My mind still can't wrap around the person I met becoming the person he was after I turned. Like two polar opposites. But then . . .' I pause, running my tongue across my teeth as I try to formulate my thoughts into words. 'Sometimes, the other him slips through, and it makes me wonder whether the cold persona is an act. I thought the charismatic man I first met was the act, but sometimes I wonder if it's the other way around. He says and does things that make me think he is purposely pushing me away. He doesn't want to like me. He doesn't want to depend on me. So he pushes me away, and hurts me, so that I hate him and it makes it easier to keep his distance.'

When I turn to face Theo, he is staring at me, and I realise how much I just poured out. Shit. I wasn't supposed to say *any* of that.

'Or he is just a fucking sociopath who enjoys using others as pawns in his own game,' I say, shrugging, attempting to appear nonchalant. 'Who knows.'

Exiting the room – ignoring the fact I didn't even do the job I came in here to do – I walk back out to see the diner has filled up considerably. I rush to help Mya keep up with the wave of orders coming through, not allowing Theo to catch up to me, and respond to my outburst.

'I'm heading out,' Theo tells me. 'Let me know if you wanna hang.'

'Uh-huh. Bye.'

I move around the tables, picking plates up a little too quickly and completely startling a young couple. Mentally shaking myself, I take a moment to focus, and slow down.

'Hey there,' Eli says as I walk by his table.

He is sitting at a booth, his laptop perched in front of him, and a notebook on the side. Lost in the whirlwind that is Kian, I completely forgot that Eli knows who I am, and my previous compulsion hasn't worked on him. I need to figure out what his deal is.

'Hey.'

'How are you?' he asks, leaning back onto his elbow, his eyes roaming up and down my body. This overly confident act is giving me the serious ick.

'Fine.'

'Oh my God . . .' I hear a voice trail off. 'Cora?'

Turning, I face a girl whose face I immediately recognise. She's gotten older, her hair is lighter, and she is staring at me like she has just seen a ghost. I swallow nervously.

Because she is seeing a ghost.

'Sorry?' I say, feigning ignorance.

'What the hell?' she whispers, looking like she is ready to bolt out of here, but is too curious not to stay and ask questions. Her eyes search mine, and she shakes her head in bewilderment. 'You were missing . . . you . . . you died . . .' She blinks rapidly, forehead crumpling. 'I went to your funeral.'

I freeze, unsure what to do. I feel the eyes of Eli burning holes into the side of my head, his gaze ping-ponging between me and the girl I went to school with. What the hell is she doing in a town like this? How is she here?

'I'm sorry, I think you've got the wrong person.' My voice sounds distant, and the roar of the conversations, heartbeats, utensils scraping around me feels impossibly loud, making it hard for me to focus.

'It can't be . . .' She trails off, her face draining of colour. The hand clutching her phone trembles, and the sound of her heart-beat is like a sledgehammer inside my skull. Her sweat coats the air, even though it is cold in here. She is absolutely terrified right now, and it's as obvious as a neon sign flashing above her head.

Eyes latching onto hers, I let my compulsion unleash.

'You're mistaken.' My voice is strong and firm, and I see the moment it basically slaps her in the face. She blinks.

'Sorry. I'm mistaken.' Turning her back to me, she walks over to an empty table, dropping into the seat.

I watch her for a moment. Eli clears his throat. Slowly, I pivot, clenching my jaw as I stare down at him.

'I think we need to talk.' Eli smiles sweetly, leaning forward. 'You should sit down.'

Shakily, I sit.

'Let's not pretend that I don't know what's going on,' he says.

'How long have you known?' I ask, tone even as I try to read his expression.

'Once I moved in. I recognised you and did some research.'

My stomach churns. When Kian orchestrated the accident, I don't think he predicted that my face would be shown on all the local news stations. Or perhaps, more than the local channels, since out-of-staters appear to be recognising me.

'Okay, and what did your research say?'

'You died, which your little friend just confirmed.'

'Then you know what I am, and that I can kill you. Very easily.' I link my fingers together, sitting back, my composed poker face neatly sliding into place.

'Right,' Eli says, not seeming concerned about this. 'I've heard you and Theo talking. You're trying to be a better person and all that, so I think I'm pretty safe.'

'Right.' I produce my very-obviously-fake smile, agreeing. 'So then you'd also know I have a really unhinged maker that makes anything I do his business.' My smile widens when I see him pause. Lowering my voice, I lean forward. 'I'll let you in on a little secret. He has no remorse, and no conscience. If he wants you dead, you're dead. You're already on his radar, so I would be very careful with what you say to me next.'

The confidence dries up. Eli slowly nods. 'I see. Can I ask how I'm on his radar?'

'You touched what's his.' The words fall from my lips, and I don't know why I said that. I also don't know why I feel satisfied about it. I'm truly fucked up.

'So?' I ask, leaning back once more. 'You were saying?'

'I co-run a website,' he replies. 'I just wanted some info from you to put on it.' He gestures to his notepad, and the laptop. 'I research vampires, and post about them online. On forums and whatnot. That's all.'

My eyes move to the bracelet he is wearing. As quick as a whip, I snap the thread and toss it to the side, ignoring the way the magic it possesses burns my skin. He flinches, eyes darting around to see if anyone noticed, but every person around us is consumed in conversation, or too busy eating.

'Was that the only anti-compulsion charm you have on?' I ask.

I should be thankful Kian trained me so well. He forced me to consume blood, even though my body rejects it. He forced me to build a tolerance up to silver. He forced me to endure the pain of an anti-compulsion charm. At the time, it was exhausting, and sometimes excruciating, but now, I am powerful, and I can protect myself.

'Yes,' he replies.

'Stab yourself in the leg with your fork,' I say. 'Do it quickly, and do not make a sound. Ignore the pain.'

In one fluid movement, he picks up the fork, and rams it into his leg. He chomps down onto his lip but makes no sound. His face darkens to a beetroot colour and sweat immediately dots across his forehead as he struggles to comply with my rules. I smile. I can compel him now.

'Tell me the truth, Eli,' I say. 'What do you want from me?'

'I do run an online forum,' he explains, and shoves the laptop toward me, doing well to speak clearly, given the circumstances.

I click on the web browser, and see an online forum filling the screen.

'They walk among us?' I read, staring up at him. I snort. 'Your username is "SoulEater888"?'

'Yes. I record things, and make notes of my findings.'

'And what else?' I demand.

'I work for someone. I don't know anything about them, but they want me to report on any vampires I know about in town. They're looking for someone.'

'Who?' I ask, my interest piquing.

'A really ruthless vampire, they say. Apparently they have been trying to track him down for a while.'

My stomach clenches. 'Did you find him?'

'No.' He shakes his head. 'But I was told to move next door to you, to watch you, and find out more.'

'Me?' I ask.

'Apparently you're his weakness.'

The blood in my veins freezes. Swallowing down the bile threatening to climb up my throat, I fix him with a narrowed stare, ignoring how my fragile heart trips at his words.

You're his weakness.

'You're after Kian.' I let out a humourless laugh. 'You're wrong. He has no weakness.'

He gives me a pointed look, like I'm naive, or delusional. 'He does now. The people I work for want him dead.' Reaching for the laptop, he drags it back across the table, flipping it shut. 'And they want to use you to do it.'

28

KIAN

The Enforcer

MY BLOOD POOLS ON the dirty cement floor. My arms are extended above my head, as I hang from a rope attached to the ceiling. My left shoulder is dislocated, and the white-hot agony that is flowing through my body keeps making me lose consciousness.

'Kian,' a voice whispers. 'Hang in there.'

Cas. The one who convinced me to go out the other night. We partied hard, which isn't unusual for us. We were plastered when the man stood in front of us, and practically yanked us off the street. We made it all too easy for him.

Now we have been here for what must be at least two days. Tortured, beaten, fed on. Cas's legs are broken, and he lies on the floor, propped up on his elbows. His skin has taken on a greyish colour, and his white-blond hair makes him look even more off-colour than usual.

'I am hanging,' I grunt.

'Ah, there you are,' Cas says, and somehow has enough energy to smile. I can't do that. My lips are split open and I can barely move my face. 'Thought you might have died on me.'

'I wish,' I mutter.

I don't know if I've reached a point of delusion, but the man who kidnapped us is not human. He has fangs, incredible strength, and inexplicable capabilities that makes me feel like I've been transported into some reality show and someone is going to jump out from behind one of the random bits of broken furniture and tell me I've been punk'd.

'This really sucks.' Cas sighs, rubbing a hand down his face.

'That's the understatement of the century,' I reply dryly.

'I had jury duty today, if today is Wednesday, which I suspect it is.' He exhales noisily. 'I'm going to be in so much trouble.'

I can't help but laugh. It's a bitter chuckle that falls from my lips, and my entire body is in agony as it sways.

'Think that's the least of your troubles, Cas.'

Suddenly, the door swings open, and my heart plummets into my stomach. The man strides in, and my eyes widen as he approaches me. With movement so quick I barely catch it, he snaps the rope, and I drop to the ground in a painful sprawl. He stares down at me, upper lip curling. I lift my chin, meeting his gaze, almost egging him on.

'Do it.' I sneer. 'Fucking kill me.'

The man smiles, and it possesses about as much warmth as melting snow.

'Not yet.' Keeping my eyes open just to look up at him requires so much strength, I almost give in to the darkness begging to consume me. Flipping me onto my stomach, he lifts my shirt and I grimace. 'Beautiful,' he marvels, and I fist my hands as he admires his handiwork. I've learnt he is particularly fond of whips. 'They're getting infected. I love the smell of it.' He kicks my side – several of my ribs are already broken – and I grunt as I flop backward, unable to stop my chin hitting the ground, my body too weak to move.

Turning, he walks over to Cas, whose eyes drift shut. Dropping to his knee, he yanks Cas toward him and plunges his fangs savagely into his shoulder. Cas's screams fills the air as the man takes and takes from him. Cas's head lolls to the side, and when the man shoves him, a bone protrudes from his leg.

The moment the man exits the room, I'm heaving. There is nothing left in my stomach to come up, and every muscle in my body screams as my body jerks and convulses.

'Cas,' I grind out, forcing my eyes to remain open. 'Wake up.'

He is unnaturally still, and his head is turned away from me, not allowing me to see whether his eyes are open or shut. Narrowing my eyes, I focus, and notice the very gradual rise and fall of his chest.

The door opens again. Turning my head, a man I don't recognise stands there.

'Well,' he says, looking around at the sight before him. I can't imagine what it must look like to him. A horrific crime scene, and the smell of death coating the air. 'You both look terrible.'

'Who are you?' My voice is barely a whisper at this point.

'Just a guy who happens to be at the right place at the right time,' he says, eyes focusing on me for a heartbeat longer than is considered normal. He strolls toward me, crouching down. I flinch when I see the blood on his hands. 'May I?' He holds out his hand. Grunting, I twist, and he lifts my shirt. He lets out a low whistle. 'That is a nasty lot of cuts you've got there. I'm afraid they won't heal.'

'I doubt I'll live for them to heal.'

He tsks. 'You shall live. I will make that happen.'

'Who are you?' I ask, head foggy with pain.

'My name is Aithan.' He pulls me over, so that I'm sitting up. He smiles. 'I think I quite like you. I'm going to save you, if you want it.'

'Save me?' I expel a breath.

'I admire strength,' he says. He is a tall, broad-shouldered man with long, unruly hair that is tied back from his face. He has

*an old-fashion style about him, like he doesn't quite belong to this
era of time. 'You should probably be dead by now. He's had you
here for days.'*

'You've known about us for days?'

*'I wanted to see if you'd last. I only create vampires if I think
they are of use to me.' He tilts his head. 'Are you going to be useful
to me . . .' Opening my wallet which was discarded to the side on
the first night the creature brought us here, he pulls out my licence.
'Kian?'*

Spitting out blood, I laugh. 'I'll be whatever you want me to be.'

*'Good,' he says. 'Then it's settled.' Pushing to his feet, he looks
over to Cas. 'This one has a different kind of strength to you, but
is strong nonetheless. It's your choice whether I turn him as well.'
He faces me once more, placing his hands behind his back. 'What
will it be?'*

'Yes,' I whisper. 'He's with me.'

*'All right then.' Dropping into a squat, he rolls his neck,
and his fangs snap out. I don't recoil like I have when the other
vampire did it. As absurd as everything has been these last few
days, I'm not shocked by them anymore. 'This is going to hurt, but
it probably won't hurt as much as what you've suffered through
already.' His fingers curl around my arm and when he pulls it,
I grit my teeth, pushing through the pain as it threatens to knock
me out again. 'Kian, you will be loyal to me, and you will be a part
of my army. You understand?'*

'I understand.'

*'Good.' He smiles, and it's a smile that makes a shiver roll
through me. 'It's a deal, then.'*

I wake with a gasp, and run my hands over my body. The pain
that felt so real is gone. Exhaling, I slump back against the bed.
I look over to the vacant side of the mattress, running a hand
through my hair.

Peeling myself off, I head into the bathroom. My eyes shift to the dark lines on my chest. Having Cora's blood certainly slowed the rate at which they were growing, but they're still there, as prominent as ever.

Twisting, my eyes roam over the raised scars on my back. When Aithan turned me, it corrected my broken bones, and recharged my strength, but the deep wounds on my back had scarred to a point that even turning me into a vampire was not enough to rid them.

It is a reminder of where I was, and where I am now.

I will never be vulnerable like that again.

Despite my thoughts, my body feels weary, and instead of going about my day like I should, I drop back into bed. I'll have to go back to Cora, and get my next fill of her blood. With the rate I've been consuming it, all the reserves I had are gone now.

She is the only thing that is able to help me right now, since locating this witch is proving to be far more difficult than I predicted.

Exhaustion rolls through me, and my eyes flutter closed once more.

'Take a walk with me.'

I eye the street. I couldn't forget this place if I tried. Only a week ago was I stumbling down this road, Cas by my side. Drunk, laughing, not a care in the world. Then, I was dragged into a basement. Tortured, fed on, and placed on the brink of death.

'Come on.' Aithan smirks, nudging me. 'I have a surprise for you, since you have exceeded my expectations so much already.'

Aithan has been studying us. I can tell he is looking for someone exceptional. He has an army of loyal vampires that work underneath him, but he is searching for someone to be by his side. I can be that someone, and he knows it, too.

Cas is taking a little longer to adjust to the vampire way of life, but he is doing well, considering. My need to survive and adapt is a little more developed than others, since I have had that mindset for a long time.

I'm a little cautious as Aithan leads me toward the house where I was held. Clenching my jaw, I meet his gaze.

'We're going inside?' I ask.

Aithan nods. 'We are. Are you ready?'

Nodding, I follow him. The air is damp, and reeks of blood, and the smell of death has climbed insurmountably. My nose wrinkles when we pass dead bodies slumped across the floor. In the week since I was a human, I have seen more dead bodies than someone should ever see in a lifetime.

My shoulders are tense as we walk down the stairs, into the basement. My eyes widen when they land on the vampire who tortured me. He is hanging from the very ropes he had me draped from.

'You have two choices. You can let him go, and hope to never see him again.' Aithan prowls closer to me, but my eyes don't leave the vampire in front of me. His eyes are black, and dead as they blink back at me, his upper lip curled into a sneer of hatred. 'Or, you can get revenge on him for what he did to you and your friend. What do you choose?'

'You told me to do it,' the vampire hisses, directing his glare at Aithan. 'You told me to snatch them, and torture them.' His eyes switch to mine. 'He wanted to see how well you handled it.'

I look back at Aithan. He is watching me carefully.

'He may be lying, he may be not. But you're by my side with the world at your fingertips. Can you accept what he says?'

Swallowing, I nod. 'What's done is done.'

Aithan's lips curl. 'What's done is done.'

My eyes settle on the whimpering vampire in front of me. He swings lightly, and I can almost feel the pain of my shoulder *popping out, and the burn on my skin from the rope. I remember his fangs dragging through my skin, the way his hands pummelled me. The feel of his foot crunching into my side, cracking my ribs. The fact that I was completely at his mercy. Vulnerable, defenceless.*

'What will it be?' Aithan asks, and his fingers dance across the edge of my shoulder. He touches the muscles there, and smiles, as if he is fond of my physical strength. Something ripples through me. A feeling of enjoyment at his praise. 'Free him, or get revenge?'

'Revenge.'

Lurching forward, I use the blade Aithan gave me to cut the rope. It's a black blade, with my initials carved into it. KC. Kian Cattaneo. It's sleek and weightless in my palm, but lethal.

Curling my hand around the vampire's throat, I drag him toward me, so we are eye-to-eye.

'Why did you torture me more?' I ask, eyes piercing into his.

The vampire smiles a slow, eerie smile. 'You had a fire in your eyes I wanted to extinguish.'

My jaw tics. Aithan moves, coming around behind the man. I nod at him, and he curls his hands under the vampire's armpits, securing him to the ground. The vampire jerks in his hold, trying to break free, but Aithan is much older and stronger than him, effortlessly pinning him to the spot.

'Okay,' I reply, popping my knuckles. 'Hope it was worth it.'

My hand strikes as quickly as a snake. My fingers latch onto his bones, and I begin ripping them out. His scream splinters the air, and it's like music to my ears. After his bones, I move on to his organs. The feel of his intestines in my hand has a thrilling sensation shooting through me. One by one, I yank out each organ, tossing it behind me, creating a pile of his body parts. The vampire is slumped forward, only being held up by Aithan.

Then there is only his heart left.

The vampire's face is as white as a piece of paper, and I love the feeling it gives me, watching the life drain out of him.

'Enjoy hell.' I smirk, before my blade pierces through his heart.

I cleave it straight in half, and pull both halves out. As he falls forward, gasping on air, he collapses. By the time he hits the ground, he is dead. My fingers sink into the pieces of his heart, and I continue to slice my blade through it, like I'm cutting a piece of cake. When it's in pieces, I toss to them onto the ground.

After licking my hands clean, I turn to face Aithan, who is beaming across at me like he is having a proud father moment.

'How did it feel?' Aithan asks, folding his arms across his chest, assessing me.

'Satisfying,' I reply, my lips twitching as my eyes flick back to the dead man, a surge of delight flooding through me. Flexing my hands, the blood drips off them, hitting the ground softly. 'And extremely powerful.'

'Sure, come on in.'

I glance at Sofia, who is staring at me with her brows raised.

'What?' I ask. 'I came through the front door this time.'

'There's a thing called knocking, and people do that so they can be let inside,' she says slowly, talking as if I may have difficulty understanding her.

'But I can easily let myself in.'

She rolls her eyes. 'What do you want, Kian?'

'I need answers. About the bonded blood situation.'

'No shit.' She sighs. 'What do you think I've been doing?'

'Well?' I demand. 'Are there any updates?'

'I am so close to figuring it out, but I can't tell you anything until I know for sure. I will come to you when I know. Okay? Stop harassing me, you impatient shit.'

Groaning, I collapse onto the lounge. 'No updates, then?'

'No.' She huffs in frustration. 'And I have a lot to do today, so if you don't mind . . .' She trails off, shooing me from the lounge. I side-eye as I push to my feet. She frowns, peering up at me. 'You don't look so good, Ki.'

'Thanks,' I mutter. 'You sure there isn't any witchy voodoo stuff you can do to slow this thing down, or make me feel better?'

She exhales, shaking her head. 'It's a death curse, Kian. There isn't much to be done. The best you can do is visit your bonded mate and let her blood make you feel better.'

'Right,' I say, a little uneasily.

Blood sharing with Cora is dangerous. As good as it makes me feel, it's drawing us closer to a line I've been adamant I can't cross with her. I don't have friends, or lovers, or anything in between. I have allies, because they're essential.

I don't let anyone in, and I don't permit myself to have any weaknesses. She is a giant fucking weakness, and I don't want things developing any more than they have. People are starting to notice. That note was a clear threat to me, and it can't go ignored. Cora isn't safe, unless I force her to be with me at all times. It may reach a point that it comes to that, although she didn't exactly enjoy the lack of freedom last time. It would be different this time, though. I can't keep lying to her, and keeping her at a distance.

I'm losing my ability to walk away from her.

Sighing, I rub a hand down my face. It might be time to start treating her exactly as she deserves: as my equal. I almost laugh. I never expected to find anyone that I would ever deem as my equal.

'All right then,' I lament, offering her a two-finger salute. 'Catch ya.'

'Pleasure, as always,' Sofia mutters.

The detour to Red Thorne doesn't take too long. I'm thankful it isn't a full moon tonight, because I'm already feeling agitated and reckless. My body gravitates to her house, and I'm slipping in through the window within a few minutes of crossing over into the town. This is infuriating. I don't want to give in to this. I don't want to always go to her, but I'm powerless to stop it. I've spent so long refusing to be vulnerable to anyone, but I'm incapable of keeping this distance between myself and her. Honestly, I don't think I want to anymore . . .

She twists in her sheets, chest heaving. I watch her. She jerks and spasms, the fear rolling through her blossoming inside my chest. Her nightmares are so similar to mine. I recognise the feeling all too well.

Sitting down on the edge of the bed, I place a hand on her arm. She stirs, her eyes slowly fluttering open. The hardness behind them is momentarily vacant. She smiles softly, her fingers curling around my bicep.

'You're here,' she whispers.

'I'm here.'

'I need you to stay with me,' she murmurs, voice laced with sleep. 'I'm sick of being alone.'

Everything inside me is screaming at me to walk away.

But I can't.

'Okay.'

Moving beside her, I lay back. She curls into me, resting her head on my chest. Breathing her in, I pull her closer to me, resting my cheek on the top of her head.

Just for tonight, I'm going to ignore every rational thought inside my mind, and let myself give in.

Just for tonight.

29

The Prisoner

MY BODY IS SORE AND TENDER.

It feels as if I've simultaneously run a marathon, and performed a round in a boxing ring. But when I look down at myself, there are no physical marks on my body.

My head is cloudy.

A memory from earlier flashes through my mind. A woman. I try to remember something about her, but it's like every time I think I can visualise her, the image floats away.

Questions. She asked me questions.

Questions about what?

Twisting my fingers together restlessly, I frown, attempting to recall the conversation.

The memory seems so distant and distorted that I'm starting to doubt whether it truly happened today, or whether it's a memory that's resurfacing from my past.

'Do you know who you are?'

I sit up straight, whirling around, before I realise the voice was from one of my memories, but it was such a clear thought, it sounded like the person was right here in the room with me. My eyes sweep over the bare walls, falling on the door.

Stepping toward it, I try the handle a few times, but like always, nothing happens.

'You really don't remember anything?'

Spinning around, my eyes dart up to the ceiling, to the window, and back around the room.

'This might hurt . . .'

As if reliving it, the pressure builds in my head, and I cry out, my knees buckling. Cradling my head, I hold on to it, as if it might burst.

And then everything stops.

No more memories. No more questions. No more pain.

Just a quiet sort of numbness, which I have become accustomed to.

Silently, I walk back to the bed, dropping onto it. My eyes lower to my hands, tracing over the scars there.

None of this is making any sense.

30

CORA

The Fighter

I'M IN KIAN'S ARMS.

It's somehow not a dream.

He is *really* here.

And fuck, it makes me so sad and angry that I don't hate that fact.

His fingers brush the hair back from my face, and he stares down at me with that look like he is analysing me, while also considering exactly how to say what he wants to say. Every word is deliberate with him. I'm starting to see through the cracks of his foundation. The wall he keeps around himself.

'Hi,' I whisper.

His cheek twitches, as if he is fighting off a smile. 'Hi.'

'You're here,' I say, because that seems to be the first words that come to mind whenever he turns up.

'Yes.'

'Is everything okay?' I ask slowly, acutely aware he hasn't moved away, and his arm is still holding me close to him.

His head falls back against the pillows, and he gazes up at the ceiling. Running a tongue across his teeth, he is silent for a moment.

'No,' he eventually murmurs. 'Not really.'

'You're dying, and you can't find the witch.'

'Correct.'

'People are hunting you down because they know you're weak, or they've heard about our connection and know I'm their way to you.'

'You're good at this.'

My eyes flutter closed, and I let myself continue lying on his chest. It's hard and smooth beneath my palm. My hand moves to his, and I trace the black rings across them. For some reason, he allows it. I'm partly convinced I'm still dreaming. This is feeling very similar to how it was before he turned me. It's jarring.

'I keep listening to people. At work, in class. There is never anything said that points fingers to any witches, except the boy next door. He said he is working for someone, and they want to use me to kill you.'

'The boy who touched what was mine?' Kian asks, upper lip curling in distaste.

I roll my eyes.

'I need to interrogate him.'

I wince. 'I don't like the sound of that.'

'It must be done. It doesn't have to be painful, if he cooperates. What else were you able to find out?'

'Not much. I had to go back to work, and I haven't seen him since. I can find him though, and will try to discover more.'

'Good. Okay. I'm happy you found something.' He sighs. 'Every person that appears to be a lead is a dead end. This is what I'm best at, tracking people, and yet, she's . . . elusive.'

Listening to his voice is soothing a part of my soul. I surreptitiously inhale, drowning my senses in his scent. As much as I hate to even think it, I wish I could bottle it up and store it for later, when my raging hormones make me crave him.

'Why are you here?' I ask.

'I need your blood.'

'Okay . . .' I trail off, the room feeling impossibly small, like there isn't enough oxygen suddenly. I don't know how I go from feeling nothing, to basically becoming a human again. I swear it feels like my pulse is thrumming, and my skin is hot, and yet, I know realistically none of that is possible. I wait for him to move away from me, to unfurl his arm, but he stays where he is, watching me with that intensity that makes me want to squirm. 'You could have just taken it and left.'

He says nothing.

'Why didn't you?' I ask, my voice barely a whisper. I'm desperate to know why, but a part of me is expecting him to shove me back, and stalk out of the room, like he has done so many times before when I 'get too close'. A beat passes, and I wait, expecting it to happen any second, but it doesn't. Instead, a muscle in his jaw flexes, and his finger moves, tracing an invisible pattern on my arm.

'You know why.'

'I need you to say it.'

'I can't do this, *mio tesoro*.'

'Kian . . .' I whisper.

He rolls onto his side. The morning sun peeking through the blinds lights up his eyes, and they almost look a dark grey. His straight nose, that perfect jawline, his ruffled dark hair. He is so handsome to look at, I almost can't stand it.

'I'm dying, Cora,' he murmurs, and the way he says my name makes a ripple of desire roll through me, despite the words he speaks. 'I'm dying, and the more my strength depletes, the more dangerous I'll become. I can't have you near me when that happens.'

I shake my head. 'You won't hurt me.'

He barks a short, bitter laugh. 'I hurt you all the time. Over and over, in the worst possible ways, and yet, you say that to me.'

'I mean, yes, you hurt me,' I correct. 'You hurt me all the time, but when it comes down to it, you would never cause me true harm. Everything you've done so far has been for a reason . . . even if I'm yet to put all the pieces together.'

Kian eyes me, studying me carefully, his gaze narrowing. 'You speak like you have any clue about me at all.'

'I do, and you hate that I do.'

He shakes his head, looking like he is torn between disbelief, and acceptance of my words.

'I'm not who you think I am. There is no good in me. Stop trying to find any.'

'I don't believe that.'

'Then you're utterly wrong,' he drawls, dropping his gaze, following his finger as he carves tender patterns up my arm. Such a soft gesture, compared to the harsh words he is throwing at me. That's Kian – a complete contradiction.

'You have a soft side but you're terrified for anyone to see it, because you don't want anyone to think you're weak,' I say, the words that have been on my mind spilling out of me. I tell myself to quit while ahead, but as usual, my mind and my mouth don't see eye-to-eye. 'But guess what? I see it, and I don't think you're weak.' I stare hard at the side of his face. 'There are . . . gaps in my memories, or at least that's how it feels. I'm piecing things together, Kian, and I want you to stop shielding me from things. You have a soft side, and I need you to be honest with me. I want to see it . . . I *need* to.'

His hand stills, and his cheek spasms, as if he is fighting his natural reaction to my words. He is always fighting for control, always wanting to be cold, and unaffected. I see through the bullshit and it's time I start calling him out on it.

'You're more delusional than I thought if you think I have a soft side,' he says in a low voice, but there is no menace in it. It's just hollow.

My lips quirk upward. 'You're a good liar, but it doesn't work on me. Not anymore.'

'I didn't come here for a heart to heart. I need your blood.'

'Take it, then.'

His eyes snap to mine, and I stare back, challengingly.

His hands strike toward me, and I'm flattened onto my back. He straddles my waist, pressing his delicious weight down onto me, and I love the feel of it. I've been craving it more and more.

I smile. He groans.

'You're not meant to be like this,' he growls. 'You're supposed to hate me. I've done everything I can to make you hate me.'

I lift a shoulder, moving my hands so that my palms flatten on his chest. 'I do hate you.'

He scoffs. 'You hate me as much as I hate you.' His eyes are full of depth, and are endless pools of darkness. 'We're both liars.'

'That's the most honest thing you've ever said to me.'

'My God, *mio tesoro*, you are a stunning creature. As beautiful as you are stubborn. As witty as you are fiery. A damn challenge.' His head dips toward me, our lips brushing. 'The only challenge I'm willing to lose.'

He crashes his mouth to mine, and I loop my arms around his neck, pulling him closer. I fumble for the bottom of his shirt, and I yank it up over his head. My hands skim over his broad shoulders, down his muscled back, and my fingertips graze over the raised, scarred skin. He shivers under my touch, breaking the kiss and pressing his forehead to my temple.

'You can be strong, while being kind, Kian,' I whisper, tracing his scars. 'You don't have to be a monster.'

'I am a monster,' he whispers.

'You don't have to be.'

He presses harder into me, his breath cool against my skin. He moves his mouth to kiss my temple, down my cheek, and across my jaw. His lips move to my neck, and I arch my back. He kisses my neck for a moment before his fangs slide into the tender part of my throat. A sharp gasp emits from me, and I dig my nails into his back – the unscarred part, since I have memorised his skin like a world map.

He drinks from me, and my eyes roll into the back of my head at the sensation of it. When he draws back, my blood painted across his lips, he tilts his head and exposes his neck to me. I inch forward and bite. The sound of his groan sends pure bliss through me, and I find myself pulling him even closer, grinding against his hard length.

'*Pregate alle stelle, mio tesoro,*' he sighs, digging his hands into my hips.

With our bodies flush, and my shirt rising, I realise all too quickly that I'm completely bare underneath this shirt. As if realising it at the same time, his hands slide up my stomach before travelling back down my sides. They move to cup my ass, and he makes a soft growl at the back of his throat.

I release my fangs from him, slumping back into the pillows. He stills, breathing hard, and I curl my legs around him.

'No,' he chokes out, voice low. 'We can't do this.'

'No,' I agree, tightening my legs around him. 'We can't.'

'I can't let you in.' His voice is pleading, and it's almost like he is having a conversation with himself.

'No,' I murmur. 'That would be terrible.'

His fangs drive into my throat as his hard body presses against mine. The bite transforms into a hot kiss that trails down my neck. Moving across my jaw, his lips capture mine and I groan against his mouth. He moves his hand to the side of my face, tracing my lower lip.

'Thanks for the blood, *mio tesoro*,' he murmurs.

By the time I've blinked, he has gone.

*

I spend far too long in the shower, reliving the last hour in my mind.

There are dark circles under my eyes. I lean closer, inspecting my reflection. Shaking my head, I step back. I've been sleeping terribly lately. It's not unusual for me, the nightmares are truly awful. I have a lot of fuel for them. My mother, Alex, the dead bodies we find, other humans I've killed, the way the bodies burn after Theo and I light them on fire. An endless repetition of the horrors I've lived, always there to remind me of what I've done, and how I will never forgive myself for it.

I do what I do best. I push it all away, and focus on something else.

Once I'm dressed, I walk back into my room, and gasp. My entire bed is covered with rose petals with a familiar black border. Rolling my lips inward, I slowly make my way to the bed. I pick one up, running my thumb over it. Tears burn my eyes. He hasn't given me one of these since *before*.

Shaking my head, I stroll out to the kitchen, and the empty glass in my hand drops from my hand, shattering across the floor.

'Hey, big sis.'

'Is this real?' I whisper, gaping at my sister. 'Are you really here right now?'

Raya beams at me. 'Yup.'

Looks like this day is going to be full of surprises.

Launching myself at her, she laughs as we fall to the floor in a tangle of limbs and hair. I clutch her to me tightly, squeezing her so hard I hear a rib pop.

'Ow,' she whines.

'Sorry,' I say, but by the time I've let her go, it's clicked back into place. I vaguely pay attention to Hunter quickly cleaning the glass with his vampire speed, having the job done within seconds.

Clambering to my feet, I look over to Hunter, who is smiling at me.

'Hey, Cora.'

I nod at him. 'Hunter.'

Raya narrows her eyes at me. 'Can I smell . . . cologne? Have you had a guy here?'

My stomach bottoms out. My sister is far too observant for her own good. I shake my head, giving my best incredulous look.

'A guy? No way. The most action I've gotten is from the dude next door, and it turns out he was just trying to gather intel on me for some juvenile online forum.' I pointedly leave out how that was a mere cover story, and he is in fact working for someone who is planning to use me to hunt down Kian.

'What?' Raya exclaims.

I wave my hand dismissively. 'I'll fill you in later. What are you doing here?'

'I was worried about you,' Raya admits, casting a glance to Hunter, doing that annoying exchange where they don't need words to communicate. 'I felt like you weren't being entirely honest with me on the phone.'

'Well, I was. There's no need to worry about little old me,' I say brightly, clasping my hands together. 'But either way, I'm glad you're here. Theo is annoying me no end.'

'Hey!' he grumbles, and I flinch, not having realised he was at the door.

'You're freakishly silent,' I snarl at him. 'How do you do that?'

'They don't call me the Stealth Ninja for nothing,' he counters.

'No one calls you that,' I mutter.

'Ray Ray.' Theo points to Raya. His eyes shift to her side.

He steps in and barrels toward Hunter, whose eyes widen as Theo leaps on top of him. They crash into my table, sending it flying across the room. I huff out a sigh, watching it scrape across the floor, leaving a mark.

'HUNTER!!!' He throws his arms around him and squeezes. Hunter chokes, and attempts to push him off, but Theo clings to him tighter. 'I know you must have missed me so much, but don't worry, I'm here.'

'Get. Off. Me,' Hunter drags out, and successfully shoves him off.

Theo beams at him. 'You have gotten even more handsome.'

Hunter looks uncomfortable as he gets to his feet. Raya rolls her eyes, and I smirk at Theo. I'm really starting to think Theo is in love with Hunter, in a way that goes beyond being friends. It's most likely they were close and then the bond between a maker and the vampire they created heightened that, but either way, it's entertaining as hell to watch.

'Er – thanks,' Hunter says, scratching the back of his neck.

'I missed you so much, I could just kiss you,' Theo blurts, smiling so wide I swear I can see every single one of his teeth.

Hunter looks alarmed. 'Please don't.'

Theo takes a step closer and Hunter flees toward the back of the house. Theo chases after him, and Raya and I exchange a look before bursting out laughing. We have barely sobered up when Hunter storms back into the room, a look of fury swirling in his eyes. The smile from my face vanishes when his gaze lands heavily on me.

'Kian has been here,' he says, and it's not a question, his voice thick with accusation. Folding his arms across his chest, he fixes me with a penetrating stare that reminds me of his brother. He raises a brow, looking confused, frustrated, and disappointed all at once. Dread circles in my gut. 'What the hell is going on?'

31

KIAN

The Enforcer

WATER RIPPLES OVER MY skin as I float, gazing up at the moon.

Since I've been feeling considerably worse as the days go by, stopping for a moment and soaking up the moonlight feels almost as good as when I drink from Cora. Well, not quite, but it's something I enjoy, nonetheless. It's very rare I allow myself this kind of relaxation, but with everything going on, it seems there's no time like the present.

Allowing my eyes to close, I let my mind wander.

She snapped my neck. I've never been prouder.

Getting to my feet, I rub my neck, glancing at the mirror, catching the genuine smile on my face, and the hint of amusement in my eyes. No one ever sneaks up on me, but I truly underestimated her. I just simply didn't expect her to do that. She's a fast little thing.

Exhaling, I shrug into my leather jacket and step outside, peering up at the sky. It's overcast, so I don't need to worry about her burning out here. Thunder rumbles in the distance, and the first fall of rain is starting.

A pit hollows in my stomach, but I'm getting better at ignoring it. Whenever there is distance between Cora and I, it hurts, and I feel very ill, but since I purposely distanced myself often when she was human, I can handle the pain. It seems to be stronger now that she is turned, but I can handle it. We already had an annoyingly strong connection, and now that I have piled a maker-and-vampire attachment on top of it, it has made everything significantly worse.

She is very mad at me.

I don't blame her, but I need it to be like this. It's the only way I can control her, while simultaneously keeping her away from my very closely guarded heart. I breathe a laugh. Some might argue there is no heart in my chest. Sometimes I don't believe there is.

As clever and cunning as my Cora is, I know exactly where she would be going. To visit that sister of hers. Sighing, I begin the journey back to Ocean Port, where Cora and Raya live. Well, Cora lived. I thought I was being clever with the blood oath, and she threw that at me, once again taking me by surprise. Not that I would actually kill her sister, but I don't like being told that I can't. Well. I could hurt her, but I couldn't kill her. I'm pretty sure turning her is a loophole that I perhaps will explore one day.

Pausing, honing my senses, I feel where she is. She's at the apartment. Gritting my teeth, I speed up my pace. If she goes back to Raya, the whole plan will unravel. My veins tingle, and I freeze, coming to a complete stop.

She's using compulsion.

At least I taught her how to perfect it. There will be no issues with Raya, then.

When I get to the apartment, I hover outside, peering from behind a tree. Cora appears at the door, nervously casting her eyes around. I smirk. She knows I'm after her, and would have no clue how long I'd be down for.

My smile widens. She might even think she actually killed me.

As she takes off toward the woods, I follow her. When we are far enough in not to be seen by anyone, I drop in front of her. She screams, skidding to a stop. Sticks and dirt fly out from around her feet and she falls backward.

'Boo,' *I drawl, smirking down at her.*

'Fuck,' *she mutters.* 'You found me.'

'No shit,' *I growl.* 'You went to the one fucking place I asked you to never go back to.'

'You tore my mother away from me,' *she screams up at me, getting to her feet so fast, she sways.* 'I needed to make sure you hadn't killed Raya, too.'

I roll my eyes. 'I promised you your sister would be fine. You made me promise, remember?'

'Promises don't mean shit when it comes to you!' *she seethes.*

'It does when it is a blood oath, sweetheart.'

'Don't call me that.'

I grin, flashing my fangs. 'I can't kill her, okay? No need to stress.'

'You can still hurt her,' *she snaps.* 'And turn her, right?'

'Huh,' *I say, considering her words, acting as though I hadn't thought this myself only moments ago.* 'I suppose I can. That's a neat idea.'

'Fuck. You.'

Ah, she is so angry. I can taste it in the air.

'Nice little move you did back there. I haven't had anyone successfully break my neck for a while. I genuinely didn't expect that from you.'

'That's on you. You're the one who says never underestimate your opponent.'

'Didn't see you as an opponent, mio tesoro.'

She stiffens, jutting her chin, eyes blazing. 'I'm done with this. With you. I don't care if I'm condemned to death or hell for breaking a blood oath. I'm already there.'

Pushing my tongue against the inside of my cheek, I nod. 'If only it was that easy. A blood oath can't be broken. Why do you think I tricked you into it?'

'You're a fucking monster.'

I glance down at my watch. 'Okay. Sure. I'm a monster. Let's get going, we have a dinner reservation. I want to introduce you to a friend of mine.'

'I'm not going anywhere with you!' she hisses, scrambling backward, her eyes flashing with rage that is barely being contained.

'Well, you are.' I shrug. 'Either voluntarily, or . . .' I trail off, my lips curving.

With speed that I actually find quite impressive, she pulls out one of the daggers I gifted her and launches it straight at my chest. I dance out of the way, unable to stop the smile forming.

'You're so beautiful when you want to kill me,' I drawl.

Growling, she throws another. And another.

Darting out of the way with ease, I avoid each of her throws, before plucking one from the air and flinging it back at her. She screams, stumbling back into the tree behind her. Her hand trembles as she steps away from the tree, blood trickling down her neck from where the blade nicked her.

There's a storm glittering in those now-black eyes, and it makes the wretched organ in my chest melt a little at the sight of it. I need to lock that down. I can't let her get inside any more than she already has, but when she stares at me – like she wants me dead – harnessing the lethal weapons I gifted her, it really turns me the fuck on.

'I always win, mio tesoro,' I purr, leaning in close, my mouth an inch from hers. 'Don't forget that.'

I step away, turning my back to her.

'*Come along now,*' I toss over my shoulder. '*We have a date to get to.*'

'Where the hell have you been?'

Sofia eyes me, a very clear unimpressed expression on her face. 'Shut up and let me through my goddamn door,' she snaps, pushing past me. 'I hate when you turn up unannounced. Believe it or not, Kian, it's actually very rude.'

'Never said I wasn't rude,' I argue. 'Answer the question.'

'The supermarket,' she gripes, pointing at the grocery bags.

'Before that.' I lean closer, flattening my hands on the counter. 'You paid a visit to my prisoner. Didn't you?'

'You wanted answers. I'm getting you answers.' She lifts her chin, levelling me with an unwavering gaze. 'You got a problem with me doing what you asked me to?'

'I have a problem with you doing things without asking me.'

'I didn't realise I had to run every single thing by you.'

'Yes, you did,' I growl, leaning further forward, my eyes flashing with anger. 'You deliberately went behind my back. Why?'

'Oh fuck off,' she snaps, turning her back to me as she begins to unpack the bags. 'I'm getting shit done, like you asked. If there's a problem, then leave me the hell alone and find someone else to do your dirty work for you. Believe me, I could do without your invasive ass all up in my face.'

Unclenching my jaw, I nod stiffly. 'Do not do that again.' Focusing on calming down, I meet her eyes. 'What did she say?'

'She doesn't know a damn thing,' Sofia huffs. 'I tried every spell on her to draw out the truth, but she doesn't know. I was able to extract some blood, though, and I am going to do some spells with it. Find out someone who is related to her. Once I know more, I will contact you.' Turning to face me, her eyes shimmer. 'If you barge into my house uninvited again, you won't like what happens.'

'Right,' I say, unfazed. 'You do that.' I eye the ice-cream container. 'You eat a lot of ice cream.'

'You're getting on my last nerve, Kian,' she mutters through gritted teeth.

'Oh.' I smile. 'My favourite place to be.'

She rolls her eyes so hard, I'm surprised they don't fall out of their sockets.

'Is that all?' she demands, planting her hands on her hips.

My expressionless mask slips back onto my face, as easy as putting on a t-shirt at the start of the day. 'Mmhmm.'

'By all means, see yourself out,' she says with a flick of her wrist, and the front door swings open. It collides with the wall dramatically, further proving how annoyed she is with me.

'And you say *I'm* rude,' I mutter, walking out.

As I head over to Cas's house, I take my time, trying to think about where to go, and what to do next. Panic is starting to well inside my chest. I swear I'm starting to hear the sound of a 'tick-tock' in my head, as if my mind is reminding me that there's a time sentence on my life, and that sentence is getting shorter by the minute.

The air is unnaturally cold when I step inside his house. A guy who looks to be in his early twenties is sprawled across the lounge, his eyes closed, blood smeared down his neck and chest. His heartbeat is slow and steady as he sleeps.

'Hungry?' Cas asks, strolling out from the kitchen, pointing toward the man. 'He's delicious.'

'Nah,' I say. 'I want to know how it went today. When Sofia was here. Did you listen?'

Cas nods. 'Yeah. She just asked her a bunch of family questions, and it got a bit intense. I genuinely don't think she knows, man. I'm sorry.'

I grunt, collapsing onto the lounge, shoving the man's leg out of my way. The guy is so out of it, he doesn't even stir.

'Nothing appears to be going my way.'

'Witches,' Cas grumbles. 'They're a pain.'

'You don't say.'

There's a heavy silence, and I let my eyes close.

'Are you going to tell me what's going on?' Cas asks, and there's a slight edge to his voice.

I know he hates being left in the dark, especially when I ask him to do things and don't provide any context as to why. I understand that, but I like doing things alone. The fewer who know about my plans, the better. Less risk of information leaking, or plans getting interrupted, although Cas is one of the very few people I do trust.

Trust means everything to me, and I don't give it out lightly. But Cas just happened to have been in the exact same situation as me, and now we both have each other's back because of it. There will always be the faintest link between vampires when they have the same maker. Faint, but it's there.

He has proved his loyalty to me several times. One of the more significant times was with my brother. I sent Cas to befriend him, to gain his trust. I wanted to be able to use that later, but I also liked that Hunter had someone to lean on, who could help him if he needed it, since I could never be the person for him. Not that I would ever admit that out loud.

I hesitate. 'I'm just trying to find out answers to something.'

'Thank you for being painfully vague.' Cas exhales. 'Answers to what?'

A muscle in my jaw tenses. 'Do you really need to know?'

'I am babysitting a prisoner for you. I have a witch turning up unannounced on my doorstep. I'd like to know what the hell is going on since I'm doing you a *favour*.'

Damn. He has me there.

'I'm doing research about the prisoner, and it's easier if I know exactly where they are. I don't have the time to worry about their whereabouts.'

'And?' Cas probes. Eventually, I open my eyes, staring up at the dark ceiling. 'Why are you doing research?'

My hands clench and unclench as I battle with the urge to strengthen the walls around me, or just give in and tell him.

'Come on, man,' Cas says softly, leaning forward, eyes narrowing. 'I'm not blind. You're pale, you have dark circles under your eyes, you're fatigued.' He pauses, considering his next words. 'You're doing very un-Kian-like things. Something is wrong with you, and I want to know what it is.'

Turning my head, I stare at him. 'I'm dying.'

Cas physically jerks back as if I've slapped him. His mouth opens and closes a few times as he gapes at me. I keep my face stony as I stare at him for a few moments longer before returning my gaze forward, unable to stand the shock and pity in his eyes. I fucking loathe having anyone pity me, especially not someone I actually consider a *friend*.

'*What?*' he chokes out, sounding more broken than I expected. Cas and I are allies, and we have been through everything together, but at the end of the day, vampires look out for themselves. We have one goal: survive.

'A witch cursed me, and it's slowly eating me away. I'm trying to figure out how to find the witch to get her to undo it, but as you can see' – I gesture to myself – 'time is running out.'

'Fuck,' Cas whispers. 'You should have told me. I could have been helping you.'

'You are helping me.' I shrug. 'You're keeping an eye on the prisoner.'

'What has she got to do with it?' Cas asks.

'Could be nothing,' I say. A loud creak has Cas snapping his head toward the door, and I follow his gaze, knowing she is behind there. Her heartbeat is strong, and a little distracting. 'Could be everything. That's what I'm trying to work out.'

'Ki,' Cas says, eyes snapping to mine. He leans forward, touching his hand to my arm. I stare down at it, a little shocked by the gesture. His fingers bite into my arm, and I reluctantly meet his gaze. 'I'm going to help.'

I nod, disbelief swimming in my eyes. 'Sure.'

'I promise, Ki,' Cas says firmly. 'We will fix this.'

32

The Prisoner

THE PENCIL I HOLD lightly slides against the paper.

My hand moves slightly as I shade in the eyes of the drawing in front of me. A pencil, a sharpener, and a notepad were left for me, and I have almost filled the entire notepad. There is nothing else to do, and this makes me feel at peace.

Blowing across the page, I shake it lightly, and lean back, admiring the work.

Demonic black eyes stare up at me. A shiver rolls down my spine.

Flashes of those eyes boring into mine jolt me, and the notepad falls from my hands, clattering onto the floor. Leaning forward, I press my head against my hand, rubbing slow circles across my forehead.

Every day the memories try to force their way in.

Every day it gets more painful.

The door opens. My breath hitches and I scramble to my feet.

A woman smiles at me, and my heart trips at the coolness in it. I've met this woman before. I don't know when, or where, but I somehow know that I have. Those eyes, that smile; they have a familiarity about them.

'Hello,' she murmurs, her voice low, and a little hesitant as she steps closer. 'Do you remember me?'

I shake my head. I don't point out the fact that I'm positive I have met her, but I don't recall any details surrounding that, so I'm not exactly lying.

Her smile widens. 'That's okay. I'm not here to ask you questions this time.'

Something clicks in the back of my brain. She was here once before. Questioning me. Odd questions that I had no clue about . . .

'It will all come to an end soon,' the woman says, her tone soft, and soothing, as if speaking to a nervous child. 'I'm going to make it all go away.'

'Make what go away?' I ask, my throat dry as I step backward, the heels of my feet hitting the wall.

'Anything of use,' she answers. 'They won't be able to hurt you.'

'Who?' I whisper, my brows pulling together. 'Who are you? And who do you speak of?'

'Hush . . .' Her voice trails off and she shakes her head almost dismissively.

'Don't do this,' I beg, leaning back into the wall, unsure what exactly I'm even pleading for. A calculated smile spreads over her face, making my blood run cold. The air seems to shimmer and pulse around her, making my skin feel prickly.

'Don't worry,' she murmurs, a wicked kind of grin forming on her face. 'You won't remember a thing.' .

33

CORA

The Fighter

PANIC CLOGS MY THROAT.

Shit, shit, shit.

The rose petals. They're everywhere. His scent would be clinging to the sheets. His presence would have felt like he had grabbed Hunter by the shoulders and basically shouted in his face. My heart plummets into my stomach as I blink at a furious-looking Hunter, a wide-eyed Raya, and Theo, who emerges from around the corner, a grimace on his face. He is probably feeling guilty that he basically pushed Hunter in that direction, but he really isn't to blame. No one would have suspected Kian would have been here, like this.

'He does this,' Theo says after a moment when I fail to reply. Hunter's head whips to face his friend, and Raya eyes me a heart-beat longer before turning to face Theo, too. He shrugs, looking so casual, I almost believe what he is saying. 'Leaves her littles notes, or gifts, taunting her. Making her feel paranoid and on edge that he is just going to show up anywhere, anytime.' Theo exhales, shaking his head, looking disgusted. 'He's tormenting her, just because he can.'

Hunter's face falls, and Raya looks sick.

'Really?' she whispers, turning to face me, a hand over her mouth. 'That is awful, Cor. I'm so sorry that you're dealing with all of that.'

My stomach clenches. A part of me is relieved that I don't have to admit to her that something seriously weird is going on with Kian and me – she would never understand. The other half of me is wracked with guilt over the lie. And a smaller, tiny fraction, feels bad for painting Kian as the bad guy, once again, when he has a softer side to him that he just doesn't allow anyone to see.

Nodding slowly, I can't find words to reply. Ducking my chin, I head toward the fridge and draw the curtains closed, since it seems to be bright outside. Brighter than usual, and I don't feel like having sore, itchy skin today. I also wanted something to occupy my hands, since I feel weirdly restless and agitated.

'No wonder you look so stressed,' Raya murmurs, and I look back at her.

'What?' I ask.

'You look so pale . . . and . . . like you're sick,' she says softly. 'Sorry, I know that's not a very nice thing to say.'

'You do have darkness under your eyes,' Theo adds, unhelpfully. 'Getting worse and worse, actually. What's up with that?'

'Theo,' Hunter exhales. 'Have some tact, would you?'

'You guys know how to make a girl feel good,' I mumble, skulking back to the lounge and flopping down onto it. Midnight trots out from the spare room, and freezes when her eyes land on everyone. Backpedalling, she sprints back into the room. I guess two vampires are more than enough for her, let alone four.

'I'm worried about you, Cor,' Raya says nervously, coming to join me. The cushions dip under her weight and she swivels to face me. Compared to me, she is glowing. Her eyes sparkle, her hair is long and glossy, her skin smooth and shimmery. She is flourishing.

The corner of my mouth lifts, and I feel a sense of irony flood through me. Just like old times. The weight of the world is getting heavier and heavier for me, while she shines. I accepted that this is life for me – a long time ago – but I thought I was getting away from it. I thought becoming a vampire would save me. Instead, it condemned me to an even worse fate.

'I'm fine.' Frowning, Raya casts a nervous look at Hunter, disbelief clear on her face. Reaching for her hands, I circle mine around them. 'I'm really glad you're here. I missed you so much.'

She offers me a watery smile. 'I missed you, too.'

We spend the rest of the day wandering around town, talking, enjoying the music that drifts out of the stores we pass. I can't remember the last time we simply had a sister day to hang out, and I had no idea how much I needed it.

By the time we get back to my place, the boys meet up with us and we spend the night swapping stories, playing board games and ending the night with a movie. It all seems so incredibly *normal*. Having Raya back here makes me so happy. Like my heart is slowly mending just by having her close.

They decide to stay with Theo as his house is much more generously sized, and Hunter still has some of his things there. When they leave, an emptiness fills my chest. I stare at the front door for a moment, and then look around. The warmth and cosiness of the place seems to dry up right before me, and I exhale, the awful sensation of loneliness gnawing at me. I could have asked her to stay, or I could have joined them. Either option would have been good, but as usual, I insisted to everyone I was fine on my own, even though being alone is the last thing I feel like right now.

After taking a shower and spending longer than I should have scrubbing myself with bodywash and washing my hair, I step out into the room and almost choke on my breath when Kian is casually climbing through the window. Since it's raining outside, water droplets slide down his skin and his hair is damp, sticking to his forehead. Dressed in all black, his eyes as dark as coal, his t-shirt clinging to his muscles deliciously, I can't help but stare at him, my gaze travelling over every inch of him. He is so handsome, it hurts.

Sweeping his hair back, his lips do that half-crooked grin that always makes my stomach flutter.

'Oh,' I say, unable to form any other words. 'Hi.'

'Hi,' he replies.

'You're here.'

'You like to point that out.' He grins. His smile quickly fades as he looks around my room, and then back to me. 'Hunter's home.'

'Yeah. They're worried about me.'

'Ah.' Kian nods. 'Wouldn't have anything to do with me, would it?'

'Of course not,' I reply, sarcastically. 'Nothing I do ever involves you.'

'Perfect. Do I need to know anything?'

I shake my head. 'I don't think so.'

'Okay,' he says. 'Come here.'

Unable to deny the request, I cross the room and fall into him. His arms wrap around me, pulling me in tightly, and we both simply hold each other, in silence, as if we are tethered on the edge of a cliff and will fall if we don't cling on to each other.

He smells like rain, and pine, and a delicious scent that is simply just *him*.

'Why do you climb through the window?' I ask.

'It's easier to break in that way. The deadbolt is rather annoying.'

'That's fair.'

Neither of us speaks for a while. We don't question what we are doing. I don't want to fight with myself today, and it looks like he doesn't either.

I lead him into the bathroom where he undresses, and I can't look away. He steps underneath the water and it sprays down his body. His eyes lift, and he beckons me to him, with a sharp curl of his fingers.

Stepping out of my nightie, I slip inside after him. Turning, he buries his face into my shoulder.

He leaves a burning trail of kisses up my neck before dipping my head back and kissing my mouth with an intensity that has me stumbling back into the wall. It's all we do. Kiss, and touch, and loop our arms around one another. I drink from him, he drinks from me, and it's an endless cycle of kissing, and feeding, and savouring tender touches and soft, blissful sighs.

When I fall into bed later, I expect him to leave, but he crawls in beside me.

'You're staying?' I whisper.

His fingers tenderly brush my hair out of my eyes. 'There is no point denying that there is nowhere else I'd rather be.'

My eyes flutter closed, and I lean into him, and within seconds, I'm asleep in his arms.

When I wake the next morning, the space beside me is empty.

Raya flops down beside me underneath the shade of the tree, her thick waves billowing out around her head. 'Being back here is triggering.'

'Yeah?' I ask, turning my head, so that I'm looking over at her. It still hasn't sunk in that she is here, and how quickly she dropped everything to come check on me. As the one that has always been the protector, the one who worries, the one who always checks on *her*, it seems so . . . odd . . . that she is now doing that to me.

'It's just so cold and eerie here. The people in this town are creepy.' She shudders. 'In the UK the weather is absolutely perfect for us.'

'And this isn't?' I laugh, gesturing to the gloomy sky.

'Well. This town is notorious for that, I suppose, but I mean you can be out and about always, not confined to this one place.' She exhales. 'I know you can cover up and avoid the sun, but what I'm saying is that it's a lot easier to do there.'

'I'll come visit one day.'

I should. I want to explore the world, since I have seen so little of it, but while I have my life sold to Kian for ten years, it seems pointless to waste time wishing and planning for travel. I just need to survive these next years, and hope I make it out.

As I hug my knees to my chest, the breeze blows strands of hair across my face. Propping my chin on top of my knee, I watch Hunter and Theo tossing a football back and forth, doing long, hard-hitting shots that would look outrageous to the human eye, but the field is relatively deserted, give or take a few dog-walkers who have passed by.

My head spins, and I press it back on the tree, trying to re-centre myself. When I open my eyes, Raya is watching me closely, frowning.

'What's wrong with you?' she asks, narrowing those pretty eyes of hers. Similar to mine, except for the glowing silver ring that borders them, linking her to Hunter. 'Wait . . . let me guess . . .' she mocks. 'You're fine?'

'That's right.'

'Vampires are strong, and perfectly healthy.' It makes me feel uncomfortable, the way she looks at me, like she can read every thought spinning around my mind. 'And here you are, looking ill. Even worse than yesterday.'

'I'm really enjoying everyone saying how terrible I look,' I snap, pushing to my feet.

'Cor,' Raya warns, frustration leaking into her voice. 'Don't walk away from me. We are not finished.'

'We're finished when I say we're finished.'

'Stubborn as usual,' she mutters.

'My hearing still works fine!' I gripe, stomping away from her.

Theo and Hunter are looking over at me, but I ignore them. I make my way to our pile of things, shrug my jacket on and step into my shoes. It was nice relaxing under the tree, but I can't stand to be around them when it feels like they're nit-picking me all the time. All my life there has always been something wrong. My hair was too long, I was too thin, I was too pale, I worked too much, then I didn't work enough, I didn't try hard enough at school. I was always late to events, and then I was too early. I dressed too boy-like, and then I dressed too slutty. This mainly stemmed from Mum, but I'm getting flashbacks to it now that Raya is saying these things, and I'm growing angrier by the second.

There. Is. Always. Something.

I don't recognise this anger uncurling inside of me, rising at such a rapid rate, I swear I can feel my heartbeat drumming in my ears, but I know that's not possible.

'Cora,' Raya says, appearing behind me.

I whirl around, eyes flashing. 'Back off!'

The bite in my tone makes her flinch and she stops, eyes widening. She seems to pale as she steps back from me.

'Woah . . .' she murmurs. 'Cor, something is definitely going on with you.'

'It wouldn't have something to do with those dark lines on Kian's chest, would it?' Theo says, and we turn to look at him. He stares at me.

'Dark lines?' Hunter echoes, stepping forward, brow furrowed.

'He has a weird mark on his chest. I have been doing some digging about it and I think it's a hex or something. Because he doesn't look right, and he has been visiting you and now you're not right either . . .' He trails off, and if I could shoot daggers with my eyes, he would be dead.

'Kian has visited you more than once?' Raya whispers.

'Oh no . . .' Theo says slowly, eyes widening as he looks at me in shock. Concern fills his gaze as his brow creases. 'You've been blood sharing with him, haven't you? He's transferring the hex onto you to make himself live longer.'

My stomach feels like it lands at my feet. That can't be true. Surely not . . . surely he wouldn't be doing that to me, not when he's finally showing his soft side again. Unless, of course, it is all a part of his game.

He did tell me that it helps, but I didn't realise it was transferring the curse to me . . .

Of course it is. Yet again, he has fooled me, and I've played right into it.

'What the hell?' Raya exclaims, looking perplexed.

Turning, I flee. I run fast and hard, desperate to get away from them. Thankfully no one follows me, because the anger surging inside me is bordering on dangerous, and I shouldn't be around anyone right now.

Finally stopping, I find myself on the edge of the woods. I brace myself against a tree, trying to control the rapid pace of my spinning thoughts. A group of people wander past, and I grip the tree, fighting off the urge to spill blood. The group moves past, but one of them breaks away from the pack, walking over.

'Oh, hey!' a voice says. My head jerks up, and a boy I don't recognise strolls toward me, waving at me like I'm a friend of his. He grins, giving me a once-over, looking impressed. 'You turned? That's awesome.'

'Who are you?' I frown, trying to recall who the hell this person is, but I'm positive I've never seen him.

'Brax?' he says. 'We met at that party a while back. Look, I get that we got off on the wrong foot, but hey, you're a vamp now. That's sick.' He beams at me. 'I still haven't had any luck getting someone to turn me. Sorry for the . . . er . . . whole wanting to sacrifice you, and whatnot.'

I stare at him, dumbfounded. Then it clicks. Raya told me about this boy. He threw her to a hungry vampire to be a sacrifice for his own plan to be turned. Hunter killed the vampire, and saved her life. It was then that they bonded with each other.

Brax has mistaken me for Raya, because of how similar we look. I bare my teeth at him.

What an incredibly bad time for him to have run into me.

'So,' he continues, casually digging his hands into the pocket of his hoodie. 'Wanna do me a solid and turn me? I'd totally owe you one.'

'You almost killed her,' I say in a low voice, stepping toward him. 'If it wasn't for Hunter, she'd be dead because of you.'

He looks puzzled. 'Huh?'

The anger takes over. I lunge at him, whipping out a dagger, and I plunge it into his chest. He screams, and it fuels me. I stab him over and over again, enjoying the wicked flare of delight that fills me with. An anger I've never quite felt takes complete control of me, and I can taste the darkness wrapping around my blood.

'Cora!' a voice screams.

I'm yanked off the boy by two strong hands, and I fight to get out of the hold. Vaguely, I see Raya and Theo standing off to the side with horrified looks on their faces. Well, Raya looks horrified, Theo mildly entertained. The hands gripping me spin me around, and shake me.

'Cora!' Hunter barks at me. 'Snap out of it.'

His biting grip and strong voice break through, and the anger subsides, like a wave that crashes and smooths out to a flat horizon. I slowly blink, the world materialising around me. I have no clue where I am. I stumble back, and Hunter releases me.

I stare down at my hands which are coated in blood. Slowly, I look over to where the dead boy lies, completely mutilated by over a hundred stab wounds. It is a horrific sight.

So, so much blood. And it was all *me*.

'Oh my God.' Raya sinks to her knees beside the boy. 'I remember him.'

A rush of emotions hit me like a tonne of bricks. Anger, hurt, betrayal. I desperately wish Kian was the person I need him to be, but of course, he just uses me, and controls my life. Why can't I get that through my head?

He doesn't want me. He doesn't care for me. He doesn't love me.

I feel hollow as the thought of this rings through me. A part of me is heartbroken all over again. I know I can't trust him, or let myself fall for him any more than I have because of the things he has done, and continues to do, but another part of me knows there is more to the story. Do I really believe he is doing this to me? Why wouldn't I? He hurts me over and over. He's cruel, cunning, possessive, and does things only to benefit himself, so why do I have this traitorous feeling inside of me that is so sure I'm wrong, and I'm missing something?

I turn, ready to run again, but Hunter reaches for me.

The sound of my neck snapping fills my ears, and then, there is only darkness.

I'm chained to the floor.

The fucking *floor*.

I've only been down here once or twice before. The basement in Theo and Hunter's house. It's dark, and neglected. In fact,

I didn't know it existed for a while until Theo randomly moved a few spare fridges into it. Ironically, I thought it would be the perfect place to hold someone hostage. I never realised it would be *me*.

'You know how I said I'm glad you're home?' Leaning forward, I narrow my gaze at Raya, who hovers by the door, looking at me with a guilty but determined expression on her face. A face I want so badly to punch right now. 'I take it back. I wish you'd fucking never come here. I'm better off without you dragging me down.'

Raya's eyes flash with a barely contained storm, and she lifts her chin. 'That's the hex talking.'

'No,' I hiss, jabbing a finger at her, and the chains around my wrist rattle, but she's right, I can feel the darkness inside me, like a kiss of a shadow, boiling through my blood, heating it to an impossible fire. 'That's how I truly feel, and for the first time in my life, I'm being honest with you.'

'Come on,' Hunter says softly, wrapping his arm protectively around Raya, not even dignifying me with a glance. 'She's not herself right now.'

'I'm more myself than I've ever been,' I spit, the darkness blossoming inside me. 'He's coming for me.'

'That's what I'm hoping for,' Hunter replies, still with his back to me.

I laugh, and it is cold, and cruel, and manic-sounding. I rock back and forth, crawling forward to the point where the chains pull, gripping my wrists in a harsh hold that pinches my skin.

'He will kill you. He will kill all of you.'

Finally, he turns. Hunter offers me an inch of a smile, and at this moment, he looks so much like Kian, it's startling.

'Not if we kill him first.'

They step out of the room, and the iron door slams shut. Dust stirs, and I watch it rise and fall, settling back onto the ground of the basement. I yank and pull on the chains, screaming until my throat is raw, and I feel delirious from hunger.

I have no idea how much time has passed, but a light touch on my shoulder jerks me awake. I don't remember falling asleep. Theo blinks down at me, holding out a blood bag. The earlier hysteria has ebbed away, and I'm feeling more like myself, but fatigued, and starving.

'Thank you,' I whisper, taking it from him. My hands look sickly pale, and more bony than usual. Theo's hands look large and strong compared to mine. I hate feeling weak.

It's difficult to determine what is true and what isn't, in my mind. What actually happened, or what my foggy head may have made up. I remember fighting with Raya, and then everything is blurry after that.

'Cor,' he says urgently, gripping my face and forcing me to meet his eyes. 'They're planning to kill him. They know he will come for you because you're helping hinder the curse. They think killing him will stop the torment for you, and allow me to be free, and of course, bring safety to all the future humans and vampires he may kill.' Theo grips my arm, shaking me. 'They want revenge for your mother, and everything else he's done. Do you understand what I'm saying? This is going to affect you and me. They've shut me out of the plan because of my attachment to him, but I know it's taking place soon, and he won't be far off coming for you.' His stare is intense, and he fades in and out of focus for a moment.

His grip tightens on my face, and I groan, coming back to reality. 'I know you haven't been honest with me about everything between the two of you, but I know it's significant.' Flashes from earlier slam into my mind, and I try to work through what's real, and what's not. 'Cora, I need you to understand what I'm saying!'

Blinking slowly, I drag the blood bag to my lips and take a long drink. Resisting the urge to bring it back up, I force myself to swallow it, knowing I need the strength.

'He should be here by now,' I whisper, leaning back onto my palm as I continue to sip, ignoring how bitter it tastes. 'Maybe he suspects something.'

'I wouldn't be surprised. He is always a step ahead of everyone else.'

'How did you get down here unnoticed?' I ask.

'I'm very quiet when I want to be,' Theo replies.

I nod. 'I've noticed that.'

'You good?' he asks, pulling out a key from his pocket.

'Yeah. Get them off.'

He removes the cuffs from my wrists, and I rub them lightly, the skin raw underneath. It only takes them a few seconds to heal, now that I have blood in my system. I still don't feel one hundred percent, but I feel more myself, and a lot stronger than I did a few minutes ago.

Quietly, we head up the stairs, and hushed voices meet our ears. I recognise Hunter and Raya's voice, but a few others as well. I focus, trying to recall where I know the other male's voice from.

'Dante,' Theo murmurs. 'Hunter and Raya brought him in to kill Kian, and Dante brought reinforcements. Don't underestimate them.' Pausing, he looks back to me. 'You were right, you know.'

'About what?' I whisper, my brows pulling together.

'Dante. He's a bad guy.'

I blink at him. 'What makes you say that?'

'You were right. He has been stalking you, trying to figure out a way to Kian through you.'

I bristle. That's the story of my life right now.

Theo exhales, looking disappointed. 'Dante, and his friends, have been the ones killing people around town. Trying to get Kian's attention.'

A slight gasp leaves me.

Destroying Kian is Dante's entire life's purpose, and that is no life at all.

My lips tug down, and for some reason unknown to me, my eyes fill with tears.

'That's so sad,' I whisper. 'Dante has become a monster.'

I recall what he said when I first met him. *To beat a monster, you must become one.*

Theo looks away, his jaw clenching. 'Happens to us all at some point.'

'It doesn't have to be like this.'

'I know,' Theo murmurs so softly, I barely catch it. 'Ready?' he asks, giving me a quick look over, as if double-checking I'm not about to collapse. 'We need to get on top of this situation before it escalates, but Dante is out for blood, so he may need to be taken down first. I'll go for him, you go for the two females he brought with him. We just need to temporarily kill them, so we can talk to Hunter and Raya. They need to know *everything.*'

'Got it.' I nod, glad that he is able to think clearly and formulate a plan, as my head still feels fuzzy.

'I need you to be quick and efficient, just like he's taught you. Can you do that, or do you need more time?' he asks, and I'm so taken back by his seriousness, all I can do is nod. He levels me with a look.

'Yes,' I say, looking blankly ahead, honing my focus, and making everything else simply background noise. 'I'm good to go.'

We step out into the room, at the exact moment the front door opens. Kian strolls in, looking like he doesn't have a care in the world. Pushing his sunglasses up, he smiles his sadistic, blood-thirsty smile that he saves for special occasions. My stomach does a flip-flop motion at the sight of him, and I crave being close to him.

I am speechless as I stare.

I can't believe he has just walked in *through the front door*, and alone. Well, I shouldn't be surprised, it *is* Kian. He is confident of his abilities, and nothing much fazes him, even with the fact he is seriously outnumbered.

'Hello,' he says, and then nods toward Hunter. '*Fratello*, good to see you.'

Everybody is unnaturally still as they gape at Kian, probably wondering the same thing as I am: where the fuck does he find such audacity?

'Dante,' he says, and makes a clicking sound with his tongue as he points at him. 'Looking good.' He turns to face me, smiling. 'Just here to collect what's mine and then I'll be on my way. Come along, Cora.'

The air crackles with tension as everybody stares at Kian.

And then everything happens at once.

Dante lunges for Kian. The silver-haired vampire beside him follows his lead, whereas the one with dark hair turns to me. I'm already moving when I see several knives spinning, one whizzing right past my ear. I hear a grunt, as one of the knives finds Theo, but I'm quick and weave in and out of the attack easily, as if it's second nature. They don't have the precision and speed Kian does – it's like a walk in the park.

From the corner of my eye, I see Kian fighting the two vampires. His movements are so familiar, taking me back to the hours and hours he spent training me to be the perfect weapon for him. Despite everything, those were my favourite moments. Because he made me feel powerful, and strong – like no opponent could beat me, and as someone who hasn't felt strong most of my life, it's an addictive feeling.

Stealing the move from Kian, I pluck one of the knives out of the air and spin it back in the direction it came from. The woman's eyes widen a fraction as it hits her straight in the chest, sinking into her heart.

Brutal and precise. Exactly like Kian taught me.

'No!' Raya explodes, rushing toward the woman as she crumples to the floor, clawing at her chest. Raya desperately reaches for her, but the damage is done. The woman stares ahead, with no life in her eyes, and once I confirm she is dead, I keep moving, not sparing a glance at a sobbing Raya, who doesn't understand that this is all her fault. 'Cora! Stop!' she is scream-ing at me, over and over, but I tune her out, as if her screams are merely sounds from a radio I can turn down.

All I can focus on is protecting Kian. It's like something has taken over my body. Something wild, overwhelming, and out of my control. I was so confused and mad at him what only feels like minutes ago, but now nothing else matters to me except his safety, and I have no idea where this sudden drive is coming from.

Kian is grappling with Dante and the other vampire, and when I look around, Hunter is on the floor, head bent at an awkward angle, as Theo steps away from him, yanking the knife out from his own shoulder. Shock courses through me. Hunter is too strong, and too fast to not be watched at all times. Now that he is tempo-rarily out of action, it will make things a lot easier. But he would never have expected that from Theo, and it was why it worked. The element of surprise.

I don't have time to focus on why Theo would do that as the woman spares a glance over her shoulder and shrieks when she notices the other vampire dead on the ground. The scream that leaves her echoes inside my skull, and I temporarily lose focus of everything around me.

Turning to me, the woman screams, running at me with lightning speed. Darting out of her way, I yank my dagger out of my pocket, and continue evading her attacks. She is quicker than the average vampire, and I'm surprised to find myself struggling to just make it out of her way in time.

Theo is tying an unconscious Hunter to one of several small metal rings at the bottom of the fireplace. Whatever cable-like thing he is using must be incredibly powerful if he thinks it will hold. Raya is still crying over the woman she probably doesn't even know, and I can barely stand to look at her. It's difficult keeping an eye on Theo as I try to keep out of the other vampire's snapping hands, and I see him drag Raya over. She hardly even fights him as he begins to chain her as well.

She's always felt everything so strongly, and now that it is all heightened, she would feel it ten times more.

The knife I don't realise was in the vampire's hands sinks into my side, and I hiss, recoiling from her. Agony bursts through my side, and I realise the dagger is laced. That's becoming a popular weapon of choice, apparently.

She comes at me, faster than before, slamming her palms into my chest, sending me flying backward. I smash into the coffee table, glass erupting around me, biting into my skin with more brutality than I expected.

I gasp, reaching for the blade sunk so deep into my side, I can feel it has punctured my kidney, but the sound of my skin sizzling has me yanking my hand back.

The woman is on top of me before I can even blink. She yanks me up by my hair and holds another knife right against my heart. A scream erupts from me when I feel the tip of the dagger pressing into my skin, unleashing another vicious round of poison into me.

'Don't. Move,' she snarls, and everyone freezes.

Theo raises his hands in surrender, and Kian's eyes darken into an eerie blackness that is as cold as ice. His gaze darts around the room, assessing the situation. Dante strikes at him, but Kian easily evades him. He whips out his dagger – an exact replica of mine – and locks eyes with me. The miniscule nod he gives me is all I need. The speed with which he propels the dagger forward, and the shift from me, puts her right in its firing line. The dagger lodges into her forehead, and she screams so piercingly loud, my ears bleed.

Twisting on my heel, I shove my hand into her chest and rip her heart straight out.

I'm moving on autopilot, as if someone has taken over me. Like a supernatural force is inside me, possessing my mind, and my body.

Almost like a bond . . . a voice whispers in my mind.

My head is spinning, trying to catch up with what my body is doing. Raya is hysterical, her screams flooding the room, and even Theo covers his mouth with his hand, shocked at the scene before him. Raya's screams slap me back to reality. I look down at the blood on my hands, stumbling in surprise, as if the last few moments are coming back to me, like I'm watching a livestream with a slight delay in it. Except the main character is *me*, and I'm unaware of what the hell just made me do that.

By the time I turn back, Kian has Dante against the wall. Dante's eyes are filled with acceptance. He knows he has, yet again, lost the battle against Kian.

'No!' I cry, shaking my head, and Kian looks over at me. I rush forward, the darkness that soaked my mind only moments ago has faded, and I feel like myself again.

I press my hand to my side, and it burns as the skin melts a little. I wince, quickly releasing it, as I hobble forward. Blood is everywhere, and it's making me dizzy with hunger. The few sips I had earlier were not enough, and the poison is ravaging my system with horrifying speed. 'We have done enough damage. You have destroyed his life enough. You don't need to kill him. You can walk away, and let him go.'

Kian runs his tongue across his teeth, staring hard at me, those calculating eyes on the sound at my side before eventually hooking back onto my gaze.

The silence is suffocating, and every pair of eyes is on us. I don't know when Hunter woke up, but his eyes are burning holes in the side of my head, and thankfully, he has made Raya quiet.

'Kian,' I whisper, stepping forward, shaking my head. 'You can be good. Please. Let the past remain in the past, and walk away.'

'He won't walk away,' Kian hisses, pressing harder into Dante's throat, and Dante lets out a strangled sound. 'He has an obsession with me. He knows my weakness. He will not stop until I'm in the ground.'

Eli's words float through my mind. *You're his weakness.*

'Kian,' I plead, cautiously drawing closer to him, the pain of the poison hitting me with another wave that has my head swimming, and my muscles beginning to spasm. 'You can be good, and you can stop this, and let him go.'

Hesitation flickers across his face, and for a brief moment, I feel hopeful. And then that cruel smirk of his twists onto his lips. The one I despise.

'I never claimed to be a good man, Cora.'

He drives the blade through Dante's heart. The pain on his face is unbearable, and when he falls to the ground, tears spill down my cheeks.

All of the strength leaves me.

Dante's lifeless eyes stare up at the ceiling, and bile rises in my throat. Another day, another dead body. That seems to be my life now.

'I can't do this anymore,' I whisper, truly looking at him, and seeing the undeniable darkness shimmering in those eyes. 'Killing is second nature to you, and now you've turned me into a monster, too. I can't let that go. I can never forgive you for killing our mother. No wonder they wanted to end you. You're cruel, and unstoppable.'

He wanted to push me away. He's done it. He's really done it this time.

Kian wipes the blood off his dagger, taking his time, and I stare at him, waiting for him to dignify me with an answer. When he finally lifts his eyes to meet mine, he is smirking, looking far too pleased with himself.

And then he says the only words in the entire world that I never expected to ever come from his mouth.

'Who said your mother is dead?'

34

KIAN

The Enforcer

I STEP OVER DANTE'S BODY.

Casually, as I continue cleaning my daggers, and neatly pocketing them in their designated areas, an eerie silence filling the room. When I finally look up, Cora is gaping at me. Raya is as white as a ghost, Theo is scratching his head in confusion, and Hunter is looking between everyone like he is watching a tennis match, trying to figure out what the hell he missed while being temporarily out of action.

And then the poison reaches a point that makes Cora collapse.

She's in my arms before she hits the floor, and I carry her over to the lounge. Sliding to the floor, my back against it, I place her onto my lap, her eyes fluttering as she struggles to keep conscious.

'Don't you dare blood share with her and transfer that curse even more than you already have,' Raya hisses, pulling harshly on the rope that binds her to the metal ring it's wrapped around, but it doesn't budge. I compelled Theo to break Hunter's neck and tie the both of them with a magically enhanced rope I've had designed for special occasions such as this. Theo doesn't remember that I asked him to do this, however, and is probably wondering why the hell he temporarily killed his best friend. Though the way his eyes are watching me carefully makes me wonder what he knows.

Looking Raya in the eyes, I drag my fang down my wrist and

press it against Cora's lips. She glares at me, furious. Cora moans softly as the first few drops of blood trickle into her mouth, and then she is taking long, greedy gulps. My veins tingle, and I can *feel* the poison retracting.

'I'm not transferring the curse to her, you misguided twat,' I say dryly.

'Watch it,' Hunter snaps, and Theo tries to cover his snort with a very fake yawn, earning himself a withering glare from Hunter.

'Yes, she absorbs some of the repercussions of the curse, but it isn't transferring to her, and it will not kill her, or cause any serious harm.'

According to my witch friend, anyway. She has been doing quite a bit of research, and I've reached out and asked a few vampires about it, and they've backed it up.

'I don't believe a word out of your mouth!' Raya snarls.

'I don't care what you believe, doll. You're the least of my concerns.'

'You're on thin ice,' Hunter growls, eyes flashing with a familiar rage I am quite accustomed to.

'Oh.' I smirk, flashing my fangs at him. 'Am I? And what do you think you could do to me?'

Hunter doesn't rise to the bait, although I wish he would. I love tormenting him. He is so easy to rile up.

Cora wakes with a gasp, and I brush the hair out of her eyes. She gazes up at me, and I can sense her mind running wild. She grips my arms.

'Did you mean what you said?' she whispers, hands trembling. 'Is Mum alive?'

Dragging my thumb across her lower lip, I clear her skin, shifting her so that she is more comfortable. I nod.

'She is.'

*

No one has tried to kill me in the last hour, which is weird. I keep my eyes peeled though, never letting my guard down.

Turning into the street, I pull up at Cas's house. Cora hugs her arms around herself, still not quite feeling one hundred percent. Going to her, I place a hand on her back and rub soft circles into it. She is staring at the house blankly. She doesn't flinch away from me, or step out of my touch, which I take as a good sign.

She has gotten good at controlling her emotions. She is careful and guarded, which means she can focus during stressful moments, and keep her head during battles and attacks. It's a strength that doesn't come easily, and I admire that she has picked it up so well. Even dealing with the guilt and overwhelming feelings that come with all the things we have done, she compartmentalises it with a control not many possess.

Reluctantly, I pull my gaze from her when Hunter, Theo and Raya pull up behind us, exchanging weary glances amongst each other as they climb out of the car.

'I swear, if this is a trap . . .' Hunter breathes, glaring at me.

'You're the one who tried to kill me today, *fratello*.'

Before we left the house, Raya forced everyone to make a 'truce', which is comical because they were the ones intending to end my life today, but it is also fair, given the past. I conducted the experiment with Raya and Hunter all those months ago because I was curious about the bond, and wasn't able to find answers on my own. I do realise it was an extreme way to go about things, but *they* hunted *me* down, and led Dante straight to me. They obviously didn't know Dante was stalking them at the time, but ultimately, I needed to test the bond to its limit, and there was no other way to get the information I needed than to have everyone believe they were truly in danger. It's a long game I've been playing.

An image of the expression on my brother's face, and the way Raya's windpipe crushed under my fingertips, haunts me.

Swallowing down the bile rising in my throat, I push it all away. I can't feel guilty over that. I did them both a favour. She would have died if he didn't turn her, and the bond would have killed him, too. The experiment and turning her came as a package deal, and I don't regret it.

I hadn't had the intention of having Raya turned when I first started the experiment, but I knew she needed to become one. It was inevitable, so I just sped up the process. She is much safer as a vampire than not. Vampires who fall for humans and keep them human are deluding themselves. They will never be safe if they can't protect themselves.

Climbing the porch steps, I make a sweeping gesture with my hand. Cas has many houses scattered around that he moves to and from, but this is the one he has been at the most, given he has been holding my prisoner here.

'After you,' I say, fighting off a smirk, and being entirely unsuccessful.

'Fuck no,' Hunter counters, shooting a suspicious glare at me. 'You're going in first.'

'Suit yourself,' I shrug, pushing the door open.

Cas strolls around the corner, grinning at me. 'Oh. We have guests.' He flashes a smile at Hunter. 'Good to see you, Hunter.'

Hunter's lips spread into a thin line. This is the first time they are all seeing each other since Cas double-crossed them. Hunter reaching out to Cas to help find me couldn't have worked out better if I had planned it myself. When I had Cas befriend him, I never predicted it would lead to that, so it was a pleasant bonus.

'You two really are buddies, then,' he grunts, eyes switching between Cas and myself. 'That would have been good to know.'

'Apologies about that, my friend.' Cas smiles, not looking the slightest bit fazed that more than half the group hate him. 'Anywho, let's all move on and leave the past in the past.'

'Yeah,' Hunter scoffs, shaking his head, barely containing his rage.

'This way,' I say, walking past Cas, leading the group through the loungeroom.

The same guy who was here last time is yet again sprawled half-naked across the lounge, eyes closed, blood smeared down his neck and chest. Cas must like this one, as he has kept him around for a little while now. Raya wrinkles her nose at the sight, and Hunter touches her shoulder.

Pausing at the door, I turn, placing a hand on Cora's elbow. 'You good?'

Feeling the eyes of everyone in the room on us, I ignore them. It probably seems strange since I've gone out of my way to cut everyone off and show indifference, but at this stage of my life – and the limited time I have left – I can't be fucked to keep up with the act. I do care about Cora, and I know this day has been a lot for her, and it's all my doing.

'Yeah,' she murmurs. 'I don't believe this is really happening.'

Tucking a piece of her hair behind her ear, I tilt her chin up, forcing those haunting dark eyes to meet mine. 'I'll explain everything to you. I promise.'

Her eyes search mine, and I give her a brief nod. Accepting my words, she nods back, and I release her.

Pushing open the door to the bedroom where I keep their mother, I step inside, and the others follow. As we enter, she slowly sits up from the bed she's on, blinking at us. Raya sharply inhales, reaching for Hunter. Her fingers bunch up his shirt as she grips him. Theo's eyes are wide as he peers around the room, gauging everyone's reactions.

'Oh my God,' Raya blurts, her hands flying to her face as she releases a sob. She raises a shaky hand, which Hunter takes, steadying her, as if fearing she might collapse. Stumbling forward, she reaches for Maree, grabbing her hands. Maree stares down at their entwined hands, her brows creasing.

Cora is frozen. Her lips are parted, eyes wide, and she stares down at Maree, as if seeing a ghost. She swivels her gaze to mine, her eyes filling with tears, her brows pulling together as she tries to understand.

'She's alive,' she chokes out, staring at me in disbelief. 'She is really alive.'

I nod, and with no control over it, I reach out, touching her arm. My thumb strokes the material of her sleeve. I stare into her eyes, attempting to ground her, so she doesn't go into shock. After a moment, she pulls her gaze from me, staring down at Maree, who is still mutely staring around the room, looking dazed.

'Mum?' Cora whispers, dropping to her knees beside Raya, staring up at the woman she never thought she would see again.

Maree's forehead crumples as she looks straight at her.

'I'm sorry?' Their mother says, frowning, eyes flitting between us, before landing back on Cora. 'Who are you?'

It doesn't surprise me that their mother is confused. That's understandable.

'What's wrong with her?' Cora whispers, tears filling her eyes.

'Temporary memory loss,' I say dismissively. 'It'll wear off.' She's always seemed vague when I've seen her in the past, but it concerns me just how much she is today, as if she is completely blank. 'Maree,' I say in the tone I often use with her. 'I need you to think clearly, and remember.'

Maree has been facing temporary memory loss during her time here, but she has always been compelled to remember when I tell her to.

I stare at her, waiting.

She slowly blinks at me, looking unnervingly blank. I turn, poking my head out the door. She has never appeared this off before. A frown tugs at my lips.

'Cas,' I say.

'Yes?' he asks, appearing practically out of thin air.

'When was the last time she ate?'

'Um.' Cas pauses, raking a hand through his white-blond hair, making it stick up even more oddly than it was before. 'This morning, I think. When Sofia was here.'

Straightening, I stare at Cas, who tenses, frowning back at me.

'Sofia was here?' I question.

Cas nods. 'Yeah. I assumed you knew.'

'What did she do?' I demand.

Cas shrugs. 'She was in and out pretty quickly. I didn't really pay much attention.'

My stomach sinks. Sofia came here – again – without permission. What is she up to? My gut churns as worst-case scenarios flood my mind. I often believe the worst in a person, and this time, it's no different. When you expect less from people, it's less likely you'll get disappointed. I just didn't realise I needed to do that with Sofia.

This is why I don't fucking trust people.

'Fuck,' I growl, storming back into the room, swerving around Raya who has parked herself in front of her mother. 'Maree, do you know who you are?'

Everyone's eyes are on me, and I look down at the woman who is staring vacantly ahead.

'I can't remember anything,' she confesses. She finally meets my eyes. A face, so similar to Cora's and Raya's, lined with age, her hair having turned a little grey since her time here. She doesn't have the fire in her eyes like she used to. It's like . . . no one is home. 'Where am I? Who are you? Who are these other people?'

Running a hand down my face, I turn, throwing my fist straight through the wall. Sofia has erased their mother's memories.

The fucking bitch has betrayed me.

A few hours later, I'm pacing the room, and Cora is watching me, an expression on her face I can't quite decipher, and her feelings are even more muddled to try to work out.

Raya and Hunter are with Maree. They took her to Theo's house, making her comfortable, trying to go over things with her, all the while trying to keep her calm. I dragged a reluctant Cora back to her house.

'I'm confused, Kian,' Cora whispers, rubbing circles into her temples. 'Why have you done any of this?'

'I need to know,' I say, my fingers tapping restlessly against my thighs as I think, my mind racing, my self-control barely hanging on by a thread. I need to find Sofia and get things settled, but there is something deep inside me that can't walk away from Cora right now. 'There is something going on with your family, and I have been trying desperately to find answers about it.'

Looking weary, she raises a brow. 'Why did you convince me, and everyone else, that you killed my mother?'

'Because I couldn't give in to this,' I answer, throwing a hand between us. 'I needed you to hate me with every fibre of your being because I did not want you to see any decency in me.' I exhale, scrubbing my hand across my jaw. 'I didn't want to fall for you, or you to fall for me. It was the most effective way to kill whatever was happening between us.'

'Well,' she half-scoffs, half-laughs. 'It certainly worked.'

'Obviously. I'm good at what I do.'

'She looked dead . . .' She frowns, peering up at me. 'I saw the blood on her, and her head bent at an angle that wasn't natural.'

'Sofia cast an illusion over her. I wanted you to believe it.'

She shakes her head, staring at me, incredulous. 'I can't even wrap my head around any of this, but I have to know, what did you find out?' she asks. 'Is that why you kept her locked up all this time?'

'There was something strange about your mother's blood, and I couldn't figure out what. She was human, but her blood was . . . strange. And then so was your sister's.' I pause, trying to work out how to say what I want to say. 'It's impossible,' I explain, 'for both Hunter and I to have been drawn to two sisters and both bonded. Bonding is so rare that it is practically unheard of, and yet we have both done it. Seems weird, right?'

'But we haven't bonded,' Cora says, forehead crumpled in confusion, but I see a spark in her eyes. She has suspected it for a while. She has questioned her own sanity, her thoughts, her feelings. The thought of us being bonded is not new to her. It's clear in the way she hesitates, brows pulled together, her eyes staring hard into mine, as if she can see straight through me, and into my soul.

Chewing my lip, I continue pacing. 'We have, but the curse has hindered it, so it is not as strong. Fully formed, rather. Not like Hunter and Raya.'

Cora leans forward, digging her elbows into her thighs as she shakes her head, trying to absorb all of this. 'That can't be right.'

'It is.'

'It sort of makes sense,' she murmurs after a moment. 'There is an undeniable connection, and we both have tried everything to sever it. I've been thinking about this a lot. How I feel one way toward you, and then completely opposite the next. Back there . . . with those vampires . . . it was like something took over me. Your safety became my entire life's purpose.'

'Mmhmm,' I reply. 'The bond.'

'Did you find answers?'

'No. I have been researching it for months and months. Nothing is clear, but now, I'm wondering whether Sofia has been sabotaging me for some reason. Perhaps she doesn't want me to find out the truth. She has wiped your mother's memories clear to hide something from me. I need to track her down and find out what game she is playing.'

'We need to focus on getting my mother better!' Cora snaps. 'That should be your main concern right now.'

'My main concern?' I respond, whirling around to face her, incredulous. '*You* are my main concern. Your health, your safety, your wellbeing. That is all in the hands of witches right now. Any moment, I could drop dead, and take you with me,' I snap, glaring at her. 'That's what Hunter and Raya are for. They can help your mother right now, because we need answers, Cora.'

Her mouth drops open, fury, shock, and rage rippling across her features as she glares daggers at me. 'My mother is in this state because of *you*. You need to take responsibility for that, and you owe me a big fucking apology!'

I crack my neck, trying to release the pressure and tension accumulating from my shoulders, trying to keep calm. Darkness caresses me, and the urge to give in to it has me quaking.

'I don't have time for this. I need to find Sofia.'

'Go then.'

Stalking toward her, I lean forward, bracing my hands either side of the bed. She glares at me, visibly shaking.

'I'd really like to, but I am incapable of leaving unless I know you're okay.'

'I'm fine,' she says snarkily. 'Go. You have certainly kept me in the dark for long enough, why not continue to do so? Who cares about me and what I want?'

'I fucking do,' I growl. 'And I need you to understand that this is really important, and that your mum is in safe hands. Wouldn't you rather she have someone like Raya helping her right now, over me? Hm?'

She narrows her eyes. 'This changes nothing. I can't forgive you for anything. Bond or not, it's never going to work.'

Exhaling sharply, I drop my head, gathering my thoughts. My head feels light, and my gut is churning uncomfortably, like I might throw up any second. The skin across my chest feels tight and prickly.

'Just . . . let it go, Cora. I don't have time for this.'

Tears fill her eyes and her mouth twists into an angry scowl. 'Are you serious, Kian?' She steps forward, shoving me backwards in the process, jabbing a finger toward me. '*Let this go?* You made me think you killed my mother! You've hidden everything important from me, taking away *my* right to know about my life, and I should just forget about it, because you don't want to waste your precious time explaining anything to me?'

She's breathing hard, and I don't move, and I say nothing.

Dragging my eyes to hers, I stare at her. With a steadying breath, my eyes pierce hers. 'I need you to remember.'

She jolts backward, landing on her back, and I study her as she shakes, her eyes fluttering before they close. All the memories I've hidden from her are bombarding her.

Closing my eyes, I can see them.

She leans in close, studying me, as I tell her about my family. Her pretty smile, the way we can't stop staring at each other.

Us lying together on the floor of her room, her tucked into my side, as I tell her all about my relationship with Hunter, what I've done to protect him, how I convinced him I hated him, how I have to do the same to her. About how I run a business that saves vampires, and that I have enemies because of this. A few of the tender moments we shared where I completely let my control go.

I see myself through her eyes, and my heart squeezes. She adores me as much as I adore her, and we have both been fighting this for so long.

'I can't walk away from you, but I can't let you in.'

Reaching out, I stroke her cheek, and the spasming in her body eventually stops. Her eyes snap open, and she sits up, blinking at me in shock.

'Do you remember?' I whisper, searching her eyes.

'Kian,' she whispers, tears filling her eyes. 'I wish . . .' Her eyes close briefly, tears slipping down her cheeks. 'I wish you hadn't done that to me.' Her eyes snap back open, her jaw ticking. 'You took that right away from me. You should not decide what I get to know, and what I don't.'

Swallowing, I nod, looking down. 'I know.'

'You hid the sweetest parts of yourself from me.'

'I know, *mio tesoro*.' Swallowing, I press my forehead against hers. 'I'm sorry. I know I made you believe it, but I would never kill anyone that is close or important to you. I hope you know that.' Breathing her in, pressing my hands to her face. 'I wish there had been another way I could have made you hate me that hadn't involved your mother, but it was the best way to allow me to get answers, while also keeping her safe.'

Linking her fingers behind my neck, she kisses me. It's soft, warm, and perfect. She touches her hand to my cheek.

'There's so much I'm feeling right now, and so many things I need to say . . .' She exhales, shaking her head, her eyes two endless pools of darkness. 'But you need to go. You're sick, and it's getting worse. We can discuss this later. Go find Sofia, and figure out what is going on. I'm going to go check in on the others.'

Rolling her lips inward, she inhales, as if steadying herself. 'Call for me, if you need me.'

'I will.'

Pushing back, I turn, feeling an immense weight off my shoulders. She knows everything now, and finally, I can let her in. Like I've been wanting to for so long.

'Kian,' she calls after me. I turn back to her. She places a hand over her heart. 'Be safe. Come back to me.'

Smiling, I nod. 'Always.'

35

CORA

The Fighter

I STARE AT KIAN like it's the first time I've ever seen him.

With the memories back in my mind – where they should be – it's like everything I've thought up until now has been a total lie.

It has been.

Kian presses two fingers to his lips and then moves them forward, as if sending the kiss to me, and my heart falls to my feet. That gesture. One I didn't remember existed until now. The gesture he does to me when what he is saying is real.

He disappears through the door and I hang my head in my hands, the tears I've been holding in spilling down my cheeks.

He kept everything from me.

He made himself a monster so that I wouldn't love him.

But he isn't a monster.

He never has been.

He might be more morally grey than not, but he is nowhere near as horrible and disturbed as I had been led to believe. Like always, everything he does is deliberate, and cunning.

What a lonely life he has chosen to live, but that's all about to change.

Because I remember now, and I will *never* forget again.

*

Mum is finally asleep.

She's been restless and confused. Raya can't understand what is going on, and is trying to force photos and memories onto Mum, as if she will have a light-bulb moment and it will all come rushing back.

Like it did for me . . .

Hunter is sitting in the corner by himself, staring at the wall. I info-dumped a whole hell of a lot onto him about Kian, and he has gone into this weird, quiet state. He hasn't moved a muscle for about an hour now. His mind must be reeling.

'You know . . .' Hunter says, and Raya finally steps away from Mum, heaving a sigh. Dropping onto the spot beside me on the lounge, we both look over to Hunter, who is twisting his fingers, eyes still staring ahead in that vacant way they have been. 'It makes sense.'

'What does?' I ask.

'I always thought my brother had a very particular way he killed, and he would leave a trail behind, almost as if he wanted to be discovered. I always thought it was a weird thing in his mind how he wanted to risk getting caught. To show fearlessness. To invite people to chase him, because he craved that kind of drama and chaos. It never made sense how he would leave a trail of bodies, and yet he could never be found. Almost like he was in multiple places at one time.' Hunter brings his hand to his jaw, rubbing along it, frowning. 'And that's because the mark he leaves on his victims, the one Raya has, is not just his. It's his entire company's symbol. Because he has been finding and saving vampires, and he leaves a trail of dead bodies behind to show others – the witches, vampire hunters, whoever else is planning these kidnappings – that it was *his* corporation that shut it down.' Shaking his head, he breathes a laugh. 'All this time, I thought he was soulless, killing people mindlessly. For fun. I never knew he was saving lives, too.'

Raya stares down at the mark on her wrist. 'Then that means this is not actually a sign that I was meant to be his intended victim,' she says slowly, rubbing her thumb across the half-crescent moon shape that scars her skin. 'This is a sign of protection.'

My eyes move down to my wrist, where I have the same mark.

'But he killed you,' Hunter murmurs. 'He ended your human life in such a brutal way, and he chained me up. Why did he orchestrate it like that?'

'He needed to experiment with the bond. There was no one else to test it on.'

Hunter grunts. 'That's one way to test it.'

'He wanted to understand it. He suspected we'd bonded, but ours was so different from yours and Raya's.'

'And he wants to know why we have bonded with two girls from the same family when a bond is so unbelievably rare, hardly anyone knows anything about them.'

'Yeah.'

'And?' Hunter questions, seeming to take all this info in stride, even though it is seriously overwhelming. Theo gave up understanding and disappeared to get a drink. He hasn't returned, so I imagine he has ended up in a bar somewhere making out with someone. That's how he deals with his problems. 'What has he found out?'

'That's what the witch and Mum were supposed to tell him, but now Mum has no memory, and Kian is tracking down the witch to find out what the hell is going on.'

'In what world does my brother not hate me?' Hunter muses, shaking his head, somehow looking in wonder but doubtful at the same time.

Raya smiles softly. 'So everything we have ever learnt about him has been a lie.'

'Pretty much.' I nod. 'It's all his own doing though, so don't feel too bad.'

'Well. He still snapped my windpipe, so I don't know if I will ever truly warm up to him, but I'm understanding him a lot better now.' Raya flashes a smile at me, and I smile back. 'He's totally messed up, though.'

'Oh yeah,' I agree, the corners of my mouth lifting.

'In a way, I get why he has done everything the way he has, but it's still bloody twisted,' Hunter remarks, sighing. 'Could have saved himself a lot of trouble if he'd just let people in and been honest, but I understand it was to keep everyone safe and out of harm's way. But you can only push people away for so long.'

'Yeah,' I mumble.

A heavy silence fills the room, everyone wrapped up in their thoughts. The sky darkens outside, and I lift my eyes to look out the window, wondering where Kian is, and how everything is going. I hope he can find answers soon, so we can restore Mum's memories, lift Kian's curse, and try to make life somewhat normal, but I know it won't be that easy. It never is.

'I don't know about you guys, but I'm wrecked.' Raya yawns, pushing to her feet. 'I feel mentally drained.'

'Me too,' Hunter mutters.

I unloaded everything onto them. The secrets of Kian, the curse, our attachment to each other, his hunt for the witch, and everything else in between. No wonder why they seemed exhausted. It's a lot for the mind to process.

'You're staying here, right?' Raya asks, as I stand and make my way to the door, where my shoes are.

'Yeah I'll come back here, but I need to get a few things.'

'What things?' she inquires, arching her dark brow.

'My cat.'

Raya laughs. 'Of all the bizarre things you've told me since

I've been home, going back to your place for your cat is honestly low on the list at this point. Do you want me to come with you?'

'Nah, I'll be fine. I'll be there and back before you know it.'

'Okay,' she mumbles, fighting off another yawn.

Stepping outside, I glance up at the moon peeking from behind the clouds. I instantly feel better as my skin is exposed to it. I don't know what it is about walking in the moonlight, but it always feels like it's rejuvenating a part of me. Like recharging my batteries.

The moment I open my front door, I feel uneasy. My skin prickles, and my eyes swing around the room. I jump in alarm when I see Mya sitting cross-legged on my lounge, tears running down her face.

'My God, Mya, you scared the shit out of me!' I exclaim. 'How the hell did you get in here?' My eyes turn to the deadbolted front door in alarm, wondering if I had somehow forgotten to lock it. Although vampires can get in easily enough, it certainly shouldn't have been possible for a human to just walk on in. 'What's wrong?'

'I had a huge fight with my family,' she whispers. 'And you're the only person I felt I could come to. I haven't been truthful with you though, and you're going to hate me for it, but I need to tell you anyway. To warn you . . .'

With my eyes trained on her, I approach cautiously, lowering onto my knees in front of her, squeezing her hands in mine. Her skin feels cold, and the hairs on my arm rise in response.

'What's going on?' I ask.

'I've been a terrible friend to you, and I'm really sorry.'

I laugh. 'Mya, you're the most normal thing in my life. If anything, I'm not truthful with you. Whatever is going on, I'm sure it's not nearly as absurd as the week I've had.'

'I've been running from something for a long time, and it's caught up to me.'

I stare at her. 'Running from what?'

'My family. My lineage. Everything I'm supposed to be.'

'I'm not understanding.'

Huffing out a breath, she tilts her head back, staring at the ceiling, as if looking me in the eyes is too difficult for her.

'I need to tell you the reason why I had a big falling out with my family, and everything has been really tense between us.'

'Okay . . .'

'I didn't want to be a part of the coven, or practise any kind of witchcraft, so they kicked me out.'

My mouth forms an 'O' as I gape at her. 'This can't be right. I'd know if you're a witch.'

'My whole family is a part of a coven, and I refused to have any part of it, and since I haven't been practising, my body sometimes . . . forces it onto me, and things happen out of my control. I'm extremely terrified and vulnerable when it happens, so, I come to you . . .'

Frowning, I stare at her as she finally lowers her gaze to meet mine. 'You mean, when you're upset?'

'Er – sort of.'

'I'm not following.'

'It might be easier if I show you.'

Scrambling to my feet, I step back, as she does the same.

And then I blink, and Midnight is sitting at my feet.

I inhale sharply, stepping back in shock. She blinks up at me.

'Oh fuck no,' I say, stumbling back, gripping the door frame for support.

A second later, Mya is standing in front of me, no cat in sight.

'Yeah,' she says casually, shrugging, as if being able to transform is completely normal. 'So. That's me.'

My mouth opens and closes for several moments as I try to comprehend what the hell I just witnessed and what it means.

After the day I've had, I feel dizzy. Leaning onto the wall behind me, I gaze at her.

'Say something,' she pleads.

'You've been spying on me.'

'No!' she quickly says, holding out her hands, attempting to appear as non-threatening as possible. 'I haven't been spying on you. I was just scared and didn't know where to go.'

'If that was true, you would have come to me for help. You clearly know what I am, and that I was capable of helping you.'

'I didn't want him to know,' she whispers, tears sliding down her flushed cheeks.

'Who?'

'Kian! I didn't want him to know I was a witch. He would want to use me.'

'Oh my God,' I whisper. 'You know everything about me. About my life. You fucking wormed your way inside here, spied on me, betrayed my trust. You showed up here, crying, and I stupidly always let you in and gave you advice!' Turning around, I slam my palm into the wall, and it shakes on impact. 'Fuck! Why is no one fucking truthful in this goddamn town?'

'I'm so, so sorry, Cora,' she sobs, barely able to draw a breath as she cries. 'I promise I didn't mean to invade your privacy.'

'What the hell do you think you were doing then?' I hiss, seething.

'I wasn't thinking about any of that! I was scared and needed to protect myself!'

'Get the fuck out of my house!' I bark at her, pointing to the door.

'Cora . . . please . . .' She chokes on her breath, hastily wiping at her cheeks. 'I came here to warn you about something I heard —'

My door bangs open, and Eli stands there. Someone steps out from behind him, completely shrouded in darkness. They wave their hand around, and a ripple in the air causes everything inside me to tense. My fangs drop down as I snarl, my eyes darting between them, trying to figure out what the hell is going on.

Mya gasps, shrinking into her cat form at the sight of the people in front of us. I'm distracted by her making a run for it, and by the time I realise what is in the figure's hand, it's too late.

They aim the gun right at my chest, pulling the trigger.

There's a sharp sting, and everything is black before I hit the ground.

36

KIAN

The Enforcer

KICKING OPEN THE DOOR, I stride inside.

Since coming to Sofia's house earlier and finding the place deserted, I tracked all over town trying to find any sign of where she had gone, but turned up empty-handed. Now, I'm back at the house, and everything is gone.

Rage fills me. I trusted Sofia, and I do *not* choose to give out my trust lightly. She betrayed me. She is letting me die. She has sat by, watching this curse slowly destroy me, and has done everything she can to prevent me finding the witch that can undo it.

Turning to the few plants that she left here, I kick them violently, splitting the pots. Dirt spills across the carpet and I pick up the pieces, hurling them toward the wall. A furious scream leaves me as I let the darkness pour out of me. I throw and break anything I can find until I fall to my knees, weak and drained. My stomach clenches as I heave. Vomit explodes from my mouth, spraying across the floor. A thick wall of blackness, looking like death in liquid form.

Collapsing onto my back, I shiver, twitching.

With shaking hands, I reach for my necklace, clutching it.

'*Mio tesoro,*' I whisper, desperate for her comforting touch and steady hands. Those pretty, demonic eyes that seem to fill me with warmth and ground me in a way nothing else ever has. I crave her to be close to me.

I squeeze the necklace tighter, so tight, I fear it might snap right off. After a few long minutes, I push myself into a seated position, staring down at the necklace.

Something is wrong.

With my energy depleting faster than I can keep up with, I stagger to standing, forcing my feet to propel me out the door. Tripping down the stairs, I collapse, but the feel of the moon on my skin makes me feel a lot better.

After a minute, I stand once more, and make my way to Cora's house.

The door is open, and when I step inside, I can sense the eerie coldness that comes from witches. The smell of magic is in the air. Someone has cast a spell here, and I'm guessing it has severed my connection to Cora somehow. I can still feel her there – the bond is too strong even for a witch to overcome – but the necklace is not working, and the sense of her feels almost muted somehow. Like I can vaguely feel she is there, but I can't reach her.

A note sits on the floor, next to the spray of blood up the wall.

My upper lip curls in fury as I stumble over to it, swiping it off the floor.

YOUR TIME IS ALMOST UP, KIAN.
WE HOPE YOU FIND HER BEFORE IT'S TOO LATE . . .

My hand trembles as I scrunch it.

I'm too weak for any of this to be happening right now, but the bond courses through me with as much strength as it has left, making me turn and exit the house with a briskness my body shouldn't be able to endure, but somehow it does.

Barging through the front door, I find Theo with a girl wrapped around him.

'Well, hello there, Maker,' Theo says, drawing back, flashing me a grin as he gently lowers her back onto the table behind him. 'Care to join me?'

'Move,' I grunt.

Theo stands immediately, stepping away from the girl. She has a blissful smile on her face which widens considerably when her eyes rake over me. I don't look at anything except the vein in her neck. Yanking her to me, I drive my fangs into her neck and she screams, the high-pitch of it making my blood curdle.

I take as much as I can handle and drop her back onto the lounge, feeling incredibly unsatisfied, but thankfully stronger than a minute earlier. She chokes out a sob as she reaches for her neck, blood running down her skin.

'Leave,' I command. 'Forget about all of this.'

Nodding, the girl clambers to her feet, quickly yanking her dress down before sprinting out the door. Theo pouts, staring after her.

'Why'd you do that? I was having fun.'

'Get the others,' I order, my voice thick with authority.

Sensing my untamed fury, he swiftly leaves. I'm assuming they'd be awake after that scream, but they might assume Theo is simply being Theo. A moment later, Theo emerges with Raya and Hunter behind him.

'They've taken her,' I bark at them, my hands shaking as I tug my hair, pacing back and forth, trying to get my thoughts in order. 'The curse is close to finishing me, my strength is all but gone. I need you to come with me, and get her back.'

'Slow down,' Hunter says, stepping toward me. 'Someone took Cora? What happened?'

'The witch I was working with has turned on me. She wiped Maree's memory, and she disappeared. My necklace – it's linked to Cora's – is not working. She made them, so she has the ability to disable them, too. She must be working with the witch who cursed me, and now they've taken Cora to lure me to them. They want to finish me.'

Raya's eyes widen and she looks at Hunter in alarm. Hunter nods, always the logical one in a time of crisis.

'Where is she?' he asks.

I shake my head. 'I don't know for sure, but I'm hoping if I can go around town, I might be able to sense her if I'm close enough. The bond is still there, it's just . . . quiet.' Exhaling, I turn, glaring at Theo. 'Put some fucking pants on, would you?'

'Oh,' Theo says, looking down, as if only then realising he is basically naked. 'Right. Forgot about that.'

'Okay, well, let's think this through,' Raya says, pulling her hair back from her face and braiding it so quickly, her fingers are a blur. 'We don't know who exactly has her, or how many of them are there. Being witches, they could have all sorts of spells, hexes, enchantments spread all through the place. Will we need weapons? Will they even be useful? We need a plan.'

'Find wherever it is, get inside, and kill every fucking one of them,' I growl, cracking my knuckles.

'I like that idea.' Theo nods.

Raya ignores me, turning to Hunter. 'Hunter, what's the best way to get in there?'

He chews the edge of his thumb as he looks at the floor, brows dipped in concentration. 'It depends on the location.'

'Let's get moving. I'm running out of time, and I have no clue what they are doing to her. Let's just hope I can find her through sensing her proximity.'

Raya looks concerned, but nods. 'Okay.'

Everyone is dressed and ready to go within five minutes. As I descend the stairs, a wave of nausea hits me, and I stagger to the side, gripping my head. Hunter is in front of me, his hand touching my shoulder, and it's his touch that stops me toppling over. We both glance up at each other in surprise, and he steps back, dropping his hand.

I haven't allowed myself to think of Hunter as my brother for a long time. Not in the way I should, anyway. I've forced myself to hate him, and after a while, I began to believe that I did, but all of that just seems pointless now. I'm too far gone with Cora, so I can't live the solitary life anymore, and frankly, I don't really want to.

'We'll get her back,' he says firmly, nodding at me, eyes intensely staring into mine, as if he is able to see right through me.

Jaw clenched, I nod.

Red Thorne is busy tonight. There are people *everywhere*. They all appear to be dressed in spooky costumes, like someone is throwing a Halloween party, but it isn't Halloween. The black, brick buildings cast an ominous feel over the street, and the air is crackling with tension, and the faint hint of magic.

When a group spills out from a small diner, I step forward, yanking one to me.

'Where are you all going, and why are you dressed like that?' I demand, pressing a little too tightly on the boy's arm, knowing it will leave a bruise.

Wincing, he tries to pull his arm free, but the moment his eyes hook onto mine, the compulsion hits him like a wave. He straightens, face morphing into a blank stare as he gazes at me.

'The bar, Code Red. It's a party they're throwing. The owner of the bar sent out flyers around town earlier today. It's to celebrate "the capture of his greatest treasure".' The boy successfully yanks his arm out of my grip, and turns to follow his friends.

A low growl emits from me.

My weakness. Mio tesoro.

Swallowing, I turn to face the others, cheek spasming as I grapple with my self-control. Theo stares after the group, while Hunter and Raya exchange a glance, looking concerned and determined. They face me, and I nod at them.

'Looks like we know where she is.'

37

CORA

The Fighter

EVERYTHING HURTS.

The first thing I hear is the loud thumping of music, some techno sound that seems to be blasting from speakers on an upper level. The next thing I notice is the damp smell of the air, as if I'm deep underground somewhere that hasn't breathed fresh air in months, or perhaps years.

Footsteps bang overhead, loud chatter, and the occasional clink of a glass. Forcing my eyes open, I sit up, staring around me. With the way my head is pounding, it feels like the music is screeching inside my head.

My fingers fumble to my chest, and I look down, seeing the bullet still jammed inside me. Gritting my molars, I sink my fingers into my flesh and bite down hard on my tongue to stop myself crying out as I find the bullet and pull it out. It drops to the floor with a clatter, rolling away from me.

The ground is cold, harsh concrete, and drops of blood are everywhere; given the state of my clothes, I imagine they are mine.

Panic washes through me, and I quickly reach for my necklace, but my fingers enclose empty air. My stomach hollows out, before I quickly remember that he will find me, because of the bond. Whatever happens, Kian always comes for me. He always finds me.

'Hey, you're awake.'

My head jerks up as Eli strolls into the room, hands in his pockets. He grins at me, looking like he is enjoying seeing me sitting on the ground in a cage. Metal bars stand between us, and I am also shackled to the floor. How I am chained to the floor for the second time in a week is beyond me.

'Of course you're here,' I mutter. 'You just keep turning up.'

'Yeah, that's me.'

'Why are you here?' I ask, arching a brow. 'What's in it for you?'

The corner of his mouth lifts, his smile offering a casual bravado that is asking for trouble. There is being confident – like Kian, and Theo – and there's this. A false sense of entitlement. It will be his undoing.

'They've promised me something.'

I try to keep the bark of laughter that is threatening to release at bay. Of course they did, and of course he blindly accepted it. Humans, they can be so painfully naive. I should know better than anyone.

'And? What is it?'

His smile widens. 'They're giving me a gift.'

'A gift?' I echo.

'Yes.'

'What kind of gift?'

'A supernatural one.'

'For fuck's sake, Eli, no need to be cryptic. Just tell me what it is.'

'They're giving me exceptional health, and strength.'

I blink at him. 'What?'

'You wanted to know. There it is.'

'So . . . you're becoming a vampire?' I frown. 'That seems . . . er . . . counterproductive to everything you've all been doing.'

He has the audacity to roll his eyes. 'No. They're giving me some vampire gifts, but I'm not becoming one.'

'That's not possible.'

'Oh, honey,' he laughs, sounding condescending as hell, making my hands curl furiously around the bars in front of me. 'You have no idea what these witches are up to. What they can do. What they can offer to people. The things they have been able to . . . manipulate.'

'Sounds like they're feeding you a tonne of bullshit and you're eating out of the palm of their hand.'

He shrugs. 'I wouldn't expect you to understand. You're on the wrong side of the war.'

I scoff. 'War? I never asked to be in anything of the sort.'

'Sure you didn't.'

I exhale, growing tired of Eli, and this entire conversation.

'So, what's next?' I ask, leaning back onto my hands, rolling my shoulders to release the slight stiffness in them. I've been without blood for a while and my body is feeling a little achy. 'Wait for Kian to kick the door down and rescue me? Your little witch friends are going to try to kill him?'

'They won't just *try*,' Eli answers, slinking toward the bars and leaning on them, smirking down at me as his eyes not-so-subtly land on the chains on my wrists. 'They *will* kill him.'

'Ah,' I say, nodding.

He quirks an eyebrow. 'You don't seem to be bothered by that.'

I smile. 'I wish them luck. They're going to need it.'

'Yeah?' Eli laughs, looking amused. 'You think one vampire – on the brink of death – is going to take on an entire coven of angry witches?'

'He's done it before.'

'Not this coven.' Eli smirks, and the confidence of him makes me laugh. His eyes snap to mine as he scowls at my amusement.

With a speed I've mastered due to much training, I snap the chains from my wrist with an expert manoeuvre, and I reach through the bars before he has time to even hear the chains hitting the floor. My fingers curl around his neck and I pull him roughly forward, his face smashing into the bars. He screams as blood pours down his face.

Footsteps thunder down the stairs and I grin, digging my fingers into his neck, tearing the skin.

'Should I wait and let him kill you, or should I get it over and done with?' I laugh, sounding a little manic as I press my forehead into the bar, running a tongue up the side of his face, collecting his blood.

'Get her off me!' he bellows, desperately trying to get out of my grip, and I further sink my fingers into him, watching the blood spurt out of the slits I've created.

A witch flings her hand out, spraying my face with silver, and my grip tightens as I hold my ground. My flesh burns and sizzles, but it's a pain I'm accustomed to. My grin widens as my skin melts, and I meet their eyes.

'It's going to take more than that to hurt me,' I sneer. 'Kian created me, and you best not underestimate him, or me.'

My hand closes around Eli's throat. His muffled, strangled cry fills the room and then a witch shouts something incoherent. Vines twist around my hands, thorns piercing my skin, and they rip my hands back, forcing me to release him.

Eli crumples to the floor, gasping, and the witch beside him gapes in horror, stumbling back at the sight of the blood spilling from him. Raising my bloodied hand to my mouth, I lick it clean, staring her straight in the eyes. Calmly, I brush away the silver, feeling myself heal as Eli's blood infiltrates my system, plucking the vines off my hands. My skin is blistered and burnt from them, but they begin to heal.

'You're a demon,' she hisses, her heart thundering wildly in her chest. The sound is delicious. 'You're just like him.'

'Thank you,' I say, and she shoots me a cold look as she assists Eli to his feet. His jaw trembles, his eyes narrowing into hateful slits as he glowers at me. Gone is the cocky boy who I enjoyed having banter with. His true colours are on full display, and he is just as ugly as my gut feeling was telling me. 'He will be happy to hear that.'

The witch helping Eli spits at me, but it doesn't make it past the bars. I finally tear my eyes off Eli's bloodied wound, releasing a sharp bark of laughter, and it sounds dark, and wicked, and so much like Kian that she backs up further, looking over her shoulder. Another witch stands there, studying me with her head slightly tilted. She doesn't seem as terrified as the one in front of her and, instantly, I can tell she is far more powerful, and perhaps could be the one who cursed Kian, but it's difficult to know for sure.

Stepping closer, I wrap my hands around the bars, and begin to pull. After a few seconds, one of the poles bends. The witch before me looks like she might faint, and the other appraises me with narrowed eyes.

'He will come for her,' the scared witch says, turning to face the other, her hair a pretty auburn colour. 'Is everything ready?'

The woman steps down, eyes piercing mine. She has honey-coloured hair, and dark-brown eyes. She nods slowly, still not taking her eyes off me as she edges toward me, chin jutted out as she surveys me, and the damage I did to Eli, who is still coughing and spluttering, desperately trying to place pressure on the wound.

'Yes. I'm ready,' she says.

'Sofia, is it?' I question, realising who it is, now that she is closer. We haven't met, but Kian has told me bits and pieces about her, now that my memories are back where they belong.

'You've heard of me?' She smiles, her mouth twitching slightly. I can't tell if that pleases her, or if she is annoyed about the fact. Maybe she wishes I knew nothing about her so I'd be completely unprepared for what she may throw at me.

'As you've heard of me.'

'Mm.' She nods, growing silent, but her eyes continue to track every movement of mine. It reminds me of how Kian watches people, studying everything there is to know about them.

'Were you always planning to stab him in the back, or did the opportunity arise sometime during?' I ask sweetly, yanking once more on the bar, and it makes a horrible creaking sound as it bends further.

'Always the plan.' She eyes me for another moment, before her gaze drops to Eli.

'Was he always going to be collateral?' I question. 'I almost got him.'

She shrugs. 'There is always collateral in war.'

'Seems you are no better than Kian.'

Her mouth twists into a scowl as more footsteps descend the stairs. Three more witches enter, and the air crackles.

'He's here,' one of them squeaks, eyes wide.

Sofia flicks a hand to me, and I'm launched backward. Snarling, I rush forward, and hit an invisible barrier. I'm knocked back into the wall, hitting my head so hard, I see stars. Blinking, I try to rid myself of the dots, but my head pulses, and the magic in the air is making me feel nauseous.

Screams erupt from the top of the stairs, and then a dead body slides down them. A man. Whether he was just someone meant to guard the door, or if he is in on this, I'm uncertain, but either way, he didn't last long.

A blur of movement captures my attention, and then there is a blood-curdling scream as Hunter appears, his arm wrapping around one of the witches, knocking her unconscious instantly. Her heartbeat falters, and I realise his attack was a little more precise than I thought. It was made to look like she has just gone unconscious, when in fact, she's dead.

Hunter has a hard look of determination on his face as he sweeps around the room. The witch who stopped me attacking Eli twists her hands, encasing Hunter in the same snake-like vines she tied me in.

He slashes through them, lunging to her, but the vines multiply each time he breaks one apart, constricting around him like a snake. Hissing, he tries to pull them off, and using his lapse of focus, the witch pins him against the wall with some sort of magic that I can't see, though the air around him is shimmering, indicating there is something holding him.

Raya appears next, rushing to help Hunter, when the witch begins striding toward her.

'Raya!' I scream, banging against the invisible barrier. 'Watch out!'

She swings around and ducks, missing a bolt of magic that has exploded toward her. Rolling, she's back on her feet. As if my shouting jolted Eli back to reality, he makes a pained moaning sound.

'You bitch,' Eli snarls, staggering to his feet, eyes on me. For a moment, I'd totally forgotten about him. Reaching for the gun at his side, he turns to aim it at me. Those vicious vines find their way to me again, curling around my arms and my neck, locking me into place.

Eli's expression tightens in rage as he raises his arm, the gun pointing at my chest. I can tell by the way all the witches are watching him, there is something significant about this gun. It's designed to kill vampires, not only wound them, like the last one had been.

His finger curls around the trigger. Raya spins, noticing the gun, her eyes following the path between it and me, and a cry of panic leaving her when she realises I'm being held by the vines, just like Hunter is.

A loud crash upstairs has both the witches glancing that way, and Raya strikes.

She moves in front of Eli, slamming the palm of her hand against the gun, sending it skittering across the floor.

Eli freezes, his eyes blinking rapidly, locking eyes with me over the top of Raya's head before he looks down at his chest. A gaping hole is there as Raya steps back, his heart clutched in her hand.

He collapses with a hollow *thump*, and Raya stumbles back, hands trembling.

The witch who has control over the vines throws her hands out to Raya, and the scream that leaves my sister's mouth makes my blood run cold. Her screams ring in my ears as she drops to the floor, convulsing, blood smeared across her as she flails, trying to remove something I can't see.

Hunter is pinned against the wall in a similar position to mine, and he snarls in fury, watching his bonded being tortured right in front of his eyes.

A loud crack echoes through the room and one of the witches falls to the ground, her head bent at a horrible angle, her now-lifeless eyes gazing ahead. Theo smiles around the room, looking rather pleased with himself.

'Who's next?' He grins.

Sofia snarls at him, shouting words I can't decipher, and Theo clutches his head, falling to the ground, releasing a devastating sound that makes my insides curl.

Raya, Hunter, and Theo, all down.

But where is Kian?

'Where is he?' Sofia snaps, whirling around to face the others.

Another witch appears at the steps, practically tripping down them. 'All the witches upstairs are dead. He's here, but I can't find him!'

Sofia releases an enraged sound, and my body stiffens as her magic seems to suck the air out of the room. My head is swimming, and my stomach churns. The screams from Raya echo around my head, making me feel dizzy, and light-headed.

The vines bite into my flesh, eating away at it, and I try my hardest to stay still, as it seems they attack harder the more I move.

'Keep looking!' she snaps, baring her teeth. 'Find him before he kills you, too!'

Gulping, the man turns, rushing out, and then there is an ear-splitting scream moments before he is launched back down the stairs. Everyone goes still as we wait to see if Kian is going to appear.

Sofia's phone rings, and everyone in the room jumps, Raya's wailing finally subsiding to an exhausted, soft groan.

Sofia's cold, withering glare swivels to me, her upper lip trembling in rage as she pulls the phone from her pocket. She answers it, and although she doesn't put it on speaker, every one of us vampires can hear it perfectly despite the raging music above us.

'Sofia,' Kian drawls. 'Been trying to get a hold of you all day.'

'Where are you?' she asks, sounding much calmer than she looks. Although she appears in control, the other witches around her look pale and distraught, struggling to hold whichever vampire they have while keeping their eyes trained on the stairs.

'You have something of mine,' Kian says, tone dripping with indignation. 'I'd like it back. Preferably in one piece.'

Sofia scoffs, whipping her head around to look at me, those dark eyes of her scrutinising me, as if expecting me to break free from her invisible barrier and lunge at her. Tempting my luck, I try to push through it, but it's like trying to penetrate a metal door.

'Come get her,' she hisses.

'I will,' Kian replies conversationally. 'But first, I'd like to know what caused all this. Why double-cross me? What's your involvement in it all?'

'My family has a long history with Aithan, and we thought ending his life would be the end of the reign of terror he bestowed on us, but no . . .' She trails off, anger curling around each word, making them sharper and firmer with each breath. 'You took over for him, and you killed my sister.'

Ice filters in my veins when I hear Kian's dark laughter bubble through the speaker.

'My bad.'

Sofia's hand trembles with rage as she holds the phone to her ear, eyes darting around the room.

'I will fucking kill her, Kian,' Sofia screams into the phone, magic crackling the air around her, and a whimper escapes Raya as the witch twists her hand, causing more cuts to slice across her skin. I run forward and growl furiously when I hit the invisible barrier. 'Come to me *now*.'

'Answer this first,' Kian continues, tone as mild and carefree as ever. He has an incredible gift for sounding completely at ease in the most chaotic of situations. 'Did you ever find out the answer to their family blood, or did you never intend to find out, and instead send me on a wild goose chase and drag it out long enough that the curse ended me?'

She swallows, eyes moving to the ceiling, as if she is trying to see through it, to determine whether he is inside the building or not.

'Answer me, and I will come to you,' he presses.

Her jaw clenches. 'Many years ago, vampires were rampant, killing off hundreds of humans, witches, anything they could get their fangs into. A few witch families got together, casting a spell on some of the humans' blood. Making them so incredibly sweet, it would be impossible for vampires not to be drawn to them.'

A loud clatter has everyone jumping. As if something was knocked over. A distraction? Or is there someone else up there he is fighting?

Sofia grits her teeth, struggling with the amount of magic she is using as she whirls around.

'And?' Kian presses, not sounding out of breath at all, but I'm sure he was the reason for that loud crash just now.

Her jaw twitches. 'Depending on the country, and the vampire, some blood was tainted to a particular vampire lineage so that they could pinpoint what vampires were killed, and which were still out and about.'

Sofia pauses, sweat sliding down her neck as she continues to use more magic to maintain the barricade in front of me as I push through it, and briefly feel it give a little. She grunts, hand shaking as she holds it out toward me, obviously working harder on keeping the wall up.

'I believe that Cora and Raya's family were one of the ones used in this experiment. Their mother knew nothing of it, being adopted and all, but there are the faintest bits of magic in their blood. Somehow, in the past, your family was targeted. There would be no one alive today to remember, most likely, on your side of things, but the magic has been passed on. From what I can tell, it's only the tiniest amount still in their blood, but it was potent enough to draw you both out.'

'And it caused the bond?' Kian inquires.

'I don't know. I think it potentially increased the chances of a bond happening, but I'd never heard of that with anyone else. I think it was a mix of magic blood and carelessness on both your parts.'

'I see.'

'Aithan's father knew one of your ancestors,' Sofia continues, and I think she is enjoying unloading information on him, answers he was so desperate to find out. She must feel powerful having held on to them for so long, dangling them over his head. Big, bad, Kian. At her mercy. I almost smile. She forgets, *he always wins*. 'That's why he targeted you, and turned you. He knew your strength. The eldest brothers in your family are known to be particularly wicked.' Her eyes flicker to Hunter, who is staring at her with wide eyes, taking in all the information. 'He knew he could train you to take over for him if the time came. Your little *business*,' she snarls the last word, like it's a curse.

Kian – for once – is silent. Sofia's mouth twists into a satisfied smirk, having finally rendered him speechless.

'So, there you have it. The answers you've been seeking,' she spits. 'Now, come to me, or they're all dead. I'll skin her sister alive and make her watch.'

Panic twists in my gut and I bang against the barricade with all my strength, but nothing happens. The vines are vicious. There is more blood than not covering my skin, but the pain of it all is nothing to me right now. Not when everyone I love and care for is in harm's way.

'One more thing,' Kian finally says. 'The witch who cursed me. Your sister's lover. Where can I find her?'

Sofia cackles, throwing her head back. 'You think I would ever tell you that?'

'No harm in asking,' Kian says, voice snide. I can practically *hear* the smirk on his lips.

'You won't be around much longer, Kian, so I wouldn't worry about it,' Sofia snaps, her voice venomous. Swallowing hard, a bead of sweat slides down her forehead, making it evident just how much power she is harnessing right now. 'All we want is to end you. You dying will end Cora's life – the bond won't let her survive it – but the others are free to go. Come to me, lay down your weapons, and they will be released.'

Suddenly, blood bubbles out of one of the witch's mouths, and when she falls, Kian is behind her, a savage, brutal smile twisted onto his lips. Hunter steps forward, the barrier no longer holding him in, and the two of them side by side is a deadly combination.

Sofia's lips flatten into a line as she steps back, eyes bouncing between them. Hunter knows he has to be very careful about what he does next. If he goes for Raya, he risks the life of everyone else in the room, but it must be unbearable seeing – feeling – her pain, and not being able to get her out of it.

'How did you get through the ward at the top of the stairs?' she hisses, staring at Kian with a mixture of fury and astonishment swimming in her eyes. I notice now that Kian is covered in a lot of blood, and while a lot of it is not his own, a lot of it is, too. 'It was designed specifically for you.'

'I'm more than used to pain, Sofia, you know that,' he says, walking slowly toward her, blood dripping from his hands. 'It takes a lot to injure me.' He places a hand over his chest. 'Even this curse should have had me on my deathbed right now, but you know what?' He continues walking toward her, and she back-pedals, hitting the bars. 'You underestimated your opponent.'

'The almighty Kian has his limits,' she hisses.

Kian's eyes dart to Hunter's, and the way his chin juts forward, I know immediately he wants Hunter to go after the witch holding Theo. It happens so quickly, it is almost like it never actually happened.

'Tell me where the witch is,' Kian growls.

'Over my dead body,' Sofia sneers, jerking her chin up in defiance.

Kian's lip twitches. 'If you could tell me before I kill you, that would be ideal.'

Hunter moves. Swiping his arm, he knocks the witch backward, effectively breaking her concentration. Theo scrambles to his feet as quick as a blink, locking eyes with Kian, as if confirming a plan, and he quickly disappears up the stairs.

Sofia screams, lunging forward, and the other witch curses at Kian. He stumbles back, as if hit with someone that can't be seen by the naked eye. Sofia's hand whips toward Hunter, and he makes a choked sound, clawing at his throat. Raya screams for him, desperately trying to get to her feet, but something is holding her down, and there is just *so much blood* coming from her, it's like a river of burgundy, pooling at her sides.

I run at the barricade, banging and barging my way into it, but nothing helps. I cry out, feeling hopeless as everything before me escalates, and there is nothing I can do to help.

Kian's eyes dart between Sofia and Hunter. If he goes for the other witch, Sofia will kill Hunter. If he kills Sofia, he saves his brother, but ends the one and only lead he has to ending his curse, inevitably signing his own death sentence.

My heart sinks as the horror of the situation settles through me with harrowing force.

Hunter's face is completely drained of colour as he falls back against the wall, hands at his throat. So much screaming, so much chaos, and Kian hesitates – just for a moment – and then Theo is halfway down the stairs when he tosses an axe toward Kian. Kian captures it and flies forward as he swings.

The blade slices through Sofia's neck, her blood showering red droplets across Kian and the ground in front of her. My stomach roils as her head completely separates from her body, landing with a heavy *thump* on the ground, rolling for a moment before her wide, lifeless eyes stare straight at me, chilling me to the bone.

Hunter drops to his knees, gasping for breath, and the barricade in front of me collapses. Rushing forward, I smash through the bent bar, ignoring the pain radiating through me at the feel of it.

The last remaining witch flings a hex of some sort toward Kian, but he sidesteps it, and Theo gets launched backward from it, only just having gotten to the bottom of the stairs before he is thrown back up them.

Kian meets my eyes fleetingly, and we turn to the witch at the same time, and she screams, turning, attempting to run.

We throw our daggers; they glide through the air with identical precision. Kian aims for her back, and I aim for her head. They plunge into her at the exact same time, and she falls forward, blood spraying the floor.

Raya splutters, getting to her feet, her blood streaming down her skin, looking like she has just stumbled out of a horror movie set, but the wounds are slowly healing. Theo groans, rubbing his head as he manages to wake, his skin having a greyish tinge to it, like he hasn't fed for days.

'Raya,' Hunter rasps, using the wall for support as he stands. He stumbles over to her, helping her up, and she stares wide-eyed at Kian, like she has just seen a ghost.

'You just killed the only person who knew where the witch was that could have undone your curse,' I whisper, my voice small, the realisation of what he just did sinking in.

My heart squeezes when Kian stares down at Sofia's disfigured body for a long moment, before his eyes turn to his brother, a sad smile on his face, then looking over at me.

'There was no choice.'

38

KIAN

The Enforcer

THE SOFT CARESS OF her fingers jolts me awake.

My eyes are crusty and sore as they open, and I stare at the stunning girl beside me. Her hand is wrapped around mine, her thumb stroking my knuckles. My eyes lower to my hand, seeing the colour of my skin is sickly pale, and my bones are jutting out. Swallowing, my throat feeling dry, I tilt my head back, admiring her.

'You are more beautiful with every day,' I murmur, attempting to squeeze her hand, but even that feels like it is using too much energy. 'I wasted so much time . . . when I could have had you.' A wheezing sound escapes my lips, and I attempt to swallow, but the lump in my throat doesn't allow it. 'I wanted to give you everything and more, but I couldn't let myself be happy. I'm so sorry.'

Tears run down her cheeks, and she nods, lower lip trembling. 'I can't say I forgive you for that, because I don't.'

A ghost of a smile flickers across my face. 'I've always been the one to ruin everything for myself. Self-sabotage is my strongest skill.'

'I often think back to those times, when you were real with me. You offered me a sneak peek into what life with you could have been like, and my God, I wish I could have that with you.'

'I'm sorry I didn't allow it,' I croak. 'I regret so much of my life.'

Moving her hand to my face, she cups my cheek. 'It's okay.'

'It's not. I'm dying, and I never got to fulfil any of the promises I made you.'

'Maybe we will meet in another life.'

She strokes her hand through my hair, and I make a soft hum in the back of my throat at the feel of it. It's soothing. Leaning forward, her lips meet mine in quite possibly the most tender kiss I've ever felt. Her hands run lightly over my chest, and my eyes flutter, and everything around me dims.

Memories of us dance through my mind. The soft moments when she was still a human.

'You're going to ruin me,' I whisper.

Her hands glide over my shoulders, lightly touching my scars, making me shudder.

'Not if you ruin me first,' she murmurs.

Reality creeps back in. Cora's thumb rubs soft circles on my cheek. Her long dark hair covers her face like a curtain. I reach for the red ends, curling a lock around my finger as the world loses focus again.

'Promise me it will be like this forever,' she whispers, looping her arms around the back of my neck, keeping me flush against her. 'I've never been so happy.'

When I wake next, it's impossible to tell how much time has passed.

The room around me swims in and out of focus, and when I see Cora walking toward me in a flowing white dress, I think I'm hallucinating. Then I blink, and I am alone in a dark room. It's quiet – unnervingly so – and for a moment, I have no clue where I am, or what is going on.

'Easy,' a voice says, and I jerk in alarm, snapping my head to the corner of the room, where my brother stands, eyes narrowed as he watches me closely, as if fearing I might launch out of the bed and attack him. 'You're at Theo's house.'

'Cora,' I choke out, eyes darting around the room. 'Where is she?'

'She's safe, she's okay,' he reassures me.

'They took her,' I say, panic swelling inside me, and I push from the bed.

Hunter is in front of me in a blur, his firm hand pushing against my chest, forcing me back down.

'You got her back,' he says quietly. 'I promise you, she is safe.'

I fall back against the pillows. 'I got her back.' I let out a puff of air, relieved. 'I got her back.' Everything catches back up with me, and I remember it all. My body aches like I've been run over by a truck, and I feel so fatigued, I fear if I blink, I may never reopen my eyes.

Hunter nods. 'You did. You saved her, and you saved me.' My eyes move to his, and he presses his lips together, touching a hand to my shoulder. 'A debt I can never repay.'

My lips twitch. 'I forced Theo to turn you because of decisions I made that put you in danger. I'd say we're even.'

'Okay.' Hunter nods. 'We're even.'

'I haven't been a very good brother to you.'

'You have been a great brother. You just had a terrible way of showing it.'

I breathe a laugh, and my chest tightens uncomfortably, making me cough. My stomach roils, and blood splatters across the bedspread. Hunter jumps up in alarm, quickly reaching for something to wipe it away. Collapsing back onto the pillows, I listen to the sound of my breathing with each wheezy inhale.

'Is it true you hacked my security cameras?' Hunter smiles

wryly. 'The cameras I set up to keep the family safe from you, and you were monitoring their safety the whole time.'

A half-formed, lazy smile takes over my face. 'Yeah. You suck at security control. I hacked everything of yours, and you never even knew.'

'Bastard,' he mutters. 'I wasted so much time hating you.'

'Yeah. Well. Join the long line of others.'

Hunter exhales, shaking his head. 'I wish everyone got to see the real you. I wish you'd let them.'

Running my tongue down the inside of my cheek, I nod. 'It was easier this way.'

'For you, maybe.'

'Hm,' I quietly hum.

'I must ask you something.'

'Go ahead.'

Hunter chews the edge of his thumb, a terrible habit he has had since he was a kid. 'There was a time when I was feeding, feeling totally out of control, just after I had turned. I was in some random alley, in a place I don't even remember the name of, and a vampire attacked me. I was so close to dying, but someone pulled them off me, and killed them. I thought it was Theo – I couldn't see their face – but he assured me it wasn't him, and all this time, I assumed it must have been a random vampire, and somehow all of us just so happened to be in the same area.' A muscle in his jaw jumps as he swallows. 'But it was you, wasn't it? You were always keeping an eye on me, making sure I was safe.'

'Downtown Los Angeles,' I say faintly. 'It's a notorious spot for vampires. You were on a bender. Everyone knows not to feed down there, but you and Theo were too new to know the street rules.'

Hunter's eyes lift. 'That's right. That's where it was.'

'You kept me busy, that's for sure.'

Shaking his head, he laughs. 'All this time, I thought I had to run from you, and you were always right there, protecting me.'

'Does it count when it was mostly from my enemies?' I counter.

Hunter nods, his dark eyes unfathomable as he gazes down at me, a thoughtful expression on his face as he studies me. 'Yeah. It counts.'

There's a brief silence between us, and Hunter taps his fingers together. 'I have another question.'

'Go ahead.'

'You and Cas were turned at the same time. Right?' he asks. 'Tell me about it.'

So I do. With frequent breaks, and a few more coughing fits, I tell my brother the story of how it all began. He listens, eyes never leaving my face as I recall every detail.

'You sent Cas to befriend me. Why?'

'I needed someone for you to turn to, and trust, who had knowledge and experience that could help you.'

'He misled me. Made me think he was much older than he was.'

'Yeah,' I grunt. 'You're annoyingly observant, and quick-thinking. I didn't want you to think he was associated with me in any way.'

'I see.' His eyes flick toward mine. 'You really thought of everything. Didn't you?'

'I'm not just a pretty face.'

He breathes a laugh. 'What you did to Raya, and myself, it was all a big test to the bond. You were trying to understand it, and needed to see it tested to the best of its ability.'

Running my tongue on the inside of my cheek, I nod. 'Correct.'

He points to his head. 'Just trying to wrap my mind around it all.'

'Understandable.'

'Cas is a good actor,' he mutters, rubbing a hand across his jaw, looking thoughtful. He's probably recalling the time they met. It was completely staged, how Cas bumped into him at a nightclub, and they shared drinks together. Cas looked after him – because he needed it.

'Don't be too hard on him. He's a good friend,' I say, giving him a pointed stare, since I don't say that about anyone. Ever. 'He's loyal. Loyalty is everything.'

'Yeah. He's loyal to *you*.'

'Which extends to you.'

Hunter makes a sound in the back of his throat, lowering his gaze to the floor. It's a lot for him to try to understand. More confusing than not, probably.

'Do me a favour,' I murmur. 'Make it easy on her. If the bond kills her after my death, I need you to look after her, and make it as comfortable as possible.'

'Of course.'

'Promise me.'

'*Te lo prometto, mio fratello, mio tutore.*'

Hunter's gaze is unwavering as it holds promises I know he is honourable enough to keep.

Giving in to the darkness, I fall further back into the pillows, a faint smile on my lips, my mind revisiting the only thing that matters to me.

Mio tesoro.

39

CORA

The Fighter

MY FOREHEAD IS PRESSED against Kian's chest.

I clutch his hand in mine, but there is no strength in his. My cheeks are patchy with dried tears as I breathe in his scent, wondering how much time we have left like this. Lightly, I trace my fingers over his perfect jawline, admiring how handsome he still looks, despite quite literally being on his deathbed. A soft laugh spills through my lips. Technically, he already *is* dead.

Pressing my lips to his, I lean back, staring down at him, the sinking sensation of his declining health hitting me harder and harder with each passing moment. Being here, seeing him like this, it's literally killing me.

I startle when the door opens and Mya enters.

'Hey,' Theo barks, storming in after her, looking furious. Blood is smeared around the corner of his mouth, and I assume he was mid-feed when she let herself in, probably in cat form. 'I told you not to go in there.'

Theo reaches for her and she slaps his hand away in irritation.

'Easy, kitty cat, don't touch the precious cargo,' he gripes.

'Mya,' I say, scrambling to my feet, quickly glancing down at Kian, but he doesn't move. Reluctantly, I drag my gaze from him. My heart hurts looking into her sad round eyes. With everything that has happened, I've almost forgotten about what she admitted to me before I was taken. I don't have the energy in me to even feel angry at the moment. I'm just confused. 'What are you doing here?'

Hesitantly, she takes a step toward me.

'Cora, I'm so sorry that I was never honest with you. I didn't do any of this to spy on you, or be malicious in any way. You are a genuine friend of mine, and I really value our friendship. You weren't honest with me about you being a vampire, so I'm hoping you can understand why I kept this hidden from you, too.'

'I can't do this right now, Mya.' I sniffle, gesturing to Kian. 'I'm a bit preoccupied.'

Releasing a steadying breath, she presses her lips together for a moment, taking a small step once more toward me. 'That's why I'm here. I want to help.'

'Help?' Theo echoes, arching a brow. 'How do you plan to do that?'

'I might not be practising magic . . .' She trails off. 'Well. I transform, but it's not exactly that same thing, but I want to try to undo the hex. It's easier if it's the witch who did, but since no one knows where she is, I'd like to try.'

I don't know what to say. Tears burn my eyes and I look help-lessly over to Kian, just about willing to try anything at this point.

Walking around me, she touches my arm briefly, and that eerie feeling rolls through me. The one I have felt around her before. I inwardly sigh. The signs were there, I was just too preoccupied to look close enough. Mya sits down on the mattress. She turns toward Kian, and hovers her hands over him, murmuring some-thing so low, even with my vampire hearing, it's inaudible.

Seconds stretch into minutes, and time seems to be crawling by at a snail's pace as her hands shift and move over his chest. Eventually, her shoulders slump, and she stands, wiping sweat from her brow.

'Damn it.' She sighs heavily, barely able to meet my eyes. 'I . . . thought I could help.'

I feel sick. Turning from her, I press a hand to my mouth to stop myself from vomiting. The thought of losing Kian is making me feel sick to my stomach. Life without him simply doesn't exist.

'She will die, you know,' Theo says firmly, jaw set tight as he stares hard at Mya. 'Bonded vampires can't exist when the other dies.'

Mya pales impossibly more, her skin as white as paper. With wet cheeks and sodden lashes, she peers over to me, looking as broken as I feel.

She looks like she wants to reach out to me, but she decides not to as she slowly makes her way to the door, looking dejected and defeated. A sob breaks from me and I steady myself on the wall.

Darkness rises up inside me, caressing me, whispering at me to reach out for her and force her back to his side. Terror clogs my throat and my eyes burn. My fingernails sink into my palms as I resist the bond's temptation to snap at her, and scream, and force her to fix him.

'Cora . . .' Theo says slowly, stepping between Mya and me.

I had turned to face them, unaware that I had. My head jerks as the bond fights for my control, urging me forward.

'You can fix him,' I snarl in a low, dangerous voice.

Whatever colour was remaining on Mya's face completely drains as she cringes away from me in fright. My fangs drop, and Theo's eyes widen in alarm, stepping forward again, looking hesitant to come too close.

'Cora!' Theo snaps, holding his hands out.

A choking sound has all of us turning, snapping me out of whatever trance the bond had thrown me in.

Then Kian screams, and it's a sound of raw, pure agony, and my heart splits into two at the sound of it. Something out of my control tugs me toward him as desperation fills me to the point where I can't think.

My eyes roam over him, his inky-black hair slick on his pale skin. His chest is heaving as he spasms, fingers gripping the sheets as he fights with whatever the curse is doing to him. It's unbearable to watch, panic heavy in my chest, climbing up my throat.

Kian's body jerks and convulses as he clutches his chest, his eyes open for the first time in hours. A scream rips from my throat when I see the same dark marks from his chest are now streaking down his face, as if leaking from the darkness his eyes possess.

'Kian!' I cry out, about to rush toward him, but recoil in horror.

He sits up abruptly, upper lip curling back into a snarl as those demonic-looking eyes sweep the room.

This isn't Kian. It's some unhinged, zombie-like version of him. A monster created from the curse. With his speed, he moves from the bed, launching toward us.

It all happens so fast.

Mya throws her hands out, a golden beam of light shooting out of them. It fills the dark room, so bright I gasp, shielding my face. A sound I've never heard before fills the room, and the windows shatter. I'm flattened onto my back, the air in my lungs knocked out of me by some supernatural force, and the air shimmers and crackles.

After a few moments, I wake, not even realising I had somehow been knocked out. Pushing myself up, I stare around the room. It is deadly silent. Everyone is on the ground, and Theo groans. My eyes turn to Kian, who is a metre away from me. Rushing to his side, I drop to my knees, my hands flitting across him.

A loud scream echoes through the room, one of despair and panic, and it is only a moment later that I realise it is coming from me.

He's dead.

Kian is *dead*.

The second scream that leaves me is shattering. I desperately touch my hands over him, feeling his hard muscles. The dark lines have gone, but he is motionless, as if there is nothing left inside him.

'Please,' I beg, distraught. 'You can't leave me.' I can barely speak through my cries as I sob over his body. 'Please, Kian. I need you to come back to me. Live for me.'

I'm heaving, choking on my tears, barely able to think coherently, when there is a minor movement beneath me, making me freeze. Leaning back, I stare down at him, my vision blurry from the tears.

His eyes snap open.

'What the hell was that?' he croaks, a hand on his head.

I blink in surprise, watching the colour returning to him as he propels into a seated position, rubbing his eyes. They have returned to the swirling darkness I know them as, his lips a dark red, and his skin shimmering. The too-perfect, marble-like texture.

Shock and confusion course through me. Climbing onto his lap, I yank his shirt over his head.

My eyes roam his chest.

His bare, unblemished chest.

'Kian . . .' I whisper. 'The curse. It's gone.'

Brows pulling together, he looks down. There are no more dark lines. His lips part in surprise, and his fingers touch the spot where they used to be. I let out a sob of relief, dropping my head into his chest. Curling his arms around me, he holds me to him, kissing my hair. I relish being this close to him, when he is truly *him*.

'Er . . . guys . . .' Theo says, breaking the eerie silence that had settled. I startle, having forgotten where we were, and that we aren't alone. His sorrowful expression makes my stomach sink. 'Mya's dead.'

Scrambling off Kian's lap, I look over to where Theo is crouched beside a lifeless Mya. Blood is streaming out of her ears and nose, her fingers have black edges on them, as if she has been electrocuted. Her skin is pale, her lips purple, with a hint of blue, meaning she has been dead for a little while. We must have all been out for longer than I realised. Quietly, I step over to her, and undo the first few buttons of her shirt. Horrifying black marks scatter across her skin, like blackened tree branches, running down her body, disappearing underneath the fabric.

Somehow, she reversed the death curse, but instead of undoing it, she took it on herself, and it killed her instantly. My heart clenches, and I reach out, touching her arm, sick with guilt. The overflowing sensation of the bond is almost blinding me from everything else, but I force myself to focus.

'Thank you,' I whisper, moving my hand up to her face, closing her eyes. 'I'm so sorry . . .' My hands shake as I lay them over her.

My eyes burn, and I lean over her body. I sob, unable to handle even more blood on my hands.

It's a cold, dreary day.

Typical Red Thorne weather.

Folding my arms across my chest, I continue watching Mum as she wanders around the garden, a relaxed smile on her face. My hair whips around me, and I brush it from my eyes in irritation.

We have determined Mum has a normal understanding of how life works, she just doesn't remember who she is, or who we are. At least she believes us that we are her daughters. She listens carefully whenever we talk about the past, and I think it makes her sad to think about the life she no longer remembers.

Like me, she wasn't happy before, so maybe it's a blessing in disguise. A way to completely start over, fresh, without the baggage of her former life weighing her down. She looks young again, and content. It's not until now that I realise just how bad her mental health must have been. I think we were both spiralling and couldn't see a light at the end of the tunnel.

'I forgot what her smile looked like,' I murmur, and Raya glances at me, before gazing out to where our mum is. We held a small funeral for Mya this morning, so this is the only part of the day that has brought me a moment of happiness. A small distraction from the bleak world around me. 'Her genuine, real smile.'

'I wish you'd both shared the burden of everything,' she whispers, eyes shimmering with unshed tears. 'I feel awful knowing now how much you both were struggling, and how far you went to ensure I had everything I needed, even if it cost you your own happiness.'

'It seemed unfair to share it with you when I could protect you from it.'

'I'm strong enough to handle this, you know,' Raya says. 'I know you have spent your entire life being my hero, but I'm strong, and I can protect you, too. It's okay to let someone help you.'

Rolling my lips inward, I nod, unsure what to say. Kian and I are similar that way, both wanting to do everything on our own, ensuring we aren't a burden on anyone, sheltering everyone around us from everything. It's exhausting, and it's time we both embrace the fact that we don't have to do everything alone anymore.

My heart throbs at the thought of Kian. Ever since the curse lifted, our bond is strengthening to the point that I can hardly think about anything else other than him. Forcing ourselves apart this morning was excruciating. Since he has had to take a step back from the business with everything going on, he is spending the day going to its headquarters, while I spend some much-needed time with Raya, and Mum.

Hunter and Theo went with Kian, which seems so odd to think about. Them, all together, like they're . . . *friends*. It must be difficult for Kian to let his walls down. I don't know if he will ever be completely open with them, but this is certainly an incredible first step.

Apparently, Kian has offices everywhere, and one of the main buildings happens to be here in Red Thorne. It's tucked away, out of sight, and it's not easy to stumble across, but now I know it's there, it makes me wonder how the hell I missed it.

'You know, I was distraught after everything that happened when I found you. With Kian, you, and . . . Alex . . .' She forces his name from her lips as if it is difficult for her to say out loud. My stomach roils at the mention of him. I will never forget the look in his eyes and the feel of his neck breaking in my own hands.

It's something I could never get rid of as much as I pushed it away. Forcing the thoughts away and becoming numb helped, but only so much. For months, I felt like an empty shell of myself because of it, but now I'm learning to live with the guilt, as much as it still hurts to think about everything. It's the only way I can survive.

'I never actually thanked you for saving my life. I was so caught up with Alex . . . his death haunts me. I blame myself for it because he only came on the journey to find you because of me. He was only there because of *me*.'

Swallowing, she looks ahead, and for the first time, I really acknowledge how much she has grown up. She isn't the little kid sister I remember. She is strong, brave, and can hold her own.

'I never understood . . . not completely . . . until I was in the same situation. Eli – a stranger to me – is now dead because

I chose to save you. Like you said to me . . . there was no choice.' Turning to face me, she collects my hands in hers. 'I'm so sorry it took me so long to understand this. I can't ever repay you for saving my life, and sacrificing your own for so many years for me to be happy and carefree. I don't know how I can ever make it up to you, but I just want you to know that I understand now. Everything you've done, why you did it, and even your complicated relationship with Kian. I see you, I understand, I support you, and I love you so much.'

Pulling her to me, I wrap my arms tightly around her and hold her to me, just like I used to when she was little. We stay like that, in a tight embrace, before I finally release her and sit back, resting my hand on her shoulders.

'There is something I want to show you,' I murmur. 'Let's take a walk.'

As we head downtown, the sun attempts to peek out from behind the clouds, but the sky is still as grey and dull as ever. It's silent as we walk, neither of our steps making any noise.

'I love your hair, by the way,' Raya says, reaching out and touching the red ends. 'It suits you.'

'Thanks. I really needed a change.'

'I'm sorry about your friend,' she continues, offering me a sad smile.

'It's horrible,' I admit, exhaling, remembering the way Mya's eyes stared lifelessly up at me, and the blood trickling down her skin. 'I was *so* mad at her, I didn't even let her explain things, and everything happened after that . . . she came to the house to help Kian, *for me*. She never wanted to use her magic, or tell me about it in case she was forced to use it, and then she did . . . and it killed her.'

Squeezing my eyes shut, I stop walking, placing a hand on my stomach. I haven't slept since it happened, and I feel so uneasy about it all.

'She just . . . died. So suddenly. It was just . . . done.' I shake my head, forcing my eyes to reopen, my gut churning uncomfortably. 'Everywhere I go, something terrible happens, and it's always *my* fault. No matter how hard I try, I can't do anything right.'

'Cor,' Raya says, touching a hand to my back. 'You didn't know that was going to happen. You didn't force her to turn up, and you didn't ask her to do any of that. No one expected that to happen.'

'She didn't want to practise witchcraft, but she did it for me, because I made her feel like she was a bad friend, and then she died because of it.'

'I understand how you're feeling – the guilt of knowing your involvement in the end of someone else's life is something horribly tragic that you will never truly get over it, although you *didn't* force anyone to do anything.' We begin walking again, and she hugs her arms around herself. 'We just have to do our best to live with the guilt and move on from it. We need to learn from this experience, and do our best to not repeat mistakes.'

As we make our way down the street, Raya's gaze shifts toward her old apartment building, the one we shared briefly with Alex. Quickly averting her eyes, we keep walking, and I guide her toward the bench. With the breeze, the autumn leaves of the tree behind it have swept across it, making it look even more aesthetically pleasing than usual. I gesture to it, and she frowns at me in confusion.

'What is this?' she asks, tensing slightly.

'Go take a look.'

Raya falls silent as she steps toward the bench and freezes, her eyes landing on the words written in front of it.

'*In loving memory of Alex Valenti. Forever in our hearts.*'

'Oh . . .' she says softly, gaze lingering on the words for a little while longer before jumping back to the bench. 'You did this?'

'Yeah,' I reply. 'I wanted there to be a spot for him here, for us to easily remember him by. A place where you can come talk to him when you need to, since Paradise Bay is a little too . . . sunshiny . . . for us.'

'It's beautiful, Cor,' she whispers, eyes glittering with the tears that do break through this time, and suddenly, I'm crying, too.

The clouds shift, and a warm golden beam of sunshine moves across the bench. Raya gasps, and my eyes widen as we both gape at it.

'I didn't organise *that*.' I choke out a bubble of laughter.

Raya joins in, leaning forward and touching her fingers to it.

'I love you,' Raya says after a moment. 'I miss you every day. I hope you're at peace.'

The silence is heavy around us, but a comfortable one. After a few moments, she turns, walking over to me and resting her head on my shoulder. Curling my arm around her, I pull her into me tightly.

'Thank you,' she whispers. 'He would love it.'

Running circles over her back, I kiss the top of her head.

I've missed this. The closeness between us. The feeling of us against the world.

We got lost there for a little, but we have finally found our way back to each other, exactly where we were meant to be, all along.

40

KIAN

The Enforcer

A BLARING ALARM PIERCES THE AIR.

'Stop touching shit,' I growl at Theo, smacking his hand away as he presses a button that activates the panic alarm, causing everyone to leap out of the chairs and dive for the floor. Theo's eyes widen as he looks around the room, an amused smirk lifting the corner of his mouth.

'Whoops?' He shrugs, offering me a very insincere apologetic grin.

'Bringing Theo along anywhere is how I think a parent would feel bringing their child to work for the day,' Hunter says, shaking his head at his friend.

'Hey!' Theo grumbles, shooting an offended look at Hunter, who goes back to ignoring him as his eyes survey his surroundings.

'Wow,' he comments, eyes shifting to look at the ceiling. 'This is impressive, Ki.'

I can't help but tense a little at the nickname. It feels so strange being here with my brother. After spending so long ensuring there was so much distance between us, there never seemed a chance it would be crossed.

Guilt floods me when I think about all the times I pushed him away, hurt him, and made him hate me. I thought it was the best thing to do, to ensure his safety, but I fear I've caused irreparable damage between us now. But Hunter seems relatively relaxed, as if he is taking this new development between us in stride. Hunter has always been very adaptable to any changes, so it shouldn't surprise me. He is a very logical, level-headed man, which has only sharpened since he turned. I feel he has thought of every possibility, weighed everything up in his mind, and has come to the conclusion that he believes my intentions were not as evil as I led him to believe.

'How does it work, exactly?' Hunter asks.

'I have people networking all around the world, gathering intel, researching. Once we find out where a suspected operation is, we figure out a way to extract the vampires they have there,' I answer, pointing to the screen where a map materialises, highlighting all the suspected areas of kidnappings.

'What do they do with them?' Theo questions, looking alarmed at how many red dots appear.

'Torture them, starve them, experiment. Sometimes they force them to do things for them. It really depends on who is running the operation, and what their intentions are. Sometimes it's hunters who just want to kill vampires. Sometimes it's werewolves, witches, shifters. Honestly, we have seen everything. Everyone has their own game they play, but the most common thing they have in common is capturing vampires and wolves. Vampires more so, since we have a bad reputation for killing. Werewolves are a bit better at coexisting.'

'And the operations are most often unrelated?' Hunter inquires, scrubbing a hand down his jaw as his eyes scan the map, as if memorising all the locations.

'Sometimes unrelated, sometimes connected very closely. It really depends.'

Theo's face twists in outrage when the screen changes, showing an aerial view of one of the farms, and how many cells are there. It pans across it, showcasing all the blood on the dirt, the chains, and other torture devices.

'Makes me sick.' He scowls, shaking his head. 'Can't we all just fucking live our own lives?'

'There's always consequences to murder,' Hunter says, looking contemplative as his eyes continue sweeping the room, taking everything in, his brow creased. He sighs then, appearing as though the topic of the vampire race is a subject that drains him – which it most likely does. He has very strong opinions about vampires. It's sort of comical how much he hates them when he *is* one. 'And vampires don't stop doing that.'

Theo rolls his eyes. 'Everyone needs to lighten up.'

Hunter doesn't bother replying – knowing it will only start an argument – and walks down the hall, looking over at the other vampires who are at their desks, working away.

An ache forms in my stomach and the urge to return to Cora is almost unbearable. Fisting my hands, I grapple with my self-control. I can overcome anything if I put my mind to it, this is no different. She needs the day with her family, and I need to be here to make sure everything is still running smoothly.

There is an energy buzzing through me – my connection to Cora – demanding attention, and I close my eyes, grinding my molars almost to dust as I force the feelings surging inside me to a corner in the back of my mind. I will absolutely deliver on these urges the moment I can, but I need everything sorted before I do that, because I will *not* be interrupted.

'Kian,' Lance says as he approaches me, a no-nonsense expression on his face, as usual. He comes to a stop before me, placing his hands behind his back. 'I'd like to propose some new plans with you, when you have a moment.'

Nodding, I glance at Theo and Hunter, who wordlessly nod, moving out of the way. I go into work-mode, overseeing and approving as much as I can, in the hope that I will be left alone for a few hours, or days, preferably. I need all the time I can get with my girl, to make up for lost time.

When I'm done, I begin wandering through the rooms, looking for the boys. I find Hunter first, who is back in front of the screen, looking over it. Moving to his side, I join him.

'It's pretty impressive,' Hunter murmurs. 'You must have saved thousands of lives.'

'I end plenty of them, too. I'm no saint.'

'Maybe you used to kill for fun – a lot of newbie vampires do – but I see it now. You kill when you deem it's necessary.' He pauses, flickering that pensive gaze to mine, those dark eyes so similar to my own. 'Basically what I'm saying is, thanks. For everything you've done. I don't forgive you for some things, and the way you didn't allow me to make any decisions, but I appreciate all that you have done, and what you have sacrificed. I want a clean slate from here on out. You can't meddle with my life any longer.'

Running a hand through his hair, he half-turns, facing me, and my shoulders are stiff. I don't like doing this kind of thing. It still makes me feel icky having to discuss feelings, and whatnot, but I suppose we need to clear the air and get it out of the way.

'But I'd really like us to be good, Kian. I want us to be brothers, and have the relationship I've always wanted from you. I know it's not in your nature to let anyone in, but you've seen how lonely it is on the top, all by yourself, and you have Cora now, which means she will always be around Raya, who is always around me . . .' He trails off for a moment, eyes scrutinising mine with an intensity that makes me uncomfortable. He holds out his hand. 'I want to start fresh. Can you do that?'

I look down at his outstretched hand, and force my own hand out in front of me, shaking his. 'Fresh start.'

He nods at me, and quickly lets go. My head is spinning with how fast everything has changed, but it feels like a weight has been lifted off my chest. Like . . . it's a relief to know I have someone in my corner. To have someone I can call if I need help. Of course, Cora is everything to me and more, but having my brother back feels like it's mending something inside me I wasn't aware was broken.

'So, are you doing okay?' Hunter asks, pinning with me that stare again, the one that makes it feel like he can pull my thoughts out of my head. My brother is far too observant, and even after all this time, can read me too well. 'Is it completely gone? The curse?'

Looking away from him, I nod. It still makes me uncomfortable to think about. How weak I became. How many people witnessed it. My death was so close. 'Yeah. It's gone.'

'You must feel loads better.'

'Yeah,' I agree. 'I have never felt anything like what I went through with the curse. I've been kidnapped, tortured, beaten half to death – and I would go through all that again to never experience how that curse made me feel.'

Hunter grimaces. 'Yeah, you weren't in good shape, that's for sure.'

'Now it's just trying to handle the bond,' I say, unable to help bringing up Cora, since she has consumed my mind all day. It's been incredibly distracting. All I see in my mind is her on top of me, with her glossy long black hair, and the way it feels when she grinds up against me . . .

'It's worth everything.' He grins, clapping me on the back. 'Enjoy it.'

Oh, a voice in my mind whispers as a dark, possessive sensation rolls through me. *I will.*

*

Curling my hand around the back of her neck, I yank Cora toward me.

I have been craving having her in my hands all day and, finally, she is in front of me, we are alone, and the bond is *happy*.

Her breath fans across my lips as my mouth dives toward her. She moans, slipping her fingers around my neck, and I pull her flush against me, the incessant need to be closer still roaring through me.

'You are fucking perfect, and you are *mine*.'

'Yes,' she agrees, pulling back enough for us to lock gazes, voice pure husk and smoke as she draws her lower lip between her teeth. 'Yours.'

Hearing those words – the acceptance – falling from her lips strokes something primal inside me. Capturing her face between my hands, I kiss her, and kiss her, and kiss her some more. It's fire, ice, and everything in between. Longing and lust. Rough, and yet tender.

Keeping one hand against her cheek, I use my other to pull her up. She tightens her legs around my waist and I sink my fingers into her hair, tangling them, while keeping a firm hold on her ass with the other.

'I fucking love you,' I whisper, pulling back, lips still brushing hers as those glimmering dark eyes snap to mine. 'I've loved you since the moment I laid eyes on you, and it terrified me no end.' We fall back onto the bed, and I slide my hand down to her neck, stroking it possessively, her legs tightening around my waist, sending a pulse of desire through me. 'There is nothing and no one that will ever take you from me. I will love you endlessly, without fault, without limit.' Swooping down, I kiss her once more. 'You. Are. My. *Everything*.'

She lets out a soft gasp – which almost sounds like a sob – as she crashes her mouth to mine.

'I love you,' she whispers, and her lips taste of salty tears when we kiss.

'They say I'm heartless but here I am, bleeding for you, offering you all of me. Every broken, scarred piece.'

'And I don't plan on ever giving it back,' she murmurs, smiling up at me, her fingertips light as a feather as she traces them across my jaw.

'For so long, I wanted to be alone. Nothing else mattered except power, survival, and making sure I had *no* attachments to hold me back.' I swallow, circling my thumb over the most tender part of the throat. 'But nothing – and I mean *nothing* – matters, if I do not have you.'

'You have me.'

'For how long?' I question, searching her eyes.

'Forever.'

There is no self-control left inside me to stop myself throwing her back onto the mattress and kissing her like an animal. She groans into my mouth, deepening the kiss, curling her fingers around my hair and pulling on it. I fucking love the feel of her mouth on mine, and her fingers through my hair.

Suddenly, her hands slam into my chest, and the world tips as I'm flipped. She lands on top of me, fangs dropping and, fuck, it turns me on even more, which doesn't seem possible at this point.

'Be a good boy and let me ride you,' she purrs, and my eyes snap up to hers.

Grinning, she is enjoying my look of shock far too much. Before my mind can scramble together a reply, she tears my pants clean off, the material falling in pieces around my legs. I raise a brow, enjoying the show as she tears my shirt off, flinging it over her head.

Reaching for her dress, I pull it up over her, drinking in every inch of her. I groan as my eyes roam over her naked body.

My hands – having a mind of their own – fondle her breasts, and she hisses when my thumbs skate over her pebbled nipples.

As quick as a whip, she lifts her hips and sinks onto me. A sound I don't recognise leaves me as I grip her hips hard enough to bruise, and when she moans, I sink my fingers into her flesh, enjoying seeing blood trickle down her smooth, marble skin.

When she slides up and down my length, we both throw our heads back, our groans completely in sync.

'Fuck me,' I growl, voice pure gravel.

'I am.' She smirks, and a chuckle escapes me.

My eyes are trained on the point where our bodies meet, and seeing her moving up and down me makes me *melt*, as if the possessive beast inside me is getting bigger and stronger simply by watching it.

Gripping her, I thrust into her hard, and she yelps, throwing her hands out onto the headboard as I continue to fuck her.

'Kian,' she warns, but it comes out like a moan, and her eyes roll back into her head. 'You're meant to be a good boy. Are you being a good boy?'

'I am not a fucking good boy,' I sneer, and suddenly, we are mid-air and I slam her hard onto the floor, wrapping my hand around her neck. 'You want a good boy? Keep looking, *mio tesoro*, because there are only villains in this room.'

She chokes on a gasp as I drive into her. She arches off the ground, raking her hands down the unscarred parts of my back. My fangs explode from me and I plunge them into her neck, drawing a hearty gulp of her delicious blood.

Rearing back, I tilt my head, exposing my throat to her, and the delicious sting of her fangs sliding into me almost has me exploding.

As she sucks me, I thrust into her harder and faster than I ever have before.

I kiss her with a savage brutality that has our tongues clashing together, my breaths sharp and ragged as I trace every curve she has to offer with my hands.

'I'm sorry for everything I've done,' I choke out, voice hoarse and thick as I caress her face. 'I wanted to give you the world but I was terrified of what it might do to me in the process. I didn't want to bow down to anyone, but here I am, at your mercy.' I press my forehead to hers.

I love her *violently*.

The intensity of my feelings for her is terrifying, but also thrilling.

We have the rest of our lives together.

This is just the beginning.

My name falls from her lips moments before I feel her clamp around me, and I thrust forward as we release at the same time. Black dots swallow my vision and I genuinely black out momentarily.

When I wake, we are both on our backs, trembling. I don't even know how I ended up here. Rolling over to her, I grip her chin, forcing her gaze to mine, and warmth trickles through me when I see vibrant silver rings bordering her eyes.

'Your eyes,' I gulp, staring at them in astonishment. 'They're beautiful.'

'Oh . . .' she whispers, lightly touching her fingers to the corners of them.

'I don't deserve any of this.' Kneading my fingers through her silky strands, I push them back from her forehead. 'I don't deserve you, but I'll be damned if I'm giving you up now.'

She smiles. 'Then we will be damned together.'

41

CORA

The Fighter

MY APPETITE IS INSATIABLE.

I cannot get enough of him, his blood, and the way his hands feel on my skin.

I have lost track of time, having no clue how many hours, days, weeks have passed. I'm confident it isn't weeks, but I genuinely don't know, since I haven't breathed my own air for what feels like an eon.

And I'm still desperate for *more*.

We finally detached from each other to visit the real world again. We completely missed it, but apparently Cas has disappeared and left Hunter a note – that seems to be his signature move – having left his mansion in Rose Hills to Hunter and Raya, apologising for the role he played in everything that happened all those months ago, and said they can use the estate as they please.

Hunter loves it there. He has said a few times he would consider living in Rose Hills. After discussing it with Mum, she has agreed she likes the idea of being close to the beach. She doesn't remember much about her old life, but she remembers wanting to help people, and dedicating her life to it. Since there is a massive hospital in Rose Hills, it might be the perfect place for her to start over. It's far enough from Red Thorne, but close enough that we can get to her quickly if we need to, although we will hire a security team to watch the house. Kian has connections everywhere, so it won't be a problem finding someone who will keep her safe.

We have spent the day filling the mansion with everything we think she will enjoy and love. It doesn't take nearly as long as I expect, since there are so many of us here, and we all have super-human speed.

The house has transformed from a gothic mansion to a warm home, and it is so nice seeing the shine back in my mother's eyes. She's happy. Truly happy. Alive and safe. Healthy, and ready to begin her life again.

It makes everything that she has been through worth it.

Sitting around the loungeroom, the fireplace crackles. It seems surreal – all of us in the one room – watching a *movie*. It seems so normal and completely out of this new world we have found ourselves in.

It's just . . . perfect. Everything I have wanted for so long.

'When do you head back to London?' I ask, leaning back into the lounge. Kian throws his arm around my shoulders, bringing me closer to him. Resting into his upper arm, I release a content sigh.

This, right here, is my new happy place.

'Well,' Raya says, glancing at Hunter. 'We have decided to stay for a little while.'

'You have?' I exclaim, smiling.

'Yeah. I want to spend more time with you all, and make sure Mum is settled.'

Mum smiles softly at Raya. She is quiet, not talking nearly as much as she used to, but she seems more relaxed. I think once she is around us more, she will be more talkative. It must be quite overwhelming being thrown into a brand-new life with strangers who insist they are your family. A family that isn't even human.

'And . . .' Hunter says, clearing his throat, sliding his fingers between Raya's. They do that annoying thing where they silently communicate, and I eye them both. 'We have an announcement.'

They both smile, looking around the room.

'We're getting married.'

The music pulses through me.

I feel the vibrations under my skin as I throw my head back, the neon lights of the club flashing over me. Tilting my chin forward, I lock eyes with the dark gaze of the man across the room.

Tall, impeccably dressed, brutally black eyes, even darker hair, and the sexiest smirk I've ever seen, and he's all *mine*.

Running my hands down my sides, I sway my hips to the beat, moving slow and sensually, feeling every single thrum of the music.

A tall guy steps in front of me, blocking my stunning view of the villainous creature basking in the shadows. Forcing my gaze up to meet his, he grins down at me, eyes glued on my chest.

'You are the hottest thing in here,' he shouts at me, and I cringe away from him, given that I have impeccable hearing.

'I know,' I reply, planning to step around him, when his hand snakes out, gripping my wrist.

'Wanna ditch this place and go back to mine?' he asks, and I stare at him incredulously, shocked he hasn't even attempted small talk, or to buy me a drink, before trying to take me home.

Pushing to his feet, Kian crosses the room, invading my space with his intoxicating scent. Looming over me, his lips curve, and I feel his presence like a warm embrace. The guy in front of me abruptly lets go, stumbling back.

'You lay a hand on my girl again, I will cut up your limbs piece by piece and feed them to you. Do you understand?' he asks in a cold, deadly voice, his thin smirk inching across his mouth.

The guy pales, noticing Kian's darkening gaze. Gulping, he spins, taking off toward the door, and I release a loud laugh.

'Seeing another man's hands on you makes me want to snap bones,' he seethes, swinging to face me. 'But I get extreme satisfaction knowing that I will be the one inside you later tonight.'

Biting my lip, I shake my head, his dirty words always making my stomach flutter, and my insides burn.

'You look as sinful as you taste, *mio tesoro*,' he purrs.

Liquid heat ignites through me like a wave of hot lava. Shivering under those endless black eyes, I flutter my eyelashes, offering him a coy smile. 'Oh yeah?' I ask.

'Yeah,' he grunts, yanking me toward him possessively. 'I'm not sure I can last a second longer without being inside you.'

Yep, I think, grasping his hand. *That'll do it*.

Dragging him out of the club, we stumble onto the street, the cool night air blasting over my face after being inside that stuffy, stale-aired club. We have been going out every night, drinking, dancing, and having fun. We have been doing all the things I've wanted to do. Bowling, ice-skating, sharing an ice cream – which didn't have much taste, but was just for the experience of being on a date with Kian – and then all the other fun things like being out in a club, dancing all night until the sky brightens and the birds start chirping.

Sweeping me off my feet, he carries me through the front door of the house we are staying in and deposits me on the dining table. Stepping between my thighs, he peels my dress off. His eyes rake over my body, and it makes me feel like I'm on fire.

The shoes I'm wearing sparkle underneath the light, and I bring my knee up, ready to remove them when his fingers press against my ankle, stopping me. They're the shoes he bought me when we first met.

'Leave them on,' he rasps, fingering the strap of the heel. My lip twitches as I nod, leaning back onto my palms. 'Spread your legs for me, *Tesoro*, and show me what's mine.'

Doing as I'm told, I lean further back, and he drops to his knees, gazing at me with pure lust and adoration.

'So pretty,' he murmurs. 'So perfect.' His gaze lifts. 'All for me.'

'All for you.'

I don't think I will ever get over the feel of his tongue dragging up the centre of me. My moans fill the air as he nips, sucks, and bites me until I'm writhing beneath him.

I'm still riding my post-orgasm high when he stands, yanking out his dagger, his eyes travelling back to mine slowly, his smirk inching across that perfect mouth.

'Do it,' I pant.

He drags the dagger down the inside of my thigh, and I watch the blood spill across my skin. Continuing to cut, when there is a steady stream of blood, he flips the dagger, smearing it across the handle, right over his initials. He holds it out to me. Wordlessly, I accept it, and Kian leans forward, bracing his arms around my thighs, caging me in.

I love it when he does that.

I push the dagger into him, and a rumble pulls from his chest, his fangs descending. I push it in deep, completely covering the dagger in blood from us both, and then hand it back to him.

He lightly dances the end of the blade across my tender nipples, dark eyes piercing straight through me, and I suck in a harsh breath, my eyes dropping to the blade, loving the feel and sight of the sharp edge dragging across my skin, leaving a red ribbon in its wake. The sting of it is delicious, and I want to feel more of it.

Excruciatingly slow, he drags the tip of it between my breasts, all the way down my navel, before flipping it in the air, the blade landing in his palm, slicing straight into his palm. I love seeing him bleed.

'Wet and needy,' he drawls, rolling his tongue across his bottom lip. 'Always so eager for me, aren't you, *Tesoro*?'

'I'll never get enough,' I promise him.

Moving it to my entrance, he pushes the handle inside me, and I moan loudly, my head dipping back. Kian presses his face against my breasts, his fangs sinking into the soft swells of my breast as he moves the handle in and out of me, making me pant and beg him for more as he does.

My hands move up his arms, caressing and squeezing those rock-hard muscles before they slide over his scars. My touch on his scars always causes a shiver to roll down his spine, and I love seeing that reaction from him. Moving up my chest, he kisses my collar bones, neck, across my jaw, leaving delicate, soft kisses on my cheekbones.

As he travels back to my mouth, I snake my tongue out, dragging it across his lips, tasting my own blood before we kiss. It's deep, and raw, making me feel desperate and reckless as he increases the speed of his hand, kissing me like he is devouring me – like I'm his last meal.

We break the kiss, and his eyes flash with desire, lowering to watch the dagger move in and out of me, and I follow his gaze. His hand is so tightly wrung around the blade, his blood drips all over my thighs, and the table I'm perched on top of.

He is everything I have ever wanted and more.

Pulling the dagger out, he tosses it over his shoulder, and pushes inside me with an almost violent thrust. I whimper at the feel of it, almost unable to have lasted another minute without feeling him inside me.

Kian makes a soft moan that sounds husky, making my insides melt. Leaning over me, he drags his tongue across my breast, collecting the blood, and moves to my neck, where he bites me again. Reaching over, I bite into his shoulder simultaneously, and the feeling of my blood leaving and his flowing into me is a dizzying sensation that makes me light-headed. He pumps into me erratically, thrusting into me so hard, he has to wrap an arm around my back to keep me in place as we move harder and faster, blood smearing *everywhere*.

As usual, we release at the same time, and it's a euphoric high I have never felt until being with him. A high I will crave for the rest of my life. No matter how many times I quench my thirst for him, I will always come back for more.

When he finally pulls out of me, we are both soaked in each other's blood. The scent of him wraps around me, having me in a chokehold.

Curling his fingers around my throat, he pulls me toward him, squeezing so tight, it feels dangerously possessive. The fire in his eyes makes him look utterly *feral*, and I love every second of it.

'You still hate me, *Tesoro*?' Kian asks, those glittering eyes dipping back to my mouth as he leans closer, grazing the tip of his nose against mine.

'Of course,' I whisper, tracing the muscles of his chest.

'Excellent,' he purrs, before flattening me onto my back.

I'm in for a long night.

42

KIAN

The Enforcer

THERE'S A KNOCK ON MY DOOR.

A small smile threatens to emerge as I sense my bonded is here.

'Come in,' I say, and one of my men opens my office door, revealing the stunning woman behind him. My eyes ravage her. Long, silky black hair, with a vibrant red tingeing the tips. Those glittering black eyes find mine, and a ripple of satisfaction rolls through me at the sight of the silver rings bordering them, showing the world that she is *mine*. 'Hello, love.' I beckon her to me.

'Hello,' she murmurs, stepping inside, her voice that smoky tone I adore so much.

Pressing two fingers to my lips, blowing the kiss to her. Smiling, she strides over to me, rounding the edge of my desk and planting herself straight into my lap. Placing my hands on her hips, I tilt my head back to meet her gaze.

Cora insisted she wanted in on everything, and after being in the office for only a week, she practically runs the place. Not often people surprise me, if anything, I expect the worst from them, but when it comes to Cora, there is no doubt in my mind that she will succeed at something once she puts her mind to it. She has proved as much.

I must admit, it's easier having her here. I like working, keeping busy, doing what I do best, tracking people, and now that she is here, I'm not preoccupied wondering where she is, what she's doing, or if she is safe. Honestly, she's proved herself to be better and more competent than half my staff, so it's actually quite good business-wise, too, except when we can't keep our hands off each other, which, admittedly, is a lot.

Whenever my eyes fall onto those silver-ringed orbs, I'm reminded just how much time I wasted forcing her away, when I should have been cherishing her from the moment I met her, and if it wasn't for that damn curse, I probably would have.

Drumming my fingers on her thighs, I push the thoughts from my mind. There is no point dwelling on the past now, not when the curse is gone, and I have the girl of my dreams literally in my lap.

I won't ever make my past mistakes again.

There's another knock, and I swivel the chair, facing the door as it opens.

'Hi, Kian, can you please look at these forms —' a voice says and the woman abruptly stops, eyes widening as she takes in Cora. 'Oh – I'm so sorry, I should have waited for your permission to enter.'

'Oh my God,' Cora blurts, her mouth dropping open. 'Lucy?'

Lucy straightens, eyebrows shooting up. Her raven-black hair is pin straight, falling down her shoulders. 'Cora? Hi.'

'Hi.'

Lucy used to live in Red Thorne, and dated Theo for a while. I don't really know the details of the break-up – I really don't care – but it means she knows the whole gang, and appears to have met Cora sometime during all of the drama a few months ago, when I turned Raya, and let Cora momentarily slip through my fingers, when I was desperate for the space and time away from her to get my shit together. Which was clearly very unsuccessful.

'How are you?' Lucy asks, her smile a little warmer than it usually is, since she usually dislikes anyone she meets for the first time.

'Good!' Cora answers, returning the smile. 'I had no idea you worked here. I thought you might have left the country, after you and Theo . . .' She trails off.

Lucy shrugs, a guarded expression on her face. 'I thought about it, but I ran into a friend who was working for Kian, so I switched sides.' She winks. 'No hard feelings.'

'Clearly, none taken.' Cora laughs, gesturing to me. 'Well, it's nice to see you. We will have to go out one night. Have a drink, or something.'

'Sure,' Lucy agrees. 'Sounds great.' Striding over to the desk, her heels click-clacking on the marble flooring, she places the folder down. 'If you could take a look at these, Kian, when you get time.'

'Sure,' I reply. 'Any news on the farm up north?'

She shakes her head. 'Not yet. Working on it.'

'Okay.'

Shooting Cora one last smile, she disappears through the door, shutting it behind her. Cora turns, placing her hands on my chest.

'You have way more staff than I realised. I didn't expect this to be a proper business.'

I raise a brow. 'What did you think it was?'

'I don't know, a shady warehouse with a bunch of torture devices, or something.' She shrugs, laughing. 'I didn't expect this super modern building and high-tech equipment.'

Tsking my tongue, I frown up at her. 'How dare you think I would operate a business out of a "shady warehouse". Who do you think I am?'

She grins. 'I never know what to expect when it comes to you.'

'Hmm,' I hum, walking my fingers up her thigh. 'Do you like your office?'

'It's beautiful. Especially all my stunning rose petals.'

I flash her a smirk. 'I thought a little personal touch might make it feel more like *yours*.'

'I love it, thank you.'

The past month has been a wild ride of partying and living life carefree. I never knew how much fun it could be doing it with someone by my side. Someone to share things with, to talk to, to laugh and have fun with. I had forgotten what it felt like to be young and free, and goddamn, I had missed it.

Collecting her hands in mine, I bring them to my mouth. I kiss across her fingers, across her knuckles, and then give her hands a brief squeeze, meeting her gaze.

'I love you. More than life itself.' Tugging her closer to me, I secure my hold on her. 'No one will ever take you from me.'

A slow smile crosses her face. 'I love you.' Leaning forward, she kisses my forehead. 'Good luck to them if they try. They will have just signed their death wish.'

A predatory smirk lights my lips. 'Yes.'

Her eyes soften as she runs her fingers through my hair. Tilting my head back, I enjoy the feel of it for a moment, our eyes locked on each other's.

For the first time since I was turned, it feels like my life has meaning.

43

CORA

The Fighter

AS THE MUSIC BEGINS, I turn, seeing Raya walking down the aisle.

My heart is in my throat as I take in her stunning white dress, which shimmers underneath the twinkling fairy lights. Since Hunter and Raya are bonded, there really is no need to solidify their commitment with a wedding, but there is also no reason *not* to.

Planning a wedding when you have money at your fingertips, an ability to command others to do anything you want, and the superhuman strength and speed to get shit done, is actually a total breeze.

Her dark hair tumbles down her shoulders, and Mum meets her, guiding her to the front, where I'm standing, down a little further from a very dashing Hunter, who is smiling from ear to ear. I've hardly ever seen Hunter smile, so it looks a bit odd on his face.

Mum kisses her on the cheek, releasing her to Hunter, who embraces Mum briefly. She heads over to the front of the seats. I'm smiling so much, my cheeks are aching. I look over to Kian, who nods back at me, looking fucking *edible* in his charcoal suit that matches his hair and dark eyes perfectly. Forcing my gaze from his, I look to Theo, who childishly sticks his tongue out at me.

Typical.

The ceremony is relatively quick, and I end up a sobbing mess by the end of their vows. They are sickeningly sweet to each other – it's so cute, I might throw up.

After the ceremony, we get hundreds of photos, and by the time we end up back at the hall, I'm eager for a drink, my face feeling stiff and sore. I'm not one to smile much and Raya made me, so now my cheeks hurt, but the strained muscles will heal in a minute or two. As if he has read my mind, Kian beelines for the bar, ordering us two drinks each. We wordlessly down the first and clink glasses, downing the second. The bartender observes us silently, and pours another without either of us having to say a word.

'Cheers,' I say to the bartender, before linking arms with Kian, and leading him to the table where the others are seated.

Considering we left our lives behind, it's a relatively small wedding, and by small, I mean *tiny*, but it's stunning and we wouldn't have it any other way.

It's nice to do something so normal, and for everyone to be here together, and *happy*. After the mess that has been our lives for the past two years, I never expected this to be a reality. I assumed I was condemned to a life of misery, but here in this moment, I'm the happiest I've ever been. I'm still haunted and plagued by the horrible things I've done in my past, but I'm learning to deal with that. It will take time, and I will never completely get over all the things I've witnessed and been a part of, but I'm here, smiling, surrounded by my friends and family. That is all I need.

Dropping into the seat, Kian beside me, I lean my forearms on the table. Theo looks devastatingly handsome in a tie, his hair stylishly messy. He winks at me as he brings his glass to his mouth, taking a long drink of the bourbon.

'I got the couple a wedding present. Wanna see?' he asks.

'Not really,' Kian mutters.

'Sure!' I say at the same time.

Theo places his drink down, and stands, yanking his tucked shirt out of the waistband of his pants. He pulls his shirt up, revealing his muscled stomach, and my eyes catch onto the patch of new tattoos near his hip. Theo already had tattoos on his arms, but I notice he has new ink, including a stunning snake that curls around his forearm.

'I had to go to this special tattoo place in town that is designed to make tattoos for us, with the healing and all. Never knew it existed until I walked in there, thinking it was a bar.'

I roll my eyes. 'That doesn't surprise me.'

'So. This is for Hunter.' Theo points to two little bats that have a love heart drawn around them. I attempt to cover my snort. Theo ignores me, moving on to the next. 'This is for Ray Ray. A little paintbrush. For her art stuff.'

'Aw,' I croon. 'That's cute.'

'This is for you,' Theo continues, tapping his finger on a small dagger, and a genuine grin takes over my face. 'This is for Alex.' He points to the outline of the car that Cas gifted him, the one that sits in Theo's garage now. Theo has kept it in good condition. It's really thoughtful of him to have included Alex since he didn't really know him. 'Then this one is for Mya.' He moves onto the next, a small black cat. An iron fist circles my stomach, and the room spins for a moment. *Mya.* Theo continues obliviously, pointing to the last tattoo. 'This, Kian, is for you.'

The last tattoo is a skull, with two roses as the eyes. The detail in the petals is impeccable, and my eyes widen.

'Wow, Theo. That's incredible.'

'Why did I get included?' Kian frowns.

'You're my maker, and in the gang now, *duh*,' he replies in an obvious tone, and Kian scowls at him, as if the thought of being a part of the group makes him feel sick. I nudge him, and his scowl lessens. Slightly.

'Anyways,' Theo says, shoving his shirt back to where it was before, collapsing onto the seat. 'I'm sure they will love it. Especially Hunter. His is extra special.'

'Uh-huh,' I reply, shaking my head.

I look at Kian pointedly. Rolling his eyes, he drapes his hands across the table, nodding at Theo, effectively gaining his attention. Theo raises a brow, sitting up a little straighter. It makes me a little sad how desperate Theo is to have approval and attention from Kian, but Kian is getting better at showing Theo, well, I wouldn't call it kindness, but he isn't such a dick, at least.

'Thank you for watching over Cora while I took care of things,' Kian forces the words out, but his eyes are soft, and even a little warm as he gazes at Theo. 'I appreciate it.'

'Sure.' Theo nods, spinning the glass, trying, and failing, to hide how delighted he is at the praise. 'Happy to.'

Kian leans back, propping his elbow up on the back of his chair, turning his gaze to look out at the trees around us. I kick him lightly under the table and his expression tightens, shooting me an annoyed side-eye.

'And?' I probe, narrowing my eyes at him.

Kian exhales. 'And . . . you're free to leave Red Thorne whenever you'd like. You are able to come and go as you please.'

Theo brightens, a child-like smile taking over his face. 'Really?' He stands abruptly, pushing the chair back so quickly, it topples over. 'I'm going to hug you!'

'If you set one foot toward me I'll break your fucking neck,' Kian warns in a low voice, eyeing him wearily.

'One hug. Please.'

'I will puncture your spleen, Theo,' Kian grunts. 'I can revoke what I just said any time I like.'

'It's happening!' Theo says, leaping over the table, crashing into Kian.

Kian is halfway out of his chair, but Theo manages to take him down, throwing his arms around him. He is silent and quick, that guy. I manage to save the two glasses that almost go flying off the edge of the table.

'Ugh!' Kian exclaims, looking horrified. He slams his elbow into Theo's gut, sending him sprawling onto the grass. Theo winces, rubbing his stomach. I finish my drink, enjoying their little moment.

'Worth it,' Theo mumbles, looking victorious.

Kian stares down at him, but I don't miss the slight twitch in his lips, which makes me smile. Glancing to me, he notices my glass is empty, and heads toward the bar. Theo pushes to his feet, taking his seat once more.

'What are you going to do with your new-found freedom?' I ask him.

'I don't know.' He shrugs. 'I want to spend time with all of you, and help Kian find this witch.'

Nodding, I exhale. Now that Sofia is dead, it's impossible to know where the witch is that cursed Kian. It makes us both uncomfortable that she is still out there somewhere. Possibly watching us all, waiting to make her next move. I can't think about any of that right now, though. For the first time in what feels like forever, I just want to enjoy this day.

'And I'll venture to some places I've never been before. Who knows, the opportunities are endless,' he continues.

'That they are,' I agree.

'Thanks for that. If it wasn't for you, I might have been stuck here forever.'

I roll my eyes. 'Don't be dramatic.'

'Kian is the definition of dramatic, girlfriend.'

'Don't call me that.'

'It's really nice to see you happy, Cor,' he says, looking genuinely pleased as he offers me an easy grin. 'You're the best thing to ever happen to him.'

My eyes follow Theo's gaze to where Kian is leaning against the bar, looking over to where Hunter and Raya are. They flew out some friends from London, and they're currently sitting at their table. I love that Raya has friends, and is out here living as normal a life as she can. As wild as this ride has been, it's somehow worked out for the best.

'I don't know how we both got here, but I'm rolling with it.'

Theo smiles. 'You're happy. It's good.'

'Are you?' I ask, studying him. 'Happy?'

'I don't know what I am. I just vibe.'

An unladylike snort escapes me. 'Well. That sounds fine to me.'

He tips his chin toward me. 'I'm going to ask your mum for a dance.' He winks. 'Catch ya.'

Theo has barely left before Kian returns. Theo dances over to Mum and whisks her off her feet. She thinks he is very charming, and it's cute to see how she blushes as he leads her to the dance floor. Without telling any of us, Theo opened a bank account for her and filled it with more money than she could ever dream of. It was such a thoughtful thing for him to do.

I hope he finds someone that makes him happy. He deserves it.

I sip my drink, eyes roaming over Kian's beautiful face. This feels like a dream. This moment, with him, and everyone who matters to us.

Placing his glass down, he turns. His cool fingers trail up my bare arms, skimming over my collarbones, tracing the curve of my throat.

'You are fucking stunning,' he murmurs, eyes darkening the further they travel across my skin, eventually landing on mine.

'Somehow, you've completely wrapped me around your finger. Thought that was impossible.'

'I think that might be the other way around,' I confess with a small smile.

'I would do anything for you, you know that, right?' he asks, voice silken, his thumb skating across my cheek, so feather light, it is barely a caress. 'I would go to the end of the earth for you. I would *kill* for you. Anyone, anywhere, anytime.'

'You're so romantic,' I tease, but my heart trips inside my chest.

Having these hands, hands designed and crafted to kill, able to touch me so tenderly, it does things to me.

A predator in the wild, who has me in his clutches, but I wouldn't have it any other way.

Circling my hands around his, I bring them to my lips, kissing them softly.

'That's me.' He smirks, gently dropping his hand back into his lap.

Kian's hands rest on me as we glide around the dance floor sometime later. I feel buzzed from the alcohol and content, enjoying being in his arms. I've never seen Raya so radiant, and it makes me so happy.

'I'm glad we found our way through the mess, to each other,' I say to him.

He nods, bringing my hand to his mouth, kissing my knuckles. 'Me too, *mio tesoro*.'

'I want to go to Paris,' I blurt.

'Easy done. Where else?'

'Everywhere. I want to go everywhere.'

'And everywhere, we shall go,' he replies, stepping back, our hands still linked, his eyes meeting mine. 'I hereby redact the blood oath we made to each other. You are free to leave me, anytime you wish to.'

I blink, a slight tingling sensation rippling through me. My lips part as I gaze at him in surprise. He smiles, placing pressure on me to keep dancing, since I had come to a sudden stop in the middle of the dance floor.

'I know the bond ties us together, but I want you to know that if you do not want this life with me, you can walk away any time you want. I will always be here, to protect and care for you, but I understand if you ever change your mind.'

Stepping toward him, I loop my arms around his neck. 'I will be by your side, forever, Kian. You won't be getting rid of me now.'

Pressing our foreheads together, he tenderly presses his lips against mine.

'I wouldn't dream of it, *mio tesoro*.'

EPILOGUE

THEO

THE LEAVES BRUSH OVER my skin as I climb.

Flicking twigs out of the way, I swing onto one of the wider branches, lightly walking across it. Throwing myself through the air, I land easily on the next. My eyes survey the dense woods. I love prowling the woods at night. The moonlight shimmering overhead, the crisp night air, the rustling of the leaves in the wind. It's calming.

The familiar sound of the train approaching pulls my attention toward the entry to Red Thorne.

It's funny how I was so desperate to leave this place, and now I'm able to, and I'm still here. Because they are all here, and I enjoy being around them. After I do one final train run, I plan to go out on my own for a while, to see what lies ahead.

Anticipation tingles through my veins.

Dropping to the ground, I make my way to the train, slinking through the shadows.

The brakes release an ear-splitting wince as it comes to a stop, and people begin spilling out. Three groups. My eyes track their movements as they all go in different directions. After a minute, there is a couple left, who are waiting for an Uber.

I smirk.

Perfect.

'Do you have a signal?' the woman asks, frowning down at her phone. She is tightly bundled up in a large brown coat, a beanie on top of her head. The man beside her is tall and wiry, with glasses perched on his nose.

'Hmm,' the man beside her replies, squinting at his phone. 'No, I don't.'

Huffing, the woman turns, holding her phone in the air as she walks around the bench they dumped their belongings on in an attempt to get her phone to increase its signal. I move silently, wrapping my arm around his torso and yanking him back into the shadows. He doesn't even get a chance to make a sound before I slam my hand over his mouth, diving toward his neck.

The blood is hot and delicious as I drink greedily. His hands grip my arms, and after a moment, they grow weak, falling to the ground.

The woman groans in frustration, looking comical as she waves her phone into the air, cursing under her breath. Spinning, she opens her mouth to say something, and freezes, eyes wildly darting around.

'Oliver?' she calls out, and the sound of her heartbeat hammering in her chest is delightful.

Oliver chokes, drawing in a ragged breath, and I slowly release him, dropping him onto the dirt. Blood spills down his neck, soaking through his pale-blue shirt. He claws at his throat, desperately trying to slow the bleeding, but it is impossible to.

In full panic-mode, the woman begins desperately trying to get a signal on her phone. Faster than the human eye can detect, I place Oliver onto the bench, and am back in the shadows when she glances around her. She screams, the sound ringing so loudly through the air, a few bats fly out of a nearby tree.

'Oh God . . .' she whispers, a look of horror painting her face as she grows paler by the second.

Turning, she goes to run, but I'm standing in front of her.

Blood is smeared all over my lips as I smirk down at her. She's panting, unable to catch her breath. She shivers as she backs up, eyes spinning, trying to find a way to get around me.

'You okay?' I ask, tilting my head, offering her a cold, calculating smile.

'You're one of them,' she spits at me. 'Those monsters!'

Running my tongue around my mouth, I lick the blood clean, and her eyes widen as she staggers back, running into Oliver's legs as they dangle off the side of the bench.

'So you've heard the rumours?' I ask, lips tilting. 'The whispers about the creatures of the night.'

'I thought it was bullshit,' she whispers, skin white as snow. 'It can't be real.'

'And?' I press, stalking closer to her. 'What do you think? Does it seem real enough now?'

Turning, she runs. Grinning, her adrenaline coating the air makes me feel alive. Sprinting after her, I almost have my fingers around her throat, when I hear a faint whizzing sound, and then something strikes me in the shoulder.

Launching backward, I land hard on the ground, completely blindsided. An arrow protrudes from me, and whatever it is laced with completely immobilises me. My muscles lock up, and I'm paralysed as I hear the woman scream, sprinting away from me. My eyes roll to the side, and Oliver slinks down onto the bench, his heart stopping with a booming silence.

Well. I wasn't *actually* going to kill him. That's unfortunate.

The sound of footsteps thunder toward me, and men dressed in all black, masks covering their faces, rush toward me. Two of them have weapons raised at me – one a gun, the other a crossbow.

'Get him in the truck,' I hear one of the grunt.

My head lolls to the side as my body is lifted, eyes heavy as darkness eats at my vision.

The last thing I see is the '*You are leaving Red Thorne. We hope you enjoyed your stay!*' as I head in the opposite direction, back toward the town.

I never even made it past the damn sign.

THANK YOU

THANK YOU SO MUCH for reading *Live for Me*. I really hope you enjoyed the story. I love writing romance stories with emotional, angsty characters that draw you in. I had so much fun exploring the romantasy genre, and had the best time with my morally corrupt bad guys. I loved creating this world and I hope you enjoyed reading it as much as I enjoyed writing it.

ACKNOWLEDGEMENTS

FIRST AND FOREMOST, I'd like to thank the readers – thank you from the bottom of my heart for picking up this book and embracing Cora and Kian's story. Thank you for your love, support, encouragement, and reviews. I will be forever grateful for your support.

I really enjoyed writing this book and delving deep into the mindset of someone who is considered to be the 'villain'. It was a really fun journey, and I think there will definitely be more morally grey characters in the future!

Thank you to my friends and family who have dealt with endless questions, ideas, and offered me much appreciated feedback. Thank you for always listening to my rambling voice notes, my looooong phone calls where I ended up telling five different stories just to explain the one simple point I'm trying to make, and always being so proud of everything I've achieved.

This book wouldn't exist without my best friend, Becka – my real-life Cora. My rock, my ride or die, the yin to my yang. Becka was the person I pitched the idea to, and from there we spent endless hours messaging, voice-noting, FaceTiming at all different hours of the day and night, since for the entire writing journey of *Live for Me*, she was on the other side of the world! This has been the first time I shared my chapter-to-chapter thoughts and feelings as I wrote, and it was incredible having someone there with me every step of the way. Becka, I honestly can't thank you enough for your support, your guidance, and every single idea you helped with. Thank you for being my inspiration. No question was too difficult for you to answer, no plot hole was too big for you to overcome, and without you, this book wouldn't be where it is today. I'm endlessly thankful for you being in my life.

I will always thank my beautiful friend Genicious, who supported me so much when I first began the journey of self-publishing. If it wasn't for her and all the help she provided me, I would never have taken the plunge and ended up with the deal of my dreams from Penguin.

Thank you to my incredible friend Sydni, who is a godsend in my life. Thank you for always being there for me, supporting me with everything, and always being ready to jump on for a call. I am so grateful!

To my beautiful friend Nicole, who is also subject to my long voice notes of rambling thoughts. Thank you for being such a kind, generous, and wonderful friend to me. I am so glad we found each other, even though we live on opposite sides of the world!

My amazing 'Team No Sleep' girls, who have given me feedback and crucial advice that has helped shape me as a writer and has motivated me to be where I am today – thank you Kenadee, Jess, and SJ.

Jordan – my wonderful beta reader, advice giver, editor, and creative genius – who is always down to work on my next project with me, always has the best way to word things, always has a new idea or title in mind when I can't think of one. I really look up to you and rely so much on your advice. I've been a fan of your writing since I was in my early teens, and I'm honoured you've become one of my closest friends.

Thank you especially to my amazing friends Haley, Chloe, and Tamika for always listening to me, offering me advice, and always being there for me.

Thank you to my amazing Book Club for supporting me! I am so thrilled to have found such a wonderful group of people to share my bookish adventures with. Creating our online book club gave me the confidence to be bold with my reading and helped me take the dive to branching out on my own Bookstagram.

To my wonderful friends Jane, Rachelle, and Marnie, my close friends who have always given me help when I've asked, and always gone above and beyond to support me, by turning up to my book events, telling so many people about my books, and so much more. I love you girls.

To all the bloggers, reviewers, and BookTok accounts that shower me with support. To anyone who has followed me on Wattpad and been a part of my writing journey. I can't ever tell you thank you enough.

Last and certainly not least, a massive **thank you** to the amazing team at Penguin Books Australia for your support, and the incredible opportunity you have given me. Chris – you are wonderful. I appreciate how kind you are, how supportive you've always been, how prompt you are to answer or follow up any questions I have, and everything you've done behind the scenes to make this the most perfect experience. I will be forever grateful!

Can you ever really
run from your past
or change your destiny?

MEANT
to be

LAUREN JACKSON
AUSTRALIA'S OWN ROMANCE WRITING SENSATION

A steamy new adult romance perfect for fans of Ana Huang, Lucy Score, Tessa Bailey and Monica Murphy.

Josie Mayor fled Fern Grove after a scandal that rocked the town, turning her back on her friends and family. She disappeared with no contact, no forwarding address and abandoned the only life she knew.

Now she's back and has to confront what she left behind. When Josie runs into her ex-boyfriend, Nick, and Harley, the boy who stole her heart, she is faced with the pain and heartache of a past she's desperate to forget. Josie must make a choice in doing what's best for her, or risk repeating history once more.

A HUMAN SEARCHING FOR HER SISTER,
A GRUMPY VAMPIRE BODYGUARD,
AND A PREDATOR ON THE HUNT.
WHAT COULD GO WRONG?

DIE
FOR
YOU

A RED THORNE NOVEL

LAUREN JACKSON
AUSTRALIA'S OWN ROMANCE WRITING SENSATION

RED THORNE BOOK 1

Twilight meets *The Vampire Diaries* in this steamy
new adult romantasy.

A girl searching for her sister, a grumpy vampire bodyguard in
charge of keeping her alive, and a malicious creature hunting
them down. What could go wrong?

THE SURVIVOR

The death certificate says my sister died two years ago in the
accident, but her body was never found. I was the sole survivor.
Then I saw her. Someone lied. Now, I must travel across the
country to find answers from a blood-thirsty vampire with one
thing on his mind. I will find out the truth. Even if it kills me.

THE PROTECTOR

I didn't mean for this to happen. I didn't mean for any of it to
happen. Now Raya is here. She is mine, and I must protect her
at all costs. If she dies, I die. It doesn't add up, and it's all a mess.
It's my job to fix it and find my brother. She knows I'm hiding
something, but I'm terrified to tell her the truth.

THE PREDATOR

It's been years since I had a lead. Now, I have one.
I will watch. I will wait. I will strike. He will be mine.

Read on for an extract of *Break the Rules*,
Lauren Jackson's forthcoming steamy second-chance
college sports romance – the first in her
Stratton University series

1

ANYA

BEING YELLED AT BY an incoherent drunk man isn't how I wanted to spend my Friday night. I also didn't particularly want to pack up my life and move an hour north because my boyfriend decided my best friend was a better option than me. I guess we all have bad days, though. Or weeks, in my case.

My heart hurts at the thought of Dylan – my now ex-boyfriend – and Phoebe, my ex-best friend, sneaking around behind my back and lying to me. Forcing them from my mind, I try to focus on the situation in front of me.

The man shouts at me again, spit flying from his mouth and landing on my face. Wrinkles line his forehead and the corners of his eyes. He waves his hands, swaying so much he almost topples over. I have no clue what he is trying to say, but I'm guessing I'm at the wrong place. I flinch away and sigh as I step back from the kerb, looking down at the address I saved in my notes, which is supposed to be the share house I'm renting a room in. This is where the maps on my phone directed me to.

The street is quiet, which makes the drunk man's voice sound ten times as loud. I'm positive I'm in the wrong place because a street full of student housing wouldn't be this calm. I turn, leaving the man to yell at my back as I retreat to the car. The first fall of rain hits my cheeks. Tilting my head back, I glare up at the darkening sky.

I slide into the driver's seat and retype the address into my phone, and this time, it tells me my destination is five minutes away. Exhaling, I pull away from the kerb, trying to keep my shit together, but the tiny thread of hope I'm holding onto is getting thinner by the second.

Tiredness gnaws at me as I battle to keep my eyes open. This is the last thing I feel like doing tonight, but I had to get away from there. From them.

I swing the car into a busy narrow street, littered with cars parked haphazardly in places they shouldn't be parked. Cutting the engine, I peer through the window at the small, weathered share house I'm meant to be moving into.

Neon lights shine through the windows, and music floats down the driveway as I wander up it. A guy sits on the front porch, his legs dangling from the railing as he blows out a cloud of smoke.

'Hi,' I say when he stares at me for a long, awkward moment. 'Are you Johnny?'

'Yeah,' he says wearily, his voice with a husky edge to it.

'Hi,' I say again. The rain is starting to fall heavier now, so I move onto the porch step, trying to avoid my shirt getting any damper than it already is. 'I'm Anya.'

'Who?' His brows draw together.

'Anya Stark? We spoke on Messenger. I'm renting room three.'

He raises an eyebrow, looking a little surprised. 'Not anymore.'

My heart does an awkward jolt in my chest. 'What do you mean, not anymore?'

'You were supposed to pay the two weeks of rent in advance, but you never did. The room has been rented to someone else.' His face fades back into the stoic expression he was wearing before as he inhales a long drag from the cigarette between his fingers.

I blink at him. 'What are you talking about? The money left my account.'

'Never came into mine.'

'What?' I frown, reaching into my pocket and pulling out my phone. I log into my banking app and stare down at the red digits that indicate the withdrawn amount. I shove the phone under his nose. 'See?'

'It was withdrawn. Not transferred to me.' I stare back down at the screen, realising he is right. My heart plummets to my stomach. 'You also would've gotten a confirmation message from me once it went through.'

Swallowing, my shoulders sag in defeat. Once again, I'm furious with myself for giving Dylan access to my bank account because – as usual – he didn't have any money. He was meant to pay the deposit for me on the day it was due. A fiery ball of anger burns in my chest as I realise that he stole from me.

'Well,' I say bitterly, stepping back into the rain. 'That's just great.'

'Yeah. That sucks,' he says flatly, flicking the cigarette to the ground in front of me before disappearing inside the house, slamming the front door behind him.

Running my tongue across my teeth, I try my hardest to stop the tears welling in my eyes from spilling over. I stiffly walk back to the car and exhale a shaky breath before I settle behind the wheel. I dial my brother's number. My left leg jitters restlessly as I listen to the phone ring out.

After a moment, a text comes through.

Zayden: Dodgy reception. Everything ok?

Anya: Are you home? Or if not is there a spare key?

My brother sends through where his spare key is kept, no questions asked. I sink my teeth into my lower lip, still trying not to burst into tears. After a ten-minute drive, I pull up at my brother's house. There are several lights on, and an unfamiliar black truck parked in the driveway. I double check the number as I'm getting out and head to the front door. After moving a few pots around, I exhale when the spare key isn't where my brother said it would be. Pressing my lips into a line, my eyes bounce from the truck in the driveway to the lights on inside.

Blowing out a hot breath, I knock and step back. Just as a traitorous tear slips out, the front door opens. My breath gets trapped in my lungs when my eyes land on Mason.

My brother's best friend.

The boy I had always loved, until I hated him.

He's aged well. Really fucking well. He's tall, packed with muscle, and with broader shoulders than when I'd seen him last. His eyes seem darker, his jaw more defined, his hair longer. Tattoos that once painted only part of one arm now cover every inch of skin that I can see, except for his face and some parts of his neck. He's dressed in all black; that's something that hasn't changed. The shirt shows off how big his biceps are and how defined his chest is. He had always been very attractive, and I hopelessly wished he would get worse with age. Damn.

After all this time, he's seeing me dishevelled and crying on my brother's doorstep on a Friday night.

'What are you doing here?' I ask, my voice betraying me by coming out in a whisper. All the feelings and reassurances I've convinced myself of over the years flash before my eyes, and I realise how much of a lie they all were. Because I am very, very much still affected by this man, and he hasn't even said one word to me yet. In fact, I bet he doesn't feel a damn thing. That's where the problems began.

Those dark, whisky-coloured eyes settle on me, and I feel every inch of my insides curl in on themselves. My heart feels like it' s twisted into a ball of lead in my chest and plummeted down into my stomach, knocking against everything in its path along the way.

He quirks an eyebrow, eyes scanning my face, as if reassuring himself it really is me standing here in front of him, shivering and looking on the verge of a mental breakdown.

'I live here.'

My eyes widen as dread spreads through my veins. His words ring loudly in my ears, repeating inside my head, as if stuck on a loop. 'Since when?'

'Since Leasa moved out.'

I didn't consider the fact that my brother would have found a roommate after his girlfriend of three years moved out. I should have guessed Mason would be the replacement. It makes sense, but in my defence, I try my best not to think about the boy who ripped my heart out of my chest and stomped on it.

Could this night get any worse?

'Oh,' I mumble, attempting to swallow, but suddenly my mouth and throat are paper dry. My body has always had such an extreme reaction to being near Mason, and it drives me crazy. It's like he owns the remote to my body and knows exactly which buttons to press.

The corner of his mouth twitches as his eyes openly roam over me, not caring in the slightest how obvious it is.

'No "hi"? "How are you? What have you been up to?"' He smirks, leaning on the door frame. My heart jackhammers in my chest at the familiarity of the movement. He used to do that exact thing in the doorframe of my bedroom.

I definitely don't want to be thinking about him and me in my bedroom right now.

'No, that wasn't my first thought when I saw you,' I say, hoping my voice sounds stronger than I feel.

'What was that thought, then?'

'I don't want to deal with this asshole.' I fold my arms across my chest, trying to look the opposite of how I truly feel.

Mason grins at me, flashing his teeth. Handsome smile lines appear around the edges of his mouth. The lines that I loved so much. The very ones I've trailed my fingertips over...

'Good to know you still have that giant crush on me.'

The memory shatters, and I'm forcefully jolted back to reality. My face must reflect my true feelings, because his smirk falters for a moment. I force a blank expression. As best I can, anyway, since he is doing a marvellous job of not revealing his thoughts.

'You wish,' I spit back, trying my best to mask my hurt.

'Mmhmm,' he murmurs, eyeing the bare bit of skin where my shirt has slipped off my shoulder. My stomach does a flip-flop motion. 'If you say so. Why are you here?'

'I've had a hell of a night. I need somewhere to crash,' I say, rubbing a hand down my face. 'Zayden didn't mention you would be here.'

'Would it have made a difference?' he questions, sounding genuinely curious.

I don't want to do this. I wasn't ready to face him, nor the feelings that I've forcefully shoved deep down into a file labelled: Do not open. EVER.

'Can you just let me in?' I huff, shaking out the hair that has fallen across my eyes.

His dark- brown eyes – two smoky quartz – hover over my glistening cheeks for a moment before he steps back, allowing me access through the door. I haul my bag inside and he reaches around me to grab it, easily slinging it over his shoulder. I wipe my cheeks and avoid his gaze as I scan the room, taking in what is possibly the cleanest apartment I have ever seen. My brother is not a clean person, but I imagine this is Mason's doing. It must drive him crazy, always having to clean up after my disaster of a brother. Hurricane Zay, my mother used to call him.

'Weren't you meant to be moving into some share house downtown?' he asks, gesturing to the stairs.

They talk about me? Interesting.

Sighing, I walk in front of him and start to climb, taking in everything around me. A lot has changed since Leasa left.

'My asshole of an ex really wanted to make sure the knife he dug into my back wasn't getting out easily.'

I feel the heat of his gaze on my skin as we trail down the upstairs hallway. I pause, seeing a photo of Zayden, Mason and myself. We're at the beach, and I'm holding my arms out, showing where a line of starfish is sitting on my forearm. Zayden is beaming at the camera, pointing to the starfish. Stepping closer, I squint, looking closely at how Mason's eyes are on me. I never noticed that before. His lips are tilted up in a crooked smile, his cheeks flushed from running down the beach. I remember that day so clearly. It was one of the last fun days we had before things got complicated. I stand so close to the frame that the tip of my nose grazes the glass.

Why did I never notice he was looking at me like that?

'Heard about Dylan,' Mason says, brushing past me and opening a door, revealing a neatly kept spare room. I startle, having been so focused on the photo, I forgot for a moment where I am. Shaking my head, I follow him inside the room. It looks different – bigger than I remembered, with a soft-looking brown comforter that is calling my name. 'And Phoebe,' he adds after a moment.

A sickening feeling washes over me at the mention of their names. The two people in my life who I love so much. Or at least, I did.

I have been extremely unlucky in the love department.

'You keeping tabs on me, Mase?' I exhale, bringing my hair around over my shoulder, feeling how damp it is from the rain.

He lowers my bag onto the bed, and it groans briefly under the weight of it. The bag is practically bursting at the seams, and there are three more just like it in the boot of my car, but they can stay there for now.

'Of course, Blush.'

Heat burns my cheeks and races down my neck at the familiar nickname. Blush. Every time Mason looked in my direction when we were growing up, my cheeks would shine a bright, noticeable red, as vibrant as a neon sign above my head telling the world I was crushing on him. Since he loved to enjoy my misery and discomfort, he quickly nicknamed me 'Blush' to further torment me.

I haven't seen him since everything went down over two years ago. Or heard that nickname. As much as it was meant to be teasing, over the years it became something a little…flirty. Which is where the true trouble began.

And now we're staring at each other, the air between us crackling. My cheeks warm impossibly more, and I step back from him, even though there is already two metres of space between our bodies. No distance is enough when it comes to him. His presence feels like a physical touch, and his hold on me is stronger than my will.

'So. You're back,' I say, just to say something, and I desperately hope he can't hear how loudly my heart is hammering in my chest.

His lips tilt in the sexy way they always have. 'Obviously.'

'How was Mexico?' I turn towards him, following him back out to the hall, certainly not looking at how tightly his shirt clings to his back muscles.

He throws a smirk over his shoulder. 'Looks like you've been keeping tabs on me, too.'

If only he knew I had to block all his stories from my social media so I couldn't see anything. I couldn't bear seeing his face and crying over it, like I had so many times. I never went as far as blocking him completely. That would raise questions from my friends and family that I had no intention of answering.

'More like the only person Zayden likes to talk about more than himself is you,' I point out.

'Uh-huh.'

My eyes roam over those delicious arm muscles, down to the ass that's been burned into my memory for years. Yup. Still as good as ever.

'Unusual for you to be in on a Friday night, isn't it?' I ask, padding into the kitchen and dropping onto one of the bar stools.

'Stalker, much?'

'Get over yourself.'

Mason effortlessly moves around the kitchen. He flicks the kettle on, withdraws two mugs from one of the cabinets and leans back onto the kitchen bench.

'You're not…' I start, a slow smile spreading across my face. Since Mason was at our house every weekend throughout high school, he would go out of his way to cook or do something helpful around the house. I assume it was a thank you to my family for always taking him in. He knew his way around a kitchen, and often added unique extra touches on simple meals, making them somehow taste ten times better.

'Making you the Mason Special? Why, of course I am.'

'Since when are you nice to me?' I narrow my eyes suspiciously.

His eyes look a little brighter under the kitchen lights, which cast a golden glow over his skin and a shadow across the slight stubble that's growing across his jaw.

'Since you've had a fucking terrible time lately,' he replies, way more honestly than I expected. His gaze lingers on mine for a heartbeat too long. 'But just tonight. Game over from tomorrow.'

I breathe a forced laugh, tugging the sleeves of my jacket down over my hands before I bring them up to cup my cheeks. I hate the fact that they are still extremely warm despite the cold temperature.

Just seeing his face makes me miserable. I thought I would feel angrier than I do, but I just feel crappy. I hate what he did to me, and I hate even more that I can't let go of all the feelings I've been harbouring for him all my life. I don't want to feel anything, but that's impossible when it comes to him.

'Wouldn't expect anything less.'

It's silent for a moment between us. Only the sounds of metal clanging on the bench top and his footsteps as he moves across the tiled floor fill the room. I try everything I can not to stare at him.

'It was amazing, by the way.'

'Hmm?' I murmur, drawing myself out of my thoughts.

'Mexico.'

'Oh,' I reply, my eyes slowly trailing down his tanned forearms and those swirling dark tattoos. 'That's good. How long have you been back?'

'Almost a month.'

'Just in time for a vacant room, hey?' I say with a tight-lipped smile.

'I've always had great timing.'

Ugh. Ouch.

'I know Zayden and Leasa had been rocky for a while, but I still feel like the break-up happened so fast,' I say thoughtfully, desperately trying to stop my mind from thinking back to everything that happened between us as he turns and slides a mug across the bench top. 'Seemed like she was just up and...gone.'

'Pretty much how it happened, by the sound of it.'

'You must be glad to get your sidekick back,' I tease, circling my hands around the cup and embracing the warmth of it, even though I feel cold and empty inside.

'Zay falls head over heels for every girl he meets. He's a useless wingman.' Mason grins lightly. 'I'm just glad to see he seems happier.'

I don't know why I said that. The last thing I want to think about or discuss is Zayden being Mason's wingman. The thought of Mason with anyone makes me want to empty my stomach.

'He is?' I ask, leaning forward. 'Happy?'

Mason considers this. 'Honestly? I'm not sure. I think this break-up has been good for him in a lot of ways. They were toxic for each other in the end, but no. I'm not sure that he is happy, just happier.'

'They were always toxic,' I agree with a dry smile. My brother and his girlfriend had a relationship that made no sense to me. Powerful and passionate, but a whirlwind of extreme highs and the lowest of lows. 'The way they would scream at each other gave me nightmares.' Bringing the mug up to my lips, I take a small sip. An explosion of warmth and flavour takes over my tongue and I moan, having missed this. It used to be a weekly tradition of ours.

I'm surprised to see Mason's eyes travelling down my body as he watches me. The tension from two years ago feels as strong as ever. I want to be able to look at him and not think about everything we once were, but it's too difficult not to.

'I've missed this,' I whisper, breathing into the mug.

I honestly don't know if I mean the hot chocolate or him. Both, really. Mason was a huge part of my life and then suddenly he wasn't. The hole he left behind is still gaping, as much as I tried everything to fill it up.

'Me too, Blush.' He offers me a small, sad smile. 'Me too.'

He turns, disappearing from the kitchen.

Powered by Penguin